The Sixth William

for Betty & Jim

[signature]

John Davis

The Sixth William

John Neely Davis

AuthorHouse™
1663 Liberty Drive
Bloomington, IN 47403
www.authorhouse.com
Phone: 1-800-839-8640

© 2012 John Neely Davis. All rights reserved.

No part of this book may be reproduced, stored in a retrieval system, or transmitted by any means without the written permission of the author.

Published by AuthorHouse   2/16/2012

ISBN: 978-1-4670-4030-3 (sc)
ISBN: 978-1-4670-4029-7 (hc)
ISBN: 978-1-4670-4028-0 (e)

Library of Congress Control Number: 2011917431

Any people depicted in stock imagery provided by Thinkstock are models, and such images are being used for illustrative purposes only.
Certain stock imagery © Thinkstock.

This book is printed on acid-free paper.

Because of the dynamic nature of the Internet, any web addresses or links contained in this book may have changed since publication and may no longer be valid. The views expressed in this work are solely those of the author and do not necessarily reflect the views of the publisher, and the publisher hereby disclaims any responsibility for them.

DEDICATION

For Jayne, the woman whom I loved even before she was born.

ACKNOWLEDGEMENTS

The gestation period of a human is nine months, a whale more than a year, and an elephant just under two years. Conceived in the spring warmth of southern Arizona and after a gestation period of five years, *The Sixth William* was born on a winter night in Tennessee. A number of people acted as midwives, and I will be grateful to them forever. Jerry and Gayle Henderson cheerfully offered their eagle-eyed grammatical and syntax skills, and I still managed to scatter errors throughout the book. My sister Karen loaned her considerable business acumen and gave me access to professionals in the literary world. My family and friends gently prodded.

Behind, they say, every good man is a good woman. My wife Jayne read and reread dozens of drafts, pointed out errors, frequently disagreed with my rambling mind but always laughed and cried in the appropriate places – time and time again.

ANCHORAGE 1986

The Prospector was cool and dark, with only a couple of regular customers and Willie, the bartender, watching the flickering TV. I sat down, and when Willie didn't turn, growled in my best Humphrey Bogart voice, "What does a poor, thirsty brush pilot have to do to get some service around this dirty joint?" Willie turned, held an index finger across his lips and pointed to the TV.

The picture was a mountain stream contained by high bluffs. A tanned newscaster decked out in a yellow polo shirt pointed at an outcrop on the cliff about a hundred feet up from the riverbed.

"… and it was at this point where, late yesterday afternoon, three kayakers paddling down the Findhorn River discovered the body. Sheriff Roy Ruby Fox said the dead man had been identified, and the identity will be made public after the next of kin is notified. The body was taken into Cedergren. The cause of death has not yet been determined. Sources tell us the dead man may have been scalped. He wore an amulet of plaited leather and willow bark which we understand contained a small gold figure that resembled a bird in flight."

The cute, young woman sitting at the anchor desk was wide-eyed. "Jeff, isn't this the same area where another body was found earlier this year?"

"Yes, Jackie, it is the same area, and that man was wearing a similar amulet." The camera panned away from the reporter and showed churning rapids. "The cause of that death is still being investigated also. One other fact adds to the mystery. Reportedly, an ancient stone fort is atop the escarpment very near where the dead men were found. The fort may have no significance but it does thicken the mystery."

An aerial photograph of a wooded plateau almost surrounded by a river flashed briefly on the screen.

"You can see the isolation of the area from the photograph. The Roman Company owns this plateau as well as thousands of acres of woodland in this mountainous part of Tennessee. Locals have named the area The Arn because the plateau is shaped like an old fashion iron – the kind used by rural people before they got electricity."

"Thank you, Jeff, for that report." She grinned, "By the way, do you plan to spend the night along the river?"

Jeff removed his sunglasses, "Are you kidding me?" He smiled and said, "This is Jeff Boozer in the Findhorn River canyon near Cedergren, Tennessee.

Willie slid a mug of beer to me. "Well, hillbilly boy, ain't you from there? Ain't I heard you talk about the Arn, Roman Company, Cedergren, and the Findhorn River?"

"Son of a bitch," I muttered. No contact, nothing for more than half of my life. I am thousands of miles and thirty years away, and damned if it's not as if it was yesterday, the river, the purple mountains, and the Arn – always the Arn.

I looked down at my frosted beer mug and watched the ice loosen and slide onto the wooden bar top, leaving an irregular wetness. Like images on film, the past started to loop through my mind. I had no more control of my thoughts than the blood coursing through my veins.

*****

Like many Alaskans, I am not a native. We folks that chose to move here are a mixed group. Some came here simply for the adventure, others seeking a different life style, and others running from their own personal demons; I was one of the latter.

Had I been smarter, I would have known that you can't hide forever and eventually your demons will find you. Or you might become a demon yourself.

JUNO 1981

I'd come up here with Ken Bishop and his family. He moved up through the bureaucracy of the Forest Service and became a big shot there at the end. He towed me like a trailer through the ranks of the Service and across the western half of the Lower-48. At some point, the employee-employer relationship changed to that of a family member. I never called Mrs. Bishop, Mama, but I would have been comfortable using those words. The Bishops only had one child, Josh. I was seventeen years older than Josh and he was the brother I never had. I taught him how to fish, canoe, hunt, and run trap lines. If folks didn't know different, they usually thought we were blood related.

Mr. Bishop constantly encouraged me to enroll in college. "You don't have to get a degree, just take some courses – English, history, economics, some math – I don't want you to walk around sounding ignorant all your life. You might have to apply for a real job someday." He usually laughed when he said that.

Living in Alaska was not always easy. Sadness invaded my long nights. Nightmares were frequent overnight guest. Sometimes alcohol helped, sometimes it didn't, and when it didn't they could turn real nasty.

"Melancholia," the doctor said. "It'll go away when spring comes." Probably I was not the first patient he misdiagnosed.

I had a few girlfriends. The ones I wanted to marry didn't want to marry me. The ones that wanted to marry me, I wouldn't have. One wanted to move in. "See how it works," she said. But I thought of Mrs. Bishop and knew she would disapprove.

I watched Mr. and Mrs. Bishop age. Gray crept into their hair, and wrinkles grew around their eyes. Age is not selective. As the Bishop family grew older, so did I and developed my own wrinkles and expanded waistline.

Twenty-five years after I first met Mr. Bishop, he called me into his office. He was riffling through papers on his desk, dropping some in a briefcase and others in a wastepaper can. He looked up. Without enthusiasm, he said, "I wanted you to be the first to know. I'm hanging it up. I've worked 35 years for this outfit, and it's not the same as it was when I came. It's being run by a bunch of political dumb asses, folks that don't know a bitter weed from a pine tree. I have accomplished more than I ever thought I would, and old friend you have been a great part of my success. You've been like a son, never disappointed me, never let me down, ever."

I stood at the window, looked out at the tall fir trees nodding in the wind, and did my best to keep my voice from breaking. "What are you going to do?"

"We're going to move down to Florida. I'm going to sit in the sun and enjoy being an old man. Try to put some polish on this life, you might say. Josh has accepted a job in Atlanta, just about a day's drive from where we'll be living. By the time I get my fill of sunshine and the ocean, I hope to spend some time rocking grandbabies. Hopefully, Josh and his new wife will get in gear on this baby business."

Mr. Bishop started taking pictures off the wall. He handed me a black and white photograph of men unloading a bulldozer. "I want you to have this one. I want you to remember how young I looked once upon a time. Look at the young man sitting on the dozer. See how skinny he is? Look at how he's reaching for the throttle. That's you. I've never known you to do anything but reach for the throttle your whole life, always moving forward. We've both changed. A lot of water has run under our bridges."

I couldn't look at his face.

He put his arm around my shoulder. "I want to tell you about a book I've been reading. A chapter that tells about a young man that kinda got on the outs with his daddy. The young man left home and after awhile, when he'd sown his wild oats, he wanted to go back and be with his family. He was worried about how they'd take to him. His daddy saw him coming and ran to meet him. They had a big celebration. I haven't finished the whole book, but I think they're going to live happy ever after."

I nodded, "Yes sir. I know that story."

"Creight, I may be an old man but I didn't ride into town on the last wagon load of turnips. Years ago, when we were living in Colorado, a Tennessee sheriff and a detective came by questioning me about a young man. Said the man's name was William Creighton Roane."

"William Creighton Roane?"

MEMPHIS 1956

Filled with a mixture of hurt and misery, I turned west out of Cedergren. I had no idea where I was going and I didn't care. I was just going.

I drove through the darkness and stopped at daylight in a patch of woods near a creek where I made coffee, eggs and toast on a Coleman stove. Without even thinking about sleep, I got back on the road and pointed the nose of my wreck of a pickup toward Memphis. I had never been there, but I knew it was a big town. I could get some kind of job – I hoped.

I crossed the Cumberland River at Nashville and wondered if the Mississippi was bigger. Later crossing the Duck and the Buffalo Rivers, I thought their sluggish and muddy waters were ugly compared to the rapid and clear Findhorn. The Tennessee River was much larger than the Cumberland, and I decided the rivers got bigger the further west.

Darkness approached and an hour east of Memphis I ran into a tremendous downpour - my homefolks would have said it was raining bullfrogs and bull yearlings. Muddy water had filled the ditches and then overflowed and covered the highway. Traffic slowed to a crawl as the cars inched carefully forward through the driving rainstorm.

Ahead, the taillights of a car blinked rapidly. The car veered to the right and swerved onto the shoulder of the road. In almost slow motion, the car tilted over into the rain-swollen ditch. It floated on its side for a few seconds, rolled over onto its top, and then was swept away.

Ahead, the ditch emptied into a small river. Spinning wildly as it reached the swifter flowing water, the car came to rest against a bridge.

I stopped, jumped out, and ran to the bridge. Two men wearing raincoats were leaning over the metal banister of the rusty bridge looking down at the car.

I yelled to them through the driving rain, "There's somebody in that car!"

Brush and other debris washed against the car on the upstream side. With enough buildup, the car would either sink or roll over and wash under the bridge.

I shouted at the men again. A reply came back through the rain, "We can't swim."

I struggled down the limestone riprap to the edge of the river and crawled out onto a drift of debris. The car was filling with water. A woman clawed against the driver's side window, her face twisted in panic and terror. I kicked the window with my heavy lumberman's boots and it gave way in large pieces. I reached inside, grabbed the woman's blouse, and pulled her outside and onto the drift.

With the window gone, muddy water flowed into the car and it started to sink.

The woman screamed, "My baby's in there!"

I shoved her toward the bank, turned, and reached inside the car again. The baby was in a small basket just out of reach. I pulled myself inside the car, grabbed the basket, and started back through the broken window. The woman had not gone to the riverbank but was clutching the side of the drift and reaching out toward the basket. I shoved it toward her. She grabbed it and fell back onto the drift just as the car filled with water and sank.

The car tumbled along the bottom of the river. Disoriented, I thrashed around trying to find the broken window. The car lodged between the bank and a tree. Rolling over on my back, I kicked against the windshield. Running out of air, I gave one last kick.

The windshield collapsed, and I was sucked out into the muddy stream. Gasping for air, I washed against the bank and clutched the limbs of a willow. Blood was flowing from cuts on my hands and arms. Too exhausted to pull myself up on the muddy riverbank, I hung on to the willows, gasping and sucking damp, night air into my oxygen-starved lungs.

I was vaguely aware of sirens, flashing lights, and men with flashlights running along the bank. Retching and throwing up muddy water, I heard a man shout, "Here he is, over here!" More dancing lights along the bank and then with muddy water exploding from my stomach once again, the lights faded, and everything went fuzzy.

*****

"It's time for you to wake up now. You're going to sleep the whole day away. For a while, we thought we were going to lose you."

I opened my eyes and stared up into the face of a nurse who was not much older than I. Liquid was dripping from a large bottle through a plastic tubing, then into my arm.

Things were a long way from being clear in my head, "What happened?"

The nurse brushed a wisp of red hair from her face, "Well, this is what I was told. I wasn't here right in the beginning, but I came on the floor at the shift change. The ambulance people were just bringing you in. They said you almost drowned in the Loosahatchie. Said somebody ran off into the river and you were trying to help. You were washed away. You were cut up some and had drunk a whole lot of that old muddy Loosahatchie, so we pumped you out and sewed you up. As soon as we can get some food in you, you'll be bout good as new." She paused for breath then said, "Whatever that is."

The nurse had a way of ending all her sentences with a high note and a question mark. If I hadn't been so sick, I might have found it irritating.

I raised my good arm, "I know all that. What happened to the woman and the baby?"

"Oh," she exclaimed, waving her hands and smiling. "Some men standing on the bridge got down into the water and saved them. Some folks say it was a miracle, cause if they weren't there that woman and little baby would have died. They were angels. I tell you I have never been so excited in all my life. Newspaper folks were here last night, talking to the woman and making pictures."

Her smile became a scowl, "A sheriff's deputy brought the two men here to see the woman, and she had a fit. The newspaper wanted to make a picture of them together. She must have been out of her head cause she screamed at them. Told them to go away and leave her alone.

"Then her husband got here. He was a really big man and was wearing some kind of green uniform and one of those Smoky Bear hats. He talked to her a while and got her calmed down some. They had to give her a shot. He slept all night in a chair beside her bed. The baby - it's a little boy - is fine. Doctor Paul says babies are tougher than boot leather anyway, and if folks will just let them alone they will grow up fine on their own.

"You just lay here right still and I'll go and get you some dinner. We're having fried chicken and creamed potatoes. You'll just love them. It's one of my favorites." She left, starched uniform making little crinkling sounds.

My ears were ringing from her chatter. I was glad to see her go. But I was glad to know the woman and baby were okay.

After I found a comfortable position, sleep or whatever was running from the bottle took me away.

*****

It was almost dark. A pale woman with blond hair and a large man were standing at the foot of my bed. The man was holding a baby against his chest with its head resting on his shoulder.

"My name is Ken Bishop. This is my wife Margaret and my son Josh. These are the most precious things in my life, and you saved them. I thank you more than I can ever express. If you are a husband and a father, you will understand what I'm saying, and if you're not, no way I...," his sentence trailed off.

I felt embarrassed. "Anybody else would have done the same thing. The whole thing just kinda blew up when I kicked in the window and water started running into the car. Probably was a better way of getting your family out."

The man came around to the side of the bed, "If you had not acted when you did ... ." He swallowed. "Other people might have just stood by like those two men on the bridge. They certainly didn't act, but they were glad to take credit." He smiled and went on, "I guess you heard how Margaret straightened out the reporter and sent those two men packing."

"Yes sir. The nurse told me."

"What's your name, son? They have got you registered as John Doe. You had no identification on you, and they have not even been able to find your vehicle."

"What do you mean, find it?"

"Most of the road washed away, along with your truck. The whole shooting match just caved off into the river and left. They may never find it."

I felt the presence of a new horror entering my life.

"You do remember your name, don't you?"

"Yes sir. It's uh, uh, William Creighton…folks call me Creight for short."

The man asked, "Where are you from, Creight?"

I stammered, "Far eastern part of the state, northeast of Knoxville … in the mountains."

"Well, Creight, that covers a pretty good area. What town?"

"Just a little mountain town. You probably never heard of it."

Mrs. Bishop gave her husband an elbow as he questioned, "You're not giving out much information. Is everything all right?"

"Sure. I'm kinda on my own right now."

"Kinda on your own?"

"Yes sir. Kinda on my own."

His wife spoke for the first time, "What is the matter with you, Ken? Don't you understand? He's on his own, just like he said."

The man nodded and gave the baby to his wife and said, "Honey, why don't you go back to your room and feed Josh his last bottle. I'll be along in just a minute."

Margaret left, closing the door behind her. Mr. Bishop sat on my bed. "I've made some big mistakes in my life but yesterday tops them all. I work with the U.S. Forest Service - been transferred from the Allegheny National Forest to Golden, Colorado. The movers have already taken our furniture. I wanted to have one of our vehicles shipped so we could travel up in one car, but I had to attend one final meeting here in Memphis. Margaret wanted to spend some more time with her mother in Nashville."

He took a pipe from a hand-tooled, leather holder attached to his belt, filled it, tamped the tobacco, and inspected his work. He took a worn Zippo lighter from his pocket, lit the tobacco, and sucked the smoke down into his lungs.

"So things just kinda got out of kilter and we ended up with two vehicles. I really wasn't worried. Margaret's a good driver and does a good job of taking care of herself. So I came on down to Memphis, and she was to meet me here. Damned near cost me my family."

He stood and smiled, "Well, that's the short and dirty. Guess I'd better check on the wife and baby. I'll stop in tomorrow."

*****

I didn't have a very good night, lots of things going through my head and none of them very comforting. Things like no money, no job, no place to go, no truck. But I was sure of one thing. I wasn't going to call Daddy and ask for help.

At eight o'clock in the morning, the chatty, redheaded nurse took the IV from my arm and I drifted off to sleep. Just before noon, Mr. Bishop tapped on the door.

"How'd you rest?"

"Oh, pretty well, I reckon."

"Good, good. Stopped by the desk. They still have you listed as John Doe. They tell me you're gonna be released today. After you pay your bill, you'll be free to go."

"Pay my bill?"

"Yep, these are good folks, but their services don't come free or cheap, for that matter."

Things were going from bad to worse. Now on top of everything else, I had a hospital bill to pay.

"Tell you what, Creight. Margaret and I talked about this some. It's our fault you're in this mess. If you want to leave this hospital known as John Doe, it's none of anybody's business."

Bishop searched his shirt pocket and found two sticks of peppermint. He peeled the paper from one and handed me the other. "Look. Some things have come up in Colorado. It's fire season and they need me now.

If I had somebody to drive my truck, I could take Margaret and Josh, fly on up, and get started. I know you've probably got a lot of things to do, but if you could do this for me, I'll give you the cash to pay the hospital bill and I'll pay you for your time."

I was dumbfounded, "Well, I don't know but …"

"I know that it's asking a lot, but you can't ever tell. I'll bet you just might like Colorado."

JUNO 1981

"Yeah. William Creighton Roane. You'd told me you were kinda on your own. I figured that you didn't want to be found so I lied, a big black one. Told them I didn't know anything about anybody with that name."

I couldn't believe what he was telling me, "Thank you for doing that."

"In my line of business, I've conducted a lot of investigations; I've had the ability to reach way out. Dig deep. One time I dug into something that was none of my business."

He looked down at the floor and continued almost sheepishly, "I know who you are. Where you came from. I've even kinda kept tabs on things around Cedergren. Your daddy's lumber company, The Roman Company, is big. Biggest in the southeastern part of the U.S. I know some Forest Service men that have had dealings with him. They all say good things about him. Say he's tough but fair. Creight, he's an old man. I don't know what went on between the two of you and it's none of my damn business. But sometimes you have to let bygones be bygones and just suck it up."

I nodded in agreement.

"I'm not preaching to you, just giving you some advice from an old gray-headed man. You don't have to do like the boy in the story who wanted to go back to his family, but I think you should give it some thought."

ANCHORAGE 1984

Even with the Bishops gone, Alaska was still my home. I loved traveling through the backcountry on a snowmobile, a "tin dog" the natives called it. Local rivers were great for canoeing and, after spending a lot of time upside down underwater, I became better than average in a kayak.

I enjoyed helping load the aerial tankers when they were going out to drop fire retardant and developed an interest in flying. After scraping together a little extra money, I started taking flying lessons. In a couple of years, I got my pilot's license, then my commercial license. The freedom of flight, being up with the eagles, the solitude; it was enough to take your breath.

Seasonal workers made up a large part of the Forest Service work force. One of our seasonals, Jamiesie Cotterill, lived down the street from me. He was an Alaskan of the Aleut people. He was a good-looking fellow with the dark skin of the natives, and his hair had a startling auburn hue. "We were here before the land bridge closed," he boasted. When not working with the Service, Jamiesie hung around the local airport, swapping odd jobs for flying lessons.

We were camping on the Inlet one night and had just finished eating supper when Jamiesie said, "Tell me something about you, where you came from, about your people."

"What brought that on?"

Jamiesie folded his sleeping bag against a log, leaned back, and opened a beer. "I just want to know what makes you tick. I know more about the mating habits of otters than I know about hillbillies." He laughed and held up his hands, "Skip the mating habits of hillbillies and just tell me about your people."

"All right. Tell me when you've had enough."

Watching the moon rising over the bay, I sorted through my memory. "We've lived in the same place in the edge of the Smoky Mountains since before eighteen hundred. That's when one of my distant granddaddies, William McCree Roane, and his brother Joseph came over the mountains from the Carolinas. A lot of other folks with names like McDholl, Kelly, McCall, Grainger, Person, Shannon, and Dwyre. The Grainger family, they were cousins of the Roanes. Don't know why these folks chose to live in the mountains. Guess it might have reminded them of the highlands of Scotland."

Jamiesie leaned forward, "So your folks were Scots?"

"Mostly, I reckon."

"You one of those mountain folks that were always feuding?"

"Yeah, that was us. Guess you could say we were born with a chip on our shoulder. We were always waiting for something to be insulted about. Never forgot or forgave any kinda slight. Sociologists call it a warrior ethic."

"Hatfields and McCoys!" Jamiesie exclaimed, pretending to aim a rifle.

"No. Not like them. Hell, that's up in Kentucky. Anyway, the Roane tribe must have liked the wooded plateaus along the mountain rivers. Sometime in the early 1800s, the Roane brothers built two log cabins and a barn near a place they named Christian Springs.

"The Roane brothers married. William McCree married an Indian woman named Ella Blueleaf. Most of his descendants were dark and had dark hair. Joseph went back to North Carolina and brought back a wife, Herna McCamy. She was a contentious, freckled, redheaded woman, meaner than hell. Six months after she got to the mountains, two of her brothers, Hermes and Artemis, showed up with nothing more than the shirts on their back. Bad seeds, daddy called them. "'Somebody should have castrated all the males and spayed the females. Except seed ticks, they are the worst things in these mountains.'"

"Where did they get those names? Hermes, Herna, what in hell is that?

"Greek mythology. One of the old McCamy women had a book on Greek mythology. She thought the Greek names would make them important."

"Did it?"

I grinned. "What do you think? You ever heard of any of them?"

Jamiesie shook his head.

"Daddy said he had always heard William McCree was an easy-going man, just wanted to run a few cows and hogs, using the scattered balds on the plateau for pasture. Joseph didn't like such hard work. He added a large room to his cabin and opened the Christian Springs Tavern."

"I got a question," Jamiesie interrupted. "You came from the side of William McCree Roane and the Indian woman?"

I laughed. "How did you guess?"

It had started to get cool. Jamiesie turned the collar of his jacket up, "Just didn't want any associating with somebody with those weird McCamy names."

"Our side was always pretty straightforward about names. They always named the first son William and gave him his mother's maiden name for a middle name. Course pretty soon it became kinda confusing with so many of the men named William. So all those first sons started being called by their mothers' maiden name. More in my family to worry about than weird names," I said.

"You hillbillies are strange people, fighting each other all the time and really screwing up names."

"Yeah, I'd talk if I was you. Your folks mostly got names that nobody without a double tongue can even start to pronounce. And they eat raw, fat meat and run around trying to poke sharp sticks into fish and seals."

Jamiesie's white teeth flashed in the twilight, "Okay, okay. Sorry. Go on with your history lesson."

"Joseph's tavern business was pretty good cause the local men liked to come down out of the mountains, bend an elbow, and play cards. They would load up on the local moonshine and get into fights. Law enforcement didn't even exist. Most of the men agreed that the last man standing was probably right in any argument.

"Herna got tired of Joseph and announced she was moving west with a local blacksmith. The night before she was to leave, a barking dog spooked her mule. She was thrown headfirst into an oak tree, bashing her brains out. Herna was a good rider but that was Joseph's story."

Jamiesie raised his hand like he was taking an oath, "That's my story and I'm sticking to it."

"You asked for all this."

"Sorry, go on."

"Three nights later, the tavern burned. They found Joseph's body in the ashes, with a blacksmith's hammer buried up in his head. A couple of weeks later, a circuit judge declared Joseph had taken his own life and no need for further investigation.

"Hermes and Artemis McCamy, were in full agreement with the judge. They whooped, hollered, and toasted the barrister til daylight. Six months later, coming back from mink hunting, they were ambushed. Their killer or killers were never found. Most of the mountain people, except the McCamy tribe, forgot about it pretty quick."

"Just like that," Jamiesie snarled, with a snap of his fingers.

"Pretty much, but you've got to remember, I'm giving you the short version."

Jamiesie slipped down into his sleeping bag and folded his jacket into a pillow, "Go on with your story."

"Daddy said Herna would probably have rather been buried in some other place, but Joseph had picked out a site just above Christian Springs. William McCree figured Joseph and Herna would probably rest better with some distance between their graves. So he planted Joseph about fifty yards higher up the hill from where Herna had been buried just days earlier. He stood by his brother's grave, recited a few verses from the Bible, and played *Amazing Grace* on his battered fiddle. After that it became customary for the Roane men to be buried in a location separate from their wives.

"Daddy once showed me the grave of great-great-granddaddy William McCree Roane, great-granddaddy William Blueleaf Roane, granddaddy William McFadden Roane, and a plot for himself. He told me, 'Us Williams got to stick together and we'll do it to the end. I expect you will be buried here by me, and when you have a son, he'll be buried beside you, and his son will be laid to rest beside him.'"

I waited for another question from Jamiesie but the only sound that came from his lips was a soft snore.

The Prospector wasn't the fanciest bar in Anchorage. But the management tolerated the lies bush pilots told: dangerous landings, scary takeoffs, running out of gas, mountain crashes, and some of the nastiest weather on earth. An old pilot called Lefty usually waited to tell his story last. He claimed he was hauling a grizzly cub, it got loose and bit off his right hand. Nobody could ever top that story.

Late one afternoon, Jamiesie and I drew up a business plan on a Prospector bar napkin. If we could scrape enough money together, we would buy a used bush plane and open a little flying service. Nothing big, a little four-seater that could make short take offs and landings, something we could set down on a sandbar or a short strip in the bush.

We tried every bank in town with no luck. Not only had we never been in business, but we didn't even have enough money for a down payment. I called Mr. Bishop to ask his advice, which was, "Just take it easy and try the same banks again in a couple of weeks." It didn't make a lot of sense, but I had never known him to be wrong.

Two weeks later, the first bank we walked into approved our loan, saying they had checked around and thought we were a good risk. We walked out of the bank with our heads in the clouds and a substantial letter of credit.

Our new business was slow in the beginning but we had enough clients to make the monthly payments on the plane. Usually, one of us would take anglers out into the backcountry and drop them off. The next weekend, the other would go out and pick them up. Jamiesie grumbled, "We're just running a flying taxi."

Reviewing our clients at the end of the year, we found most of them came from the southern part of U.S. - Florida or Georgia. I smelled the handiwork of Mr. Bishop. After all these years, he was still looking out for me.

The Service's budget was cut and I took an early retirement. Now that I was able to fly full time, our little air service bloomed and we became busier. We bought a second plane, a floatplane this time. We needed a name for the company and decided on Aleutian Air. "Pretty impressive sounding," I kidded Jamiesie, "considering we started our business on a beer-soaked napkin."

ANCHORAGE 1986

One of the drawbacks of operating our bush flying service was spending so much down time in the flight lounge of outlying airports, reading old magazines.

One night, while waiting for clients to finish their supply purchase, I thumbed through an old *National Geographic*. The featured spread chronicled a man in the mountains of eastern Tennessee who had introduced woodland bison into a remote area, a secluded plateau called the Arn. A map and a larger map showing more detail followed the introductory page. I found myself looking at the familiar serpentine route of the Findhorn as it flowed around the perimeter of the Arn. The article explained that a security fence at the southern end of the plateau and the steep sides of the escarpment permitted the bison to roam freely over the area without any fear of their escaping.

On the next page, a photo of an old stone fort and a thumbnail relating the legends around it. The final page showed a gray-haired man standing in a mountain meadow unloading a block of salt from a battered station wagon. Two men, one white and one black, were working in the background cleaning out a hay trough. Painted on the opened door of the station wagon was the profile of a Roman centurion.

I folded the magazine and put it in my jacket. Outside in the cold Alaskan night, I watched the northern lights undulate across the dark sky.

So that's what Zeale Roane looks like, I thought. My daddy is getting old.

*****

A cold rain had been falling for a long time. The ground was muddy and it clung to my boots making them as cumbersome as ski boots. Walking across the mountain meadow, I felt a trembling in the earth, turned and looked over my shoulder as the first of the bison emerged from the timberland. They turned and came straight toward me, led by two large, shaggy bulls. They looked like some primitive beasts, maybe mastodons, and now the two were followed by thousands coming toward me in a wild stampede. I couldn't run because of the mud on my boots. My feet and legs felt like they were made of concrete. Lightning blazed and thunder roared atop the timber. I fell, then got up and tried to run again.

Ahead of me in the center of the meadow, a man dressed in khakis was motioning me to come toward him. He represented safety from the thundering herd, and with my lungs filling with fire, I ran toward him. He disappeared in the mist that rose from the ground. Like water flowing around a rock, the bison herd separated where he had been standing. The herd came back together into one mass. I could see the foam running from their mouths and hear the rumbling of their cloven hoofs. I knew I was going to be trampled in the muddy field. I fell again. Then the bison were upon me.

I woke up on my hands and knees, gasping for breath.

I finished servicing our floatplane and was sitting in our small office when Jamiesie walked in, greeting me with his standard, "How's it hanging, hillbilly?"

The normal reply would have been, "Way below normal!" But not this morning. I'd had trouble going back to sleep after last night's dream. "Don't know, Jamiesie, I feel like I'm just barely ahead of the hounds this morning."

Jamiesie poured a cup of coffee. "Nightmares again?"

"Yeah."

Our charter clients were starting to unload their gear from the back of their green jeep as we walked out to the aircraft.

"Same kind?"

"Pretty much. They are hell on sleep. Anyway, time for me to saddle up and make these folks happy."

Just before sundown, after a successful day of fishing in a large lake about two hundred miles to the north, I landed under overcast skies and taxied up to the mooring space we leased. The fishermen left our parking lot shouting cheerful goodbyes. I was glad to see them go.

Our office was dark. One of my hunting coats had fallen to the floor and Clawed had snuggled up on it. He was, in my opinion, a handsome cat with a superb personality. I'd picked him up in the alley behind my house two years ago when Ellie decided I would never be husband material and moved on. Clawed was just a mangy kitten with exposed ribs. He was a tuxedo cat, black and white with a triangular shaped goatee, and as he filled out, his coat became glossy. Such a great looking animal deserved a title. I gave him one: Clawed the Magnificent. Trading Ellie for Clawed was one of the best trades ever made in Alaska, ranked right up there alongside the Seward's Icebox trade with the Russians.

A note from Jamiesie on my desk: "Got a two-day charter up to Caribou Falls - spend the night in the lodge - want to do a little fishing and a lot of drinking. Told them I was their man. See you late tomorrow. Sleep tight. Try not feeding the nightmares."

I gathered up Clawed, climbed in my old pickup, and started home through the misty rain with the cat in his accustomed place atop one of my wool caps. We picked up a six-pack of Bud and a half-pound of sharp cheese. Clawed and I would share a can of sardines. At my house, I fired up the gas heater and opened the beer and the sardines.

Most people would have thought Clawed and I lived pretty rough. Bachelorhood seemed to suit both of us. I had picked up an old dresser and a bed at a second-hand store. They didn't match but that didn't seem to cramp our style. We had a kitchen table and two chairs, a stove with two working eyes setting over a worthless oven, and a fridge that wheezed like an old woman with asthma. We spent most of our time at home in the living room where I had a couch that over the years had developed depressions where I had protrusions. We had a good reading light and a brown recliner spotted with spilled Bud. Most important, we had a satellite dish and a color TV.

I liked hunting and fishing shows. Clawed mostly watched cartoons. His second choice was basketball games. He perched on top of the TV, swatting at the players as they ran up and down the court. We had reduced our collection of furniture after Clawed, with a lot of encouragement on my part, learned he no longer needed a litter box and could pee outside like a big boy.

I was well into my third beer and second package of crackers. Clawed was standing in the center of the living room floor, licking sardine-oil off his lips, staring at me. "All right, don't glare at me like that. I'll find us a cartoon." He climbed up into my lap and burrowed under my newspaper. I started channel surfing.

The *Discovery* channel was showing an old, rerun program on wild turkeys, not hunting them but how this one man was reestablishing them on some isolated generational mountain. A great shot showed wild turkeys strutting across a pasture. The late afternoon sun struck the turkeys' feathers and turned them to bronze and deep purple. The camera focused on a man sitting astride a red sorrel mule, a burlap bag across the pommel of his saddle, feeding the turkeys shelled corn.

The old man's voice was rough but his words were smooth and rounded. "Six years ago we brought this strain of wild turkeys back into these mountains. They are one of two strains in the United States that has not been corrupted by domestic stock. The Cherokees and our ancestors hunted this kind of bird. They're original, a lot more original than we are here in Tennessee."

The narrator commented about the beauty of the area, the pristine woodland, and the clear streams. The camera swung across the pasture and focused on a single bison bull at the edge of the escarpment, rubbing his horns against a large shagbark hickory.

The camera panned again to the old man. He had dismounted and a dark-haired young man was loading the mule into a horse trailer. I could just make out the faded logo on the door of the white four-wheel drive pickup pulling the trailer, the profile of a Roman centurion.

The narrator concluded by saying, "This is as real as it gets."

Scratching between Clawed's ears, I mouthed the narrator's final words, "…as real as it gets."

Bored with the *Discovery* channel, Clawed decided it was time for his last pee of the day. I let him out with the admonition, "Watch out for the meanies, old buddy."

*****

Wild turkeys visited my dreams that night. They filled my den and attacked Clawed, tearing his body to shreds right before my eyes. I was powerless to stop them. An old man wearing khakis leaned against a horse trailer and watched.

*****

The next morning Clawed was not in his usual place outside the kitchen door. He didn't come when I called, so I left a bowl of food on the back steps. He was not around when I went outside to get the paper either. He still hadn't showed up when I left for work mid-morning.

Damned cat, I thought, I hope he had a better night than I did.

*****

It was a slow day, so I caught up on some overdue paperwork and paid some bills. We were now operating clearly in the black. It was a good feeling to lay a few bucks back. "Nookie money," Jamiesie called it.

I was enjoying the sunshine and my first beer of the day when Jamiesie buzzed the office and then set the aircraft down. He and his clients walked up to our small office, laughing like long-time friends. They loaded an ice chest filled with trout in the back of their car and shook hands. Driving off, the driver rolled his window down, gave a final wave and shouted, "Helluva trip, Jamiesie, helluva trip! See you in a month."

On the porch, Jamiesie sat on an old rickety chair, removed the rubber band that held his shoulder-length hair in a ponytail, and combed it out with his fingers. "Glad that's over, what a couple of jerks. Those guys kept me up until half past two, laughing, telling sorry old jokes, and drinking Scotch. It'll take me a month to recover."

I nodded.

"Regular Mr. Sunshine this morning, ain't you?"

"Screw you."

"What's eating at you?"

"I'm not sleeping, I've got nightmares like you wouldn't believe. Clawed didn't show up this morning. My life is heading for the crapper in a straight line. I'm not passing go, and I'm not collecting two hundred dollars."

"Hey, we've got nothing on the books for tomorrow, unfortunately. Why don't you and Clawed take the day off. Maybe take in a movie. Go out, have a couple of beers, and look for some female companionship. Spend some of that nookie money."

"First smart thing you've said this month."

I drove home in blue funk listening to some man with a nasal voice singing about home, sadness, and women crying in the grave yard on a rain swept night.

Not the kind of song for someone in my state of mind.

Clawed wasn't waiting in his usual place on the front steps. In the back yard, I found his ragged body. Something caught him and tore him into pieces, slinging guts all over the yard. I found where the first attack must have taken place. There was cat hair and blood where Clawed had come under the back fence. Then, apparently, just before he reached the opening under the house and safety, his attacker caught and killed him.

I gathered his remains and wrapped them in his favorite blanket. I sat in the dark with his mutilated body in my lap. Goddamn you, whoever you are. Just goddamn your sorry soul to Hell. Through my tears, I thought, poor old Clawed, you damned near made it didn't you? You damned near got back home.

Late night, by the light of a kerosene lantern, I dug a deep grave beside Clawed's favorite honeysuckle bush. I kept thinking - You almost got home. You'd have made it if you had just started a little earlier, just a little earlier.

*****

I was holding a Silva timber cruiser's compass and taking a sighting. It was getting dark and I knew I had less than an hour to reach my destination. I had seen the man earlier in the afternoon standing on a cliff and motioning me toward him. "Set the needle on south thirty-five east and hold the line – you'll be here before it gets dark," he kept repeating. In the fading light, I was running over the low hills trying to maintain my bearing. But I kept getting off course and had to readjust my heading. In the last bit of daylight, I reached the bottom of the cliff. I reached up and just before clutching the man's extended hand, lost my footing and tumbled backward into the darkness. I felt my body being torn apart and scattered on the forest floor.

Not much sleeping took place that night. But I did a lot of thinking about my life, the things I had done, and I thought about Daddy and all the years we hadn't spoken. Other than the segment on TV and the article in the old *Geographic*, I had not seen him in almost thirty years. Where had the time gone?

Maybe some spirit, something far out in the future or way back in time, was trying to send me a message. After all, neither Daddy nor I was getting any younger. I felt a need to try to patch things up between us. All kinds of thoughts rambled through my mind: Why had Daddy been so hard on me? Why had I been such a hothead? The "whys" were like sparrows fleeing in panic before a windstorm.

For the second time in my life, and the first time since becoming an adult, I felt lost, lonely, and afraid.

Maybe I'd found a lesson in Clawed's death. Maybe my time was running out. Maybe I needed to go home before something bad happened to me between the fence and safety. Maybe something evil and fierce was waiting for me out there in the dark.

*****

Not a good day - rainy, foggy - and by noon all my beer had disappeared. I went down to the corner, got a 12-pack, stopped by a used bookstore and bought a secondhand Bible. I spent most of the afternoon trying to find the story about the lost son. I wanted to know what finally made him go home. I found it in Luke and was relieved. I hadn't come to the point where I was eating with the hogs; not yet anyway.

I didn't sleep very well that night but at least I didn't have nightmares. I dreamed a lot about Clawed. We were at the grocery shopping for sardines. We took a sackfull home and he sat in my lap licking the last bit of oil from the can. He snuggled up against my stomach. I stroked the fur between his ears. He purred, and the tiny ragged rumble put me to sleep.

Stiff and sore the next morning from sleeping on the couch, I barely stopped myself from opening the back door and calling Clawed in for breakfast. I cooked a couple of eggs, made some toast, and brewed a pot of coffee. After eating and having a cup of coffee, I cleaned up the kitchen and took the trash out to the garbage can. I threw away five unopened cans of sardines but I kept the sixth, just in case Clawed was due another life.

Two boards had come loose from an old storage building and I made a marker for Clawed's grave. With a router, I cut on the cross arm of the marker:

> *'Clawed the Magnificent*
> *A Good Buddy'*

Afterward, I sat at the kitchen table drinking coffee and trying to calculate the difference between Alaskan and east Tennessee time.

*****

The Knoxville operator found two 800-numbers, three department numbers, an aviation number, and a general number for The Roman Company. She asked if I wanted the general number. I told her I would settle for that.

When I left, Roman had only one company number and now seven!

I looked a long time at the number. Maybe I was not ready for the next step. I got the folded *Geographic* from my desk drawer and looked at the photos of the bison and the old man again. I got another cup of coffee, poured two fingers of Irish cream in it, and reached for the phone.

A female voice answered, "Roman Company, how may I direct your call?"

I mumbled something about speaking to Breazeale Roane.

"I'm sorry, sir, Mr. Roane is out of town and is not expected back until late this afternoon."

"Uh, someone else I could talk to?"

"Certainly, sir. May I ask the nature of your business? Then I can connect you with someone who can assist you."

"Yes ma'am. Someone Mr. Roane leaves in charge when he is gone."

"That would be Mr. Luther Sears, but I'm afraid he is unavailable. Please give me your number and when Mr. Sears is available, he'll return your call."

I licked my dry lips. "No, I'll call back later. Thank you."

"Just a moment, please. Mr. Sears has just gotten off the phone. I'll connect you."

There was a brief pause. "Luther Sears."

"I, uh, I just wanted to, uh…." My voice turned into a croak.

"I'm sorry. I didn't catch your name. We seem to have a very poor connection. Could you give me your name again and your company?"

I stammered, "It's Creight and I wanted to find out about…."

Sweat rolled down my forehead, I hung up and sat staring at the phone, shaking.

*****

On learning I had southern roots, a client had given me a commemorative bottle of Jack Daniel. I took it out of the fancy wooden box, set it on the kitchen table, and broke the seal. I tossed down two shots.

"Good evening, Mr. Jack."

*****

"Creight, what in the hell is wrong with you? Why didn't you answer your damn phone? What were you doing laying under the table?"

I was hanging over the kitchen sink. "Sick. I'm sick"

He picked up the empty bottle, "You didn't drink all this by yourself, did you?"

I emptied the contents of my stomach – foul, green, evil tasting - in the sink.

"You're a damn mess. Shit-faced."

He put my arm over his shoulder and he walked me to the couch - dragged me is more like it.

"Get away," I managed to mumble. My tongue was the size of a catcher's mitt. "Let me die."

"Screw you," Jamiesie said. "Partners are too hard to break in."

"I'm serious," I whispered, "I'm not going to live through this."

I smelled coffee. Jamiesie was trying to put my fingers through the handle of a mug.

"Get a good grip on this, old buddy," he said in a voice much too loud. "You dump this hot stuff in your lap and you're going to be doing your own doctoring. I really like you, but some things I just don't do. Here are three aspirin, finish your coffee and I'll give you a couple more."

An hour later, after a pot of coffee, a cold shower, and more aspirins, I could walk a reasonably straight course. Jamiesie sat in my easy chair watching TV, which was thankfully muted.

"Thanks for the coffee," I said.

"Thank you for living. Damn what a mess! What's wrong with you?"

"I called home yesterday."

Jamiesie turned the TV off. "You what?"

I took the *Geographic* from the kitchen table and turned to the article. It took him ten minutes to read it. When he finished, he looked up and said, "Your daddy?"

I nodded.

"Damn. How long has it been since you've seen him?"

"Long time. About thirty years, I guess."

Jamiesie scanned the story again. "Damn, thirty years. Who're these other folks? You know them?"

"The black man is Luther Sears. We grew up together. He's kinda like a brother. I don't know the white kid. Guess he works with Daddy."

"Tell me about it, Creight."

I would have laughed except for my throbbing temples, "Which part?"

Jamiesie reached to the side of the recliner, pulled the lever upward, leaned back, crossed his ankles and said, "All of it."

"I was three when mother died giving birth to my brother. The baby never breathed. Daddy never remarried, and we lived out at Christian Springs in the house he had built after marrying Mother. This was right at the end of the Depression, and Daddy was busy trying to keep his timber business going. He didn't have time to raise a three-year-old. He hired a black woman, Winnie Sears, to take care of me and the house. She had a grandson that lived with her. Luther was just three years older than me, a skinny-legged boy with big scared eyes. I liked him a lot."

"So, you never really knew your mother?"

"Barely. I guess she mostly lived in my memory."

"What's this about the stone fort?"

I closed my eyes for a second. It came into focus. "Not much of it left. About five feet high and maybe couple hundred feet long. Most of it has fallen down. There's still some depressions along the north side of the wall floored with smaller stones. Nobody really knows who built it. Most archeologists think it was an early Indian culture. Maybe a ceremonial site. Lots of arrowheads scattered all over the place. But others say the east-west orientation of the wall lines up with sunrise and sunset at the solar equinox."

Jamiesie cleared his throat, "Nothing like sacrificing virgins at sunrise."

"Wrong Indians. We're way too far north. Local Indians talk about a race of fair skinned, blue eyed, and blond haired people who once lived in the mountains. The Indians called them "moon-eyes."

"Moon-eyes?"

"Yeah. They may have built the fort for protection. The Indians believe their ancestors made war against the moon-eyes. The moon-eyes took refuge behind the stone walls and the Indians laid siege. During the dark nights in August - nights with no moon - the Indians breached the walls. The defenders were killed, and the women and children were thrown off the cliff into the Findhorn River."

Jamiesie laced his fingers behind his head. "I believe I like the second version."

"There are etchings and drawings on the bluff, a couple hundred feet below the edge of the plateau. They look like flying birds.

"Luther and I used to stand on the edge of the bluff and throw chunks of wood into the river. Sometimes we were moon-eyes, killing the invading Indians and throwing their bodies off the cliff. Sometimes we were the Indians, throwing the moon-eyes into the Findhorn. But we never disturbed the ceremonial circles inside the walls. We didn't know who built them but we sure didn't want to make their spirits unhappy."

"Unhappy spirits, wooooo."

I ignored him. "The strangest time around the fort was when the north wind would blow up through a large crevice at the very tip of the bluff. The noise would pulsate between a low moan and a shriek. Luther and I pretended the noise came from broken bodies of the moon-eyes lodged in the crevice."

"Anybody ever do a dig. I mean somebody with some training?"

"Several times after Daddy took control of the Arn, amateur archeologists and professors from the University of the South at Sewanee talked with him about doing studies. Daddy always turned them down flat,

'Just let the poor folks, whoever or whatever they were, rest in peace.' That ended that and whatever the mystery there was remained a mystery."

"The night we camped on the Inlet, you talked about Yankees. Your folks have any trouble with them?"

"Not really. Most of the people who lived in my part of the mountains were poor. Didn't own slaves. So, as great-granddaddy Blue once told a Union officer, 'We ain't got no dog in this fight and we'll thank you to keep the hell off our land.' Southern raiders knew how clannish the mountain folks were and didn't send foraging troops onto the plateau. Every once in a while Yankee troops who were strangers to the area came through looking to steal livestock. Daddy would laugh and say, 'If the sumbitches got out alive, come hell or high water, they wouldn't come back.'"

Jamiesie leaned forward, "Bunch of badasses."

"I never gave it much thought. It was just the way folks in the mountains were. They were all tough. Granddaddy Fad came down with the pox. He lived but he was really disfigured. Had thick scar tissue on his eyelids. His eyelashes couldn't come through the tissue, so instead of growing outward normal, they grew inward. The ingrown lashes caused ulcers to develop on the surface of his eyes and he went blind.

"Granddaddy Fad developed a mean streak and nasty behavior. Because he was blind, wasn't much he could do. His brothers built a little store at Christian Springs and he ran it. Daddy talked about his father sitting in a straight wooden chair out on the store porch, cursing his blindness while he whittled small figurines from dried peach seeds.

"I think Granddaddy was a real pain in the ass. The older he got, he got more quarrelsome. He accused my grandmother of being unfaithful. Daddy said he didn't know how she put up with his father.

"One night about closing time, two of the McCamy brothers, Achilles and Ajax, came into the store to buy chewing tobacco and shotgun shells."

"These McCamys, they're the distant cousins with the weird names?"

"Yep, one and the same. Folks say the brothers were always looking for a fight. Granddaddy accused Ajax of trying to have grandmother meet him out at the barn and lay with him in the hay. Ajax slapped him. Granddaddy staggered to the front door, locked it, and blew out the kerosene lamp.

"Since Granddaddy was accustomed to being in darkness, he had the upper hand. He cornered Ajax behind the counter and stabbed him with a butcher knife. But Achilles slit Granddaddy's throat. He later bragged, '… contrary old bastard was dead before he hit the floor.'"

"He killed a blind man?"

"Yeah. So in the spring of 1920, they buried Granddaddy Fad beside his father, Blue.

"Two months to the day, Achilles McCamy apparently cut most of his foot off with an ax. He bled to death at his still up at Massey Springs. Four days later, Brontes McCamy disappeared. Folks said Granddaddy's first cousin, Buck Grainger, was the last man to see either of the McCamy brothers alive."

Jamiesie punched his fist into an open palm, "Yeah. Teach them to not screw around with a Roane, didn't it?"

"I don't know. Stuff like that wasn't too uncommon in the mountains."

Jamiesie looked at the photos of the Arn again, "So this is where you grew up?"

"Until I was about 14. I spent all of my free time along the Findhorn. Had a good buddy, Vaughn Blackman. His folks were bankers. They helped Daddy with financing in the timber business. Vaughn and I knew the river backwards and forwards."

"Where is he now?"

"Don't know. Don't know any more about him than anybody else in Cedergren."

"Damn, Creight, you're pretty cold. You know that?"

"Okay Jamiesie, I'm cutting you out of my will."

"I'm pretty crushed but I'm not surprised. Go on with your story."

"Just before I started high school, Daddy built a three-bedroom house and a little office outside of Cedergren. Down the road, he built a house for Winnie and Luther. It raised a few eyebrows in town, a black family living so close to white folks. Daddy said, 'Winnie and Luther are a part of our family and, if you don't like it, it's just tough.'"

Jamiesie turned a page and studied the photograph of Daddy. "I never knew my daddy. Wish I could have been around him. You're pretty lucky."

"Maybe. I grew up in Daddy's shadow. I spent a lot of time in the woods with him, using a chainsaw and an ax. I was good with a bulldozer, building a log road, pulling logs out of the woods, plowing a firebreak. Daddy was a good forester. His way of teaching was to expose me to the best practices - which just happened to be his method.

"By the time I was sixteen I was grading lumber and if the mill wasn't running, Daddy would let me drive a semi loaded with lumber to the rail siding in Cedergren."

"So you working with the Forest Service was a lot like working for your Daddy. 'Cept sounds like he worked your ass off."

"We worked hard. Fished and hunted together. Beautiful country, I'm telling you. Looking out over the mountains, Daddy would spread his hand and move it across the horizon and say, 'Son, you're looking at the heritage of the Roane family. It's ours - all of it. We have our sweat and blood and a few tears invested in it. If we're good stewards, it'll be ours until God needs it.'

"Those times sit in the back of my mind like a trophy on a shelf. One time, I heard city people felt sorry for our backward way of life. Let me tell you, one fall afternoon of quail hunting on the Arn would have forever cured them of those thoughts."

Jamiesie put the magazine on the floor and leaned toward me. "Creight, you sound like … well, something is hanging."

"As much as I loved Daddy, something was always missing. Something … a space and …it never really closed, something I couldn't put my finger on. I think it was respect and acceptance that I wanted. I needed to know that he knew I was nearing manhood."

"Validation. You wanted validation."

"Yeah, that's what folks call it today, I needed validating. I'd spend ten hours in the logwoods doing the same amount of work as any of the hired hands. But he never seemed to notice. He never said, 'good job.' Never, in any way, did he acknowledge my accomplishments.

"Over the years, looking back on my relationship with my daddy and trying to analyze what was happening, maybe I've discovered something. Daddy had been on his own since he was twenty years old. He wanted me to be his kind of man. Maybe he accomplished what he set out to do, but he never did get around to recognizing the finished product."

Jamiesie ran his fingers through his hair, "Maybe I did just as well not knowing my Daddy."

"I didn't mean for it to sound all bad, but parts of it were pretty hurtful."

Jamiesie stood, "Well, some of us have to work, to try to keep Aleutian Air off the ground. Guess it's my day in the barrel. Sides you don't need to be out in public scaring little children and dogs the way you look."

*****

I opened the magazine again. I'm pretty sure the black man with my father is Luther. I couldn't picture him as anything more than the spindly-legged boy Aunt Winnie used to switch right after she got through switching me. I was very proud of him somehow.

I spent the rest of the day putting together my next call. I thought about telling some big lie about how I was in the timber business and needed a job. But what I really wanted to know was about Daddy's health, and there was no way to work that kind of question into a job search.

I decided, Hell, I'm a big boy. I'll just come right out, tell them who I am, and ask to speak to my daddy.

The next morning, I dialed again.

"Roman Company, how may I direct your call?"

"Yes, this is Creight. May I speak with Luther Sears?"

"May I tell Mr. Sears the name of your firm, please?"

"Yes, it's Aleutian Air Service."

"One moment please."

Luther's voice came on the line, "Good morning, Mr. Crate. Sorry about the broken connection earlier. We had quite a windstorm through here and our phone service was disrupted."

Too deep to turn back now. "Luther, it's Creighton, Creighton Roane."

There was a long silence, then, "Sir, I don't find your sense of humor amusing."

"Come on, Luther. It's been a long time but you haven't forgotten me. I just want to know how Daddy is getting along."

"Sir, I don't know what kind of game you are playing, but Creighton Roane has been dead thirty years."

"No, Luther, I'm not dead."

Luther's voice was a low rumble, "No, obviously you are not dead. But Creighton Roane is. He drowned in the Loosahatchie River in 1956. I suggest you not call here again or I will contact the authorities."

For the next few hours, my emotions ranged from stunned to anger and to deep sadness. What if I never really lived? Could I just be some misty, thin plume of smoke rising out from nothing and disappearing into nothing? Maybe I wasn't real, maybe I never existed at all, maybe my memories were not connected to anything, maybe I was crazy and all my thoughts were based on nothing. Maybe I really drowned in the Loosahatchie. Maybe my state of mind was just part of death. Maybe in death my mind was searching, trying to reach back into life, trying to bring closure.

*****

I was drowning in the muddy water of a swollen, west Tennessee river. Two men stood on the bank of the river oblivious to my calls for help. They were within ten feet of me and yet they were unable to see me. I pleaded with them, "Daddy, Luther, please help me." I felt myself vaporizing into a thin mist and then I was absorbed by the low hanging clouds.

*****

I got up the next morning long before the alarm went off and made a pot of coffee. I drank three cups and poured the rest into a thermos. I was probably in no condition to fly, but I had an early morning charter. Sometimes dollars came before common sense. Besides, it would be good to get my mind on something other than my phone conservation with Luther.

We made the short flight up to the river and within three hours my clients had caught the limit of trout. I cleaned three of the smaller fish and fried them over an open fire. The two clients, both in their 70s and obviously pretty well heeled, took some pictures and by mid-afternoon we were on our way back home.

Fifteen minutes after landing the floatplane and unloading their gear, I dropped them off at the airport. With five one-hundred-dollar bills in my jeans pocket, I believed I owed myself a cold beer.

I walked into the Prospector and looked up at the TV screen: a cute young woman sitting at an anchor desk…"The Findhorn River…dead men with amulets…Cedergren…Roman Company…and the Arn."

I felt as if I'd lost control of my mind.

*****

I dreaded going to sleep that night and hoped I was too exhausted to dream. No such luck. But the dream was shorter than the other nightmares.

I was standing on the edge of the river below the stone fort looking up toward the rim of the escarpment. Clawed came floating over the side and I watched in horror as he bounced off the rocks in his downward flight. He landed at my feet. I picked up his mangled body - he had an Indian amulet around his neck.

*****

I got to work hours before Jamiesie and was on my third cup of strong coffee when he arrived. He took one look at my bloodshot eyes, shook his head and said, "Creight, I don't know what kind of bunch you are hanging around with at night, but they are obviously too young for you."

I was in no mood to listen to Jamiesie. "Piss off."

"Going to take more than that to make me feel bad, old buddy. While you were out yesterday afternoon spreading your sweetness, we got a call from some big shot in North Carolina. Wants to charter us for a week and he specifically asked for you. They overnighted a five thousand dollar retainer. Picked it up at Fed Ex this morning. Looks like we're going to make plane payments a little early this month."

Jamiesie went into a bad soft-shoe routine while snapping his fingers and did one of those Jimmy Cagney things. He sang, "Now smile, darn you, smile."

This was a pleasant surprise. "You're kidding! Who's the client?"

"North Georgia Global. They'll be here at noon tomorrow – three of them. Guy I talked with was named Logomicino or something like that. Said they'd work out the details when they got here. I tell you, it sure is nice to work with a popular feller like you. Makes my life so much easier. I may change your name to Cash Cow."

"I may change your name to Smart Ass. Why don't you be a good boy, trot down to the bank and deposit the check? I'll hang around here and see if I can develop some more rich clients."

"Yes sir, boss, I'm on my way. But do me a favor: promise tomorrow you'll shower and wear a clean shirt."

I spent the afternoon going over both planes, since we did not know which one we would need. It was nice to have something to take my mind off the death of Clawed and all the other stuff going on in my life.

Early afternoon, Jamiesie came bouncing into the office with a big grin on his face. "Sweet little girl at the bank called me Mr. Cotterill when I deposited the check. Gave me a big smile and told me how much she liked to fly." Jamiesie looked at his reflection in our office door and carefully adjusted the part in his hair with his fingers, "Do believe I've just reached first base. After we take a little spin tomorrow afternoon, I'm going for second. Of course, I give all the credit to you, Cash Cow."

*****

For the first time in weeks, I slept a solid six hours. After breakfast, I got a haircut and even had my beard trimmed. It was not an everyday occurrence that Aleutian Air had a five thousand dollar charter retainer. I wanted to make a good impression.

Jamiesie was standing outside the office, looking worried.

"Those folks got here about an hour ago. Two of them are down at International having breakfast. Guess they flew all night. Logomicino feller came up here hunting you. Apologized for being early. Seemed nice enough. Dressed well: blazer, tie, and all that stuff. Big man, go about six four, two hundred fifty pounds. Pretty much all muscle. Had a bad scar running back from his mouth to his ear. He didn't smile much. Didn't talk much either. He prowled around the office looking at the photographs on the wall. He asked if you were in any of the pictures."

"Probably need to have some glamour shots made," I said.

"Yeah, sure. I pointed out the one where you were holding up that big trout you accidently caught last spring. He studied the picture for a long time and then asked if he could take it with him back down to the terminal. Creight, here is the thing that really spooked me. He leaned over to get a cup from the water cooler and I swear to God, he's packing heat. Something big, something like folks out in the bush carry as bear insurance. Maybe a .357 or a .45. You ain't been in something bad I don't know about, have you?"

"Naw, you're probably just seeing things. Sounds like you might have a guilty conscience bout the sweet young thing at the bank. Maybe you're not ready for second base."

Jamiesie shook his head, "Nope, I know big heat when I see it and I know bad men when I see them. This old boy needs watching. I'll go along with you to this meeting. I've got accustomed to having you around. Besides, you'll need somebody to carry their luggage."

We drove down to the terminal in our ratty jeep. Once inside Jamiesie said, "I'll have some breakfast and keep an eye on you fellers. You ain't leaving with these men until I get a little more comfortable with this situation. Old-big-ugly is sitting at the table by the back window. This is the first time I've seen his little buddy. They sure don't look like they go together."

Both men stood. Jamiesie was right. Logomicino was big. He held out his hand and mine disappeared in it. "Good morning. I'm Tony Logomicino. Hope we didn't disrupt your plans by arriving early." He nodded toward the man standing to his right, "This is Belton Essary. He'll be going along with us."

Essary was slightly built with fair skin and reddish thinning hair. I didn't think he was an outdoorsman. He would have been more at home behind a desk in some air-conditioned office. Nevertheless, his handshake was firm.

He motioned for me to sit. "We've just ordered. Would you like something to eat?"

"No, but thank you, anyway." I didn't see the photo Logomicino had taken from the office wall. "How'd you like the trout?"

"Impressive," Essary said. "Our fishing buddy took it back to the plane to show to the pilots. None of us have ever caught one half that size."

Something suspicious worked its way up my spine. You're lying, I thought, but I said, "They're fairly common in some of the rivers up to the north."

Logomicino had been studying me intently. He had a slight frown on his face. He folded his hands on the table and stared at them, "Mr. Creight, you raised in Alaska?"

I couldn't help looking at his big hands and scarred misshapen knuckles. "No, but I've been here several years and am pretty familiar with all the good fishing places."

"You raised in the Lower-Forty Eight?"

"Mostly. I've knocked around a lot in my life."

Essary smiled, "I believe I detect a hint of southern drawl in your speech."

"Well, you know how it is. They say in fifty years everybody in the United States will sound the same."

Essary took a slim black case from his coat pocket and ran his finger down the page. He looked up, "Mr. Creight, since you'll be flying some senior members of our company for the next few days, Mr. Logomicino and I have done a cursory check on you and your company. We were surprised you have been in business for such a short period, and you got your commercial license only three years ago. I must say, however, you have come highly recommended."

"Well, Mr. Essary, I appreciate your approval." Watching Logomicino closely, I saw him detect my sarcasm and stiffen.

Essary resumed looking at the page in the black case. "We were more surprised that twice in the past week you've called The Roman Company office. Once hanging up and the second time attempting to pass yourself off as Creighton Roane. We find this very disturbing. Would you care to explain your actions?"

Furious, I stood up, "Who in the hell are you?"

Logomicino towered over me. With his hand on my shoulder he forced me back into my seat. He leaned forward. His face almost touched mine. He growled, "No, who in the hell are you? And why are you trying to pass yourself off as Creighton Roane?"

In my peripheral vision I saw Jamiesie starting toward our table, a metal napkin dispenser in each hand. Logomicino, without taking his eyes from mine, said, "Tell your long haired friend to stay out of this. We're not interested in him. Just you. I don't want to hurt him unless I have to."

I motioned for Jamiesie to stop, "It's okay, just a little misunderstanding. We'll be able to sort this out."

Essary smiled, "Good move on your part. I'm sure we will be able to resolve this problem to everyone's satisfaction."

"I don't know what problem you're talking about."

Essary shook his head slightly, "Sure you do. What are you after? Money? Revenge? Or are you just stupid?"

I stood up again and looked at Essary, "You tell this ugly sumbitch to not touch me again. Wherever you're from you may bully folks around, but we operate a little different up here. I'm walking out of here and you can take your retainer and stuff it sideways up your ass."

"Just like I thought, you're gutless," Logomicino said. "You try to scam an old man, but when the chips are down you cut and run."

I felt my face burning, "You big sumbitch, I'm not gutless."

Logomicino stood again. His right hand slid under his jacket.

"Pull that gun and I'll beat the crap out of you, right here in front of your boss." I said that through clenched teeth and with a lot more confidence than I really had.

Logomicino looked at Essary, who nodded. Logomicino sat down.

Essary said, "Who are you?"

I was so mad I felt myself starting to shake. I leaned forward and rested my clenched fists on the table, trying to control my emotions. "My name is William Creighton Roane. My daddy is William Breazeale Roane. I don't have to prove shit to you or anybody else. I've been on my own since I was eighteen years old, and I'll be on my own long after you are dead and gone."

Essary looked closely at me, "Where were you raised?"

"I'm not going to play this game with you."

Logomicino asked, "You think this is a game?"

"I told you who I am – game over."

Logomicino stared at me with his cold eyes, "I'll let you know when the game is over."

I had regained some of my composure, "That's it, buddy. No more third-degree. No more Mickey Mouse shit. Get you another pilot."

Essary stood and nodded his head toward the door leading out to the area where corporate aircraft parked. "I've got something I want to show you - come outside just a minute," he said.

I followed Essary out into the bright noonday sun. As my eyes adjusted to the brightness, I could see a half dozen corporate aircraft. Big, expensive stuff. Parked in the second tier was a shiny Learjet 31 with the silhouette of a Roman centurion on the vertical stabilizer.

A tall man with close-cropped, graying hair and slightly stooped shoulders was coming down the air ramp from the plane.

Essary asked, "You know that man?"

"You're damned straight I know him. That's Luther Sears."

We hugged a long time and then, without a single word, sat down on the steps of the plane with our shoulders touching and cried.

IN FLIGHT 1986

At a cruising speed of four hundred knots, the Lear sliced through the cold night sky on a southeastern bearing toward Knoxville.

Covered with a light blanket, Essary slumped in the rear of the cabin, his mouth hanging open in deep sleep. Logomicino was sitting across from me, his eyes hooded, still watching.

Luther and I were sitting behind the bulkhead, sharing a small table. Eight hours into conversation, neither of us had thought of sleep.

"Let's start a few days ago when you first called," Luther said.

I felt embarrassed. "I'm sorry about that Luther. I … I didn't know what to say."

Luther shook his head, "Wouldn't have been a good way. Over the past thirty years, on at least a dozen occasions, we've received similar phone calls. You see, because your body was never found, rumors had it you'd not drowned, that you had amnesia, that you'd joined the military, or were simply hiding in the mountains."

"What do you mean my body wasn't found? Hell, Luther, I wasn't dead."

"We know that now but we didn't then." Luther smiled and placed his hands together, only the tips of his fingers touching, "You see, the local and state authorities were able to trace you to a point just east of Memphis. There'd been a terrible rainstorm, followed by one of those five-hundred year floods."

"Yeah I know. I was in the middle of it."

Luther continued, "All of the river bottoms around Memphis were flooded. The Mississippi was out of its banks for months. Houses washed away and at least a hundred people drowned. Many bodies were never recovered. After the water went down, your truck was found. Your billfold was still in the glove compartment but there was no body. Mr. Roane maintained for months that you'd turn up."

"But I didn't."

"No. Surely you realize our frustrations. Because of the devastation and deaths, wild tales were common about survivors found on logs floating down the Mississippi and bodies found in trees. We thought we had a lead when the *Memphis Commercial Appeal* ran a series of human-interest articles about the disaster. A young man fitting your description had rescued a woman and child from the waters of the Loosahatchie. He was admitted to John Gaston hospital as John Doe, and his real name was never known."

"Ah, the infamous John Doe."

"His bill was paid in cash and he disappeared. The authorities traced the woman and child to Colorado. When she and her husband were questioned, they claimed to have no knowledge of the whereabouts of the young man. That was our last good lead."

Luther shifted in his seat and continued. "So you can understand why I considered your call just another crank trying to con Mr. Roane out of money. I didn't tell him about the call, but I couldn't get it out of my mind. I guess it was because you said you wanted to know about your daddy's health."

I needed to hide my embarrassment. "I just … couldn't think of anything else to say. Sounded kinda strange, didn't it?"

Luther smiled, "No, something about your call was different. It seemed a genuine question. It sounded like you really cared. Anyway, the next morning I called Belton and asked him to investigate Aleutian Air

Service. He is Roman's "jack-of-all-trades" and a whiz. Within an hour, he'd verified Aleutian Air Service was legitimate. Even more interesting, one of the owners of the company was a William Creight."

"Not a very good disguise, was it?"

"No, not very imaginative." Luther chuckled. "That afternoon Belton brought me two photos from an Alaskan wildlife magazine offering the services of your company. The photos resembled you a little, but thirty years and a graying beard changes one considerably. Even a childhood friend.

"Later, Belton was back in my office with a profile of you taken from your commercial license application. For the first time, I thought we might be on to something. That you might be the real Creighton Roane. The plane was available, so I thought we would just run up and have a look."

"Luther, are you accustomed to making a thirty-five hundred mile flight to just have a look?"

"Oh, I'm accustomed to traveling much further than that for a look. You see, Roman has holdings in South Africa, Venezuela, and the Persian Gulf. We are not just a peckerwood sawmill outfit anymore. I'm not bragging but it is just a part of updating you."

"Well, I'm impressed."

"On our trip up to Anchorage I gave Belton background on your disappearance. When Tony brought the photo back to the plane, I told Belton our search was ending. His questioning was just a formality at that point, but I had to be sure. Didn't have any idea that you were going to challenge Logomicino to a showdown at the OK Corral."

I had to laugh. "I didn't have much intention to engaging in anything like that."

"Funny thing, Creight, I watched you walk from your jeep into the terminal, and I thought that is exactly the way Mr. Roane used to walk."

It was strange hearing someone comparing me to my daddy; I had never heard anyone do that. Time had robbed me of that. Exhaustion was starting to set in, but I asked Luther, "You've explained Essary but you've made no explanation of Logomicino. What was his role in this?"

Luther removed his shoes, put on a pair of footies, and pulled a blanket around his shoulders, "Well, you see, Mr. Logomicino works for us on a contract basis. Officially, he's not a part of the company. That revolves around an accountability issue. Sometimes he does things with which we prefer Roman not be associated. Occasionally, we have something unpleasant to come up, and it takes a man with Logomicino's skill to handle it. He'd just returned from Brazil, and we thought a trip up to a cooler climate would be a nice reward."

"Come on Luther; quit pulling my leg. Why did you bring him?"

Dimming the overhead light, Luther closed his eyes, "If this had been a scam, Creight, it would have been his responsibility to handle the problem."

*****

The whisper of the pilot woke me. "Mr. Sears, we'll be in Knoxville in fifteen minutes. Just in case you need to freshen up."

Luther stretched his arms and yawned. He looked at me and said, "Man, it's going to be good to get home."

"I been thinking, Luther, would it be too much trouble to just swing over Cedergren before we land? And I'd kinda like to see the Arn too."

Luther looked at the pilot and raised his eyebrows.

"We've got plenty of fuel and it won't add more than fifteen minutes," the pilot said.

*****

The morning sun was banishing the fog covering Cedergren. The crosshatch pattern of the chert roads appeared and then just as quickly disappeared, hidden by either trees or the remaining haze. East of Cedergren, where the elevation was higher, the air was clear and I could almost smell the mustiness of the decaying leaves under the forest canopy. I asked, "Can you take her down a little?"

The whine of the engines lessened, the plane banked, and we lost altitude. And there it was below me: the great canyon of the Findhorn and the high plateau of the Arn. At the western edge of the plateau, the old Hematite furnace and lake cut a gash through the woodland. At the northern end of the plateau, the low stone wall of the long-abandoned fort anchors the escarpment walls and looks down on the Henderson Brothers rapids. On the eastern edge of the plateau, a narrow trail leads down to Whetstone Cave, its ominous mouth facing the rising sun.

And the Findhorn – her beauty was as dazzling as the last time I saw it.

THE FINDHORN RIVER 1956

The day had started simply enough. We dropped my old pickup off at Dove Landing, a sandy beach downriver from the southwestern end of the Arn. We took Vaughn's jeep and our canoes a few miles upriver from where the Findhorn took a northern turn at the southeast corner of the Arn. Shaded by river birch, the narrow white sandy beach was a pretty launch site. Some early boater had named it Sandy Ramp.

We had packed sandwiches and shirts in a dry bag and tied it along with a coffee pot, in the bow of my canoe. Because we usually lost or broke a paddle, we had packed a couple of extras.

The Findhorn is a beautiful river. Hundreds of boulders - some as large as small houses - are scattered throughout the river basin. The river, in almost a merry fashion, works its way over and around these boulders, down waterfalls, and dashes wildly against the rugged walls of the canyon.

The locals fished from the bank and found it mystifying that people would come hundreds of miles for the opportunity to drown themselves in the rapids. But Vaughn and I ran the river several times each summer and, while we were not experts, Vaughn boasted, "We'll do until experts come along."

*****

Late morning we cut through Greyhound, the first of the major rapids, shouting with the exuberance of a successful run. As a local river-rat described it, "Sumbitch is bigger than a Greyhound bus!"

Fifty yards downstream Terminal waited. An early kayaker named the rapids after it ended his trip. Thrown from his kayak at Greyhound, he bounced off boulders and was finally able to swim to an eddy pool downstream. His kayak, sucked beneath an undercut rock and spit out in pieces, was a worthless piece of junk. The man had walked three miles to the nearest road where he waited until a local farmer came along and gave him a lift into Cedergren. Looking like some kind of puny scarecrow, he sat shivering in his wet trunks and tennis shoes on a bench outside the drug store. Two hours later his wife arrived to carry him back to civilization and away from the grinning faces of the locals.

Downstream from Terminal the river calmed. One mile into the smooth water we passed Sycamore Shoals, a favorite spot for recreational boaters to paddle around in the calm water. At this point the river was just a lazy, slow-flowing stream, "sissy water" Vaughn called it. An automobile with a two-wheeled trailer sat in the shade beside the launching area. Vaughn remarked someone had probably brought a raft out to the still water and was just floating around drinking beer.

Late morning, with still no sign of the recreational boaters, we shot Double Bubble sluice and reached the first of the challenging rapids, Last Chance. This signaled the beginning of a series of rapids reaching almost two miles. Once past these, a boater was committed to run the next twenty miles. There were no takeout points accessible by road.

*****

With Vaughn in the lead we plowed into Last Chance, swung river left and set up to run Little Sluice. We maneuvered right and shot through a three-foot standing wave at the base of the rapids. Ahead lay Big Sluice, with a ten-foot drop half way through. Earlier today, we decided to run "the hero route" just left of The Thumb, a baseball bat sized rock that hid just below the surface. A raft butting head-first onto the The Thumb would flip stern over bow and go over the falls upside down.

Vaughn looked back, grinned and gave me a "thumbs up." With the cockiness that comes from being 18-year old boys, we braced ourselves.

Halfway through Big Sluice an aluminum canoe bent into a shallow "V" was pinned between two boulders. It had come to rest with its stern partly submerged, its bow standing up at an uncomfortable angle. Vaughn was almost on top of the wreck and was unable to change course. As he passed the wreckage, he turned and shouted back at me.

"Man pinned in there!"

I dug in with a backwater stroke, trying to change my course but the current was too strong. My canoe hit The Thumb broadside and hung for a blink before flipping. Ejected and flung into the falls I fought to regain control. Fearing I would be slammed into rocks or crushed by my canoe, I pulled my knees up under my chin and wrapped my arms around my head. At the base of the falls I was sucked under and dragged along the floor of the river, fighting my way between rocks and submerged tree limbs. Fifty feet below the falls, I surfaced. The current swept me almost five hundred feet downstream before I found slack water. Finally safe, I cringed as my canoe passed me, its aluminum sides screeching off rocks, and then disappeared down the river.

Forcing my way through heavy brush along the bank, it took me an hour to work my way back to the wrecked canoe. I crawled up the largest of the boulders pinning the canoe and looked down into the wreckage. Huddled in the floor of the canoe, a small figure wearing a faded orange life jacket was trapped and being pounded by the rushing water.

Clinging to the boulder with one hand, I reached around the side of the canoe and grabbed the collar of the life jacket. When I pulled, the body rolled to one side and almost slipped out of the jacket. Now with no weight in the stern, the canoe spun, toppled forward, and tumbled downstream. I pulled the body onto the rock and collapsed, shivering from fatigue and excitement.

The small figure wrapped both arms around my legs and whimpered, "Help us. Please help us. We're all going to die."

*****

A mile and a half down the river, Vaughn found slack water and waited there for me. He was shocked when he saw my empty canoe careening toward him, still upright. He grabbed my bowline, found a sandy shoal, and pulled both canoes to the bank.

He had not seen me fall from my canoe. Later he told me he had not prayed in the last ten years but on this day, worried I might be trapped and drowning beneath an undercut rock, he stood wet and shivering on the riverbank silently repeating The Lord's Prayer.

He took the dry bag from my canoe and, fearing the worst, started scrambling upstream through the briars and thick brush.

*****

I carried the small, shivering form across the rocks to the safety of the shore. For what seemed an eternity, I sat with the sobbing figure pulled against my body, rocking back and forth saying, "It's all right. I've got you. You're safe." Slowly, the sobbing and shivering lessened.

I removed the wet life jacket from the small figure and pushed the hair back from the bruised face. It was a girl.

She started crying again. "My sisters, have you seen them?"

I took my T-shirt off, wrung it out, and wrapped it around her shoulders. "No, no. I'm sure they're okay, we'll find them. Tell me what happened?"

Her name was Missy. She and her two older sisters, C.L. and Maggie, had put their canoe in the water that morning and planned to stay in the shallow water near Sycamore Shoals. C.L. had stood in the canoe trying to reach some wild grapes. The canoe had rocked wildly, and she had fallen overboard. By the time Maggie was able to get her back in the canoe, they had reached the swift water. They made it through the first of the rapids before the paddle slipped from Maggie's hand and the canoe, now totally out of control, slid up on a boulder. Both sisters were thrown out. Missy hadn't seen them again.

She had been sitting in the center of the canoe holding on to the gunwales. When the canoe hit the boulders, it spun and she slid to the stern. "It stood up on its end. Water ran all over me, and I couldn't get out," she told me between sobs.

I sat in the afternoon sun with my arm around the little girl trying to figure out what to do next. It was too far to go down river for help and it would be dark before we could reach Sycamore Shoals upstream.

Twice, above the roar of the rapids, I heard someone calling my name. But when I answered, there was no response.

*****

Vaughn had made his way upstream for a half mile when he saw two girls wading along the shore less than a hundred yards away. He gave a keen whistle through his teeth. The girls started running along the riverbank toward him shouting, "Have you seen our little sister? You've got to help us find her."

The girls had seen Vaughn shoot past in his canoe and had called out, but the noise of the rapids had muted their voices. It made little difference since Vaughn had his hands full trying to keep his canoe upright. Both girls had cuts and bruises on their knees and elbows. Now, with help at hand, they lost the composure they'd been clinging to so desperately.

*****

Missy and I started walking downstream, hoping to find Vaughn. I knew he would come back to look for me if he had made it through the turbulent water alive. I tried to put out of my mind the thought of him injured or dead. Missy added to my misery by crying again.

We were resting on a fallen tree when Vaughn and the two older sisters came around the edge of a low bluff. The three sisters clutched each other laughing and crying at the same time. I was happy to see Vaughn, glad to know he was alive, and glad to know I now had someone to help get us out of this mess.

Vaughn and I decided to walk back downstream to where he had secured our canoes, camp for the night, and then make the run down to Dove Landing in the morning.

My canoe had taken a good battering on its unguided trip through the rapids. One of the thwarts had buckled, and a large gash had been torn in the bow just above the water line. We decided that I would take Maggie in my canoe and Vaughn would take the two younger sisters in his undamaged canoe.

If only I had remembered the words of Robert Burns:

> *But Mousie, thou are no thy-lane,*
> *In proving foresight may be vain:*
> *The best laid schemes o' Mice an' Men,*
> *Gang aft agley,*
> *An' lea'e us nought but grief an' pain,*
> *For promis'd joy.*

CEDERGREN 1986

Our descent into Knoxville was through clouds and fog. The Lear touched down smoothly, and we taxied to a private hangar where a Chevrolet Suburban was waiting.

The copilot lowered the airstairs. We all climbed down and tried to shake the stiffness from our legs. Luther said Logomicino and Essary would be going on to Charlotte.

"Why Charlotte?" I asked.

"We have our corporate headquarters in Charlotte," Luther explained. "Mr. Roane didn't want it in Cedergren. He said he didn't want to mess up a nice little town with 'white shirt people.' So Charlotte is our main office, small staff of three dozen, mostly lawyers, secretaries, and accountants. Our oil people used to be there but we've moved them down to New Orleans, and we have an office in San Paulo. I go to Charlotte when we have some heavy lifting to do. Your father has never seen any of our out-of-state facilities."

"San Paulo – like Brazil?"

Luther nodded, "That's where the oil is."

*****

I threw our bags in the rear of the Suburban. Luther slid behind the wheel and we headed northeast toward the mountains.

At a convenience store, we got coffee and a dozen Krispy Kremes. Luther took a sip of coffee and said, "We've still got a lot of updating to do, but some things are best handled by other folks."

I opened the box of donuts. "You make this sound complicated, Luther."

"Complicated in some ways. Sad and disturbing in others. After your disappearance, Mr. Roane changed. I can't say he became soft but he changed."

"How?" I said, taking a bite of a still warm donut and savoring the sugary glaze.

"I'm not sure I can describe it. About six months after you disappeared, he came by the house one night. Julie and I had just married, and we were still living with Granny. 'I've partnered with the Blackman family for years,' he said. 'They think they can get a better return on their money in some other business, so starting next Monday, I'll have full ownership of the Roman Company. I want you to go to college. I want you to learn how to help me run this business.'

"I told Mr. Roane I couldn't go to school because I hadn't been a good student and now, with a wife and Granny to look after, school was not a possibility."

"But you went."

"Yes. You must have forgotten your daddy doesn't take no for an answer. 'I'll cover your expenses', he said. 'Winnie and I will be able to handle things around here'. So I went. I never found anything as hard in my life. But I hung in there and found I had a knack for numbers. My early grades were not the best but they got better. Just before I graduated, Mr. Roane said I needed a masters degree. It blew me away when he said our arrangement would continue. He'd supply the money and I'd continue my education."

"Man, I'm proud of you."

Luther smiled. "I probably shouldn't say this, but I surprised myself. Anyway, after being gone from Cedergren for six years, I came back to work for your daddy. I had a good education and three children and the time had come for repayment.

"Mr. Roane had not just sat around while I was in school. He'd purchased several large tracts of timber adjacent to the old Trevethan and Gunn holdings. He'd bought a new mill and had tripled his work force."

I smiled, realizing how much forethought Daddy had.

Luther took a bite of donut and continued, "I hadn't been back more than a year when some wildcat oilmen came into the county and started leasing mineral rights. They drilled a few wells. Nothing very big, but local folks got awful excited. The drillers needed additional funds to buy larger rigs so they could drill deeper. 'To where the real oil was,' they said. The banks wouldn't have anything to do with them. So they came to us for the money. Roman loaned it to them, taking the drilling rigs as collateral.

"We thought even if the drillers went belly up, we still owned the mineral rights under our property, and we just might get in the drilling business in a small way. That's exactly what happened. They drilled a few dry holes and went broke. So we backed into the oil business."

"And you're still in it?"

Luther nodded, "Oh yes, we're still in it. Our holdings have increased and we're now active outside of North America. Of course, compared to the big boys we're pretty small but we're starting to make a shadow."

The topography was getting steeper. The purple profile of mountains ahead were still shrouded in a thin mist. I thought about Clawed and how he almost got back home. I remember thinking if he had started just a little earlier he would have made it to the house and safety. A lump started somewhere in my stomach and worked its way up into my throat. Maybe I'd started soon enough. Maybe I'll get back home. Maybe I'll make it.

Luther looked over at me. "You all right?"

"Yeah. I was thinking about an old friend. We saw each other through some bad times. But he was killed trying to get back home. I'm almost home and … I just thought of him."

We rode in silence for a few minutes. Luther said, "Sorry about your friend. We never know what is just around the next bend and probably that's the best way. Part of the larger plan, so to speak. I heard a man say once that's the reason the world is round, so we can't see too far down the road. It would probably scare us to death."

I could see the mountains clearer now and could make out the gap in the mountains where the Findhorn swung west around the escarpment.

I asked, "How's your grandmother?"

"Granny's been dead nine years. The night she died, Mr. Roane came to the hospital and said if I didn't mind, he would like to have Granny buried with the rest of the Roane family at Christian Springs. 'I never knew a better woman', he said, 'I don't know what I would have done without her. I'd be honored if she could sleep with the rest of my family and you would let me handle the arrangements.'

"I tell you, Creight, Granny would have been so proud. Your father bought the most expensive casket in the state. I never saw as many flowers, probably every client of the Roman Company sent something. Your father did a eulogy about what a fine and honorable woman Granny was. When he finished, there wasn't a dry eye in the church."

I reached over and put my hand on Luther's shoulder, "I'm sorry, but I'm glad she's with the rest of our family."

"Creight, I know sooner or later you're going to get tired of hearing this, but your father has changed in lots of ways. He's still tough but circumstances have softened him. But you will find out about that in time. You'll spend the night with Julie and me. I've got some planning to do… how I'm going to break the news to Mr. Roane that you are home."

The late afternoon sun had turned the dome on the Chota County courthouse gold. "Lap the square once, Luther, let me see the changes." Luther drove slowly around the courthouse square as I looked at all the familiar names – Boswell's Clothes, Blackman's Law Offices, Shannon's Five and Ten, all longtime Cedergren names. Then, directly across the street from the northern door of the courthouse, a new name: Partner's Café.

"Looks like business is picking up, Luther. I don't remember a café when I was a boy."

Luther parked in front of the café. "Tell you a funny little story. A widow woman, Mrs. Amanda Litchfield, opened it about twenty years ago. Lots of the men here in town liked to start the day off with a sausage biscuit and cup of her coffee. They'd sit around and catch up on the news and solve most of the world's major problems before eight o'clock.

"They sat at a big table in the back and called themselves the Brotherhood of the Round Table. Then one morning she told the men at the table the business was going under, and she was going to close the café the next month. Well, that kind of stunned everybody."

"Old boys losing their hangout," I laughed.

"Mr. Roane was the last person to leave the table the next morning. 'I've been thinking bout this', he said to the widow, 'how much money do you need to make each month?' She quoted some figure. Then Mr. Roane told her he had been considering opening a restaurant himself. Of course, he hadn't, but Mrs. Litchfield didn't know. He said, 'How bout I buy this restaurant and hire you to manage it?'

"Well, she's been here ever since. I know that after her salary is paid, the café goes into the red a little more each month. But the Brotherhood of the Round Table has a place to gather, and the widow is happy."

"Doesn't sound much like the man I knew thirty years ago – losing money like that."

Luther backed out of the parking space and, teasing me, said, "Goes to show just because you can fly a plane doesn't mean you know everything."

"Okay, and just because you got a masters degree doesn't give you the right to be a smart ass either."

Luther grinned. "Now, before we call it a day, I need for us to do one more thing." He turned on the Suburban's two-way radio and keyed the mike, "This is Luther calling Mr. Roane. Can you hear me, Mr. Roane?"

A ten second delay, a lot of static and then, "Hey, Luther, where you been?"

The hair stood up on the nape of my neck. I leaned forward and stared into the radio as if I could see the face of the speaker.

"Just a little business trip up north. Got back couple hours ago. Logomicino and Belton went on over to Charlotte. Where are you? Out at the Arn?"

"Yep. Just got out here. Be a couple of hours. Need to see me?

"No, not tonight. How about nine o'clock in the morning out at your house?"

"Sounds good. See you in the morning. Glad you're back home."

I had not breathed during their brief conversation. I felt shaky inside. "You should've told me what you were going to do. I wasn't ready for that."

"Creight, it's like easing into a cold shower. It'll be easier from now on."

I hesitated, "I'm not too sure about that."

A small building, its tarpaper sides dull in the afternoon sun, stood a half block off the court square. Three battered pickups and a rusting sedan were parked in front of the building, adding to the shabbiness. Half dozen young men, shirts unbuttoned and hanging out of their pants, leaned against the sedan drinking from containers hidden in paper sacks.

I stared at the building, trying to get it placed in my mind. One of the young men apparently took offense at my stare and gave me a middle-finger salute. I turned to Luther, "I don't remember…"

Luther interrupted, "One of the McCamys built it about twenty years ago, never really finished it. It's a poolroom. I don't guess anyone except a McCamy or one of their cronies has ever been inside. Damned shame we've put up with that eyesore all these years."

"I remember the McCamys. Bunch of good-for-nothings."

Luther nodded. "That's them. Your daddy says they haven't changed in 175 years. Most of them are either in jail, raising marijuana, making whiskey, or stealing cars. You name it, they've done it."

We were at the edge of town, and I was trying to get my bearings. We turned into a gravel drive and stopped. The little frame house, the garage, and Daddy's office looked just like I remembered.

"So you just wanted to know if Daddy was home, was that the reason for radioing him?"

"I guess so, I thought you'd need to see the house again before you met your daddy here in the morning."

"Kinda easing into the cold shower, Luther?"

We turned around in front of the garage and I asked Luther to stop. I walked into the garage, and there in the twilight, my canoe was hanging from the ceiling joist. The words, *Port of Cedergren,* were barely visible on the stern.

I didn't sleep much that night. I'd doze off and the dreams would start. The theme was always the same: a little boy lost in a crowd, searching for his father. But when he found him, the man did not recognize him. The man would say, "You will have to go away and stop bothering me. My son is dead." "No, no, it's me," the little boy would cry, and the man would turn away.

*****

The next morning, Julie made a working man's breakfast: ham, eggs, grits, hot biscuits, and blackberry jelly. I was barely able to swallow a cup of coffee.

"I think this is the way we'll do it," Luther explained, getting up from the table. "We'll get over a little early. You can wait for us in the office. I'll go in the house to get Mr. Roane while you kind of get geared up. I'll break the news to your father, or at least, give him a hint … I'm still not sure how I'll handle it just yet. Just play it by ear, I guess."

We didn't talk any more on our short drive to Daddy's house. I had made landings on gravel sandbars less than one hundred fifty-feet in length, landed a float plane in five-foot swells on isolated lakes, and once chased a grizzly bear out of camp by banging two skillets together, but I had never had butterflies like this. What I really needed to do was throw up.

Luther parked at the side of the office. I went inside. He made the short walk across the yard to get Daddy.

The office had not changed: oak floors, knotted pine paneling now rich-hued from age, tall windows looking out onto the mountains, and bookshelves along one wall. This morning its fireplace was cold, but seasoned hickory was stacked beside the hearth ready to chase away any chill. Daddy's wooden swivel chair was turned so it faced the mountains. A couple of straight chairs, separated by a spittoon, were facing the desk. Two calendars hung on the wall, one current and one for the year 1956.

By the door, a pedestal table held a small sculpture of a man, a woman and a little boy. The sculpture was incomplete. The faces of the boy and the woman were finished. But the man's face was smooth and featureless, as if the sculptor was waiting for the model before finishing his work.

Two large paintings hung on the wall. In one, the woman and the boy watched a man tie a Royal Coachman fly on a monofilament leader. The man's face was hidden by the brim of his hat. In the second painting, the boy and the woman were watching a man saddling a horse. While the boy and the woman were both older than in the first painting, they were obviously the same two people. The man, his face hidden by the head of the horse, was adjusting the bridle.

Perhaps the artist was just not comfortable painting men's faces.

Boots crunching on the gravel drive and then the thumping of footsteps on the floor of the wooden porch jerked me into to the present. Luther was saying, "…so we decided to go up and have a look."

The door opened and Luther followed by Daddy and a large German Shepherd came into the room. A man in his eighties doesn't compare very well with a man in his fifties – Daddy's age when I last saw him. He was now round-shouldered and thicker in the waist. His thinning hair was gray and shaggy. His steps were short and, although it was summer, he was wearing a flannel shirt and a canvas jacket. I had never seen him wearing glasses.

He gave me a brief nod, said, "Mornin'," then turned to Luther and asked, "Now tell me again where you went?"

Luther took my father's arm and turned him toward me. "It's Creighton, Mr. Roane. We've found Creighton."

Daddy took a couple of steps toward me. His brow furrowed and he squinted as I've seen old men do when they were looking at something a long way off. "Who did you say you …?"

"Good morning, Daddy."

He took a step backward, his face contorted in shock. He would've fallen had Luther not steadied him and then gently lowered him into a chair. Daddy sat, gazing at me, slack jawed, eyes brimming with tears.

I dropped to my knees, put my arms around him, and put the side of my face against his chest. Finally, he pushed me away and stared into my face. "I never thought …, I never thought I'd …" He buried his face in his hands, and his body shook with deep, racking sobs.

Finally he said, "You're home." Then he broke down again.

I struggled to steady my voice. "Sometimes it's not easy to come home. Sometimes it's a long way, sometimes it's more than just miles and a lot of things keep you from doing it. You'll never know how much … ."

Daddy's raised his hand and his mouth moved but no words came out.

But once I got started, the words wouldn't stop, "It wasn't I didn't care; it's stubbornness, it's pride, and most of all its weakness. I'm sorry I don't have a better explanation. I guess it's just me and the way I am."

I helped Daddy to his feet as I heard Luther's car backing out of the driveway.

*****

It took most of the day to catch up: the flood in the Loosahatchie bottom, my years with the Forest Service, the years I had spent in Alaska, and our flying service. He told me how the Roman Company had grown, about his plywood mill, the nursery where he was growing hardwood seedlings, and the oil drilling. Neither of us ever mentioned my leaving home. Some things stubborn people just don't talk about. It's like an old battle where both sides lost.

I told Daddy about the magazine article, the program on the Discovery Channel, and seeing the mountains of home. We had tears, tightening jaw muscles, and staring off into space during our talk. We both chose our words carefully, not wanting to reignite the flames it had taken all these years to extinguish.

Late in the afternoon, Daddy said, "Let's wet our whistles with a bit of The Turkey, then go down to Partner's Café and get a steak. This time of day, won't be many folks eating and we can have privacy." He opened a desk drawer and took out a fifth of Wild Turkey and two glasses. Taking his handkerchief and wiping the glasses out, he looked at me and grinned, "You're old enough to drink, ain't you? My mind says you're about eighteen, but my eyes tell me something else."

I smiled. "Believe your eyes when you look at me, and I will believe my heart when I look at you."

"I'm not quite clear as to what you're saying," he said and poured two fingers- width of bourbon in each glass. "But here's to the roads that we'll joyfully travel in the future, and may we never look back over our shoulder at the roads we've traveled sadly in the past."

"Pretty good, Daddy. I'll drink to that any day."

*****

We got into Daddy's beat-up Suburban, which he had named Old Pony. "Hope you don't mind the dog riding with us, but Rip goes where I go. He usually rides shotgun, right where you're sitting, but he must think you are kinda special because he just climbed into the back like it was his accustomed place. You should feel honored that he gave up his seat without a fight. And I'm telling you, he fights dirty."

It was almost dark when Daddy pulled into Pherson Brothers service station.

A broad shouldered man with long heavy sideburns came out of the grease room, leaned against Daddy's side of the truck, and kidded, " Mr. Roane, you ain't taught this old jalopy to run on its reputation yet?"

"Naw, Errick, I think it's about like me: old, beat up and too damned dumb to learn any new tricks. Put about ten gallons in it and let's see how the gauge looks."

A blue van with red lettering on the side, *Cedergren High School Biology*, was sitting on the opposite side of the gas pumps. A woman in black slacks, white blouse, and a baseball cap was sliding in behind the steering wheel.

Daddy leaned out his window, waved and said, "Evening, Doc, where're you off to?"

The woman, her face shadowed by the cap, returned the greeting. "Evening yourself, Papa Zeale. I'm taking my six top biology students down to the Gulf. I'm going to let them study some saltwater marine life. It's a reward for maintaining an A average for the year. We're driving down to Knoxville tonight and taking a corporate jet south."

"Heck," Daddy joked, "if I'd have known about trips like that, I just might have taken biology classes myself."

"Well, they're driving me crazy. None of them have ever been on a plane. When we get back, I expect all of them to write a long letter thanking North Georgia Global for sponsoring this trip. Why don't you park that old trap and come with us?"

"Don't tempt me. You know I've got to hang around here. The boys at the Round Table would miss me something awful in the morning if I just upped and ran off, you know that. Maybe someday when I'm younger, like maybe ... sixty," Daddy laughed and sat up a little straighter.

The woman's face ran a quick circle in my mind and I asked, "Did I know her? She looked kinda familiar."

Errick wiped the suburban's dipstick on his pants, dropped the hood and nodded toward me. "Who you got riddin' copilot with you tonight, Mr. Roane?"

Daddy's brow was furrowed, and he seemed lost in thought as he fumbled through his billfold, pulled out a couple of crumpled bills and gave them to Errick.

I thought he'd not heard me, so I asked again, "She looked kinda familiar. Have I seen her somewhere before?"

Daddy hesitated for a second before saying, "Don't know, you might. She's got a doctorate in biology. Could be teaching at any university in the state. She's way too good to be teaching in high school."

"What's she doing here then?"

"She likes this part of the country, always taking students down the Findhorn in canoes to study some kind of tadpole or bug. She's a crackerjack, all right."

The woman's face still circling in my mind, "She called you Papa Zeale?"

"Yeah, well, I call her Doc. We're pretty good friends. We bounce ideas off each other every once and a while."

"I see. You pick good-looking friends. Maybe you could introduce us sometime."

Daddy had cranked Old Pony. As we left the service station, he muttered tight-lipped, "Maybe."

Partner's Café crowd was sparse. A stout, middle-aged woman greeted us. "Hey, friend, take any table you want."

Daddy smiled. "Evening, Mrs. Litchfield. Got a couple of good steaks for us, maybe a salad, two of those twice-baked, and some peach cobbler? And a smile?"

Daddy looked at me. "Medium suit you?"

"You bet." I looked around at Daddy's restaurant. Couple of booths, half dozen tables, a counter that seated eight, and in the back a monstrous round table that would seat at least a dozen.

A man wearing a suit and tie got up from his table and came to ours. He nudged Daddy's shoulder with the back of hand and Daddy scooted over. The man slid into the booth beside him.

"Evening, Mr. Roane. Did I hear you order red meat? I believe our last visit we decided you wouldn't eat red meat. If I'm not mistaken, I believe I detect the odor of …, why I believe … that's … that's Wild Turkey."

Daddy tried unsuccessfully to look irritated. "This rude man, who has just invaded our privacy and started offering unsolicited advice, passes himself off as a doctor. Around these parts, he's known as a heck of a quail hunter, a pretty fair shot, and a part-time quack. Most folks had rather he make some effort to stay out of their business. Creight, this is Dr. Adam Huntsman."

I leaned across and shook the doctor's hand. His firm handshake and toothy grin made me like him immediately. "Good to meet you, Dr. Huntsman. I'm Creighton Roane."

"Good to meet you, Creighton. You any kin to this old buzzard?"

Daddy took over the conversation, "Dr. Huntsman moved in here about ten years ago, claiming he was a heart doctor. There's lots he don't know about Cedergren. Dr. Huntsman, you're looking at my son."

I watched Dr. Huntsman's face and saw a brief flicker of surprise in his eyes.

"He's lived in Alaska for the past few years, but he's thinking about moving back to Cedergren. Might even work with Roman. He used to be hell with a chain saw. 'Course, he was a lot younger then."

The doctor smiled. "I'm sorry about you being kin to such an old fart."

Our meal arrived. Dr. Huntsman took a knife and sliced off one corner of Daddy's steak. With a playful motion, Daddy pushed the doctor's hand away, but not in time to stop him from shoving the meat into his mouth. "Don't do that Zeale," the doctor said. "I'm trying to help you with your cholesterol."

"Yeah, just like you're are always coming down to our farm on Little Olivine Creek helping us control the bobwhite population."

The doctor grinned, stood, leaned across the table, and shook my hand again. "Alaska, you say. I've got some scrimshaw I'd like for you to look at, if you've got time. I'm not real sure how good it is."

I wasn't certain, but I thought Daddy gave Dr. Huntsman a dark look.

The doctor took an appointment book out of his inside coat pocket and flipped a couple of pages, "Looks like I don't have an appointment until … quarter past nine in the morning. Think you might be able to stop by? Shouldn't take more than fifteen minutes."

"I'm not sure what Daddy has planned but …"

Daddy put both hands over his plate and made a pretense of guarding his steak from Doctor Huntsman, "Go ahead, Creight, I've got something in the morning. Be a good chance for you to start getting acquainted with some of the new folks around town. We call folks like Doc flat-land touristers and watch them like a hawk, particularly around our women. And our food!"

"All right then, Doc, I'll stop by about nine and we'll have a look at that scrimshaw. I work free. You'll be getting what you pay for."

*****

We got back home at ten o'clock. Daddy asked me to drive, saying his night vision was not good anymore. Inside the house I felt a strange sensation, almost like nothing had changed, and yet it was as if I had never been here before.

Daddy pointed up the stairs, "You'll find your room just like you left it. Well, not quite. Winnie repaired the wreckage you left. Sheets and pillowcases are in the closet where they always were. Sleep good. See you in the morning."

"My bag is still in the office. I'll get it and be right back."

At the office, the small lamp on Daddy's desk barely lit the room and caused long shadows to grow out from the desk. I gathered my bag, and I stopped to look at the sculpture. I ran my fingers over the smooth, featureless face of the man, but they were unable to solve the mystery.

*****

I lay in my old bed in my old room, happy to hear Daddy downstairs snoring. The moon shown through the window just as it did when I was a boy. I was back where I had started. But I didn't feel at home. There was an uneasiness, like I was sleeping in someone else's bed, an intruder, and I did not belong there.

I was sitting at a round table in a small restaurant surrounded by men, all strangers, all featureless. They stared at me and one of the men asked where I had been and why I had not been there years ago when he needed me. I replied that I didn't know he needed me and how could he need me because I was a stranger and had never been here before? All of the men stood up, took a piece of meat from my plate, and walked out the door into the darkness.

Daddy knocked on my door.

"Hey, boy! It's time to shake a leg unless you want to stay in bed all day. Coffee's made. I'll be free somewhere around noon. You'll need to use the old jeep. It rides rougher than hell and it's ugly, but it beats walking. See you when you get back."

*****

Dr. Huntsman and I arrived at his clinic at the same time. He unlocked the door and motioned me into his private office.

"Doc, looks like it's going to be a hot one."

He hung his coat on the upraised arm of a fake skeleton. "Call me Adam," he said as he opened a file cabinet drawer and removed a thick folder. He sat on the corner of his desk, placing the folder unopened beside him. "Guess, I might as well confess. I don't have any scrimshaw. I just wanted to get to know you better. I didn't know Mr. Roane had any children, and now he pops up with a full grown son. Tell me something about yourself."

"Not much to tell. I left here when I was eighteen, bummed around some, spent several years with the Forest Service in the west, and ended up in Alaska. That's about it."

"Really? When I got home last night I called a colleague, feller named Vaughn Blackman, who said he knew you. In fact, I had a hard time convincing him I'd had supper with you. He told me you died years ago. Drowned in some God-awful flood around Memphis."

"Vaughn! You know Vaughn Blackman?"

Huntsman stood and pointed to a diploma on his wall, "Yep, we were in med school together. Funny how things work out. Here he is, a kid from a small town with a huge practice in Atlanta, three Mercedes, member of two country clubs, big alimony and child support payments. And a third wife. I once practiced in Atlanta and here I am, small town, small practice, own a half-dozen shotguns, three birddogs, got one wife and, by far and away, the happiest. Life is strange, isn't it?"

"Yeah, we never know where a road is going to take us. When we were growing up, Vaughn and I were good friends. What did he say when you told him we more or less had supper together last night?"

"He said he taught you everything you know about white water."

"Bullshit! He didn't say that, did he?"

Huntsman laughed. "No. He said you were a hard working kid, pretty much of a straight arrow, had a temper that got away from you sometimes, and he loved you like a brother. He wants you to call him."

"I'll call him. I'm just trying to reorient myself. I feel I'm a trespasser in some strange land. An intruder in my own bedroom last night. You don't know how strange this whole thing is – it's like, I don't know - I can't explain it. It's like I never lived here at all, but in other ways it's like I never left."

The doctor smiled and poked me with his index finger, "You should feel privileged. I don't think I've ever heard of but one other feller that died and then went back home alive and that was almost two thousand years ago. You are not kin to him, are you?"

I had to smile. "No."

Adam stared at me for a few seconds, like he was assessing me. He opened a folder. "You'll make it through all this because you come from tough folks. Your daddy is as tough as they come. I first saw him ten years ago, right after he had his first heart attack. He'd been out to the Arn working on a fence. Had the attack on the Cedergren-Christian Springs Road. One of Roman's men found him slumped over the wheel of his jeep, just barely alive.

"They brought him in and I pumped him full of all kinds of stuff and got him stabilized. I left his room about midnight. The next morning he was giving the nurses the dickens because they wouldn't bring him his boots and pants. He is one tough old boy."

"I didn't know he had ever been sick a day in his life."

Adam flipped through the chart. "He has had three other episodes and last year he had a really big one. Almost got him, sure enough. I've looked after him the best I can, but he's not an easy patient. Says he'll have a steak and a drink of whiskey whenever he damn well pleases."

Daddy's medical history was scary. "How can I help?"

Adam closed the file. "Don't think there is much either of us can do. He's been a good friend to this town and me. I hate to see it happen, but I worry the next attack will be fatal.

"This is an example of how he looks at things: I play the bagpipes. It's among the silly things I confess I enjoy doing. He's made me promise that when he dies, I'll dress up in my highland garb and play *Amazing Grace* over his grave. Told me he would be listening, and I'd damn well better not mess it up. Told him I would do it and I'll keep that promise."

Adam looked at his watch and started putting on a starched white coat, "You been out to the Arn yet? You won't believe the size of the wild turkey flocks, and you sure won't believe the size of those buffalo. Come back and see me when Zeale has given you the tour. We'll have a lot more to talk about."

*****

I left the jeep parked in front of Adam's office and walked down to Partner's Café for a late breakfast. Without asking, the waitress put a mug of coffee in front of me. "Good morning, I'm Louellen. How do you want your eggs this morning?"

I scanned the worn, plastic-covered menu, "Two scrambled, sausage, grits, and a couple of biscuits."

She leaned into a window opening to the kitchen, "Two scrambled and sausage."

She started placing silver in front of me. She had short red hair, green eyes, and a saddle of freckles across her nose. "You forgot to order the grits and biscuits," I said.

She got me a glass of water. "You must not be from around here. Every breakfast comes with grits and biscuits. Where you live?"

"Alaska."

"Alaska! Mercy. You must be Mr. Roane's son. They were talking about you this morning."

"Who was talking about me this morning?"

"Men at the round table. They said everybody thought you drowned a long time ago, and somebody said Luther hunted you down. Went up to Alaska to get you. I guess you didn't know that you're almost famous."

She put my breakfast in front of me. "Famous. Nothing famous about me, I just got lost, that's all."

"How'd you get lost?"

"It's a long story and you wouldn't believe me if I told you."

*****

Breakfast settled in my stomach as I walked down the sidewalk past the stores around the courthouse square, occasionally pausing to look in windows, looking for a familiar face. It dawned on me how out-of-place I must look, wearing a wool shirt and cords in the summer. I wasn't sure how well a check from an Alaskan bank would work in a local clothing store. It might be better if I cashed a check at the bank and then went shopping.

I knew the Blackmans at The Bank of Cedergren. Stanley Blackman would vouch for me.

In the bank, things looked prosperous, leather chairs in the waiting area, thick carpet, and a large painting of Stanley Blackman with his hands folded on a mahogany desk. It was nothing like the sleepy little bank I remembered.

The receptionist smiled and asked if she could help me. "Yes," I replied. "Could I speak with Mr. Blackman?"

"Certainly. Mr. Bill Blackman, Sr., or Mr. Billy Blackman?"

"Mr. Stanley Blackman, if he's in today."

"Oh, I'm sorry, Mr. Stanley Blackman passed away twenty years ago last September. I believe Mr. Bill Blackman, Sr., is available. Would you like to speak with him?"

"If I could, please."

The receptionist stood. "May I tell him your name?"

"Yes ma'am. It's Roane. Creighton Roane."

"Right this way, Mr. Roane." She stopped at the door of a large office, "Mr. Blackman, Mr. Roane is here to see you."

Without looking up from a stack of papers, Bill Blackman nodded to a chair and said, "Morning, Zeale. Have a seat; I'll be right with you."

He signed a document, stood, and offered his hand. His eyes opened wide, "What the hell …"

"Good morning, Bill."

He wrapped his arms around me in a bear hug and then pushed me back arms length. "Just give me a minute. Let me look at you." He shut his office door, came back, looked at me again, and exclaimed, "Dang, Creight, I'm kinda flabbergasted … I uh … I don't know what to say."

"Just say, 'Good morning, Creight, how've you been since you died'? That ought to get the ball rolling. Then I'll say, not too bad considering everything. Then you can say, 'You look pretty good considering you've been dead for thirty years.'"

Bill motioned toward the couch and we both sat. "Well, tell me about yourself. What happened? Where you've been, what you've been doing."

I was starting to get the answer pretty good and gave him the polished version.

He didn't interrupt, just shook his head occasionally. "Amazing, this is just amazing."

He crossed to his desk, reached for his phone and asked, "Have you talked with Vaughn? This will just blow his socks off. He and I have been playing phone tag all morning."

I shook my head, "No, I haven't and I'd like to wait a little while before calling him. I kinda need to get my head on straight. I'm still trying to sort things out."

Bill hung up. "I understand completely. What can I do for you?"

"I need to cash a check."

Bill loosened his tie and leaned back in his chair, "Well, no problem there." He called his secretary, asked for coffee and told her to hold all of his calls. "What do you think of Roman? Can you believe how it has grown?"

"No. Luther has given me the story. Pretty amazing."

"Tell you something I'll bet you don't know. As Roman prospered in the oil business, money started to flow into the county. Through a company called North Georgia Global. You ever hear of them?"

I thought of the five thousand dollar retainer Aleutian Air had received. "Yeah, once."

Bill gave me a wry grin, "Then I guess it is no secret to you who North Georgia Global is, but not many folks around here have any idea. Over the years, Global has funded or underwritten a large number of projects here in Cedergren. You've probably heard about the biology department at Cedergren High, haven't you?"

"A little. I saw some of their students at a service station. The teacher said they were going to the Gulf for a few days."

Bill was almost like a public relations executive. "Yes sir. It is one of the best in the southeast. We've got a PhD heading up the department. Can you believe a PhD in a little high school like Cedergren? She's not too bad looking either."

"I got a glimpse of her but it was getting dark."

Bill's eyebrows shot up, "But you didn't get to talk with her or anything like that?"

"No, she was leaving as we got there."

Looking at his watch, Bill exclaimed, "Damn, we've got a board meeting scheduled in twenty minutes and I've got to go over some things. Can you come back later today? Have lunch?"

"Probably not. There are some other folks I've got to see, but I sure have enjoyed this morning. Thanks for your time. Tell Vaughn I'll call."

Bill shook my hand again, wrote Vaughn's phone number on the back of his own business card, and gave it to me. "You do that now, you hear?"

*****

Daddy's Suburban was parked in front of his home office. He and Luther were standing on the front porch, and one of Roman's pickups and the Chota County Sheriff's cruiser were driving off down the gravel road. I caught the back end of Daddy's last sentence, "… and I've told those sumbitches twice to stay out of there. They're going to get somebody killed, sure as we're standing here."

I felt like I was eavesdropping on a private conversation. "Hey, sounds pretty serious."

Daddy ran his fingers across his forehead, "Naw, nothing we can't handle. Just some damned men won't mind their own business. But we'll work it out, won't we, Luther?"

"Yes sir, we will. Even if I have to get Logomicino back down here."

"No," Daddy said. "This is a family matter. The fewer folks involved, the better. I can handle this if it has to be dealt with again."

Luther laughed, "Still feel like you're ten feet tall and bulletproof, don't you?"

Daddy made a dismissive motion with his hand. Followed by Rip, he went into his office. When he had closed the door, I asked Luther, "Anything I can do to help?"

"Probably not right now. Maybe later."

"Big secret?"

Luther thought for a second, "Yeah, I guess you could put it that way. Mr. Roane will tell you. See you tomorrow, maybe?"

I stood on the porch and mulled the new mystery.

Inside, Daddy was sitting in his swivel chair, his feet up on the desk, looking out the window. An open bottle of Wild Turkey was on the floor beside him, a shot glass of whiskey in one hand and a glass of water in the other. "Getting in a touch of early sipping, Daddy?"

Daddy took a deep breath. "Do you ever get pissed off? I mean really pissed! I've been in these mountains all my life. They don't change and most of the people don't change either. If a feller is raising marijuana today, you can bet his father made moonshine forty years ago, and his grandfather probably stole hogs forty years before that. Some folks just can't get the orneriness out of their bloodline."

"Anybody in particular?"

"Yeah, but let's not ruin a good day." He took a drink of whiskey and chased it with water. "We'll get into that stuff later. What did you do this morning?"

"I went by and spent some time with Adam. Talked some about your health."

Daddy looked up over the top of his glasses, "Adam didn't have any scrimshaw, did he?"

"No," I admitted.

"Didn't think so. He is not a good liar because he has a good heart and the two don't go together. What else did you do?"

"Went into the bank to see Mr. Blackman about cashing a check. Spent an hour with Billy Joe. He brought me up to date on most things around here."

Daddy stared at me, "Regular one-man Chamber of Commerce. Can't keep a secret any better than a woman. What all did he tell you?"

"Talked about the high school. Talked some about Roman. Some about North Georgia Global and how much they had done for the town."

Daddy continued to stare at me, "What else did he tell you?"

"I guess that's about it. I don't remember anything else."

Daddy screwed the top back on the whiskey and put it in a lower drawer. "He is a good man. Had a fine father. Sometimes he talks too much."

"What did you expect him to tell me?"

"Oh, I don't know. Just … stuff. Get in Old Pony and let's take a ride, I want to show you some of our second growth timber and our nursery. If we have time we'll take a run up to Forest Home and let you see how pretty it turned out."

I was as willing to change the subject as he was. "I'd like that. Maybe tomorrow I'll take my canoe and make a run down the Findhorn and through the canyon. See if I can still run Last Chance without flipping."

Daddy looked at me and without comment, shook his head sadly, as if he thought I was some kind of dunce.

*****

We spent the rest of the afternoon up in the mountains. Daddy drove like most old men, part of the time in the middle of the road and part of the time with the bushes along the side of the road slapping at Old Pony. He pointed out several tracts of land, gave me the history, when Roman bought the property, who it was bought from, how many acres, how many dollars per acre, and the volume harvested. I found it amazing he retained all that information in his head. While his body had obviously aged, his mind was as sharp as ever.

Daddy was right about Forest Home being pretty. The houses were neat and had attractive lawns. No longer just a workingman's town, it had matured. A real credit to Daddy's foresight, I thought. The streets were well engineered and land had been set aside at each end of town for a small park. Although the original occupants or their descendants owned several of the houses, I didn't recognize the names painted on most of the mailboxes.

"I'm pretty impressed, Daddy. I don't think I've ever ridden around in a town with the founder, and a relative to boot. I can see why you're proud of this. It wouldn't have been here if it wasn't for you."

Daddy shook his head. "Wouldn't have been here if men had not been starving to death and willing to work their fingers to the bone in these log woods. I owe these folks and their willingness to come up here in these mountains. Some of them left families and worked for months at a time without going home. Others brought their wife and children and lived in those little, two-room houses. You wouldn't find folks today that would do those things. Reckon Roman was built with their sweat."

"And you feel you still owe them?"

We'd parked on the side of the road. Daddy seemed to be searching for the right words. "In a way. I was honest with them and paid them fair wages. But I can still look back and see those skinny, hollow-eyed, little children. See their old worn-out clothes and holes in their shoes, see their chapped hands and decaying teeth. We didn't know what despair was then because everybody was in the same boat."

He sat looking down the street at two children playing with a dog. He swallowed, took a breath as if to say something and then let the breath out.

"Daddy, it wasn't a lot easier for you."

"I came out of it with something, but they came out of it with just a living. We all lost something. They lost some of their self-respect, and I lost your Mother. Maybe if I'd spent less time in the woods and more time at home, things would have turned out different. Maybe I'd have noticed that your mother wasn't doing well. Maybe she would have lived. Maybe you'd have a brother. Maybe a whole lot of damn things would've been different. No way I can tell you the hours I've gone over all this in my head, just laying there in the dark, wondering."

This sensitivity was something new. I put my hand over his. "A lot of things we'll never know. We do the best we can. We try to do right. Sometimes it turns out good and sometimes it turns out bad. But it's like ringing a bell. Once we've rung it, it's rung and we listen to whatever sound comes out of it. I've rung some bad bells in my life, probably some I don't even know about."

With just a faint smile around his eyes, Daddy looked at me, "You think?"

"Naw, on second thought, I've been perfect."

Daddy cranked Old Pony and we turned onto the road leading back to Cedergren, "Well, that's the good thing about time. When enough of it passes, we all become perfect; at least that's what we try to convince ourselves. Course, convincing others is not always easy."

"Sometimes, it's impossible."

"One other thing. That damned logo."

"What about it?"

"When I owned the company with the Blackmans, I thought it was pretty good, combining our two last names and naming the company Roman. But I wish I had never dreamed it up. It's like bragging. It's arrogant. Sometimes it makes me ashamed. What the heck has a Roman officer got to do with a bunch of mountain folks?"

"It's just a symbol, that's all."

"No, it's the sign of a big important man. It makes me ashamed. I wish I'd never done it."

*****

After eating supper at the café, Daddy and I sat on the porch at home watching the fireflies chasing each other in the hollow just off the edge of the yard. The sounds of the katydids blended with the creaking of the porch swing. I could barely make out Daddy's silhouette as he swung rhythmically back and forth in the old swing. I sat leaning back against a porch post. It was where I sat as a child.

I thought Daddy had dozed off when he asked, "What made you call?"

I wasn't following him. "Call?"

"When you called Luther. What made you call home after all these years?"

"I don't know if I can tell you. It was because of a lot of things. I'd seen the article about you raising buffalo and read something about raising wild turkeys out on the Arn. Then my old cat died, got killed trying to get home, and I started having nightmares."

The swing stopped. "Your cat died, that's what caused you to call home, your cat died."

"That was just a part of a lot of things, Daddy. I wondered how you were, and I guess I was lonesome. I was homesick. Bad homesick."

"Wish you'd got homesick sooner."

"Yeah, me too. Guess it took me a long time to grow up."

"Growing up is not always easy. In a way I've been working on it for better than eighty years, and sometimes I'm not sure I've made it yet."

The moon climbed above the trees and lit the yard with a soft creamy light. Across the valley, a car door slammed, and the sound of children's laughter rode the night breeze.

Daddy cleared his throat. "Why'd you do it?"

"I told you, I was homesick and…"

"I'm not talking about that. Why did you run off?"

There was harshness in his voice, and it nudged bad memories up toward the surface. "You ran me off."

"So … you blame me."

I didn't want this confrontation and hoped Daddy couldn't sense the queasiness of my insides. "Yes, I blame you."

"What did I do that was all that bad?"

"You treated me like a child."

"When?"

"When? Damned near every day. Then that day at the river …"

THE FINDHORN 1956

An hour before dark, Vaughn, the girls and I, reached our canoes. We made camp on a sandy beach fifty feet back from the edge of the river, I gathered wood, started a fire, and soon had coffee brewing. The peanut butter sandwiches in my dry bag were not much the worse for wear. We agreed everyone should have such a wonderful meal just once. Something to tell our grandchildren in about fifty years, we joked.

Maggie was eighteen, C.L. was seventeen, and Missy had just turned ten. Their family had moved to Cedergren six months earlier after their father, Jason Lockhart, had retired from the Marines. He was a machinist and had opened an automobile and truck repair service in Cedergren. Their mother taught the second grade at Cedergren Elementary. Maggie had just finished her first year at Georgia Tech and was majoring in biology. C.L. would be a senior in high school and Missy a fifth grader when school started in September.

The Lockhart family spent their summer vacations camping, fishing and hiking. The two older girls ran track and had been on the swim team in previous years. Because of their outdoor experience, they were not afraid of the river.

I thought Mrs. Lockhart must be a good-looking woman to have such attractive daughters. They had dark, curly hair and sparkling eyes. While disheveled from their adventure, I was struck by the good looks of the two older girls – Maggie, in particular.

A half hour after dark – "dark-thirty" to us mountain folks - the fire died down and the two younger girls spooned together and went to sleep. Maggie, Vaughn and I sat in the sand talking about our plans for the future. Having an older brother who had just returned to Cedergren to start a medical practice, Vaughn was planning a career in medicine and hoped to partner with his brother in a few years. Maggie was interested in microbiology and a career in research. Vaughn and I were impressed when we learned she was attending Georgia Tech on an academic scholarship.

While I had not given much thought to my future, Daddy had been pressing me to major in forestry and business. I could then come back to Cedergren to become a part of Roman. Sitting around the fire with two very ambitious people, I didn't want them to think I hadn't focused on my future, so I drew up some vague plan for my education and shared it.

Soon Vaughn moved away from the campfire and within minutes was snoring softly. Maggie and I continued to talk about our upbringing and our childhood. We found something in common: our fathers were dominant and demanding. I envied her because she had a mother to blunt the force of her father. When Daddy and I butted heads, there was no one in my family to act as a peacemaker. Or referee, for that matter.

"Common ground," she said. "We share common ground." I liked the thought because of the warmness to it, something I seldom experienced.

I followed her as she carried the coffee pot down to the water's edge and washed it.

The sand, still warm from the afternoon sun, made a comfortable bed and we lay close together looking up at the night sky. We found the Big Dipper, and she explained how Merak and Dubhe pointed to Polaris. I pretended that I couldn't see them. Maggie moved closer to me and pointed at the Little Dipper. "See there, just to the right," she said.

I reached up, took her outstretched hand in mine, and pulled it against my lips.

*****

Shortly after daylight, we shoved our canoes into the fog rising from the Findhorn and set out for Dove Landing. Maggie and I went in front scouting the easiest route through the rapids, and the other canoe with Vaughn, C.L. and Missy, followed our lead.

Considering the first part of our trip, the last part was uneventful. Maggie and I had to beach twice to empty water from my canoe. We took out well before the Henderson Brothers falls, carried our canoes around the thundering rapids, and put them back into the water a hundred yards downstream. Vaughn, Maggie and I walked back upstream to watch the almost inescapable hydraulic that boiled up below the rapids. "I'll run that someday," I boasted, and Vaughn said he would like to have an hour to draw a crowd and might even sell tickets. "No, I'm serious. Someday I'll run those Brothers. Just you wait and see."

Maggie was a strong paddler, and despite the hole in the bow of my canoe, we had little trouble staying in front of Vaughn and the two younger girls. Just before we rounded the last bend in the river before the takeout point, we waved goodbye and increased our pace.

We were surprised at the activity at the landing. Men wearing bright red life jackets and white hardhats, part of the Findhorn River Mountain Rescue Team, were unloading airboats. Two ambulances and three Sheriff's cars were parked by the landing. A helicopter with Tennessee Highway Patrol markings had just landed and was sitting in the parking lot, its rotors still slowly turning.

Maggie looked back at me and raised her eyebrows in a silent question.

"Must be some big deal," I said. "Something bad must have happened downstream." As we neared the landing, my daddy and Vaughn's father waded out into the river. Maggie and I took a couple of backwater strokes and glided into the shore.

I never thought Daddy might be worried about me. He knew I was capable of running the river safely with little chance of mishap. If I had given it any thought at all, I would have expected a look of relief on his face. Instead, he was furious.

"Where in the hell have you been?"

Mr. Blackman was terrified. "Where is Vaughn? Is he hurt? Where is he?"

Several people gathered around our canoe, all asking questions at the same time. A woman leaned into the canoe and hugged Maggie. She was sobbing and repeating, "God have mercy on us." Then, "Where are my other girls? Please tell me they're all right."

We pulled our canoe up on the bank. Rescue squad members, the State police, the sheriff, a newspaper photographer, and people I had never seen surrounded us. Then the sheriff saw Vaughn and the two younger girls coming around the bend in the second canoe. Most of the attention shifted to them.

Maggie was talking to a short, heavyset man. From the description she had given last night, I thought this was her father but he was acting different from the mother, and his stance was belligerent.

I was having my own trouble with Daddy. "What kind of goofy crap is this? You have scared the hell out of everybody in the county. Then you show up and act like nothing has happened. I always thought you were irresponsible and immature. Now you've proved it."

Daddy grasped the front of my life jacket and pulled my face close to his. "Sometimes you act like a damn idiot. We'll get to the bottom of this at home," he shouted. He drew his hand back as if to slap me, then shook his head in discuss. He turned and walked to the edge of the river where Vaughn's canoe was surrounded in much the same way mine had been.

A couple of deputies and the photographer stared at us, slack jawed.

I was stunned. I hadn't expected a hero's welcome, hadn't really expected anything. I just thought we would load our canoes, get in my pickup and drive back to Cedergren. Now I had taken a severe tongue-lashing from Daddy in front of a lot of people. Maggie had tried to interrupt while Daddy was shouting at me but in his rage he ignored her. Carrying my canoe and climbing the sandy bank, I was determined not to cry. The embarrassment made my skin tingle and my face blazed with shame. I kept my eyes on the ground and avoided the looks from the rescuers. Daddy's words were ringing in my ear: "goofy crap ….. irresponsible ….. immature ….. proved it ….. bottom of this at home."

*****

I drove home, my mind filled with bad thoughts, most of them directed toward my daddy. He had ridiculed me in the past but nothing like this. However, one thing was certain, it would never happen again.

At home, I threw clothes into a gym bag. I had eighty dollars in my desk; I took it, grabbed my camping gear out of the garage and climbed back into my pickup. My spinning tires left deep ruts in the graveled drive. Now, for the first time, I could cry.

CEDERGREN 1986

"What would you have done? Your son is damned near a day late getting off the river, and he comes paddling up, big grin on his face, acting like nothing unusual has happened. Got lawmen everywhere, helicopters, rescue squad. Crying women. Vaughn's daddy acting plum hysterical. What in hell would you have done?"

"I believe I'd have said, 'Son, I'm glad you're okay. We were really worried.'"

"Yeah, well I …"

I interrupted. "I know you think you were right. But you weren't. It's behind us and there's nothing either one of us can do. You keep believing the way you do; I'll keep believing the way I do. Maybe someday we can sort it out but not tonight."

Daddy resumed his swinging, "… not tonight."

Neither of us spoke. Daddy kept swinging and I leaned against the porch post, brooding. Silence can get heavy and occupy lots of space.

We needed to change the subject, get off this old hurt. "I saw something on TV about a couple of mysterious deaths out near the stone fort."

"You did? Way up in Alaska? Must have been a slow news day."

"What do you know about those killings? They caught the killer yet?"

"Stuff gets blown way out of proportion. You know these news folks are always trying to stir something up."

"So, wasn't anything to it?"

"Not that much. I think it'll take care of itself. Folks just let it alone." Abruptly, he stood. "Dang, it's after ten o'clock. I'm going to turn in. Otherwise my face will be all wrinkled in the morning."

"Good idea for both of us. If you've got time tomorrow afternoon, I'd like for you to take me up to Sandy Ramp. I really do want to make the run down the river."

Daddy grumbled. "Still hadn't outgrown that kid stuff."

We were treading on thin ice. "No, probably not. It's just something, I need to do. It'll be kinda like taking a trip with an old friend."

"Well, whatever you think, but that old friend damned near got you killed and damned near ruined both our lives."

"You may be right, but it's just something I've got to do."

Daddy was still grumbling as he and Rip walked into the house. "I'll haul you out to the put-in, even if it is against my better judgment."

*****

The next morning, I loaded my canoe into the back of Old Pony. In the garage, I found a battered coffee pot, it's sides blackened from many open campfires. I took a skillet, some coffee, corn meal and grease from the kitchen, and wrapped everything up in a piece of tarpaulin.

"Well," Daddy said, "you may drown but at least you won't die hungry. If the mosquitoes and black flies get too rough, you might wish you had a bigger piece of tarp to hide under."

We left the jeep at the service station where one of the Pherson boys had agreed to drop it off at Dove Landing.

Soon after leaving Cedergren, I asked Daddy, "We're going to be coming up on the Arn pretty soon, aren't we?"

"Yep, in about five miles." Daddy had no other comment and seemed intent on his driving.

I felt childish when I asked, "Do you think you could give me a quick tour? I'd like to see the changes, and I'd love to see the buffalo."

His brow wrinkled. "I'd really rather not go out on the Arn for the next couple of days. It's right at the end of the breeding season and the bulls can get pretty testy. Had a couple of the boys take some salt out to one of the pastures a few years ago. One of them blew the horn at an old bull that was trailing a female across the road. The horn got stuck. The bull got all worked-up. Charged the truck, turned the damned thing over and it rolled down the hill. Liked to have killed two of the best hired hands I've got. Been mighty careful since then about driving around on the Arn this time of year. What say we wait and go out a little later?"

I thought about being rolled around by a buffalo bull, "Whatever you say. You're the expert."

Daddy stopped in front of a chain-link fence topped with razor wire. "This is the entrance," he said, pointing to an imposing security gate, "and the only place you can get onto the Arn. Unless you can fly like a bird or climb a vertical rock cliff. At first, poachers tried to climb the fence but we electrified that sucker and took care of that problem. Been a couple of fellers that probably had some rock climbing skills that tried it from the river."

"Was that after the men got killed?"

"Oh, I don't know. It was some months ago. I don't keep up with stuff like that."

We swung back onto the road. I knew we had exhausted any discussion of the dead men. In less than an hour, we saw the Sandy Ramp sign and followed the narrow road down to the river. We loaded my gear in the canoe and slid it into the Findhorn. I made a draw stroke, felt the pull of the current and waved goodbye.

Daddy had been watching me, hands on hips. Now he shouted through cupped hands, "Try to keep your ass out of trouble this time, okay?"

*****

Thirty years change a lot of things, but the Findhorn may not have changed in the past 30,000 years. I take a lot of comfort in that. Man wants to think the world revolves around him and he has control of his environment. Such a man has not seen the unchanged face of the Findhorn.

It was a beautiful day. The water was clear, and the temperature was in the low-80s. After a couple of miles, I felt I had been on the river just last week. For the first time since returning to Cedergren, I felt comfortable. I knew what was around the next bend and knew exactly the next rapid. Greyhound came into view and Terminal was just ahead. Feeling the beginning of fatigue in my shoulders and back, it occurred to me I was not eighteen. Maybe the gray that had appeared in my beard was trying to tell me something, trying to get me to realize that, regardless of what I thought, I was losing the battle men have always lost against the years.

I paddled to the shore just above Greyhound, tied my canoe to a birch tree, and walked down to have a look at the first of the real rapids. Just as I remembered, the best way to run the rapid was to enter to the left, cross the standing wave, then run to the right before setting up to run the center of Terminal. I knew even if I flipped going through Terminal, I would soon be in smooth water. With any luck, the canoe would come down into the eddy and I could pull it to the bank.

I walked back upstream to the canoe, checked to see that the bag containing my gear was securely tied down, tightened my life jacket, and swung out into the current. Entering the rapid just as I planned, I plowed through the standing wave and swung back to the center of the river. Perfectly lined up for the Terminal, I slid through the rapid as smoothly as if I ran it every day. Turning the canoe in the slack water just below the rapid, I looked back upstream at the churning water. I raised the paddle over my head and shouted, "I'm here. I'm back. I'm back." The sound echoed off the surrounding canyon walls. "Backkkk. I'm backkkk."

Now in what Vaughn had called the "sissy water," I leaned back, watched the bank slide by, and tried to remember the sequence of events that had taken place there thirty years earlier. It was there we saw the automobile with the trailer. I shot the Double Bubble rapids and took the "sneak route" through Little Sluice because I wanted plenty of time and maneuvering space to set up for Big Sluice. With tired arms and back, I decided no "hero" run for me today.

Hearing the roar before I saw the rapids, it came back to me. We had first spotted the big aluminum canoe half way through Big Sluice. I wondered if it would be as scary now as it was then. I was trying to silence the voice in the back of my mind shouting, "Dumb ass, this ain't going to be easy."

Nothing to it. Just take it straight through and let the water do most of the work. "Run it like a pro, like an expert," I could hear Vaughn saying. "We'll do until experts come along."

I wanted to be eighteen again, wanted the lost years back, wanted the innocence of youth. "Want in one hand and shit in the other one," mountain folks would say, "and see which one fills up first."

Blasting through Big Sluice, I just had time for one glance toward the spot where the canoe was pinned. I saw the boulder where the little girl clutched my leg, and I remember how she shook with fear.

I wondered about her older sisters – Maggie, in particular. Was she as pretty as I remembered, with the dark curly hair and blue eyes? The excitement of the rescue that day, and the fiasco at the takeout the next day paired and muddled with the passage of thirty years. Maggie and I had sat on the bank of the river after the others had gone to sleep that night. She'd said we shared common ground. I remember the warmth I felt. I remember we kissed and then … dreams and fantasy and memories mix into a mental swirl … things all ran together … thirty years will do that.

Maggie would be well into middle age now, probably with a husband and children, maybe grandchildren. What was her memory of that night? Did she ever think about it? Different things affect different people in different ways. Maybe my memory of that night was distorted – just a teenage boy with raging hormones operating with ineptness, running on adrenalin and concocting fantasies.

Daddy might know where she and her family wound up. I'd ask him tomorrow.

*****

I camped on the opposite side of the river from the Arn. I wanted a good look at the craggy escarpment to see if it was as foreboding as I remembered, and as scary as the preppy TV reporter in the yellow polo shirt had described it.

After tying my canoe to a rock at the edge of a sand spit beach, I gathered dead limbs, dug a fire pit, and lined it with rocks. I started a fire, dipped water from the river, and put a pot of coffee on to boil. There was a still pool just downstream, and ten minutes later I was cleaning two nice bass. I moved the coffee to the edge of the fire, and soon the air was strong with the wonderful smell of frying fish. I ate with my fingers while wondering if early settlers might have camped here. Indians may have camped in the same spot, and maybe those moon-eyed folks had done the same before they ventured up onto the plateau.

Just before dark, I sat in the sand finishing my last cup of coffee. It gets dark quickly down here in the canyon after sunset. Darkness seemed to come down the river like a cloud. In minutes, stars came twinkling into view. I finished my coffee and watched the moon rise in the canyon behind me. The coals of the fire lost their glow and the river gurgled hypnotically. After scooping out a depression in the sand to fit my shoulders and hips, I placed the tarp over the depressions and lay down. Kings and queens might have finer beds, but on this night, I doubted it.

Within minutes, I was asleep.

Sometime during the night, I heard a single gunshot across the river. Briefly, a dim light bobbed like a firefly along the edge of escarpment near the stone fort. Then I heard the baying of dogs. I could tell by the long pauses between their cries that they had lost the scent of whatever they were trailing. Eventually the sound of the hounds diminished and everything became peaceful. No more gunshots and no more lights. I drifted back to sleep and had a pleasant dream of salmon frying in a cast iron skillet along a cold river in Alaska.

I woke rolled up in the tarp wet with dew and fog. I was too comfortable to get up and lay on my side watching the fog up river change from gray to pink with the rising of the sun. A few dying coals remained in the fire pit. After adding some dried moss and willow limbs, I had enough fire to make coffee. I wished I had saved a piece of the fish from the night before. Then I remembered how bad warmed-over fish tasted and decided I was content with just coffee. Surely, I could do without eating until the take-out at Dove Landing.

I took my binoculars and glassed the canyon wall across the river. I could see the east end of the fort wall. I was sure that was where I had seen the light last night. I glassed the bluff again and this time, movement, a quick flash of red. It was gone before I could focus the binoculars. But the hair rose on the back of my neck, and I had a very strong feeling of being watched. Tense, I laughed aloud and convinced myself that it probably wasn't a stray Indian or a moon-eye getting ready to attack.

What were hunters doing out on the Arn at night? What were they hunting? I'll bet Daddy hadn't given them permission and I would bet my last dollar he would not be very happy when he found out they were hunting there. "Not very happy" was an understatement. "Hissy fit" would be more appropriate.

I covered my campfire with sand and leveled the depression where I had slept. Somewhere I had read "Leave no foot prints; take only memories." There was no sign that a man had ever been there, so I guess I had done it right.

With the early morning sun warming my stiff shoulders, I drifted along in the smooth water, wondering what the rest of the world was doing this fine, peaceful morning.

From a ghostly grey sycamore standing in the edge of the river, a Belted Kingfisher streaked overhead and dove into the water in front of the canoe. In a great shower of water, the bird rose triumphal with a sunfish clutched in its dagger-like bill and hustled back to the sycamore. The excitement of seeing the kingfisher take the fish pulled me back to the present, and I became aware of the roar of the Henderson Brothers. The current was becoming stronger as it yielded to the overpowering pull of the rapids. A hundred yards ahead at river left, I could see the takeout where river runners pulled their canoes and kayaks out in preparation to portage around the rapids.

I beached at the takeout and dragged my canoe up on the sand. Maybe it was just my imagination, but I could feel the sand shudder with the power of the rapids. Fifty yards downstream, I stood on a low bluff and looked down into the churning water. A thin mist rose up from the falls, coating bushes along the river. A spider had spun an intricate web, as large as a small window, just above the falls and its threads collected the mist – maybe a sliver veil over the future . At the edge, water flowed over the falls so smoothly it looked still, just a solid sheet of water, its motion frozen as in a photograph. But at the base of the falls, the water churned and thrashed against itself: a giant machine struggling to self-destruct. An aluminum Pepsi can floated to the first of the rapids then slid smoothly over the falls and landed without a splash in a large hydraulic. The can danced on the first wave and was then sucked under the water. Ten seconds later, it surfaced just in time to tumble over the top of the second rapid. I watched for the can to resurface. It didn't.

*****

When I was twenty, I went skiing in New Mexico with some friends. They were far better skiers than I would ever be, and I envied their skill and daring. Late in the afternoon, we took the lift to the top and stood together looking down the steep runs. We agreed this would be the last run of the day and they decided to take Bambi, an intermediate slope, back to the ski lodge. "I'm not ready for that," I said, looking at the steep run. "I'm going to take Honeysuckle, it's more my skill level."

"Well, chicken-man, have it your way." They laughed and went swooshing away in plumes of powdery snow leaving me looking down the beginner's slope. With a few folks my age, but mostly kids and wobbly-legged seniors, I made the run down Honeysuckle. I am better than this, I thought, and a little blackness rose in my heart.

At the bottom of the run, I took a lift half way up the mountain where I skied down to Lift 6, then rode to the top of the mountain where the rarefied air chewed at my ears like tiny mice. Now I was at the same point where, earlier today, my friends had laughed at me. I dropped off down the mountain on Bambi, and then turned right on the black diamond Lorelei. A few hundred yards ahead, the trail intersected with another intermediate run, but to the left Lorelei intersected with the double black diamond North American, the most difficult run at Taos Ski Valley. Without waiting for fear to build in my system, insides churning with adrenalin, I dropped off onto North American. I went into a tuck and went flying down the run, the wind howling warnings in my ears, my cheeks hot with the coldness. I was upright but not quite under control. Everything was a blur until I reached the bottom and skied to the side of the trail. I stood with weak knees and trembling legs, breathless, but wrapped in satisfaction.

My friends were waiting at the lodge, sipping heated brandy. They laughed when I arrived, "We thought you had gotten lost on the bunny slope. Where have you been?"

"It just took me a while," I replied, knowing they would never understand my victory over fear.

*****

I shoved the canoe back into the water. "I wish you were here Vaughn. This would be your chance to sell tickets. But you wouldn't have five minutes to draw a crowd." I gave a whoop as my canoe surrendered to the pull of the rapids.

I rode the first drop upright. The canoe bobbed up and down on the big hydraulic. I made a forward stroke and felt the emptiness of bubbles around my paddle. The canoe was sucked down to the gunwales and then spit out into the edge of a standing wave. The roiling water ripped the paddle from my hand. Paddle gone and with nothing to maintain my balance, I dropped into the center of the canoe. Immediately it rolled to the left and slid out from under me. I felt the powerful force of the hydraulic and then the greater pull of the second rapid. As I started over the falls, I pulled my legs up under me and clutched my knees, hoping to cushion the impact from any rocks.

The drop was breathtaking; I tumbled wildly, bouncing off boulders before being sucked back up under the falls.

Immediately, the current grabbed me and pulled me down into the second hydraulic. Along with golf-ball-sized bubbles, I rode the turbulent water to the bottom of the river where the current dragged me along through boulders. My eyes were open, and in the clear water I could see the remains of a canoe caught in the limbs of a fallen tree. My pulse surged when I saw a Pepsi can trapped between two boulders. Finally, the current lost strength and I swam downstream away from the falls. I fought my way to the surface, sucked air into my burning lungs and, looking back upstream was amazed at the distance I had covered underwater. Fear makes strong swimmers, I thought.

My canoe washed up on the bank ten yards away. My tarp, fly rod, and second paddle were still in place in the bow. I sat on the bank for an hour, thinking about what I had done. Like my ski run down the double black diamond North American, I could never tell anybody about my trip through the Henderson Brothers, because they couldn't understand.

Victory over fear is a magnificent and solitary emotion.

*****

After the Henderson Brothers, the river calmed but still had enough current to take me along with minimum paddling. Twice I beached the canoe and searched the shore for muscadines. City folks cultivated the wild grapes and called them scuppernongs but that seemed blasphemy, taking something wild and perfect and trying to domesticate it.

Late morning, I paddled into Willies Cove, a small inlet named after a moonshiner who made whiskey there for ten years before being caught by the Revenuers. I could smell the muscadines before I saw them. The pungent odor dredged up childhood memories of Saturdays spent hunting them with Mother and Daddy. Mother made fantastic jelly and preserves.

Daddy said angels would sell their soul to the devil for a pint of Mother's muscadine preserves.

The vines had climbed a sweet gum tree and disappeared into the star-shaped leaves. I sat in the shade of that tree thinking about my mother. Her life cut short, she never enjoyed any of Daddy's success. Mother had been dead so long that my memory of her was dim. I still remembered her hands, her long slender fingers. Her ring finger was almost as long as her middle finger. Daddy joked with her, saying someday he would fill that long finger with rings.

She died before he had the chance.

I looked down at my hands and my long ring finger. Mother's mark. At least I still have something from her and will always have it. On this day I didn't eat any muscadines; I felt their taste might not be as good as I remembered and it might smudge what memory I had left of Mother. I searched for other memories that weren't quite there and found only bits and pieces too small to be assembled. Dream material I thought and tried to put it out of my mind. I paddled slowly out of the cove and a sense of emptiness surrounded my canoe like a floating dark veil.

I reached the Dove Landing takeout at noon. The current had increased as it swung in along the bank just above the landing. Using my paddle as a rudder, I enjoyed the free ride. Just before beaching the canoe, I heard the faint sound of a tin flute, a penny whistle the mountain folks called it. While it was not a particularly good rendition, the song was clearly *Amazing Grace*.

I climbed the steep path to the parking area. Daddy was sitting on the lowered tailgate of Old Pony, Rip asleep in the grass at his feet. Daddy hadn't heard me and was looking down at the whistle in his hand. His brow furrowed as his stiff fingers moved over the holes of the whistle.

"You'll have to blow in the end. Just covering the holes with your fingers isn't going to make any music," I said.

Startled, Daddy looked up. With a sheepish look, he slid the whistle into his pocket. "Where you been, Creight? I've been waiting on you since midmorning. Dang it, son, you really take your time coming down the river, don't you?"

"Well, I wasn't racing with anybody. What are you doing here, and where's the jeep?"

"I didn't have anything to do today, so I figured I'd pick you up myself." Then, as if it were a second thought, "Sides, the feller that was going to bring the jeep down here was busy, so I figured I'd just help out."

I laughed. "So you just brought your tin whistle along and got in some practice. I didn't know you were a musician."

Daddy seemed embarrassed, "I … uh … it's just something I picked up. Helps pass the time away."

We brought the canoe up and loaded it in the back of Old Pony. I dug into Daddy's newfound musical interest, "I can see why you'd come way out here to practice. You're pretty bad, you know."

Daddy pulled the tin whistle out of his pocket and handed it to me. "Well Mozart, let's hear you play."

Out of boredom, I'd taken some flute lessons while living by myself in Colorado. After a couple of false starts, I swung into a passable version of *Amazing Grace*. I finished and gave the whistle back to Daddy. "So what do you think of that?"

"Sounds pretty fair. Man can't tell when he might need to play for an audience. You get a bit more practice and folks might recognize the song."

Daddy reached into the back of Old Pony and handed me a bundle. "I brought you some dry clothes. Looks like you need them."

I pulled off my shorts and T-shirt. My legs and stomach were covered cuts and bruises from my trip through the Henderson Brothers.

"Damned nation son. What happened? You look like you've been drug through the briars by a runaway mule. Did Last Chance eat you up?"

"Looks that way, doesn't it," I said. My secret rested comfortably in that part of the brain that stores precious things.

The drumming of rain on the metal roof woke me. The smell of coffee brewing and the nose-wrinkling odor of frying ham caused me to hobble downstairs on sore legs.

Daddy was frying eggs. There was a platter of ham on the table and a pan of biscuits sitting on the stove. "Hey, I thought you always ate breakfast at the café. Figured you'd lost all of your cooking skills."

He looked over his shoulder, "Any idiot can fry ham and eggs and make coffee, but I'm not making any promises about the biscuits. Last batch I made, even old Rip wouldn't eat them."

I lifted a biscuit from the pan and took a bite. "Taste good to me. Guess it just shows I'm a lot smarter than Rip."

Daddy sat down across the table from me. "Maybe he's accustomed to better vittles than you are." He looked over the top of his glasses. "What's on your agenda today?"

"Nothing much. You need me to do something?"

"I was thinking about taking some salt out to the buffs this morning. Maybe they've had enough time to settle down. Last time I was out, I noticed they were pretty much out. Damned things need about twice as much salt as a cow. If they could get to it, they would probably drink Hematite Lake dry. Anyway, I hadn't checked on them for a few days and there is no telling what kind of mischief they've gotten into. Just wondered if you'd like to go out there with me."

I thought what a turnabout from two days ago, "I believe I can squeeze a trip out there into my busy schedule providing we can swing by the Christian Springs Cemetery. Maybe have a look at the old stone fort."

We put four 50-pound blocks of mineralized salt into the back of Old Pony. Without too much protest, Rip climbed into the back seat graciously allowing me to ride in the sweetheart seat.

We stopped at the security gate leading into the Arn. Daddy reached up over the sun visor and pressed the button on something resembling a garage door opener. The gate opened slowly and for the first time since I became an adult I was on the Arn.

We turned onto a road that led along the east side of the plateau. "Look like you remember?" Daddy asked.

"I'm not sure. It's been a long time. Maybe the timber is bigger, and I don't remember the road being this good."

Daddy was wrestling Old Pony down the dirt road. "I'm out here a couple of times a week, checking on the buffs, feeding the turkeys. Sometimes I stop by the cemetery and talk to my folks. I've got a lot of questions to ask them. Guess I'm interested in what they think about how I handled the land they passed down to me. I never sold any of it, never had much debt against it. Don't think I ever done too much to hurt the family name. Probably never helped it much either."

Surprised by his nostalgia, I looked over at Daddy and saw a tear running down his cheek. He brushed it aside with the sleeve of his shirt.

"Sometimes I try to believe in reincarnation, but I don't have much luck at it. I'd love to come back and give life another shot. Be a better man. Help folks more. Guess I'd try going to church. I'd try to worry less and laugh more. I'd be a whole lot more understanding - with everybody. I'd let you grow up at your own speed and not try to force you grown before your time."

Daddy continued his wrestling match with Old Pony. "Probably not, but maybe I could get it right next time. But heck, I know I'll not be back and I know what's done is done." He paused and had difficulty swallowing, "Lord, how I've missed your mother."

I didn't want to see Daddy this way. "Daddy, you've …"

"No, no, you hush and listen to me. I want to get this off my chest. I want you to understand, and I hope we never talk about this again. It's too painful, the mistakes I've made."

I tried to comfort Daddy, "It's going to be all right."

Daddy shook his head, "No it isn't. I'm dealing with something so hurtful it's killing me. I'm going to have to make a decision pretty soon." He swallowed. "And whatever decision I make will be wrong."

"I don't understand. Tell me what you're talking about. Maybe I can help if you'll just let me."

"You can't. And for the first time in my life, I don't have an answer. I'm not a praying man, but I've prayed for an answer. I haven't been sent one. If I have, I haven't understood it."

Daddy raised his right hand and made an erasing motion. "Bad timing on my part. Sometimes stuff just kinda boils over in my mind. Let's get on with our business this morning and we'll cross that bridge another day. Look yonder, isn't that something?"

Down the road, three buffalo bulls and a half dozen females stood in the shade of a white oak tree and watched us approach. I knew the bulls were big, but not that big, and not that menacing – I thought about my nightmare in Alaska and my dreams weren't that far off. Seeing a buffalo in a zoo or on TV was one thing, but this close, the perspective was completely different.

Daddy stopped, the trailing dust rising up around Old Pony. He looked over his shoulder and said, "Rip, you set and don't move." He opened his door. "Just get out real easy. Don't make any sudden moves and work your way back to the tailgate. They're not afraid of you, but you sure don't want to spook them any. The cows might run off, but the bulls will charge in a blink and I don't want them abusing Old Pony. Or you."

We dropped the tailgate and unloaded the blocks of salt, placing them along either side of the road. We got back into the truck and softly closed the doors. The cows immediately walked to the blocks and started licking them. The bulls stood and looked at us, chewing their cuds. Daddy smiled. "Old boys are pretty crusty, ain't they? They want the salt as bad as the cows do, but they want to show us they don't really give a hoot one way or the other."

Still awed, I said, "Well, I'll dang sure not argue with them. They don't have to prove anything to me. I'll believe whatever they want me to believe, no argument at all."

Daddy cranked the engine, looked at me and smiled. "Thought you might be impressed. We'll go on out and let you have a look at Hematite Lake and the furnace ruins. We'll swing by the fort and visit the buffs more on our way back."

The stone furnace and the lake had not changed. The lake was a deep greenish-blue and willows grew along the levy. Daddy said, "I put just enough fertilizer in the lake so weeds don't take over. You ought to see some of the bass I've taken out of where Cerulean Springs feeds into the lake. Course, I had to fence the buffs out or they'd have wallowed it out something awful. They wade around in the creek below the spillway enough to keep happy."

The artisanship that had gone into the building of the massive furnace was impressive. The limestone blocks, some as big as four by six feet, fit with precision. In an earlier time, the same stonemasons might have constructed pyramids. The carved lintel of the furnace mouth showed the pride of their work. Some stonemason had taken the time to chisel the profile of an Indian into the limestone.

A stone bell tower, almost a companion piece and built of the same material, supported a large cast iron bell. Probably, the bell announced the beginning and ending of the workday for the ironworkers or maybe dinner. It must have weighed a hundred pounds, and that it had survived all these years was a miracle.

Luther and I had rung the bell when we were children pretending we were on a locomotive hauling iron and timber. I grasped the crank on the yoke of the bell and started to pull. That would have caused the clapper to strike the side of the bell. Daddy stopped the motion by grabbing the side of the bell with both hands, "Some of the older buffalos are in the holler to the north, and we don't want to scare them."

"I'd love to have been here when the iron company was processing ore."

"Not me. I'd a whole lot more rather see it peaceful like it is now. Sometimes wild turkeys roost on top of the furnace. Maybe we can get out here early enough some morning so you can see them coming down off their roost. After a frost on cold mornings, they'll line up and walk across the pasture eating the grasshoppers that have been stunned by the cool weather. Pretty smart old birds; a whole lot smarter than chickens."

At the fort, Daddy sat down on one of the large rocks that had fallen from the wall. I walked around the eastern edge of the wall and looked down at the Findhorn River. Through the rising fog, I could just make out the Henderson Brothers rapids and hear its dull roar. How insignificant they looked from this distance compared to how fierce they were when I was at their level. My heart skipped a couple of beats and I thought, *I beat you. Fair and square. I took the best you had and I beat you.*

Daddy was watching me from beneath the brim of his hat, "What're you grinning about, son?"

"Nothing really, just how things don't always look the same."

"Do you remember playing out here when you and Luther were just kids?"

I laughed. "Oh yeah. Sometimes we were the Indians and sometimes we were the moon-eyes. We tried camping out here one night. We built a fire, made some hoecakes and fried some baloney. We stretched an old bed sheet over a limb and used it as our tent. A strong wind came up that night. Came howling up the bluff making that screaming sound through those rocks at the end of the fort."

Daddy nodded. "I've heard that."

"We'd done something pretty dumb. We'd been telling scary stories. I wasn't too comfortable with the moaning noise. He wouldn't admit it, but Luther wasn't either."

"But you boys toughed it out?"

"Naw. Wish I could say we did, but we didn't. About midnight we pulled the sheet off the limb and stumbled in the dark back to the furnace. We huddled up and wrapped the sheet around us. Neither of us slept much. We sure were glad to see daylight come."

"You boys Indians or moon-eyes that night?" Daddy was getting a kick out of my story.

"I don't know which one we were, but whichever one, we weren't very brave."

I searched for my campsite on the other side of the river, but from this distance, I couldn't pick it out. "The other night when I was camping across the river, I heard dogs running along the edge of the bluff. It sounded like they were trailing something. I thought I heard a gunshot, but I never heard it again. Do you reckon I was hearing things?"

Daddy stood and looked at me, "What time was that?"

"Oh, I don't know. Probably sometime around midnight."

"But you heard it just one time?"

"Yeah. The next morning, I glassed the top of the bluff with binoculars."

"But you didn't see anything?"

"No, not really. Thought I saw something red but it went away and I never saw it again."

Daddy walked along the edge of the bluff, peering at the ground in front of him. Fifty feet down the bluff line, he stooped and picked up the spent casing of a shotgun shell. He smelled the end of the casing and, almost to himself, said, "Recent. Last couple of days." He continued, examining tree trunks as he walked. He stopped, took out his pocketknife, and probed a beech tree. When I caught up, he was rolling three pellets around in his hand. He held them out and, as I took them from him, he said, "Double-aught buck shot. Somebody was trying to kill something big, but he must have missed cause I don't see any blood sign. Looks like you weren't seeing and hearing things."

"You don't think they were hunting buffs, do you?"

Daddy was on his knees studying the ground. Then he stood. "No, not at night. They were hunting something else."

"What do you think it was?"

Daddy didn't answer but continued walking and staring at the ground. He parted the leaves with his foot, squatted, and picked up a crumpled cigarette pack. "Picayune," he grumbled under his breath. "Sumbitch smoking Picayune. Sure narrows it down."

He dropped the empty cigarette pack in his coat pocket.

I asked, "Who does it narrow it down to?"

Daddy glared along the bluff line and for a second I thought he had not heard my question. "Just some real dumb asses," he finally answered. He looked at his pocket watch, and then looked at the sun as if to verify the dependability of the timepiece. "We need to go," he said as he started making his way through a laurel thicket toward Old Pony.

I was disappointed that he hadn't answered my question, and he was now cutting our trip short. "Thought we were going to go back and watch the buffalo some more."

Daddy seemed to search for words before saying, "I …uh, uh, just remembered. Luther asked me to stop by the office. Something about buying a tract of timber up above Shoals, that the owner would be at the office this afternoon. Guess he just wanted a little input from me. Probably just trying to make me feel good. Anyway, we've got to get going."

"Daddy, you think we might come back out here tomorrow?"

Old Pony was bouncing past the place where we had salted the buffalo, and the bulls were licking the salt blocks. Daddy didn't slow down. "Maybe we can get back out here in a day of two."

*****

In Cedergren, Daddy pulled into his parking place in front of Roman's office. "You go on home. Luther will bring me out when the meeting is over."

On the way to the house, I wondered what made Daddy act so strangely. I went over our conversation looking for anything I might have said. Things had gone normal until I told him about the dogs and the gunshot. After he found the buckshot and the cigarette package, everything changed.

I parked in front of Daddy's home office, went inside, fixed a drink of The Turkey, and looked at the books in the shelves. While most of the books related to timber management, I was surprised at the others. Books on architecture, sculpturing, music, painting, mental illness, and physiology. Daddy had always been a voracious reader, but I found it strange that his interest covered such a wide range of topics.

Adding more whiskey to my glass, I looked at the sculpture of the woman, the little boy, and the faceless man. I compared it to the unfinished paintings. No doubt, the woman and the little boy in each piece were the same. Since the man's face was either featureless or hidden, I couldn't be sure about his identity or age. I studied the painting of the people and the horse and for the first time, saw Hematite furnace in the background.

"Get up boy. It's daylight and I'm hungry. I need breakfast. Let's go down to the café and put away a big one. Looks like it's going to be a good day. Might be a good day to have a reunion with the folks at the cemetery. Maybe do a bit of cleanup work. "

We loaded a shovel and two brush hooks in the back of Old Pony. Rip seemed accustomed to his spot in the back seat and just barely challenged me for the sweetheart seat. As we left the house, Daddy turned on the two-way radio and announced to any of the Roman staff listening that he and I'd would be at the Christian Springs cemetery most of the morning.

The Brotherhood of the Round Table had finished their coffee and were gone when we arrived. "Let's take a table close to the counter," Daddy said. "It's easier on the waitress."

Louellen put two mugs of coffee on the table. "Mr. Roane, what can I get for you this morning? "

"Pancakes." Louellen turned to leave. "Wait! You haven't taken Creight's order."

She dropped her head and looked at me through her eyelashes, "Oh, I know what he wants: two scrambled, sausage, grits and three biscuits. He told me last time. Ain't that right?"

"Right as rain, Louellen. You're a dandy."

She blushed, "I'll have your order in a jiffy."

Daddy smiled. "Careful, Louellen. You'll have him trying to follow you home."

I unrolled the napkin from the silver. "I could do worse and probably have. She seems sweet and innocent."

Daddy took his water glass and made small circles on the table. He spoke so softly that I almost missed his question. "Are you married now, or have you ever been married?"

"No to both questions."

He took his napkin and erased the circles. "You got any kids?"

I laughed. "No, not that I know of."

"Not that you know of? What kind of answer is that?"

"An honest answer. If I've got any kids, I don't know anything about it."

Daddy didn't hide his irritation. "Well hell, looks like you'd know if you had any."

"What is this Daddy, some kind of Perry Mason cross examination? I told you I'm not married and never have been. I told you if I have any kids, I don't know about it. What do you want me to say?"

Daddy looked down at the table and mumbled, "I don't know. I didn't mean anything by it. I was just wondering, that's all."

I was sorry about my sharp answer, "That's all right. I guess you were just wondering if you were a granddaddy."

Louellen was placing our breakfast on the table. Daddy said, "That's it. I was just wondering."

We ate in silence. When we had finished, Louellen refilled our coffee and put the ticket on the table. "Ya'll mad at each other? Cause if you are, I just might have to switch your little legs, and then I'd make you hug and make up."

The tension was broken. Daddy winked and gave Louellen a smile. "No, we're still getting acquainted and kinda working the kinks out of the chain. We'll be all right."

Louellen handed me a paper sack. "I believe I saw that old Rip dog. I know he'd like to have breakfast too. So here's some table scraps for him. And remember, they're for him so don't you two get none."

I said, "I promise." Then as an afterthought, "Take care."

She smiled and said, "What a nice thing to say. I don't believe anybody has ever said that to me."

We got into Old Pony. Rip smelled the sack of scraps, and was as happy as Louellen.

*****

"Well, look at 'um." Daddy said. "All those men named William Roane, lined up like they are waiting for roll call. Wives off down the hill, bunched up like they're gossiping about their husbands."

We worked all morning cutting blackberry and saw briars that insisted on invading the edge of the cemetery. We raked leaves away from the graves and trimmed some of the low pine limbs so the sun could shine on the grass seed we had sown. The backs of our shirts were wet, and salt stains were growing under our arms. I was getting tired. I knew Daddy must be exhausted.

"Why don't you sit on that log over yonder in the shade? I'll get the water jug and the scraps for Rip," I said, wiping the sweat from the back of my neck. When I returned, both Daddy and Rip were standing at the edge of the cemetery, looking off in the woods near the edge of the escarpment.

"What you two got treed?" I asked.

Daddy turned and came back to the shade. He had taken Rip by the collar and pulled him along. "Darned dog," Daddy said. "Always thinking he's got something spotted. His eyes are worse than mine, and I probably have a better sense of smell."

"Oh, I don't know. I believe you two make a pretty good pair. But I noticed Louellen sent Rip something to eat and didn't send you anything. Guess Rip probably has a better standing with the women than you do."

"He's certainly fathered more pups than I have. You're the only pup I've fathered. You tell me you haven't fathered any, so it looks like our strain of the Roane bloodline is about to run out."

"Maybe it's time, Daddy. Maybe we need to turn the world over to somebody else. See what they can do with it."

Rip was standing again, tail wagging and ears perked forward, looking at the same place where he and Daddy had been looking when I came back with the water. I walked to the edge of the woods. The light breeze was causing the sumac leaves to flutter, little green hands waving to something unseen. "Turn Rip loose, Daddy. I think he smells something."

"No, he don't see anything. He's just pulling your leg. Something there, he'd be barking his fool head off. I believe I've worked you too long out here in this heat. Load up the tools and we'll try to catch the boys at the café. Least have a bowl of apple cobbler with them."

At the cafe, Daddy's cronies had finished their meal and were well into their dessert. The men opened up a space and Louellen brought two chairs. Daddy spread his arms out in a grand gesture and loudly cleared his throat. "Boys, I don't know if all of you know my son. I know some of you remember him as a kid, but if you don't, I'd like to introduce him to you. This is my boy, Creighton."

"This is Duff Farquar."

"That's Ros Stukly."

"Where's the McDholl twins?"

Farquar grinned. "They've gone down to Knoxville. This was their day to talk with the parole officer."

"Oh, I forgot. Anyway this puny feller right here is Buster Dwyre."

Daddy next stopped behind a man wearing an old, battered Stetson. "This is Camran Grainger. Rascal claims blood kin to the Roane clan. You probably remember him. Sometimes I feel like I helped raise him."

Grainger shook his head. "Now, Zeale, don't start that bullshit."

Daddy was enjoying himself. "Been hanging around together since about the time you were born. You've probably forgotten, but he's our local tough man. Used to hear about some bad feller living in a town around here, he'd go and look them up. Did good too. Probably somewhere around seventy-five percent. Got tangled up with an old boy up at Indian Grave Gap and Camran was beating the crap out of him. Old boy got

Camran's ear in his mouth and bit it off. Camran specializes in eating cobbler now, don't you?"

Camran pointed an index finger at Daddy, his thumb raised like the hammer on a pistol. It fell forward and he made a popping sound. "Hell, Breazeale. That all happened twenty-five year ago. You trying to make it sound like it took place last week. You better watch your mouth or I'll be telling something on you. Seen you with your hackles raised pretty high. Anyhow, you the one that's always bragging about being kin to the Graingers. I probably ain't got more than a drop of Roane blood in me."

Camran and I shook hands. Gray curls fought their way from under his hat, hid his mangled ear, and stacked up on the collar of his denim jacket. He had catlike features and cold grey eyes that looked like they had seen things they had rather forget. Something about his looks made me think plenty of fire remained, enough that he might still go to some mountain town looking for their bad man.

Before he could make the introduction, the next man stood, removed his sunglasses, and said, "I'm Roy Ruby Fox. I'm the Chota County Sheriff. Have been for more than thirty years. I've hunted you from hell to Colorado. I'm glad I don't have to do that anymore. Welcome back to Cedergren." With his Rod Steiger looks and build, he could have been cast as a lawman in any movie with a southern setting.

"This spiffy-dressed feller is our local buzzard. His name is Boyd Conall and he's the sole proprietor of Conall's Funeral Home. We always tell strangers, 'Boyd will be the last feller to let you down.' Years ago, that was funny. We don't laugh about it now. None of us know what's waitin' around the next bend in the road. Except we know Boyd will be waitin'. Ain't that right, Boyd? You'll be ready, won't you?"

Boyd tried to keep a straight face, but he lost the battle. He smiled and said, "We've all agreed we'll bury Zeale face down so if he decides to come back and starts digging he'll get deeper and we won't have to put up with him again – let them Chinese deal with him."

Daddy continued with his introductions. "This is Grant Ellar, the publisher of our weekly paper, *The Mountain News*. This feller here with his collar turned backwards spends most of his time reading the good book. His name is David Moody, but we all call him Brother."

Moody smiled, a cleft in his chin broadened revealing some whiskers that had evaded the razor this morning. "Your Daddy and I have been buddies a long time. I came here to Cedergren after you left."

Daddy sat down, motioned for me to sit beside him, and attacked his cobbler. "I guess that's about it for this straggly bunch. Some not here are a whole lot more interesting than these fellers. Maybe we'll catch them next time."

Duff Farquar said, "But we are the best looking of the bunch. Ain't we, Zeale?"

Daddy said, "I guess so, but that ain't saying much," and everyone at the table laughed.

The days slipped by aimlessly. I became a leaf drifting down a creek, swinging from one side of the current to the other with no particular destination. Most mornings Daddy would prepare breakfast. We would stop by Roman's mill or plywood factory, and then have lunch at the café. In the afternoons, we would drive out into the mountains, look at a tract of timber or travel over to Forest Home to visit with some of his old friends. The days became long.

Late one afternoon we were sitting in Daddy's office having our Turkey and water. I was reading the paper when I felt his stare.

"Getting restless aren't you, Creight? Getting tired of being retired, I bet."

"Gotten to know me pretty well, haven't you? I didn't think it was showing."

"It's pretty easy knowing what you think. Sorta like looking in a mirror, knowing what the face is going to do next, where the wrinkles are, where the hair parts."

"Am I that much of an open book?"

"Yeah. You're thinking about Alaska. We've not talked about it any. But you had a life there. You claim you don't have any kids, but I'd bet there's a woman or girlfriend or something."

"Guess I'm not very good with females. They usually run off pretty quick."

"But you had a company. It won't run itself."

"It will for a while. I got a plane there that's needing a pilot. Jamiesie can't fly but one at a time."

Daddy stared at me. "I'm costing you money. Costing you time. Eating into your life. You're wondering if I'm going to try to tie you here. Wondering if you are going to have to stay here until I die. Am I pretty close? Is that what you're thinking?"

"Maybe not exactly. But pretty close. You don't need me here. You've got all your old friends, and Luther is doing a crackerjack job. I don't know anything about the business end of Roman, and I'm not sure I want to learn. Maybe I'll hang around another week, and then …"

Daddy dropped his glass into a desk drawer. He walked to the screen door and stood, hands in his pockets, rocking back and forth. "Got all the answers, hadn't you? Got it all figured out."

"No, I don't have it all figured out. But you're right. I do have a life. I've got friends. I'm respected. I'm not near the biggest thing in Alaska like you are here in the mountains. But up there, I'm not Zeale Roane's son either. If I stay here, that's all I'll ever be. Just Zeale Roane's son!"

"That's not the truth."

I wadded the paper and threw it into the wastepaper can. "It is true. You treat me like I'm still eighteen. There's something I don't know, something you're not telling me. It's not something I can put my finger on but I can feel it. Your closest friends, they're guarded when we talk. I see them watching me, waiting for me to let them know I've solved the mystery. That I know the secret, I've got the secret handshake, or whatever the hell it is. What is it I'm missing?"

"Creight, it's not that simple."

"I didn't say it was simple. But why in the hell are you keeping me in the dark?"

Daddy picked his hat up off his desk and studied it as if it was something unfamiliar. "You're right. Will you give me a week?"

"Give you a week? Sure I'll give you a week, but for what? What's going to change in a week?"

"I don't know. Maybe everything."

*****

We had biscuits, molasses, and coffee the next morning. There was no sign from Daddy of last night's blowup. "I've got a couple of things to do this morning, run some errands, drop by the bank, stuff like that. Why don't I stop back early afternoon and we'll take a ride up to Bethanys Creek Cascade, see if we can catch us enough fish for supper?"

"That'll be good, it'll give me a chance to make a phone call or two." I hadn't talked with Jamiesie in days. "I've got a client I need to talk with. I'll be waiting when you get back."

I stood at the window watching Daddy get into Old Pony and crank the engine. He lifted the mike and I knew he was "checking in", telling any of Roman's employees who were around their two-way radios that he was out and stirring. He cocked his head listening to the radio. Now he was shouting into the microphone. His head dropped, when he raised up, he pounded both fists on the dash of the Suburban.

I walked to the edge of the porch. "What's wrong, Daddy?"

He'd gotten out and was leaning against the door. "Get my shotgun and a box of buckshot loads. They're in my bedroom closet. There's a .44-magnum in my dresser drawer. Get it and a box of cartridges too." He pounded on the top of the car and said, "Sumbitches. Dirty sumbitches."

"What's wrong?"

Daddy was standing with both hands on Old Pony's fender, head down. He didn't answer.

I came out of the house with the guns and Daddy was loading Rip into the back of Old Pony. "You drive," he said. "We're going out to the Arn. Hurry."

I asked again, "What's wrong?"

"It's … it's something out on the Arn. It's trouble. I can't explain it to you right now. Please, let's go."

As we raced along the road toward the Arn, Daddy kept up a constant chatter on the radio, all the while raising his left hand upward in a jerky motion for me to speed up.

He keyed the mike and said, "What time this morning did you see their truck?"

Camran Grainger's voice came back scratchy and distant through the radio, "Hell, Breazeale, right after daylight, probably around six or so. Figured they must have broke down or something. Came back by a little after eight, stopped and got out to see if the truck engine was warm. It was colder than a dead mackerel. Then I heard the dogs. Must been way out around Hematite, but after a while I could tell they was coming this way. Barking about every breath, like hounds do when they ain't running on scent but running on sight."

"How many do you think is running?"

Camran came back, "Can't tell for sure, believe at least three - maybe four. I seed four chains in the back of the truck where the dogs been tied. One of the chains is rolled up, might not been hooked to a dog. So, guess it's probably three. Last few minutes, I ain't heard but two. Bet one of them has fell behind."

"You're sure it's Homer and Iliad McCamy's truck?"

Camran's voice climbed an octave with irritation, "Well, hell yes I'm sure. See the blasted thing about every day – them two damned idiots going down the road throwing beer cans out the winder at signposts – it's the worst old piece of shit around here to still be running. Why you keep asking me that?"

Daddy opened the box of shotgun shells. "I don't know. I guess I just hoped it wasn't them. Just hoped it was some hunter that'd run out of gas."

Camran calmed down. "By God, it's them. I'll swear to it. Even a half carton of them Picayune cigarettes on the dashboard. You want me to take my truck and shove that old piece of shit off the bluff? We'll wait on them and kick their sorry asses when they come out of the woods."

For the first time Daddy smiled. "No. But this is what I want you do. I want you to pull their distributor wire and throw it away. That'll keep them from moving the truck before we get there. Then I want you to leave. Go up on Crooked Arm Ridge and stay around the radio until I call you."

"No, I won't do that; I'll wait here. Give you a hand."

"Now Camran, you do like I asked. Creight's with me and we can handle this. If I need you, I'll holler. You know that. This is none of your business. You don't have a dog in this fight."

Camran open his mike and I could hear him breathing. "You sure you'll call me if you need me?"

Daddy had the business end of the shotgun sticking out the window and was sliding shells into the chamber. "Hadn't I always?"

"Reckon so, but don't let your mouth overload your ass when you ketch them."

Daddy smiled again. "I'm going off the air now; we'll be pulling up in ten minutes. I want you gone, you understand?"

The radio didn't respond. I could imagine Camran disabling the truck, his old battered cowboy hat pulled low to one side of his head.

Daddy said, "Camran has been in enough trouble already. You see, after that feller bit his ear off and he got patched up some, he went back up to the Gap looking for it. Couldn't find his ear, but he found the feller bit it off. Abused him pretty bad. Roy Ruby had to lock Camran up for a while. So I don't want Camran out here. If things go bad, I don't want Roy Ruby trying to drag him off to jail. Camran don't drag too easy, and I don't want him and Roy Ruby getting crossways again."

*****

"This'll do it right here," Daddy said when we got to the gate leading into the Arn. He got out, walked around to the driver's side, and motioned for me to get out. He broke the handgun open, filled the cylinder with fat, nasty-looking cartridges, and shoved it under his belt. "I reckon this is about as far as you need to go," Daddy said. "Rip and I'll handle this the rest of the way. You just hang around here until we get back."

"Yeah? Well bullshit! You told Camran I was with you, that we could handle whatever it is that needs handling. You're not dropping me off here. We came tearing out here, loaded for bear, and you tell me to get out. That's just bullshit. Now we've got all that behind us, what's next?"

He gave me the magnum. "I don't think you'll need this, but if you do, you've got it. Let's just ease on out the road about a mile and stop. See if we can hear the hounds. If we can't, we'll keep going til we do. This part is real important. You've got to do what I say. This'll be all my show. I know these old boys we are looking for; they've got a lot of blow. They'll stir up a lot of dust, but when it gets down to the nut-cutting, I believe they'll back down."

"What if they don't?" I asked.

"If they don't, it could get kinda bad and that's when I might need a little help from you. If you have to shoot one of them, try to bust his kneecap. If that don't do it, then put a bullet in his gut. If that don't do it, then … I'll leave that decision up to you. You understand?"

"I understand. Is that it?"

"For now that's it. Roll your window down and let's move on down the road real easy so we can hear what's going on."

I never shifted from low gear for the next mile as we inched down the narrow road. Daddy had his head out the window, listening. The back windows were down. Rip was moving back and forth between them, sticking his head out, sniffing and whimpering. We'd just come out of a sharp curve when Daddy raised his hand for me to stop. "I believed they'd cross over the ridge and they have. This is where I figured they would come out. This trail leads down to Whetstone Cave. Let's just stop here a minute and see what happens."

We heard the dogs. They were in full cry. Even with my inexperienced ear, I could tell one of the dogs was running ahead of the others. Daddy said, "You hold Rip and stay here. I'm going up close to where the trail comes out on this road."

"I'm coming with you."

Daddy laid the shotgun across his shoulder and started walking up the road. "Remember, this is my show; you'll know if I need you."

I let Daddy get about twenty-five yards from the truck before I followed, holding Rip's collar in my left hand and the magnum in my right. It sounded like the lead dog was no more than fifty yards from the road and was moving toward us, barking every breath. Rip was lunging against his collar and barking. Daddy turned and hollered, "Rip, you hush. Shut up."

Rip lay on the ground flat on his belly, shivering and whining with excitement. I jammed the gun under the waistband of my jeans and dropped to my knees, stroking his head trying to calm him. The lead dog had stopped barking, and I could hear him growling like he was attacking something on the ground. I'd heard hunting dogs make the same sounds when they were killing their prey. The other dogs were closing in.

A high-pitched yelp and the growling stopped. I could hear a rustling in the leaves, and rocks dislodging along the trail. I couldn't tell what kind of animal was coming toward us, but I could hear a gasping for breath and a whimpering. Daddy was standing in the middle of the road with the shotgun cradled in his right arm. It took all my strength to hold Rip, who was lunging against my grip.

At the intersection of the trail and road, the weeds and brush parted and a man bolted out onto the road. His head thrown back, his mouth was open making gasping sounds as he tried to draw air into his lungs. His torn clothes were wet with sweat and blood. His left arm and side of his face were torn, and he clutched a bloody rock the size of a baseball in his right hand.

Daddy took a step toward him. "It's okay. You're okay. I'm here."

The man had short dark hair and beard. He was lean and maybe thirty-five or forty years old. He leaned over, put both hands on his knees, and vomited. He straightened and, for the first time, saw me. He gave Daddy a bewildered look and then peered at me again. Daddy moved toward him talking so low I couldn't understand his words. The man was sobbing - deep jerking sobs - and he moved hesitantly toward Daddy, arms reaching out like a child. The dogs were scrambling up the trail, barking excitedly as they followed the scent. The man turned toward them, his frame tensed and he raised the bloody rock in his hand. He was going to stand and fight the dogs. He couldn't run anymore.

Daddy took a step forward, put his hand on the shoulder of the man, and turned him toward the woods in the opposite direction from the oncoming dogs. In a calm voice, Daddy said, "You go that way. I'll take care of this."

The man looked again toward the approaching dogs, the rock still raised in his hand. Daddy pushed him and shouted, "Get out of here, I've got it." The man took a step backward, turned and disappeared into the thick woods.

Behind us the deep, rhythmic - ahooo, ahooo - of the hounds echoed through the trees. Together the dogs burst into the road, head down, following the scent of the man. Daddy raised his shotgun hip high and, without aiming, fired. The impact of the buckshot almost severed the first dog's head from its body. Without making a sound, he crumpled to the ground.

The blast from the shotgun caused the second dog to leap sideways. Daddy's second shot broke that dog's back. The dog whirled and started slashing at his back legs; the next shot blew a hole through the dog's ribcage, and it tumbled to the ground, twitched once and was still.

Daddy stepped away from the dogs, watching the trail as he slid three shells into the chamber of the shotgun. "You keep a good hold on Rip and come on up this way."

Using the toe of his boot, Daddy rolled the second dog over on its side. He squatted beside the dog and with one hand moved the dog's collar so he could read the brass nameplate. "Camran was right, as usual. Dog belongs to Iliad McCamy. When the dog was alive, his name was Digger. I guess even with him dead his name is still Digger, but the sumbitch won't be doing much digging any more. Or trailing men either."

I was stunned. I had just seen a man hunted by dogs, and now here Daddy was just as cool as a cucumber, trying to make a joke.

"Daddy, who was that man? Tell me what in the hell is going on!"

Before he could answer, we heard rocks being dislodged on the trail, and I heard a man curse. Daddy took a couple of steps back from the dead dogs, and once again cradled the shotgun in the crook his arm. He motioned for me to get behind him. He looked over his shoulder, "Be easy. Keep Rip under control and let me handle this. You understand?"

Without waiting for an answer, he turned and faced where the man would be coming out.

They came staggering out into the road, breathing heavily. The first man was carrying an ax. He placed the axe head on the ground, leaning against the handle, trying to catch his breath. He was the largest of the men; six feet tall and heavy built. The second man was carrying a double-barrel shotgun. He was lanky, had greasy, red hair, and needed a shave. A crazy thought ran through my head: "You look just like Jack Elam in some low-budget western movie." Both men were in their early 40s and were filthy with sweat, dirt, and leaves clinging to their clothing. They saw the dead dogs before they saw us.

"What in the hell do you think you're doing?" the man with the ax shouted at Daddy.

Daddy didn't raise his voice, "Well Iliad, I've killed a couple of dogs that were on my land illegally, running something they shouldn't have been after."

Now the man with the gun screamed at Daddy, "You crazy sumbitch, them was our best dogs. I'll sue your ass."

"Maybe, Homer. Maybe if you make it out of here alive. But maybe you won't make it. It depends on how quick you drop that shotgun and how quick you can get a civil tongue in your mouth."

Iliad was standing with his legs apart and holding the ax half way up the handle. He turned to his brother, "Don't do it Homer. Don't let that old sumbitch bluff you."

Daddy took two steps forward. He jerked the shotgun up between Illiad's legs and fired. Iliad dropped the ax and fell backwards to the ground, rolling over onto his side, clutching his crotch, screaming.

Homer started to raise his gun. I yelled, "You touch that gun to your shoulder and I'll put a bullet in your head."

Homer snarled, "By God, I don't believe you've got it in you."

Gripping the magnum with both hands, I aimed at Homer's head, "Well, you'll never know until you try. If you're wrong, you'll be dead and still won't know. Just pitch the gun over in those weeds. It's the best decision you'll ever make, I swear it."

Homer hesitated a second before pitching the gun across the road into a clump of bushes.

Daddy was standing over Iliad with the shotgun back in the crook of his arm. "Damn Iliad. Be a man and get up, I didn't shoot nothing off you can't do without. The gun barrel was sticking out through your legs. I was just trying to get your attention, you haven't lost a drop of blood and if your pants are wet, it's probably piss."

Iliad stumbled to his feet, rubbing his crotch, and staring in amazement at his bloodless hands. He turned and looked at the seat of his pants, scorched by the blast from the shotgun. With no real wound, Iliad seemed to regain his combativeness, "Damn it all to hell, Zeale. You could a kilt me."

Daddy never took his eyes from Iliad's face. "What makes you think I'm not going to do it now? This is at least twice I know of you've been out here messing around in something that's none of your business."

Homer moved over close to Iliad, "Well, it is our business. That crazy bastard of yours has killed our brother. Scalped him like some kind of damned Indian and throwed him off the bluff. You damned Roanes has always looked down on us and had it in for us since grandpa killed Fad. By God, we ain't taking it anymore and we're going to put a stop to it."

Daddy was losing it. "You're going to put a stop to it? Looks like you're not in a position to put a stop to anything. I may put a stop to it."

Iliad moved to his brother's side and shook his fist at Daddy. "Yeah, we're going to report all this to Roy Ruby. You ain't going to get out of this Zeale. We're going to have that crazy bastard of yours indicted for murdering our brother. Did you know he beat one of our dogs to death with a rock or something, right back down the trail? If we'd have got there in time, I'd a blowed that crazy bastard's head plum off his shoulders."

Homer flinched as Daddy stepped forward and pressed the barrel of the shotgun into his temple.

Daddy bit his lower lip as I had seen him do when his anger was reaching the danger point. "Go get Old Pony."

When I got back with the Suburban, the McCamy brothers were sitting on the ground with their backs together.

"We reached an agreement while you were gone," Daddy said. "We're going to take them back down to their truck, then we're going to go and see Roy Ruby."

The brothers nodded in agreement and Homer said, "Yeah, he'll straighten all this mess out."

I looked at Daddy. He wrinkled his brow and slightly shook his head.

"All right, boys," Daddy said. "Load in the back and let's get going.

*****

We neared the road and Daddy said, "Go on through the gate and turn left."

Iliad shouted, "Now just a goddamn minute. Our truck is down to the right. What in the hell are you doing turning left. You lost?

Daddy slid the pistol barrel over the back of the seat. "No, I just want a chance to talk with you boys a little more. Need to impress on you just how serious what you've done today is."

Homer was trying to open the locked tailgate of Old Pony, 'Well, I don't give a shit what you want. We ain't going nowhere with you."

Homer's eyes widened when Daddy drew the hammer back on the pistol. "You sit down Homer. I'll do all of the talking and you'll do all the listening."

Homer glanced at his brother, then glared at Daddy. "No goddamnit! You let us out right here, and I mean it."

In the confined area of the Suburban, the explosion from the magnum was deafening. Glass shattered and a hole appeared in the side of the vehicle just over Homer's head. Both brothers fell onto their sides, pressing their hands over their ears.

Daddy said, "Now look what you've made me do. The dang gun went off and one of you boys could've been killed. Worst of all, it wouldn't have been my fault. You hollering like that upset me."

Iliad sat up and pulled Homer's hands from his ears. "Homer, you shut your damned mouth before one of us gets killed, you hear me?"

Daddy said, "Now boys, I don't really care what you tell Roy Ruby. Make up any kind of story you want to. But the truth is, you were trespassing. You were hunting a man like some kind of wild animal, running him with dogs, intending to kill him. If I ever find either of you on the Arn again, I'll kill you just like I killed your dogs and it will never cross my mind again. Never. Do you understand what I'm telling you?"

Iliad glared at Daddy. "Well by God, you ain't the law. You ain't going to tell us what to do. We'll come back again and hunt that bastard down. You'll see."

We had driven several miles from the entrance to the Arn while this argument was going on. Daddy said, "Boys, I'm done arguing with you. You can't say you weren't warned. Creight, turn around at this next side road."

We reached the entrance to an old logging road. I turned and started back the way we had come.

"Stop right here," Daddy said. He unlocked the back door. "You boys get out. I'm tired of looking at you."

Tentatively, the brothers got out. Daddy jabbed the barrel of the pistol into Homer's ribs. "You boys take your boots off. That way it will take a little longer for you to walk back to your truck. It'll give you a little more time to think about what I've told you."

Iliad put his hands in his pockets, "I believe you'll shit and fall back in it. We ain't a taking our boots off. We ain't taking a step down that damned gravel road without them."

Daddy turned loose of Rip's collar. "All right. Rip'll help you get them off. While he is helping you, he'll be eating your ass plum down to the bone."

Homer took a step back. "You wouldn't set that dog on us."

"I wouldn't have to. I believe he'd just do it on his own."

Rip was in a half crouch, his ears laid back against his head, upper lip pulled up, exposing his teeth.

"It's your move, boys. But I believe you've about played this hand down to the last card. I'll leave your boots at your truck."

Homer tugged at Iliad's shirtsleeve. "I'd druther walk back to the truck than have to ride back and listen to this crazy old coot."

Both men sat and, keeping their eyes on Rip, removed their boots. Homer looked up at Daddy, "What about our socks?"

"Keep them, I wouldn't want you walking down that gravel road barefooted."

The brothers failed to see the humor. Keeping their eyes on Rip, they backed away and started hobbling back down the mountain toward their truck.

I threw their boots in the back of Old Pony. Daddy nodded at the McCamy brothers as we drove by.

Rip had his head out the back window, panting. He seemed pleased with his part in this fiasco.

Daddy looked at me and said, "Well…"

I didn't take my eyes from the road, "Well, what?"

"Aren't you going to ask me any questions?"

"I don't have any. It's been a perfectly normal day. I've seen my daddy gun down two dogs, threaten to kill two men and then kidnap them, blow the side out of his vehicle with a pistol. Pretty normal day. Oh yeah, one other thing. I've seen daddy talk with some kind of wild man. Nothing abnormal."

I looked at Daddy and saw the edge of his eyes wrinkle before he said, "Good. Glad you've understood everything. Makes my life simpler."

"Who was he? Why were they trying to kill him?"

"Is that the only thing you didn't understand?"

"No, but it's a starting place."

Daddy leaned over the back of the seat and rubbed Rip's ears, "No, that's the ending place."

"You're not going to answer anything, are you?"

"Not today, I reckon. Too much to do to get into some long, drawn-out something or other. Tomorrow. We'll clear it up tomorrow." Daddy picked up the microphone. "Where are you, Camran?"

Camran's voice came back. "Got to wondering what I was a missing so I come on back down here."

"Where is down here?"

"Dammit, Zeale. Down where the truck was."

"Truck was?"

"Yeah, was. Damned thing must have caught on far just before I got cheer, she's a cooking pretty good."

"Camran, you telling me the truck was on fire when you got there?"

"Damn, Zeale, you don't think I'd lit it off, do you?"

Daddy said sarcastically, "No, you wouldn't do anything like that." Then, "Camran, you don't have a lick of sense. You just sit tight until we get there."

Daddy took a pad from the glove box and started writing.

"They called him your bastard?"

"Yes, I believe they did, didn't they?"

"What's his name?"

"What was that feller's name in the Bible, the feller the demons came out of and got in the hogs and they ran off over the cliff? Legion. Was his name Legion?"

I threw both hands up in the air. "Shit. His name isn't Legion!"

"No, that's not his name but it might as well be. It's ironing itself out. You've got my word."

We rounded a curve in the road. Camran was sitting on the front fender of his truck with his cowboy boot heels hung in behind the bumper, a gasoline can on the ground beside him. Nonchalantly, Camran got down off the fender and put the can in the back of his truck.

We stood in silence looking at the burning truck. The tires had melted and the truck's frame was resting on the ground. Daddy looked at Camran and said, "I'll be damned. Why do you do things like this?"

Camran seemed to feel the need to roll his shirtsleeves down and carefully button them. Then he undid his belt and tucked his shirt into his pants. He cleared his throat, shoved his hat back on his head, and said, "What have you done with your other passengers?"

"What makes you think we had other passengers?"

Camran was looking in the back of the Suburban. "Well hell, Zeale, you think I'm some kind of damn idiot? I know you didn't come out of the gate. You didn't come up the road behind me, so I reckon you've been higher up on the mountain. I seed two pair of boots in the back of that old trap. You ain't barefoot and Creight ain't barefoot. You hauled them damned McCamys up the road and kilt both of them, didn't you? Sumbitches deserved it too, if you ask me. But by God, I wished you'd let me done it."

"Well, I never asked you, and no, we didn't kill anybody." Daddy said. "We did haul them a few miles up on the mountain. Wanted to give them a chance to think about their sins, so I thought they ought to walk back down here where their truck was … used to be. Took their boots so they'd walk slower and think more. I told them they could pick up their boots here at the truck."

Camran reached in the back of the Suburban and pulled the boots out, "You told them their boots would be cheer at the truck?"

"Yeah, that's what we told them."

Camran tied the laces of the boots together. He swung them once around his head, loosened his grip, and the boots sailed into the hot coals of the McCamys burned truck. "Air you go," Camran said. "You're a man of your word. The boots are right cheer at their truck, waiting on them. Sorta."

Daddy furrowed his brow and shook his head. "Camran, I swear, you hadn't got a lick of sense."

Camran grinned, "Believe you just said that a little bit ago."

"Creight, Camran's going to give you a ride back to Cedergren and you're going to find Andrew Cailean and give him this note. Then I want you to go home. In the morning, take the jeep and go by the grocery, get a couple pounds of coffee, about that much dried beans, some meal, a sack of light bread, couple pounds of bacon, a dozen eggs, some tomatoes if they got them, and a pound of stick candy – peppermint. I'll meet you here at the gate round eight o'clock. One other thing: call Roy Ruby and tell him we've had a little scrape with the McCamy brothers. You won't have to go into any details. Tell him I'll be back home tomorrow night if he needs to see me."

I folded the note and without reading it, put it in my shirt pocket. "I don't reckon you would tell me who Andrew Cailean is, no more than you have answered any more of my questions."

Daddy opened the front passenger door of the Suburban for Rip to jump inside, then he got in and started the engine, "He's an old boy that works at the mill. Been there off and on since he was a kid. He was a medic in the army. That is about all the answers I've got right now, and I don't expect Camran will be answering any more questions either. Will you Camran?"

"Hell, Zeale, way you've talked to me today, I might never say another damn word to nobody about nothing. Ever again."

Daddy activated the gate that led back into the Arn. It started to open, "Camran, I wish I could bank on that." Daddy drove through the gate, it closed behind him, and the Suburban disappeared down the road toward Hematite furnace.

*****

We rode in silence back toward Cedergren. Finally, I asked Camran, "Daddy will be all right?"

He turned and looked out the driver's side window, then back at me. "Yeah, I reckon. Why you ask that?"

"He's an old man, and he's going back … out where that …," I had to search for words, "that man is. Daddy said he might as well be named Legion. Legion was crazy. Demons had got into him."

Camran drove without looking at me. "I never saw no crazy man or nobody named Legion."

"I know you didn't see him but you know he's out there, don't you?"

"Nope."

"All right, then who is this Cailean feller?"

Camran still didn't look at me, "Your daddy told you. He works for Roman and he was a medic in the army. That's all I know."

I was becoming frustrated. "And that's it?"

Camran nodded. "Yeah, reckon that's about it."

*****

Camran turned down a dirt road and drove a couple of miles. We stopped in front of a tidy weatherboard house. A couple of beagle hounds came out from under the front porch and welcomed us, barking and peeing on Camran's tires. A tall slender man was splitting stove wood beside the house. He buried his ax in a log and took a handkerchief from his back pocket to wipe his forehead. He walked to the pickup and said, "What you fellers up to today?"

Camran and I got out of the truck and he shook the man's hand. "Andrew, this is Zeale's boy, Creight. I don't reckon you've met."

The man extended his hand. "I don't believe we have but I heard you had turned up. Good to meet you."

"Good to meet you. Camran tells me you were a medic in the army?"

Andrew looked down and scrubbed a boot across the gravel drive, "Yeah, but that was a long time ago. I've forgot most of what I learned."

I had taken Daddy's note out of my pocket and handed it to Andrew.

Andrew looked at the note. "When did Mr. Roane give this to you?"

"Just a little while ago," Camran said. "Zeale said you'd take it from here."

"Been trouble out at the Arn?"

"Yeah. How did you know where the trouble was?" I asked.

Andrew jammed the note down in the front pocket of his overalls and for the first time looked directly into my eyes. "I just kinda figured. Was he hurt bad. And was hit dogs that done it?"

"Yes, to both questions. But it's not Daddy that's hurt."

"Yeah, I know," Andrew said. "I thank you for coming by. I'd better get going."

He turned and without saying goodbye walked into his house. Camran looked at me, shrugged his shoulders, and we got back into the truck.

We were almost to Cedergren when I asked Camran, "How did he know Daddy wasn't the one hurt? And how did he know it was dogs that did the damage?"

Camran lit a cigarette and said, "Damn if I know. Maybe hit was in the note. I wished you wouldn't ask me no more questions, okay?"

We finished our trip in silence. Camran stopped in front of Daddy's house and left the engine running. I got out and said, "Thanks."

Camran dropped the pickup into reverse and started to back out of the drive, but he stopped and stuck his head out the window. "I'm going to give you one piece of advice. I know you ain't even asked, but just remember: folks that'll talk don't know the story, and folks that know the story won't talk." He drove off, leaving me more confused than when the day started.

I started a pot of coffee and sat at the kitchen table looking out across the valley toward the Arn. A small cloud had just cleared the mountains. Mare's-tails of rain hung underneath. The setting sun painted the cloud a bright red, and the mare's-tails had the same fiery color. I thought of fire dripping from a volcano.

As the coffee perked, I called Luther and learned he would be out of town for a few days. A call to Roy Ruby's office was answered by a deputy who said the sheriff had gone up in the mountains to investigate a vehicle fire and would probably not be back in the office until the next morning. He volunteered his services, but I told him it was nothing important and I would wait until the next day to talk with the sheriff. The receptionist at Dr. Huntsman's office informed me he was at the hospital. Something about a little girl with a ruptured appendix. She asked about Daddy's health.

An old-fashioned answering machine sat on the floor, red light throbbing. After a couple of false starts, I pressed the right combination of buttons. A whirling sound as the machine rewound, a couple of clicks, then a mechanical voice said there was one message and I should press seven.

"Mr. Roane," came the scratchy voice, "hope you are getting along well. This is Vaughn, Vaughn Blackman, down in Atlanta. I've left a couple of messages with my brother for Creight to give me a call. He is just as contrary as ever and hasn't called me back. I thought I might catch him at your house. Tell that old boy to call me. Tell him that he doesn't want me to come up there because I just might throw him off into the river." Vaughn left his office, home, and mobile phone numbers. He ended his message by congratulating Daddy on the acquisition of 10,000 acres of timberland in north Georgia and encouraging him to "hang in there."

I dialed his mobile phone number. A voice said with just a touch of irritability, "Dr. Blackman."

I lowered my voice as deep as I could and slurred my words, "You scabby-legged sumbitch, last time I'm going to tell you to stay away from my wife."

Very smooth and refined, Vaughn responded, "Why yes, I'm glad you called. Let me put you on hold so I can find a private spot. The gentlemen here at the poker table don't care to hear a long discussion on a surgical procedure. Just give me a moment, please." The sound of classical music, then Vaughn came back on, "Who in the hell is this and how did you get my number?"

Using the same voice, "I beat it out of my wife and now I'm going to start beating on you."

I could almost hear the wheels turning in Vaughn's mind before he said, "I can have this call traced, you know; I will not be threatened by some ignorant kook."

"You can't track a call from Cedergren. You can't even paddle a canoe down the Findhorn without spilling everything you own," I couldn't control my laughter.

"Creighton Roane, you sorry devil, if I could reach you right now I'd ring your skinny neck. Where have you been and why haven't you returned my calls?"

"It's kind of a ugly story, Vaughn, and you wouldn't believe half of it even if I told you. I've run into some strange things in the last few weeks. I think I might be going crazy."

Vaughn was serious now. "What kind of strange things?"

I told him about how mysterious Daddy was acting, not giving me any straight answers, and what happened today.

Vaughn listened without interrupting and then said, "And you don't have any idea of what's going on?"

"No. None. Nada."

"What if I come up and we talk? Say early next week?"

I felt some sense of relief. "Good."

Vaughn's voice was lighter. "Buddy, you can count on it. Maybe I can make it even sooner. Maybe we can take a run down the river."

*****

I felt better just knowing Vaughn would be here, and might be able to shed some light on the mystery. Camran had said, "Folks that will talk don't know the story, and folks that know the story won't talk." Maybe I wasn't getting any closer to the truth. Maybe I should just go back to Alaska and start over. Come back to Cedergren on my own, just get a fresh start. Maybe, somewhere there is sanity in all this.

I dialed the phone, and a sweet voice said, "Aleutian Air, this is Carol." I asked to speak with Jamiesie, and she asked my name. I told her "Hillbilly." She replied, "Just a minute, Mr. Billy," and I thought I know exactly what you look like: a great body, blond hair, blue eyes, and dumb as a fence post.

Then Jamiesie, "Hello, Mr. Billy."

"Sounds like the business has grown in my absence. You got a secretary. I'll bet she even swept the front porch."

"Damn Creight. It wouldn't hurt for you to call more often. I'm about to work my butt off. I thought you were dead."

"No, Jamiesie, I'm still kicking, just not very high. Who is sweet thing answering the phone?"

Jamiesie laughed, "Hell, Creight. With you gone and me being so busy, I had to have some help around here. I think I told you about Carol. She worked at the bank and once I took her up, she just fell in love with flying."

I laughed and replied, "Right."

I brought Jamiesie up to date on the happenings since our earlier conversations. For the first time, I had somebody to tell all my frustrations, somebody who had no connections here, somebody who could be objective. We talked for thirty minutes and Jamiesie mostly listened with just an occasional question. Finally, he asked if I wanted him to come and stay with me for a while.

"No, I'm all right. I'm going back out on the Arn in the morning. I bet I'll see that wild feller again, if he isn't dead. He was cut up pretty bad. Tomorrow I'll get the answers."

We talked a little about how the business was doing and Jamiesie said things had never been better. Carol was keeping the bills paid and the appointments straight. He told me again how he was working his butt off.

I said I had to get off this phone or Daddy wouldn't be able to pay his phone bill. Then, "Speaking of butt, let me guess something about your new secretary. Good body, blond, blue eyes, and nothing between the ears?"

Now it was Jamiesie's turn to laugh, "Creight, you are partially right – but just partially."

*****

I felt better after talking with Jamiesie and Vaughn. I was convinced that tomorrow I would get answers … determined I would get answers.

At Daddy's office, I thought how little it had changed. I sat in his chair, put my feet on his desk, leaned back, and looked at the paintings and the sculpture. Such great work but always the faceless man. Why had the artist not shown the man's face? The boy's face matured as the woman aged. What a handsome pair.

With no particular thought, I opened the top drawer of the desk. I found an old pocketknife with only one blade and it worn so thin it wasn't usable, a battered compass, some sticks of peppermint candy, bits of twine, three glass marbles, stubs of wooden pencils, and two King Edward cigars still in their cellophane wrappers. There were two small coins, maybe gold, with inscriptions in strange letters. A small leather photo album was in the back of the drawer, worn from use and showing cracks from age, the cover held in place with a rubber band.

I opened the album. On the first page, a faded, black-and-white photo made more than fifty years ago of a woman sitting in a wooden porch swing, wearing a long skirt and a ruffled white blouse. Her hands were folded in her lap and her head tilted to the side, her smile slightly crooked. I hadn't seen a picture of my mother in years. Tears welled up in my eyes. Mother couldn't have been more than eighteen, maybe around the first time Daddy saw her. I studied the photo. What a pretty woman and what a short life. How different my life might have been had she lived.

The second photo was Mother and Daddy on what must have been their wedding day. He was wearing a light-colored suit, a white shirt, and a dark tie. It was midsummer because he was dark as an Indian. His hair was brushed back and the beginning of a widow's peak was starting to form. He had his arm around Mother. They were looking adoringly at each other. Mother's dress was dark, probably blue I thought. It was belted at the waist and her breasts strained at the bodice. What a beautiful figure. No wonder Daddy wanted her for his wife.

The third picture was Mother sitting on the front steps of the house at Christian Springs. I was standing beside her, one arm around her and the other clutching a kitten. Next was a formal picture of the three of us, the first professional photograph in the book. I am sitting in Mother's lap, and Daddy is standing stiffly behind us.

The next photo was not fastened to the page. It must have been near the fort because I could see part of the stone breastworks. There was a picnic basket on the ground and I was feeding a puppy. Daddy was in kakis and leather boots. Mother, obviously pregnant, was leaning against a large boulder, fingering a broach at her throat.

I found several loose photos at the back of the book.

A baby, less than a year old, was playing on a quilt, clutching a toy puppy. I examined the photograph closely, trying to identify the location. It was the short, narrow porch of the office. This photo was out of sequence. It should have been before the one of us at the fort.

Then the pages of my mental calendar flipped, I was almost fourteen when Daddy built the house and office and we moved into Cedergren. The baby was not me; it was someone else. Why would Daddy have a picture of someone else's child mixed in with the family?

I thumbed through the remaining pictures. There was a little boy about four sitting astride Daddy's neck. Daddy and a little boy about six firing a pistol at a tin can. Daddy and the same little boy at an amusement park, and the next one dated July 1963, of Daddy and the little boy making ice cream with an old fashioned hand-cranked freezer. The next photo must have been made the same day. Daddy was dipping ice cream into a bowl held by an attractive woman in her late 20s. Then there was a photo of the same boy and another boy about his age, both shirtless and astride horses, wearing feathers in their hair and painted like Indians. The final photo was the only one in color. Daddy and the boy, now a young man, were standing in front of an impressive building, perhaps at a university. Daddy looked somewhere in his 70s, and the young man was wearing a graduation cap and gown. He was proudly displaying what appeared to be a diploma.

Although I had seen the hunted man at the Arn only briefly, I was almost certain he was the young man wearing a cap and gown in the photograph.

Who are these people and why are they in the family album? Fatigued, my mind was bouncing like a ball in a pinball machine. Why so many pictures of this young man, from baby to adulthood? Then I remembered Homer McCamy screaming at Daddy. "That crazy bastard of yours has kilt our brother." Why hadn't I see it sooner? The man hunted by dogs is daddy's son. He is the little boy in the photos. He's my daddy's son – my half brother.

*****

I lay in bed, wanting rest, but trying to avoid sleep. Sometime after three o'clock, sleep came with the dreams I dreaded. Snarling dogs and Indians had me cornered in a cave below the escarpment. I knew I was in Whetstone Cave, and I knew there was no way out except through the painted savages and the dogs. I raced along the floor of the cave and managed to get by the Indians. Then the dogs pulled me down.

Now my mind leaves my body and two men, eating ice cream, approach my remains. The younger man asks the older man what the dogs are eating. The older man says it is only the remains of a cat and it doesn't matter because no one had ever seen the cat before. It's a stray and wouldn't be missed. The young man wants to take a photograph, wants to add it to his leather photo album. The older one says it is getting dark and they must go.

My spirit follows the men, shouting, "You know me. I know who you are. I love you. Please, take me with you." The two men get into Old Pony and drive off, leaving me alone, scared and crying at the trailhead.

I was glad to see the morning. A shower, coffee boosted with a shot of Turkey, and I arrived at the grocery just after daylight. I checked Daddy's list twice to see that I had everything and loaded it into the back of the jeep. As I cranked the engine, Sheriff Roy Ruby pulled up and parked beside me. I nodded. He motioned for me to cut off my engine.

"Morning, Creight. You're stirring mighty early."

"Morning to you Sheriff. Yeah, I'm up with the chickens. Did some grocery shopping. Now, I'm going to meet Daddy out at the Arn."

The sheriff got out of his cruiser, started fumbling around in his shirt pocket, and finally pulled out a plug of Apple chewing tobacco. "I see by the office phone log you called me yesterday afternoon. Sorry I missed you. Anything I can help you with?"

I was a bit uncomfortable. "No, I reckon not. I was just going to pass along a message from Daddy."

Roy Ruby cut a slice from the plug of chewing tobacco and shoved it into the back of his cheek. "Which was?"

"Uh … Daddy had a little scrape with the McCamy brothers. Wanted me to tell you he'd catch up with you sometime this afternoon."

The sheriff worked to get some saliva into the tobacco, "Don't reckon you know what it's about, do you?"

"Well, I'm not sure. You know how he is, Sheriff."

"Yeah, I do. Got his own way of handling things." The Sheriff shot a brown stream of tobacco juice toward the front tire of his cruiser. "You don't know if it had anything to do with that truck that burned near the Arn, do you?"

I wanted this conversation to end. "It could."

Another stream of tobacco juice. The sheriff smiled. "Yeah, I reckon it could. I got up there about the same time Homer and Iliad come limping up. They was barefooted as the day they was hatched. I never heard such cussing in my life. They said they was minding their own business, hunting for squirrels back up the road. Said your Daddy and three or four other men had held them hostage. Drove them way up in the mountains and was fixing to kill them. Said they jumped out of the car and run off down through the bushes."

"Three or four men?"

"Yeah. Said your Daddy put Rip on their trail, but they outsmarted the dog by wading through Skipper's Branch for a couple of miles. I asked them where their shoes was and they said they took them off to dry, then lost them. Said they was going to swear out a warrant for Zeale's arrest. All that sound about right, son?"

I shook my head. "Well, maybe a little of it."

Sheriff Roy Ruby smiled. "Kinda like I figured. Tell Zeale when it's convenient, to stop by. I'll need to hear his side." He started to get back in his car and almost as an afterthought said, "Is Zeale and that other feller okay?"

Now, I was really uncomfortable. "Yes sir, pretty much."

Roy Ruby started his cruiser. "Good luck to you, son."

*****

At the gate leading into the Arn Daddy was sitting in Old Pony and whittling on a peach seed. He looked at his watch, "By gosh, you hit it right on the head. You've learned to be punctual. Must come from your piloting days."

"No, it comes from minding your elders."

The gate slid open and I drove the jeep alongside Old Pony. The gate shut as I got out and stretched my legs. "What are you are making out of that seed?"

Daddy handed the seed to me, "See for yourself."

"A dove. I'd forgotten you were a good whittler."

Daddy closed his knife and dusted the shavings out of his lap, "Probably one of the few things my daddy ever taught me. He wasn't the most agreeable feller, and once I learned that, I gave him plenty of room. Guess I learned something else from him. I learned I didn't want to be like him when I grew up. So I reckon I learned two things."

"Being pretty hard on him, aren't you?"

Daddy started loading groceries from the jeep into Old Pony. "No. No, I'm not. He was pretty hard on himself and everybody that was around him." He leaned up against the jeep. "How about you, Creight? You got any of your granddaddy Fad in you? You hard on folks?"

I gave it some thought. "No, not now. I might have been earlier but now I try to understand everybody, try to see their side."

Daddy whistled through his teeth. Rip came trotting out of the woods. He squatted down and played with Rip's ears before looking up at me, "Say that again."

"Say what? That I try to understand and see other folks' side?"

Daddy got back into the Suburban. "Yeah, I just wanted to know I heard right, and I wanted you to hear yourself say it again. This is not going to be an easy day for you and……." He paused as if he wanted to elaborate. "Or for me."

We bounced along the woods road for a while without talking. I thought we might as well get started. "Daddy, I know about your other son."

Daddy took his foot off the gas and slowed to let a half-grown buffalo calf trot across the road, "When did you figure that out, or did somebody tell you?"

"Last night. I wasn't prying. Well, that's not exactly right. I was looking through your desk in the office, and I found pictures of you, mother, and me. Then pictures of another woman, a young woman, and a boy. Lots of pictures of the boy. I watched him grow up in those pictures."

"How'd it make you feel?"

"Bad. Not that you had another son, but bad that I didn't know."

We stopped in a cleared area at the lower end of Hematite Lake. Daddy licked his lips. Then he took a deep breath and his mouth opened, but no words came out. He licked his lips again. "Creight, there's a little more to it than that."

"Okay"

"Let's unload these groceries, get something cooking, and make some coffee. My breakfast was pretty light this morning."

"Just like yesterday, this is another case where I don't get answers, isn't it?"

"No, there's answers coming with coffee. I promise."

We hauled the groceries down an unfamiliar trail toward the edge of the lake. I was surprised to see a small one-room cabin, something a hunter might build in a remote area to use a couple of weeks a year. There were two battered lawn chairs, an old tent fly, two rolled up sleeping bags, and a large wooden box. Off to the side was a small fire pit with an iron bar supported by two large limestone rocks. A cast iron teakettle hung from the rod by a chain. Daddy dropped a double handful of coffee in the pot and added dead limbs to the fire coals.

He took a battered skillet out of the wooden box, wiped it clean with his shirttail, put six strips of bacon in it and the smell of the fried meat soon filled the air. As the bacon started browning, he pulled it to the side and broke eggs into the skillet. He splashed the hot grease over the top of the eggs with a spatula, then removed the bacon and put two slices of bread in the grease. He looked up and said, "I don't reckon this is the most healthy grub, but it'll stop the guts from growling."

He set two tin plates on the edge of the wooden box and divided the bacon and eggs into them, then rummaged around the box and brought out two forks and a pint of blackberry jelly. He held the jar of jelly up and looked at the smooth, purple texture. "One of the benefits of being a single man. Old lady Finola gave this to me."

The smell of the frying bacon made me hungry. "Which plate is mine?"

"I figured you had already eat and I didn't cook anything for you," Daddy said, digging in the jelly.

"Then that other plate is for …"

"Yep, soon as he comes around." He took a bite of bacon, "Creight, I guess we've come to the understanding part you say you're so good at. The young feller you saw yesterday is kinda different, and you're probably going to meet him in a minute. But there's some ground rules. You have to promise me you'll abide by them. Don't act surprised when you see him. I don't want you to stare at him. Don't make eye contact. Don't want you to try to touch him either. You understand all that?"

"Well, I don't understand it but I'll try to do as you say."

Daddy shook his head. "Trying don't get it; you've got to do exactly as I said. You understand?"

"Yes sir, I understand."

Daddy searched his canvas coat and pulled out the tin flute he had been playing a few days ago at Dove Landing. He wet his lips and started playing *Amazing Grace.* He must have gone through the song two or three times when Rip stood up, looked past me toward the edge of the woods, wagging his tail.

The bushes behind me whispered. I sensed that someone had come into the clearing. Daddy put the flute back into his coat, stood, and said in a low voice, "It's all right, son. I've got somebody here I'd like you to meet. I've fixed us breakfast. Come on over here and sit down beside me."

I heard footsteps and then they stopped.

"It's okay. He's a good friend, I promise. He brought us these eggs and this bacon."

Daddy extended one of the plates, and from the edge of my vision, I saw the man reach out and grasp the plate with his left hand. Daddy stirred the jelly into his eggs and took a bite. "Come on son. Sit down here beside me and let's eat."

With my peripheral vision I got my first good look at the man. The view I had yesterday was of a raggedly dressed man, covered in sweat and blood. Today he was wearing faded jeans, a T-shirt, tennis shoes and an old Cardinals baseball cap. I was shocked at the damage the dog had done. Both forearms were bandaged. The side of his face had been cut in several places. One ear had been partly severed and was crudely stitched back into place. I could see stitches running up the back of his neck and disappearing into his hairline. He was medium height and slender, had dark hair and a short beard. I thought if his hair was longer, it might be curly.

He was wolfing down the food, the tin plate balanced on his knee, holding the fork in his left hand. He had not looked at me, so I had no idea what his eyes were like. His left side was facing me and when he turned, I saw he still had the blood-crusted rock in his right hand.

"Son, my friend brought these groceries out to us, pretty nice of him, don't you think?" Daddy said.

The man nodded and looked up at me shyly.

Daddy poured three cups of coffee and extended one to the man. "Here, Lock, give this to our friend."

The man made no effort to take the cup.

"Come on, Lock," Daddy urged. "Hand him the cup." The man took it and without looking at me stuck it out in my direction.

I reached for the cup, but before I could grasp it, he loosened his grip and it fell to the ground. The man quickly moved back and leaned into Daddy without lifting his eyes. Daddy put his arm around him. "It's okay Lock. We'll pour him another one."

Daddy filled the cup a second time and handed it to me. The man raised his head and watched Daddy who turned to him and said, "It's okay. You can trust him."

"His name is Lock?"

"Yes. He is the little boy you watched in the picture album turn into an adult. Remember, the photograph that showed two boys? The second boy was Andy Cailean. You met him yesterday afternoon."

I was trying to keep from making eye contact with Lock. "Andy is the feller that came out and patched him up?"

"Yes. They've known each other since they were just little kids. At one time Andy and Lock were best friends."

"But they're not anymore?" I asked.

"If you don't count me, Andy is still probably Lock's best friend. I'm not sure anybody but Andy could have doctored him last night. It was a bad night for everybody. We got some medication in him, calmed him down, and things got some better. Andy is a quick hand with a suture, thank goodness. We slept pretty well after midnight."

"You could probably have gotten Adam to come out here, don't you think?"

"Yeah, probably could have, but it wouldn't have done any good. You see, this whole thing revolves around trust. Lock doesn't trust many people anymore."

Lock was looking down, sopping his bread in the bacon grease, and that gave me a chance to study him. "I guess it's safe to assume he doesn't trust me."

Daddy stared at me. "Well, heck no. He's never laid eyes on you until today, less you count when he was running from the dogs. Why should he trust you? Let's turn the question around. Do you trust him?"

I looked at the rock in Lock's hand. "I guess not. Has he always lived like this?"

"No. He grew up more normal than you did."

"Did he do the painting in your office?"

Daddy refilled his coffee cup. "Yes."

"The sculpture?"

"Yes, and you haven't seen near his best work."

I tried to imagine this strange young man displaying any talent. "Where are his other paintings?"

"Private collections, museums, some are abroad. Did you see anything unusual about the paintings or the sculpture?"

"Yes, the boy and the woman aged in the paintings," I said.

"What about the man? Did he age?"

"I don't know. I never saw his face. It was always hidden."

Daddy spread the last of the jelly over his remaining bread. "Reckon why?"

"I don't know. Do you?"

"Yes. He'd never seen the man and he didn't want to guess what he looked like. He always thought he would meet the man someday, and then he would complete his face."

"How did he paint the woman's face?"

"He grew up with her. She's his mother."

I was starting to fit the pieces of the puzzle together. "She's the woman in the photo album in your desk."

Lock curled up with his head on Daddy's coat and began sleeping. Somehow, it was easier to talk with him not listening to our conversation. "So then, he is your son?"

"What do you think?"

I studied Lock. "I don't know. He's built like you, same coloring. Does he talk?"

"Sometimes."

"Were you married to the woman?"

"Does it make any difference?"

"Well, if he's my brother I need to know who his mother is. She looked very young. Maybe about my age. How old was she?"

"She is about your age. What do you think of that?"

"I don't know. If she is my stepmother, there are just some things I need…," I didn't get to finish my sentence. Lock bolted upright and looked wildly around, searching the ground around him before he found the rock.

Daddy touched him lightly on the shoulder. "There's no need to be afraid son, nothing is going to hurt you."

Lock lay back down on Daddy's coat. He turned, trying to find a comfortable position, then found one lying on his stomach with his arms stretched out above his head. His left palm was flat against the ground, fingers splayed, the right hand still clutching the rock. He took a few deep breaths and went back to sleep.

I looked at him again and thought how much he resembled both Daddy and me. His fingers were unusual. His ring finger was the same length as his middle finger. I studied them closely, looked at the exactness of his hand to mine, and then said to Daddy, "Well, I guess that proves it beyond any doubt."

Daddy looked at me, his eyes shaded by his hat. "Proves what?"

"He is your son and my brother. Look at his fingers. They are just like mine and Mothers."

"You're right. His hands are just like yours. And your mother's."

Daddy raked the scraps from the plates into the fire. "Why do you think his hands look like your mother's?"

I looked at Daddy, thinking that surely you know the answer to this question. "Well, it was just passed down like everything else is passed down, like his build and dark hair."

Daddy's eyes were probing mine. "But your mother was dead a long time before Lock was born. You've seen pictures of his mother."

"Yes, I have. But … if he wasn't kin to Mother and me, then how do you explain his hands? You don't have fingers like that, but I do. I know they came from Mother's side of the family."

"You reckon I might not be his daddy and he might not be your brother?"

I sorted this around in my mind. How could his fingers look like Mother's if he wasn't kin to her? He had to have her blood and genes. Had to, no other explanation. How could he have all the same characteristics of Mother and me unless …. . Bile erupted from my gut and came churning up my throat while water filled my eyes. I looked at Daddy, searching for something.

Daddy nodded his head slowly. "I believe you have your answer."

I hadn't been an angel growing up. I'd been in my share of scrapes, on occasion had tried out some of the mountain moonshine, and played some penny-ante poker. Daddy had kept me so busy in the logwoods I had neither the time nor the energy to get into much trouble. Girls had never been a big part of my life when I was a teenager. I found hunting and fishing more to my liking. I had some innocent sexual forays, but that's all they were. Just some groping in parked cars down at the river and a couple of moonlight skinny dipping incidents. Certainly nothing that would lead to a child … except … maybe, once. My mind was assembling segments of my memory, fumbling like someone putting a jigsaw puzzle together in the dark.

Daddy had taken the peach seed from his pocket and gone back to carving.. Without looking up, he asked, "Got all the answers, Sherlock?"

"I don't know. I think I'm missing some pieces."

"What are they? What kind of pieces?"

"Why is he named Lock?"

Daddy still had not looked up from his carving. "It s a nickname. Why am I called Zeale and why are you called Creight?"

"This is not making any sense," I replied. "What is Lock's mother's name?"

"Lockhart."

Still mystified, "… Lockhart?"

"You're not going to tell me you don't remember a girl named Maggie Lockhart, are you?

The focus came slowly. "Girl on the river. The one who wrecked her canoe with her sisters? The day of our blowup?"

Daddy went back to work on the seed. "I believe the mystery has been solved."

"Why, Daddy, there wasn't nothing to speak of between us. That night out on the river after the others went to sleep, we just talked."

Daddy looked up from his carving and raised his eyebrows – a silent question.

"We just sat and talked, maybe ..., I guess … just kinda fooled around a little. It wasn't very much … it was a long time ago … I was a kid. I didn't know…..I've thought about it some over the years and it's kinda hard to separate what really happened and … well, I didn't even get to know her. Why, it was just part of two days."

"Well sometimes, Creight, it doesn't take much knowing."

"Daddy, you didn't know her. How can you be sure he's my son?"

Daddy stood up, closed his knife and put it back in his pocket, "Creight, don't ever let me hear you say that again."

I stammered, "It's just …"

"Creighton, I've known Maggie more years than I've known you. She is …, if she says …" I could see his frustration as he searched for the right words. Daddy's face was red, and veins in his forehead swelled. He gave up and sputtered, "Goddammit! Do you understand me?"

It seemed like minutes before Daddy sat in his chair still visibly upset. Lock was awake again. He squatted in front of Daddy, making soft, cooing sounds. He had the rock in his right hand and was searching his pockets with his left. I wondered what he was trying to find. When he turned his stare toward me, I felt uneasy. What kind of thoughts are going through his head, I wondered. Did he think I had hurt Daddy? What would he do next? Finally, Daddy raised his head and smiled at Lock. This simple gesture, this smile, seemed to put him at ease. He sat down beside Daddy's chair, but continued to stare at me.

"Creight, you know how long I searched for you. I never really thought you were dead. For years I had men going through records, running down every lead, no matter how vague. But after ten years and thousands of dollars, I faced reality and gave up hope."

"I'm truly sorry, Daddy. I had no idea."

Daddy was now pacing in front of the smoldering campfire. "I know, and that's not important now. All this time I was looking, I was dealing with something here at home that I was totally unprepared to do. Parts of the story I'm probably not the person you need to talk to you. There are others, Maggie, Vaughn, his brother Anderson, and God knows who else need to fill in some spaces. But part of it is my story."

"Where is Maggie now, Daddy?"

"Here. She's living here in Cedergren. She's lived here for the past fifteen years. She's been good to me and I've tried the very best I know to be good to her. She's shared Lock with me."

"When can I see her? Will she even want to see me? I guess I can imagine what she must think of me."

"Son, you're giving yourself too much credit. She doesn't think anything about you. She's grateful that you probably saved her little sister's life and helped her out of a bad scrape. But she doesn't have any love for you, except that you fathered her child. She's given all her love to the boy."

"Did she ever marry?"

"No, but it wasn't because she never had any offers. She was too busy with her education and career. And too busy raising her son. She put everything she had into that boy. Everything."

"Does she know I'm alive?"

"No."

"I'd like to meet her, or at least, see her."

Daddy looked at me. "You've seen her. Remember the night we stopped at Pherson Brothers service station? First night you were home?"

Although it had only been a few weeks, it felt like months. "Yes. We saw that teacher and her students. I remember she called you Papa Zeale, or something, and you called her Doc. Is that the night you're talking about?"

"Yep, that's the night. Remember, you thought she was pretty good-looking and asked if I would introduce you?"

"That was Maggie?"

Daddy nodded. "That was Maggie."

"Damn, Daddy. Why didn't you say something?"

Daddy chuckled. "What did you want me to say? 'Pardon me Doc; this is my son we thought was dead. You know, the one who fathered your child. I thought you might want to say hello.'"

"Yeah, I guess it would have been pretty awkward wouldn't it?"

Daddy poured the last of the coffee into his cup and stood looking out over the lake. "I really don't know where to start. I reckon I'll just start with Lock's birth."

"He was born in Atlanta while Maggie was at Georgia Tech. It was a bad pregnancy. Complications from the start. Anderson Blackman was her physician and pretty soon he recognized he was about to get in over his head. Since Maggie was enrolled at Georgia Tech, we decided she should be under the care of a specialist in Atlanta."

"Who is we?"

"Anderson, Maggie and me. It seemed the best all around."

"Why were you in on the decision?"

"Dammitt, Creight. She was having my grandbaby, and I wanted the best care for her. Can't you see that?"

"Yes, I understand."

"We decided it would be best if she had an apartment off campus. Don't expect the university wanted pregnant girls in the dorms anyway. Luther and I hauled her stuff down in one of Roman's trucks. I didn't think anything about it at the time, but looking back I guess she should have been embarrassed at the sight. Here was this white man and this black man in overalls unloading her belongings out of a battered old truck. It was a pretty nice apartment complex and here are these two hillbillies dragging her stuff up the sidewalk. But she never said anything and if it bothered her I never knew it. After we got her things arranged, we got back in the old truck and went to the grocery store."

I wished I could have been a part of that.

"When we got back to Cedergren, I called her. She just went on and on about how nice the apartment was and didn't know how she would ever repay me. I told her repayment would be good grades and a healthy grandbaby. I made that call from the office out behind the house. When we hung up, I sat there in the dark and cried. I don't know who I was the sorriest for, her being pregnant down in that big town or me sitting here by myself."

"I guess both of you had a right to be sad."

As if he didn't even hear me, Daddy continued. "I made a decision, or maybe God made it for me. She was my daughter-in-law. It didn't make any difference that there had never been a marriage, she was my daughter-in-law, and she was having the only grandbaby I'd ever have. I wanted to be a part of their lives, and if I had made mistakes in raising you I was going to make up for it this go-round." Daddy paused. "With God as my witness, I've tried to hold up my end every day of my life."

"You thought you'd just lost a son and now you had to worry about Maggie and the baby. You must have felt life was pretty unfair. I'm sorry all this happened."

"Heck, don't be sorry. You didn't have nothing more to do with this than a bee buzzing around a flower," Daddy said with just a trace of a smile. "Anyway, Maggie started having more problems somewhere in her seventh month. I got a woman to come in and stay with her to do the cleaning and cooking, whatever needed. Maggie would laugh and say she was the only pregnant sophomore in school that had a maid but no husband.

"I'd go down about once a month just to check on her. Sometimes, Aunt Winnie would go with me. She'd carry some fried apple pies and baked sweet potatoes in a basket covered with a fresh drying cloth from our kitchen. She would bring the basket home but would always leave the drying cloth. 'Something for Maggie to remember me by,' she would say".

With some difficulty, I was starting to get a sense of how this man, who had been so hard, developed compassion for something other than his business.

"We were cutting some big poplar up in Wilson Cove when Fergus Cailean drove up and told me Doc Blackman wanted to see me. I was kinda surprised when I walked into Anderson's office and Aunt Winnie was sitting in her Sunday-go-to-meeting dress with some clean white cloths and a quart of fresh apple preserves. Anderson told me Maggie was in labor and having problems. Turned out it was a breech birth.

"Well, I had driven from the woods in my old pickup truck, so Anderson insisted I take his car, a new Cadillac. Aunt Winnie and I tore out for Atlanta. I remember her sitting beside me with her knees pressed together and the quart of apple preserves in her lap.

"We didn't talk much. I remember twice she kinda leaned over, patted me on the shoulder, and said 'Zeale, I always know about stuff like this. Miss Maggie and the baby, they'll be all right. You just have to put your trust in the Lord.' Then she started singing *Standing on the Promises*. She was an old woman and had a deep, mellow voice. I thought, God if you ever heard anybody, hear this song, hear this woman."

Daddy's hands shook, and he was to the point of tears.

"Well, it turned out Aunt Winnie was right. When we got to the hospital, Maggie was back in her room asleep. Her face was flushed, her dark hair all matted up. Aunt Winnie sat on the edge of the bed rubbing Maggie's cheeks with a damp cloth. She rocked back and forth, kept repeating, 'pore chil, pore chil.' The doctor said it was a kneeling breech birth. First one he'd ever seen. He said the baby was going to need some special looking after for a few days. He shook my hand and said, 'Congratulations on a fine baby boy. I know you must be a very proud father.' I knew he really thought, 'What is an old fart like you doing being married to such a young woman, and why are you fathering a baby at your age?' I started to say I wasn't the daddy, but I stopped myself. Instead, I said, 'Thank you, doctor.' I thought, I'd give being a daddy the best shot a man ever did."

"But the baby ... Lock ... was healthy after all?"

Daddy took a deep breath and blew it out between tight lips. "Maggie went home in less than a week. Maggie told me they had things under control. Aunt Winnie told me in no uncertain terms, 'you just shoo back to Cedergren and get out of my hair.' Lock stayed in the hospital for about a month. He spent a lot of time in an incubator. The little feller had a fever, and the doctors didn't have much luck controlling it. He would go for two or three days in really good shape. "'Bout ready to come home' Aunt Winnie would say. Then the fever would come back up and the doctors would try a new medicine."

"They didn't have any idea what was causing this fever?"

"Not really. Medicine has come a long way and I suspect today they could knock out the problem in a wink, but they never really found the cause. Anyway, Maggie finished the year and Aunt Winnie stayed in

Atlanta the whole time, fussing over both of them like an old mother hen looking after her baby chicks.

"While all this was going on in Atlanta, I got a little too familiar with the Wild Turkey. Some days I'd just hang around the house and think of the rotten direction my life had taken: I'd lost a son and now I had a grandson that might not see his first birthday. Other than Luther calling and Camran coming by, most of my companionship was my old birddog. She'd lay in the floor by my bed with her front paws crossed, looking at me with those big, sad eyes."

Daddy was painting a dark portrait.

"At the end of school, Maggie and Lock moved into the house with me. It was the best thing that could have happened. Wasn't long until Lock was crawling, pulling up by my pant legs, and chattering like a squirrel. I got a cardboard box and put in the cab of my pickup, made him a bed. He seemed pretty happy bouncing along the log roads with me, but he wasn't half as happy as I was."

"So it was good having them living with you, wasn't it? I guess folks knew he was your grandson?"

"Oh, Anderson and Vaughn knew the truth. A couple of other folks knew you were his daddy. Lots of folks wondered but only a couple of them ever asked. I guess I pretty much blew up with them, a 'shit-fit' Daddy would've called it. The word got around about my fit and that was that."

"What happened about a birth certificate? Who was shown as the father?"

Daddy's eyes twinkled. "Well, who do you think? It was William Roane, of course. Anyway, Maggie hung around here for a year, then went back to Tech and finished with honors. I was as proud of her as if she was mine. Luther was getting out of school about the same time, and I told them both the same thing. 'Don't stop now. Go on and get your masters.

Take the next step.' Maggie stayed at Tech and got her masters. Highest honors again. Drug companies were falling all over themselves trying to hire her. Some good offers, too.

"She said she'd been on my payroll long enough and wanted to take a job with some big firm in New York. I told her it was up to her, but she still had more potential, lots of stuff to learn, and I was kinda getting use to going to graduation ceremonies and seeing her march across the stage. She went down to LSU and got her doctorate. She and Lock would spend the summers up here with me. Maggie was always reading stuff I couldn't start to understand, but I understood Lock and he understood me.

"We'd rattle around in my old truck and I'd wonder what else a man could ask for. Lock was about six when they moved to Hawaii. Maggie went to work in a government program studying whales and stuff like that. I felt lost. Alone in the world - again. I'd go out once a year around Christmas and Lock would spend each summer with me. Maggie said it kept him grounded. He needed to know where his roots were, needed to know all about these mountains.

"Maggie would come back at the end of summer for a few weeks before Lock had to be back in school. We would drive down to Knoxville to meet her. I remember once just watching her walking through the airport toward us. She was wearing a white business suit and one of those Hawaiian colored blouses. She was as dark as any of the islanders. Had sun streaks showing in her black curly hair and she had a big smile on her face because she was seeing Lock for the first time in months.

"She was just a knockout. I thought, you're the best-looking woman in Tennessee. No, make that the United States"

"Wasn't much business conducted at my office when she was here. Always two or three fellers who 'just happened to drop by' to talk about timber sales or some land deal. But I noticed they were always looking over toward the house, hoping to get a glimpse of Maggie. I felt like putting up a 'no trespassing' sign."

"What about her folks? Where was her family while this was going on?"

Daddy thought about this question before responding, "I guess we had a kinda falling out, me and her daddy. When Maggie was about three months pregnant, her folks moved. I think it was to West Virginia. A few times her mother and sisters would come down and visit her, but I never heard anything about her daddy once they moved. Lock was about five when Mrs. Lockhart died in a house fire. I think one of her sisters lives around Chicago and the other up near Richmond."

"What do you mean; you had a falling out with her daddy?"

"Well, just some things I didn't agree with. She was his daughter, but she was carrying my son's baby, and … uh … let's just let it go at that."

I could tell when Daddy was finished talking about something, and we had reached the end on this subject. "So, when did they move back here?"

"I don't remember the exact year, but Lock was just getting ready to start to high school. I didn't want him going to high school here. I didn't figure they could challenge him academically. So part of the deal with them moving back would be for him to attend a private school. We decided Baylor down in Chattanooga would be about right. A good school, but not too far away.

"Maybe it was selfish. No maybe to it, it was selfish. But I wanted her in the school system here in Cedergren. I knew some bright kids here in these mountains, but when time came for college, they just couldn't cut it. I talked with Scott Graham. He was head of the Board of Education then. Told him we needed to upgrade our high school science department, particularly in biology."

"I remember Mr. Graham – little short, bald-headed feller, wasn't he? Kinda uppity."

"Same man. He gave me that old song-and-dance about budget restrictions, how they were doing the best they could, and stuff like that. The Roman Company had just hit a good field in Venezuela, and we were in the chips pretty good – the 'do-da days' we called it later when the bottom fell out of the oil market. I asked Scott what would happen if some company gave the school system a grant. Could it be earmarked for a particular part of the education system? He hemmed and hawed before saying he would check and get back with me."

"Devious steps, I believe it's called."

Daddy chuckled. "You could say that, I guess. About a week later, Scott told me he'd checked with the big shots over in Nashville. 'We can do most of it but we can't direct the grant specifically into one department. The money would have to be spread out across all of our departments.' So, I told him to get me a budget. A month later, he came back with the figures and apologized for the amount. I didn't tell him but it was chicken feed to what Roman was clearing in one day down in South America.

"I told him we could swing the money end of the deal, but nobody ever got a free lunch. There were some strings attached. He was kinda a feisty little feller and I saw his hackles rise up. He wanted to know what the strings were, and I told him. One, he couldn't ever tell where the money came from. Two, I would get to choose one teacher. I think he was relieved I wasn't going to try to take over the whole school system. All he said was the teacher would have to be well qualified."

"So you got your fingers in their pie?"

"Yep, plumb up to the elbow. Luther set up a company we called North Georgia Global. Roman pumped the money into North Georgia Global and they gave it to the school system. Not five people in Cedergren have any idea who or what North Georgia Global is.

"The system got real lucky when I made my choice of a biology teacher. There was a bright young woman who was living in Honolulu. She had a doctorate and the most handsome son you ever saw. God was in His Heaven, the sun rose and set in the right place, and I was the happiest man on this earth."

The radio in Old Pony crackled. "Zeale, we're about ready."

"Give me about thirty minutes, Camran. Creight will be coming out, and when he gets to the road, let her rip."

"What's happening, Daddy? What's Camran talking about?"

"Yesterday after you left, I got hold of two of my timber cruisers. They hunt ginseng all around the edge of the Arn down where it joins the river. And they know most of this country like the back of their hand. When I told them somebody had found a way up the escarpment and had gotten into the Arn, they figured it was probably where Browns Creek comes over the bluff. Maybe a slide or a part of the bluff had just sloughed off.

"It was almost dark when they got back to me and said it was just like they thought. A section of the bluff about a hundred feet wide had just caved off. It looked like they could make out tracks of some men and dogs climbing up the slide. Tony is going to do a little dynamite work. When he gets through, a bobcat wouldn't be able to climb it."

"Tony?"

"You've met him; he came up to Alaska with Luther. I believe you didn't hit it off too well."

"I thought he was some kinda body guard."

"Tony knows a bunch of stuff. You don't have to like him, but just remember, he is a good man to have on your side."

"Why am I leaving, Daddy? I'd just as soon stay out here with you and Lock."

"I'm not sure how Lock's going to take to the dynamiting. It's probably best if it's just the two of us here while that's going on. We'll camp back here tonight. You go home and study on what you learned today. Come on back out around noon. Bring us some steaks. Might throw in some tomatoes and an angel food cake."

"I'd really rather stay out here."

"Creight, I'm going to need to talk to Lock. Probably best done with just us two here."

Daddy took me back out to the road. Just like yesterday, Camran was sitting on the fender of his pickup with the heels of his cowboy boots tucked behind the bumper. The gate to the Arn slid closed behind me.

"Smarter than you was yesterday?" Camran asked.

I nodded, Camran said a few words into a microphone, and the ground shuttered with a long, low, stuttering explosion.

*****

Halfway between the Arn and Cedergren, there's a pullout called Hooch Point. Moonshiners used to park there to transfer whiskey to cars that would deliver to Knoxville, Charlotte or Atlanta. Now, people park here to enjoy a view of the Findhorn River where it frees itself from the escarpment.

It was late afternoon and no cars were at the pullout. I sat at the edge of the bluff and watched the sun set over the river. My thoughts were a jumble of half-completed answers and many unasked questions.

Daddy had taken care of Maggie as if she'd been his own daughter and had taken great delight in her intelligence, her success, and her beauty. He saw in Lock the opportunity to help raise a son. Because of the success of the Roman Company, he had time to devote to Lock, time he didn't have in my early years. He had single-handedly upgraded the county schools just because he wanted Maggie and his grandson to live in Cedergren.

You could look at it as selfish, but then Chota County had benefitted and everything turned out good for everybody.

Then the mystery of Maggie's family. What caused the separation from her family, and what kind of "falling out" did Daddy have with her father. We hadn't even gotten into what caused Lock to be the way he is. I was surprised about how little I'd really found out about him. How could such a promising boy develop into the man I saw cooing at Daddy's feet?

And the killings. Was Lock responsible for the murder of two men? If he was, how could Sheriff Fox continue to allow him to run free, even if he stayed within the confines of the Arn? I watched darkness rise up from the floor of the gorge. Soon it mingled with the darkness and shadows in my mind.

I stopped by Pherson Brothers service station, and bought a six-pack of Bud and some salted nuts. Not much of a supper, but I didn't want to eat at the restaurant.

A shiny black Corvette sat in the drive between the office and the house. I thought about Daddy's handgun. Maybe because of the trouble with the McCamy brothers, I should carry it under the seat of the jeep. I parked behind the sports car and killed my headlights.

The dome light of the Corvette came on and Vaughn climbed out of the car. "I'll teach you, you damned hillbilly, to call and threaten me!" We wrestled around the yard like ten-year old boys.

"Whoa, whoa," I said. "Let's stop and have a beer before I have to hurt you."

Vaughn and I sat, laughing and winded, on the office porch. "Make it easy on yourself, Hoss. I'm just getting cranked up," he said.

We sat in the darkness, drinking beer, and playing a game that I always thought of as "Remember When?" Most of our sentences started with, "Remember when old Leon fell out of the big oak in your daddy's yard" or "Remember when we tied a tin can on Mrs. Bateman's dog's tail and he ran through her little boy's birthday party." In the country, we have a saying: "And the years just rolled away." Well, they did. Places change, sometimes people change, but solid friendships last forever, and thirty years passing between friends is no more than a day.

We ran out of beer and went into the office. "I need to see you in some light, try to tell if you are as ugly as you were when you were a kid," Vaughn said.

I sat in Daddy's old swivel chair and Vaughn sat across the desk from me. I thought he looked soft, nothing like the hard-muscled kid who had fought his way through the big rapids on the Findhorn. He reeked of success from the tailored sport jacket to the razor cut of his blond hair and the heavy, gold Rolex. "I know a lot about you. Adam Huntsman said you were classmates, and you have a successful practice in Atlanta."

Vaughn rubbed his hands together and laughed. "We were in med school together. He has remained a good friend, a solid man. If I got in medical trouble, I can't think of anybody I had rather stand over my bed. He had it pretty rough growing up. He was raised on a hardscrabble cotton farm in north Mississippi. He picked cotton all through high school, and I don't mean with a machine. He pulled a twelve-foot pick sack up and down those long rows in that hot Mississippi sun."

"Daddy thinks he is brilliant."

"I don't know you could call him brilliant, but he's way above average. Good heart. The man's got a good heart. Always talked about helping people. He could've been a part of any of the finest medical practices in Atlanta, but he said he wanted to be around real people. I lost contact with him shortly after med school. Then one day I get a call from him. 'Living in the Tennessee mountains,' he said. When I asked him where, he said 'Your old home town. Cedergren.' I damned near swallowed my tongue."

"Kinda ironic, isn't it?"

"You know, Creight, in some ways I'm damned envious of him. When we talked the other night and he told me about his bird dogs and the time he spends in the field working with them, in the back of my mind I kept hearing this little voice saying, "He's living like a man ought to live."

"Adam tells me you've been super successful down in Atlanta. Big house, big cars, and all the stuff that goes with it."

Vaughn held a palm out and blew on it then watched an imaginary object float up toward the ceiling.. "Fluff, Creight. The whole darn thing is just fluff. How many cars can you drive at one time? How many country clubs do you need? Do you even need one? He probably told you about my wives. I've been married to some beauties, but I probably couldn't even remember some of their names except for the alimony checks I have to sign each month.

"Success is all in how you measure it. Sometimes I think if I had it to do over again, I'd marry one of those wild mountain women. Wouldn't make any difference how she looked. And I'd build me a little house up at the head of one of these hollows. I'd learn to play a fiddle. I would get me a pack of foxhounds and in the summer I'd lay out on the front porch in the sunshine barefooted. I'd put my feet up on a porch post. I'd play my fiddle, and then I'd stop and have a glass of moonshine."

Vaughn leaned back, laced his fingers behind his head and continued. "I wouldn't wear a shirt, and I wouldn't shave except on Sunday. We'd have poke sallet, side meat, and corn bread every night for supper. I'd drink buttermilk cooled in a spring behind the house. We'd listen to the Grand Ol' Opry on the radio every Saturday night, and we'd sleep late every morning. Tell me, my old friend, what do you see wrong in any of that?"

I laughed. "Sounds good to me. It's the makings of a heck of a country song; Nashville is just probably waiting for a man with your talents."

Vaughn crossed his legs and carefully straightened the crease of his pants. "You been out to the Arn, seen the buffalo and the turkeys?"

"Yes. I've spent the day out there with Daddy."

Vaughn leaned forward and stared at me. "See anything else exciting?"

"Well, yes, I guess you could say so. I met my thirty-year-old son for the first time. I guess that could be classified as exciting."

Vaught laughed. "Really! How would you rate it on the Richter scale?"

"About an 8.9. How long have you known about Lock?"

Vaughn smiled. "A few months before he made his appearance in this world."

"Sure you did. Tell me how you knew?"

"Creight, your daddy didn't tell you?"

"Not yet. Hadn't told me crap about anything. Getting answers out of Daddy is like pulling hen's teeth."

"Well, let's see. You'd been missing about three months. Anderson came over to the house one night, sat around and talked to Mother and Daddy for a while then asked me if I wanted to go get a Coke. That had always been a secret signal between us growing up. What it really meant was 'I've got to talk to you about something, and Mother and Daddy don't need to know about it.' We drove down the road a little bit and Anderson said, 'What I am going to do is a violation of medical ethics. You understand? I hope it is justified in this case'. Then he asked me if I knew Maggie Lockhart. It took me a second because I had seen her only that once on the river. I told him I knew her just a little."

"You didn't know her any more than I did."

Vaughn did a belly laugh that ended in a kind of snort. "Well, as it turned out, I don't believe that's quite correct. But anyway, Anderson said, 'She's pregnant.'"

"I'll bet you wondered why Anderson was telling you that."

"Heck yeah. First thing I said was, 'Well, it wasn't me.'"

"You wanted to get that clear, didn't you?"

Vaughn nodded. "Yes. Anderson had seen Maggie twice. First time he saw her, Mrs. Lockhart had brought her in. Second time he saw her, she was pregnant."

"Pregnant!"

Vaughn nodded and continued, "Maggie's daddy had beaten her when he found out about it. Anderson asked about the baby's daddy and Maggie said he was dead. He pressed her some more, and she broke down crying and said it was Creighton Roane."

"Me?"

"First thing I asked Anderson was, 'How?' He said it was the same way it usually happened. Then I asked him 'Why are you telling me all this?' He said, 'I don't really know, but I had to tell somebody.'"

"Why didn't he tell the sheriff – about the abuse, I mean?"

"He said Mrs. Lockhart made him promise not to. She said her husband would kill both of them if it ever came out." Then Anderson said, 'Hell, you and Creight have been best friends since you could walk. I just thought I ought to tell you.'"

"Sounds like he just needed to get something off his chest."

Vaughn nodded. "I asked him who else knew, and he said nobody. Then he said, and I will never forget his words, 'Her daddy is beating her and if he beats her one more time like he did last night, not only will she lose the baby, but she may die as well.' I asked how I could help. He said 'I don't know but I just had to tell somebody.'"

"You didn't go and talk with her daddy did you?"

"No. Hell no. I'd seen him in town a few times. He was a big, tough looking man, big tattoos on both arms. I'd be in the parts store and he would come and growl at the parts clerk, get his parts and leave. Mike James was on the counter, and he would say when Maggie's daddy left, 'Somebody's going to kill that arrogant son-of-a-bitch one of these days.'

Creight, I was eighteen years old, you couldn't have hired me to have talked with him about anything."

"So what did you do?"

Vaughn looked down at the floor. "I told your daddy."

"Damn, Vaughn! Why did you do that?"

"I didn't know what else to do. Anderson said Lockhart was killing the baby and the mama too. What would you have done?"

"I don't know. How in the world did you tell Daddy?"

"He'd hired me to mow his yard. I think he just wanted to have somebody, some friend of yours around. I thought all day about how to tell him. I just couldn't find an easy way. I was loading my mower in the back of the truck when your daddy came out to pay me. I just kinda blurted it out. I said, 'Creight got a girl pregnant, and her daddy is beating her.' At first I thought he didn't hear me because he just stood still, a frown on his face with his mouth slightly open. Looked like he'd been stung by a bee or something"

"I guess it was a pretty big shock to him."

Vaughn slowly shook his head, "To say the least. Your daddy looked at me and said, 'Say again.' So I said the same thing again. He sat down on the tailgate of my truck, looking at the ground, and didn't say anything at all for a long time. Finally, he asked 'Who is the girl?' and I told him he had seen her at Dove Landing the day the rescue squad was getting ready to look for us."

"So was that it?"

"No. He stood up, made a couple of steps toward his house, stopped, put his hands in his pockets and kinda rocked back and forth. I heard him say, 'Shit' under his breath and then he went on into the house. I took the sling blade and went behind the house to cut the grass around the grape arbor. When I came back to the front yard, his truck was gone.

"And then …. ?"

"I don't know all of it. I know he stopped by Anderson's office. He told him pretty much what he'd told me. Your daddy asked if he was sure the baby was yours. Anderson told him he had no reason to believe any differently."

"Hadn't been a very good year for Daddy had it? First losing a son, then finding out about this?"

Vaughn shook his head. "I guess you could put it that way. Anderson said at first he thought your daddy was taking the whole thing pretty good. Then anger started building in him, and he started pacing around. The more he paced the madder he became. The only thing he said was "Sumbitch is killing my grandbaby.""

"After Daddy left Anderson's office, what happened?"

"I don't really know. Anderson saw your daddy at the drugstore the next day buying some adhesive tape, the broad kind, and some horse liniment. He had had a black eye and a cut lip. When he asked what had happened, your daddy said he had fallen off a horse. Anderson begged him to stop by the office so he could sew up the cut lip. Your daddy just kinda blew the whole thing off. When he walked out of the store, he was favoring and leaning to one side, like a man would walk if he had broken ribs."

"Daddy went out to Lockhart's house and got a beating for his trouble, didn't he?"

"What we figured. Two weeks later, Maggie was back to see Anderson. She had new bruises and was bleeding vaginally. Anderson called Beth. She picked Maggie up and took her to their house. This time, Anderson called your daddy directly. Anderson said he had just started telling your daddy what had happened when your daddy hung up."

"Not a good sign."

"So far as I know, nobody but Ian Winchcombe really knows what happened next. Anything I say would just be a guess and nothing else."

"Who is Ian Winchcombe?"

Vaughn chuckled. His fancy silver belt buckle moved up and down, "Don't you remember Ian? He lived up just south of McKelvy Mountain and used to haul whiskey for the McDholl brothers. The Feds caught him one night with forty one-gallon jugs of lightning. They wrecked three of their cars before shooting Ian's car to pieces. He spent six months in jail in Cedergren before he was convicted. They took him to Nashville and he spent ten years in the Castle on the Cumberland."

"Yeah. I remember him."

"Well, Lockhart was the man who did all of Ian's engine work. So, far as I know, other than Lockhart, Ian was the only man at the garage when your daddy got there." Vaughn paused before saying, "Last place I knew of Ian living was up in Red Hawk Valley, almost at the Kentucky line."

"Did Maggie go back to her folks?"

Vaughn yawned and looked at his Rolex. "No. She lived with Anderson and Beth until your daddy took her back to school in Atlanta. Her folks moved from here in less than a month, so far as I know, without seeing her again."

"And that's it? That's all you know?"

"That's it. You've got to remember all this happened thirty years ago. Tell you what. Let's meet at the café in the morning. In the meantime, I'll see what else I can remember. If you've got time, we'll take a run up to Red Hawk and see if we can find Ian. Get what happened at the garage straight from him."

Vaughn's Corvette purred out of the driveway and his taillights disappeared toward Cedergren. I still had big blank areas in my mind, but at least I was starting to fill in some cracks.

I had a busy night trying to put the pieces of the puzzle together. I had a son. It seemed strange that I had seen the mother of my son but had no idea who she was, nor did she recognize me. How do you reconcile with someone you don't know? Would she even want reconciliation with me and why should she?

At least I knew the reason behind Daddy's "dust-up" with Maggie's daddy and the reason for no contact with the rest of her family. But the mystery remained as to Lock's early years and his character disorder, if that's what it was. And was he a killer?

I slept fitfully. The one recurring dream, and the one that woke me before daylight, was of Lock sitting on the ground, his heels pulled up against his buttocks, his arms wrapped tightly around his legs, looking up into Daddy's face.

*****

I got to the café just before eight o'clock. Vaughn was inside, making the circle at the Round Table, shaking hands with the Brotherhood. The McDholl brothers moved their chairs, making room for us, but Vaughn said we were grabbing something to go. 'Sides, we weren't old enough or wise enough to sit with the Brotherhood. With a lot of laughter, the men around the table agreed, and told us to come back when we were better seasoned.

Armed with sausage biscuits and Styrofoam cups of coffee, we squeezed into Vaughn's car.

RED HAWK VALLEY

In less than an hour, we were on the narrow graveled road leading up through the picturesque Red Hawk Valley.

"The McDholl brothers gave me directions. I don't think we will have any trouble finding Ian. He has a garage across the road from the post office," Vaughn explained. "After all, a legend shouldn't be too hard to find."

"Think he'll know you?"

"Yeah, I carried a couple of cartons of Winstons and some *Playboys* to him while he was in the Cedergren jail. We thought he was a hero or at least the closest thing to a hero there was around."

Red Hawk was just a broad spot in the road: a post office, a little grocery store, and Ian's metal-sided garage. The double doors of the garage were open, and we could see two men with their heads stuck under the hood of a Ford pickup. I followed Vaughn into the garage. He walked up to the back of the truck. "What you say, fellers."

The men stepped back from the truck.

If a hundred men were standing there, I could have picked out Ian Winchcombe. He was wearing Ray-Ban sunglasses, and probably wore the same size Levis as when he was in high school. He was still muscular, had Elvis sideburns and when he turned to find a shop rag to clean his hands, I saw his duck-tail haircut. In the late '80s, he was still living in the '50s.

Vaughn stuck out his hand. "I'm Vaughn Blackman from Cedergren and this is Creighton Roane."

Ian grinned and shook Vaughn's hand. "Well, hell yes, you are. I remember you. You furnished me mags and smokes while I was locked up waiting on the Feds to haul me down to Nashville." He turned to the young man standing beside him, "This is my grand boy, Munro."

We shook hands. Ian motioned us to sit down. Vaughn and I chose a ragged car seat supported by two wooden Coke cases.

Ian was crippled; both of his legs twisted and supported by metal braces. He hobbled over, stopped by a wooden chair, and slapped the outer edge of his braces at the knees. With a metallic click, the braces folded. Ian sat, and Munro dropped cross-legged to the ground beside his grandfather. Ian shoved the sunglasses up to the top of his head and said, "What brings you fellers up to these hills? Munro ain't been into nothing bad, has he?"

Vaughn laughed. "Naw nothing like that. We want you to tell us about something that happened a long time ago."

Ian rocked back in his chair until only the back two legs were on the ground. "If I can remember. What's hit about?"

"It's about something that happened between a feller named Lockhart and a man named Zeale Roane."

Ian looked at me. "Thought that name rung a bell. Air you kin to Zeale Roane?"

I nodded. "He's my daddy."

"Well let me tell you – you say your name was Creighton? – that old man was one tough sumbitch in his day."

I smiled. "I guess I should thank you for those kind words."

"No, I mean it. I hadn't thought of that day in a long time." Ian blinked his eyes rapidly, smiled, and continued. "I had a '56 Chevy with a 265 and two 4-barrel carbs with a 25-gallon stainless steel tank in the trunk. Hit was my business car. I just used hit for hauling. Revenuers had damn near caught me about a week earlier, and I figured I needed more horses. So I had took the car over to Lockhart's garage. He was going to shave the heads and drop a high-lift cam in it. I didn't like him, because I thought he looked down on us mountain folks."

I asked, "Did he?"

"Oh I reckon he did. But he knew high performing engines, so he done all of the work on my cars. I'd hoped the car would be ready, and a buddy of mine, old boy named Qbert Martin, had took me to Lockharts. Qbert had left, and I was just settling up with Lockhart when this old beat-up, pickup came tearing into the parking lot. Hit slid sideways in the gravel and before hit was even stopped, this old gray headed man jumped out like his britches was a far."

"That man must have been my daddy. He was in his late '50s," I said, somewhat in his defense and in consideration of my own age.

Ian laughed and his eyelids fluttered again. "Hell, I'm way older than that now, but then I thought he was real old. Anyways, he come running in the shop hollering something like, 'I already told you about beating that girl.' Lockhart kinda reared back and said, 'I thought I'd give you enough last time that you wouldn't be coming back nosing in our family business, you old sumbitch.' About that time your daddy was all over him."

"Hitting him?"

"Hell yeah. They went to the ground and was rolling around. They turned over a big toolbox, got into a bunch of oil cans a sitting on a shelf, and old man Roane - I mean your daddy - was just pounding hell out of Lockhart. Somehow, Lockhart shoved your daddy off and both of them got back on their feet. Then your daddy come at him again.

"I'd been around folks that toted pistols kinda regular, but I seen something I'd never seed before. Lockhart was carrying a little two-shot derringer strapped round his ankle. He pulled that pistol, and his first shot took your daddy in the side of his neck. Just grazed him, but hit was enough to draw blood. I'm trying to get the hell out of the garage. I'm in enough trouble with the law as it is, and I don't want to be no witness to no killing."

I felt sorry for Daddy. "So, I guess that ended the fight."

"No, hell no. Your daddy picked up a watering can – that kind with a long spout - and just kept a coming. Lockhart shot at him again, and this time plumb missed. Well, I guess you could say right there the fight was over and done. It was Katy bar the door for Lockhart. Old man Roane - uh excuse me, Mr. Roane - just beat the hell out of Lockhart with that watering can. Just a bam-bam-bam on Lockhart's head – blood a flying everywhere. I've always thought if I'd not been there he would have kilt him for shore. Bout now I'd kinda got into the spirit of things, and I pulled your daddy off. He just stood there heaving, trying to get his breath, and Lockhart, he laid there on the ground, bleeding like a stuck hog. He was afraid to get up, afraid your daddy would jump him again with that watering can, and I reckon he figured this time might kill him.

"You think he would've?" I asked.

"Well, hell yes. If you'd seed what I just seed, you wouldn't ask. Anyhow, I picked up that little derringer and slipped it in my pocket. I was afraid Lockhart might have some more bullets. Your daddy was pretty beat up, too. Blood running out of his mouth and nose. I helped him out to his truck, and after he'd rested some, he drove off. I jumped in my Chevy and laid rubber down for a hundred yards. Went back to the garage next day to pay Lockhart, but hit was locked. I never seed Lockhart again, and I ain't paid him to this day."

I tried to picture Daddy, at least ten years older than Lockhart, taking on the younger man in a fistfight. "Have you seen Daddy since then?"

Ian laughed and his eyelids fluttered again. "Yeah, I seed him bunch a times, even worked some at his mills. He never said nothing, and you know, the funniest thing, I don't believe Mr. Roane even knew there was nobody in that garage that day except him and that Lockhart fellow."

I stood and shook Ian's hand. "Thanks for telling me this story. You probably saved Daddy from going to jail or something worse."

Ian smiled again, his eyes doing a quick flutter. "Wasn't no big deal. But you kin do me a big favor. Fore you run off; give Vaughn enough time to tell Munro bout them Feds trying to run me down."

Vaughn always relished telling a good story. So he gave Munro a couple of tales, maybe embellishing some parts. Vaughn put on one of his better performances, and Munro laughed in all the right places. Ian's eyes sparkled.

We were walking back to the car when Munro asked Vaughn if he could look at his engine - the 'mill' - he called it. Vaughn raised the Corvette's hood and Munro buried his head inside. Meantime, Ian tugged on my sleeve and motioned for me to follow him. He hobbled back into the garage, reached up above the doorframe in the small office, and took down a cigar box. He blew the dust off the box and handed it to me without opening it. "I ain't got no use for hit, and hit might mean something to you – I'd just as soon you didn't open hit until you was way down the road. Not in front of the boy, no way."

We went back out into the mid-morning sun to see Munro sitting behind the steering wheel, the engine idling smoothly. Vaughn asked Munro if he wanted to take it for a run. Munro looked at Ian who shook his head no. We shook hands all around again. Ian shook Vaughn's hand a little longer than mine, and then said, "I want to thank you for a telling Munro them stories." He paused, "I got busted up pretty bad in a wreck a few years back and, well, you see how I am. I just don't want him to think I was always this old and crippled up, and not worth a shit."

We drove toward Cedergren, rehashing what Ian had told us. Vaughn asked, "What's in the box?"

"I don't know. Ian said to open it when we were on our way back." I unwound the string and opened the box. Inside, wrapped in an oily rag, was a two-shot derringer. I broke the gun down and there was a spent cartridge casing in each barrel. Although I would never be able to prove it, I was certain these were the cartridges Jason Lockhart had fired at Daddy.

*****

The courthouse clock showed half past one when Vaughn and I got back to Cedergren. "I feel clean somehow," Vaughn said. "I really didn't know how much I missed these mountains and the people. Just talking with those old boys at the Round Table this morning was worth more than you can ever know. And Ian. I wouldn't have missed that story for anything. Creight, I believe it does a man's soul good to be around real people. I go through a lot of crap everyday dealing with rich folks who don't know the worth of life. Trying to make beautiful women more beautiful. Stretching faces, tucking tummies, ironing out wrinkles, making things the size they weren't intended to be."

I was tying the string back around the cigar box. "Why don't you move here? Get back to where you belong."

Vaughn rubbed his hands together and laughed. "Who would support my ex-wives, pay the private school tuition for all my kids, keep up my country club dues, make my mortgage payments, my car payments, and my credit card payments? Keep all those Atlanta women beautiful?"

"So you'll just have to dream of laying in the sunshine on your front porch, looking at your dogs and playing the fiddle?"

Vaughn was getting into his car, "Old buddy, I'm going to appoint you to do those things for me. But someday soon I'm going to come back up here. I swear to God I will. Going to buy a couple of six-packs, get my canoe out of Daddy's barn, and we're going to run the Findhorn, maybe take on the Henderson Brothers. And we're going to be young and the world is going to be fresh. We're not going to know about all the bad things that are out there."

"Amen, brother."

Vaughn didn't hear me because his eyes said he was in another place, a place of roiling water and clear blue sky. "Laugh," he continued. "We going to laugh because we're not going to have a care in the world."

Vaughn left. Along with his dreams, he took some of my boyhood memories with him. I don't know how he really felt, but I felt pretty sad. Down deep, I knew we wouldn't ever run the Findhorn together again.

CEDERGREN

Late that afternoon with the food Daddy had requested in the back of the jeep, I left for the Arn. In the last little valley before starting up the mountain, I crossed the West Fork of the Joe-Pye-Weed Creek, one of the small creeks that feed the Findhorn. Camran's truck was parked near the end of the bridge. He was sitting on the tailgate skinning a squirrel. Three more, already skinned, were in the bed of the pickup beside a battered old Winchester 12-gauge pump.

"Evening Camran. Didn't know squirrel season had opened yet."

"Ain't," he said, dropping the squirrels into a paper sack. "I needed some for a stew. Damn hunting season is for city folk. Hit don't mean shit to us."

"I didn't know that."

He dried his bloody hands on his pants. "Well, you do now," he said. He pumped three shells from his shotgun to the ground, picked them up, and dropped them into his pants pocket.

"Been spending some … " Camran was interrupted by a battered Chevrolet sedan weaving from side to side as it rattled across the rickety bridge toward us. As the car approached, it swerved to our side of the road, horn blaring. Camran and I jumped behind his truck as the car roared by with less than a foot to spare.

Camran scrambled to load his shotgun and got off one shot, but the car was out of range. He waved his fist toward the disappearing vehicle, "Friggin' McCamy, I'll get you one of these days."

"What was that all about?"

"It was that cross-eyed McCamy whelp. I'll get the little sumbitch. Teach him how men play. Ugly little sumbitch."

"Camran, I'm guessing that wasn't one of your friends."

Camran stood in the middle of the road his cold grey eyes blazing with rage, "Ain't funny. I'll get him. May take a while, but I'll get him."

I enjoyed seeing Camran rail against the McCamys. "So is it just you and Daddy that don't like the McCamy tribe?"

Camran's face was still red, and the veins in his neck were popped out. "They was some of the sorriest folks that ever lived. Two year ago they set my neighbor's hay barn on far. Kilt two milk cows and a mule. Last year they broke in Dee Taylor's tool shed and let about five hundred gallon of tractor fuel run off down the hill into his pond. Killed ever fish in the pond and hit was six months before livestock could drink the water."

"Don't they get into trouble with the law for doing stuff like that?"

"Them doing and catching them doing is two different things. Sumbitches may be mean but they're slyer than a gray fox. Sheriff ain't been able to pin nothing on them yet."

"Sound like regular outlaws."

"Naw. Sorrier than that. Zeale had a shed full of walnut lumber last year. Had a buyer comin' from Memphis. Damn if the McCamys didn't burn the shed plum down to the ground. Ain't no telling what it cost Zeale."

Camran waved both hands in front of his body and shook his head, "Now where was we. Oh yeah, you been spending bunch of time around Zeale, ain't you?"

"Pretty much," I said. "Looks like he depends on you a lot."

"Yeah, we do pretty good. He's been good to me. Sometime I have to put up with some mess out of him, but mostly we do good."

I laughed. "I can't imagine y'all having a falling out."

"Did he ever tell you about the time me and him went to a baseball game in Atlanta?" he said, rummaging around in his front pocket.

"No. When was that?"

"Oh, I don't know, hit must have been twenty or twenty-five year ago. I ain't never traveled much, probably never been much further way from the house than Knoxville. Hit was a hell of a big trip to me. I'd never seed no big league baseball game and when we got there, I figured Atlanta must be the biggest city in the whole damned world.

"I've been to some big league games. They're exciting, aren't they?"

"Oh, hell yeah. Zeale ordered us hot dogs and beer and we was having a high old time," Camran said as he opened a hawk-billed knife and ran his thumb along the blade. "Air was nobody a setting in front of us, so Zeale leaned back, putting his feet in the seat in front of him. Said, 'If Creighton hadn't run off and drowned, I expect we'd had gone to a lot of games, cause he really liked baseball.'"

Camran had taken a worn whetstone, spit on it and started drawing his knife blade across the wet rock. I said, "Well, ain't no need a crying over spilt milk. What's done is done."

Almost willing to bet on the answer, I asked, "What did Daddy think about your advice?"

Camran tested the blade against his thumb again. "Made him madder than hell. He said I didn't have no sympathy, and I couldn't understand because I never had no kids. I told him that might be true but if I had, I'd a treated them a damn sight better than he treated you."

"You didn't say that!"

"Damn straight I said it. I'd heard Zeale pore mouthing about you running off a dozen times. He jumped up out of the seat and I thought he was going to hit me. I jumped up too because I had about four or five beers in me, and I wern't going to take any shit off him, even if he was my boss. Folks around us scattered because they thought we was gonna fight."

"But you didn't."

"No. Zeale kinda got a hold of himself and sit back down. I did too, and things was quiet for a long time. Zeale said, 'Air you saying, I'm to fault and I caused Creight to run off?' I said, Yeah, I am. You hollering at him like he was a kid down at Dove Landing. Front of all them people and all. He was a good boy. He was damn near a growed-up man. You never even heard his side of nothing. Ever. If I'd a been your boy, I'd have took off a long time before he did.

"Reckon a lot of hit was beer a talking. But I heard him on your ass a bunch of times. Member one time we was cutting up around The Shoals. Old boy named Tootie Green got one of our skidders hung up. You was a trying to get hit out and Zeale come up. He thought you was the one that got hit hung. He got all over your ass in front of everbody. I come up after he got there but I knowed what happened. Told him, 'Damn Zeale, Creight never done that, hit was that goofy Tootie that done hit.' Zeale never said nothing, just got back in his truck and drove off."

"I remember that day."

"'Course you do, I could see you was hurt bad. Another time I remember, bet you weren't fourteen year old. You'd took a chainsaw to cut some oak saplings that was a leaning over the mill road. One of the Scott boys had run hit out of oil the day before, plum burnt the engine up. You brought the saw back and told Zeale the engine was cooked. He got all over your ass, accused you of not checking the oil before you started hit. You told him you hadn't run the engine none. Hadn't even started it. Zeale reach over and felt of the engine and hit was cold as ice so he knowed you hadn't run hit none."

I remember the coldness of that July day.

"He was wrong and he knowed it, but he just kinda grunted and told you to get another saw. Hit pissed me off something awful. I followed Zeale when he went back up to the mill, and told him off pretty damn good. He just looked at me and told me to mind my own damn business. I just gritted my teeth and didn't say no more."

Camran squinted at the knife blade and then pulled up his shirtsleeve. He slid the blade along his arm, and the silver curly hair was shaved off at skin level. He folded the blade with a click and dropped the knife back into his pocket.

This was the first time I had ever talked to a man that stood up to Daddy and told him he was wrong about something. Except the McCamy brothers out at the Arn the other day, and they didn't get very far. Camran seemed finished with his story, but I egged him on. "Anything else happen at the baseball game?"

Camran put the whetstone in a leather case and slid it into his shirt pocket. "Nothing, not a damn thing. Zeale never mentioned nothing else about you running off, least not in front of me, he never."

"I'm glad you stood up to him."

Camran gave a short laugh, "Well, hit never mounted to anything. I don't expect hit changed his mind a damn bit. After hit was all over and done, I was kinda ashamed, but I felt better about myself right then. Tell you one other thing. Bet he don't never mention none of this to you."

*****

I bounced along the trail leading out across the rolling hills of the Arn to the camp at Hematite Lake. Old Pony was parked at the trail leading down to the camp with Rip asleep in its shade. No one was in sight. I unloaded the groceries and walked down to the lake. The water was still. Only reflections of the white oak trees along the shore disturbed the shiny surface. I sat in the grass and leaned back against a log, letting the warmth of the sun suck the tension from my shoulders.

Rip woke me panting and licking my face. We walked to the edge of the lake just as a wooden johnboat rounded the point, coming toward us. Daddy was standing in the back of the boat with a fly rod working the cattails along the shore. Lock was in the front of the boat using a wooden sculling paddle.

Lock dropped down into the floor of the boat when he saw me. Daddy said something to him so softly that I couldn't hear and, after pulling the line back into the reel, lifted up a metal stringer of bluegill and bass. "Fish tonight," he shouted. "Man can't live on red meat alone."

When the boat neared the shallows, I took the bowline. Lock stepped out of the boat, the rock still clutched in his hand. Without looking at me, he put his hand on Rip's head and walked back up to the camp.

Daddy was admiring the string of fish. "Creight, don't think anything about that, he has days like that. On his bad days, he won't even look at me. Just acts like I'm not there. Then on his good days, he will want to go swimming and he'll roll and play in the grass with Rip. But there are more bad days than good ones. Maybe they're getting more frequent – I don't know."

"How long has this been going on?"

Daddy shrugged again. "This bad? Two or three years. They kinda run together.

"Have you taken him to see doctors? Tried to get professional help?"

"You can ask the damndest questions. Sometimes I believe you don't even think about…."

"I do think. Maybe you ought to be the one thinking. I don't know much about Lock, and you damned sure don't volunteer anything. I'll ask a lot of questions because I care. We need to have an understanding on this."

"You're right. I'm sorry I popped off like that."

"You don't have to apologize. Just help me understand."

Daddy took the fish off the stringer and we started cleaning them. "Maggie and I have taken him to all kinda specialists. This behavior is not something that just happened yesterday, and we've not just sat around on our hands doing nothing. We thought we were making progress. Some new and promising medications. Mood stabilizers, they call them. They worked for a while, then quit."

"How does he act around Maggie?"

"He just ignores her. It's been awfully tough on her just watching her child slip away into a tormented place."

When we reached camp Lock walked away without looking at us. Daddy said, "Right now he is in what they call a 'depressed phase.' He doesn't have any interest in anything, has no energy, listless, and won't eat. When he's like this, I try to stay with him all the time. The doctors tell us he might try to take his own life."

"How long do these mood phases last?"

"Sometimes a couple of days, sometimes a couple of weeks. They come and they go. There's no pattern."

"Do you think he's ever dangerous to other people?"

Daddy had taken a bottle of Wild Turkey from the glove compartment of Old Pony. "Heck, yes, he's dangerous when he's in one of his high stages. I've seen him go from feeling on top of the world to a wild rage within a couple of minutes. You can't believe the change."

"Can you control him?" I asked, feeling for the first time I was getting some insight into my own son.

"Mostly."

"But not always?"

Daddy took a drink of whiskey and wiped his lips on his sleeve. "No, not always."

"Was he on a high or in a depressed stage when the men were running him with the dogs?"

"I'm not sure. He'd killed their lead dog. I believe he was going to wait for the other dogs in the road. He would have fought those dogs and if he'd been alive when the McCamy brothers got there, he'd have fought them. But he was scared. You saw how he acted."

I had a brief internal debate about my next question. "Daddy, did he kill those two men that were found off the edge of the bluff?"

"I want to think that he didn't, but … I don't know for sure but down deep, I think he did. I've let him down somehow. I should have been able to prevent those killings."

"If he was involved in the killings, do you know why?"

"Yes I think so, but with somebody like Lock, you can never be sure of anything."

I was reluctant to continue questioning Daddy since I had seen how defensive he was of Lock, but I was starting to feel responsible. After all, Lock was my son, even if I had nothing to do with his parenting. I pressed on. "Can you tell me?"

Daddy seemed resigned. "You know the legend about the old fort? About the Indians and the moon-eyes and all the killing."

I thought about playing around the fort when I was a kid and the strange night noises. "Yes sir, I do."

"About five years ago and during a very stable period in his life, Lock was spending the summer camping out here on the Arn. He was working on a new painting project and spending a lot of time studying rock formations. Andy Cailean would come out on the weekends. He and Lock would fish in the lake, play poker, drink a little beer, and just set up at night around the campfire telling tall tales, probably smoke a little pot. Just doing what young men today do."

"Is that the reason you wanted Andy looking after Lock's wounds rather than a doctor? Because of their friendship?"

"Yeah." Daddy held the whiskey bottle up, looked at how little remained and put it back in his pocket. "They were hunting groundhogs out at the fort, and Andy's dog got one hemmed up in a large crevice at the east end of the breastworks. The boys had a shovel and were trying to dig the groundhog out. Pretty soon they saw that the crevice opened into a small cave. Lock had a flashlight and went down into the cave headfirst.

"The groundhog was sitting on a little ledge. A lot of small bones were on the ledge, and at first Lock thought other groundhogs had come into the cave and died. He took a stick and poked the groundhog until it scampered back up through the crevice. When he crawled over to look at the bones, he was horrified to discover they were human - the bones of little children. He couldn't tell how many, but he found three little skulls, and maybe two others."

"So maybe the story of the moon-eyes had some truth to it."

Daddy continued as if I had not interrupted. "It just scared the heck out of Lock. He hollered for Andy to come down. It didn't take the two of them more than just a blink to search the cave. They found a couple of stone jars. One of them had what looked like corn in it and the other was empty. Lock found two little mounds that looked like some kind of animal skins. But when they tried to move the skins, they just fell apart. They were pouches and there were little gold coins in each one."

I tried to picture the scene in my mind. "Damn, what a find."

"I came out later that afternoon to bring the boys some ice," Daddy continued. "You never saw two fellers more excited. They hadn't disturbed anything in the cave, just crawled out and sat kinda stunned. It was hard to get the story straight with both boys talking at the same time. Lock was particularly concerned about the bones of the children, how they had gotten in the cave, and who they were.

"The longer we talked, the more we agreed this was something we needed to keep between ourselves - something the outside didn't need to know. They showed me the entrance to the little cave, and we rolled a big rock over the opening. Hadn't been but a few folks around the fort in the past fifty years, but I didn't want somebody stumbling up on the entrance."

"Who'd ya'll tell about what you found?"

"Nobody. We agreed to keep the find a secret. Andy was just like his daddy and most of the other mountain folks. He was secretive, suspicious of outsiders, and tight-lipped. Lock had told me Andy had some pottery shards and arrowheads that he'd never shown to anybody, so I believed the secret would be safe. I wasn't going to tell anybody. I didn't want the State trying to come in, have their archeologists blundering around the fort, messing with things, trespassing on my land and disturbing the buffalos. The longer our discussion went on, the more disturbed Lock became. He started crying, plum lost it, saying things about how the children probably starved, and how could their parents have abandoned them down in that dark cave."

"He thought the children had been abandoned?"

Daddy nodded. "Yeah. We left the fort and went back down to the camp at the lake. Lock calmed down some after an hour or so. I took Andy out the gate, and we both swore again the secret would die with us. I stayed with Lock that night. He was restless and moaned some in his sleep, tossing around, and crying out loud a number of times. With 20-20 hindsight, I should have done something right then. To this day, I don't know what. But something."

"How long was he like that?"

"A long time." Daddy said. "It started him in a depressed stage that lasted six months. I don't think he was ever the same again."

It was difficult to take a breath. "What happened when ya'll took him for professional help?"

"Nothing," Daddy replied sadly. "In fact, it was the beginning of the end of the mother-son relationship. Maggie took him to see a friend of hers, a Dr. Crawford. Lock didn't want to see the doctor and kept insisting there was nothing wrong. The doctor suggested a physical examination before their first visit and Lock nixed that. Lock saw the doctor a couple of times. She prescribed a whole handful of pills. Big mistake. Really big mistake. He went into a major depression. He was living in Cedergren with Maggie at the time. One day he just disappeared."

"So, neither the medicine nor the therapy sessions helped?"

Daddy shook his head. "No, it just made things worse, a lot worse. When Lock disappeared, we searched everywhere. We called the few friends he had, college acquaintances, Knoxville homeless shelters, Asheville, everywhere. He'd been gone for about two months, and I was out here checking on some buffalo calves when Rip started going crazy, running up and down the road, and sniffing around a big laurel thicket. In just a little bit, Lock just walked out of the thicket just as calm as you please.

"He was skinny, hadn't shaved, and his hair was way down over his ears. I don't believe he'd had a bath in the whole time he'd been gone. I'd brought some alfalfa pellets out for the buffalo, and he ate those pellets like a man starving."

"Did you find out where he'd been?"

"I've got no idea. He could have been anywhere. But to get back on the Arn, he had to either climb the bluff or come over the security gate, and I don't know how he could do either one. That gate's electric and damned hot. It'll fry you to a crisp. He might have scaled the escarpment, but that would have been about as tough as climbing over the gate. Anyway, he refused to go back home and refused to see Maggie. Somehow he'd gotten it in his mind she was the cause of all his trouble."

"He hasn't seen Maggie again?"

"Yeah, Maggie kinda got back in his good graces. She took him up to Mayo. Guess that was the final straw."

"They didn't help him?"

"No. So that was it with Maggie. He just acts like she doesn't exist."

"And he hasn't seen her since she took him to Mayo?"

Daddy furrowed his brow. "Probably not. I've taken care of him out here. He doesn't have to see anybody or deal with any stress. If you can disregard the other day, which I guess you can't. I don't know. He may be right here on the Arn for the rest of my life. What happens to him after I'm gone, I don't have any idea."

"That may be the saddest story I've ever heard."

"Yeah. It's broken Maggie's heart. But we've learned to live with it. We hope maybe a new medication will come along or a big breakthrough in treating bipolar disorders – or whatever in hell he has. But, until that time, we're just playing the cards we were dealt."

"How about Sheriff Fox? How has he got around the killings?"

Daddy grimaced. "It has put him in a really bad spot. He knows more about Lock than you do. The first feller died was an archeology student from UT. A bad apple. He was one of those fellers that was always getting into trouble, always in some place he shouldn't have been, always operating just a little outside the law. Rangers had caught him in parks at night digging in old Indian graves. He was big into selling and buying stolen relics. He'd been caught twice at Shiloh late at night with a metal detector, looking for Civil War relics."

I had known of men digging around abandoned Eskimo villages and the pain it caused. "Sounds like he should have been locked up somewhere."

"He was under indictment when he died. He was a pretty skilled rock climber, and there was some speculation he'd just fallen off the bluff.

Nobody got really excited until Achilles McCamy died in about the same place. I guess you could say that's when the stuff got in the fan."

"What about the amulet the first man was wearing? Didn't that raise any questions?"

"Not really," Daddy said. "Folks just figured he had stolen it from an Indian grave somewhere. But when Achilles had the same kind of talisman around his neck and the TV folks decided to run a series on the deaths, it became a big deal. Some of those folks who write supermarket newspapers started poking around, and then more TV folks doing those 'unsolved crime' programs showed up."

"Daddy, this thing had gotten pretty big. I saw it on the news in Anchorage. Course, it probably didn't mean anything to anybody else except me, but it damned sure wrecked me."

Daddy frowned and rubbed his temples as if he had a headache. "Roy Ruby and I had an agreement that as long as I could keep Lock under control, it was none of anybody's business about him living out here and his strange actions. We weathered the first storm with the grave robber; but when Achilles was killed, it got out of Roy Ruby's hands. And that's where we are today, in a heck of a mess. I can't ask him to keep pretending nothing is wrong. He doesn't have any choice but send some deputies out and have them look around. He keeps putting it off. It's a day-to-day thing and we are running out of days."

"Why do you think the artifact hunter was killed or whatever happened to him?"

Daddy said, "I don't have to think, I pretty much know why. Lock was sleeping around Hematite furnace that night. He heard the noise of the grave robber's pick glancing off limestone. He came up to the fort to investigate and saw the man digging. Lock gets around like a cat in the dark. The grave robber never knew he was being watched. Lock probably thought the man was after the baby bones."

"So he killed him?"

"I expect he hit him upside the head with a rock. The man probably never knew what happened. Lock was in one of his manic phases, and the grave robber is lucky he wasn't hung over an open fire and cooked alive."

Hearing something like this about my son made me feel like I was in the middle of one of my bad dreams. "Tell me why Lock scalped him, and what is it with the amulet?"

Daddy was sounding weary. "He wasn't scalped. I expect he looked like he had been scalped from bouncing off the rocks after he was thrown off the bluff."

"But then the amulet. Didn't that raise all kinda questions?"

"No. You see, unless it was Andrew, nobody had any idea. But soon as I heard about it, I figured Lock had done it. Lock used to study those petroglyphs just south of Whetstone Cave. The Indians had made them - Lord knows how many years ago. They showed men being carried up into the clouds by some kind of birds that looked like doves, like they were being carried up to Heaven.

"When the word got out the grave robber was wearing an amulet with a gold dove carving, I pretty-much knew for sure Lock had killed him. At least Lock was trying to see that the robber got to Heaven."

"After the first man was killed, why in the world do you think Achilles McCamy decided to sneak into the Arn and go poking around?"

Daddy shook his head sadly. "It was the gold found around the grave robber's neck. Achilles figured the man had found the gold somewhere around the fort and there was probably more. I'm satisfied he knew about the slide at Browns Creek, probably even told his brothers. So he comes in here one night, starts digging, and meets the same fate as the grave robber."

"Lock is pretty efficient when it comes to things like this, isn't he?"

"I guess you could call it that," Daddy said. "Both men were unlucky they happened in here when Lock was in a manic phase. If he had been in a depressed phase, he would have just hidden and watched them. Probably would have just cried."

I kept pushing out of my mind scenes of Lock sneaking up on the grave robber and Achilles McCamy. "How was he after he killed them?"

"He was depressed, couldn't sleep, and wouldn't eat."

"But you don't think he could help it. That he couldn't have stopped himself from the killing?"

"No more than you can help breathing. He thought he was doing the right thing."

"Are you afraid of him? Has he ever threatened you or anything like that?"

"Not really. When he's on a high, I'm careful around him. I try to keep him busy. We'll repair fences, sometimes cut wood. I've seen him swim across Hematite Lake four times without resting. Eventually, he'll wear himself out, and then he may sleep for a whole day and night. But I worry most about him when he is depressed. I'm afraid he'll kill himself."

I thought this over, "So what do you plan … ?"

Daddy interrupted my question. "I don't want to talk about this anymore today. If we keep this up, I may be the one to jump off the bluff. What did you do this morning? Catch up on your beauty sleep?"

In a way, I was glad to change the subject. "No, not really. I spent a lot of last night and all this morning with Vaughn, Vaughn Blackman."

"Oh yeah, the famous Atlanta plastic surgeon," Daddy laughed. "Was he driving some big sports car, and did he tell you about his wives?"

"Yeah, both of those. Then he told me about the reason you had a falling out with Maggie's daddy."

"That was a long time ago. I hope I've got a little more civilized in the past thirty years. I acted real short sighted." Daddy paused. "You could probably say down-right dumb."

"Sounds like you did what had to be done. I wish I knew I'd have done the same thing. We drove up to Red Hawk Valley and talked with Ian Winchcombe."

Daddy's brow furrowed. "Who?"

"Ian Winchcombe, old hot-rodder. Used to run some whiskey for the McDholl brothers."

Daddy shook his head. "Don't believe I ever met him."

"Let me show you something that might help your memory." I went to the jeep and came back with the cigar box. I opened the box and the pearl handled derringer rolled out into my hand. "This remind you of anything?"

Daddy took the pistol and examined it. "No, don't believe I've ever seen it before. Why would a feller carry a little peashooter like this? Heck, you couldn't stop a man with a gun this size. Maybe throw it and hit him in the eye or something."

I took the pistol and put it back in the cigar box. "Yeah, that's what I understand."

"What did you say his name was again?" Daddy asked.

"Ian Winchcombe"

Daddy shook his head again. "Name's kinda familiar but I can't put a face to the name."

*****

We sat in the late afternoon sun watching Lock and Rip walking along the top of the levee, Lock skipping flat rocks across the lake and Rip watching each splash as if he were keeping count. "Believe I'll catch forty winks," Daddy said and was asleep within minutes

I walked out onto the levee toward Lock. He stopped skipping stones and stared at me before looking away. Rip came to me sniffing at my hand. I was surprised when Lock began to move slowly toward me. He passed me, turning sideways and leaning away, a man trying to slip by in a narrow place without touching anything. I thought he almost smiled, and I watched as he walked up the incline toward Daddy. Pulling his cap over his eyes, he lay down in the grass beside Daddy. It was a small victory because he'd acknowledged my presence, but the most important thing was that he was no longer carrying the rock he'd used to kill the dog.

Thank God for small favors.

It was almost dark when Daddy woke up. He looked at Lock asleep on the ground beside him. "A really good sign", Daddy said. "Shows he is comfortable with you around, he is not afraid or suspicious, and doesn't feel the need to be guarded. I think we can consider this a day of progress."

"Do you think he knows I'm his father?"

Daddy shook his head, "No. I don't believe his mind is capable of grasping that right now. Maybe later but not now. Let's do this. You go back home and give me one more night out here. We'll play tomorrow night by ear and see what we need to do then."

A real meal was in order and a six-pack didn't fall under that category.

The parking lot by Partner's Café was empty except for a beat-up, flatbed truck. Inside, an old man was sitting at a rear table. Louellen was refilling catsup bottles and glad to have company. "Hey, hon," she said. "You want breakfast this time of night? Do I need to wake up the hens?"

"You know that old saying, Louellen, let a sleeping hen lay. Bring me a porterhouse, a salad and a twice baked."

She set a mug of coffee on the table in front of me and said, "That ain't no old saying, it's dogs that you are supposed to let lay. Can I get you anything else?"

"I believe that's about it."

"Back in a jiffy."

The steak and potato quickly followed the salad. I wondered how long it had been since I'd had a full meal. Louellen freshened my coffee. "Okay, you've got your steak. Anything else?"

"Just sit down and talk to me."

She slid into the opposite side of the booth, propped both elbows on the table, leaned forward, and smiled. "What do you want to talk about?"

"Let's talk about you. Tell me something about yourself?"

"Well, I'm from Harrogate Gap. Bet you're wondering where in the world that is. It's a little place up near where Kentucky and Virginia join at the Tennessee line. Real mountain country, lots of timber, close to coal mining. Folks hunt ginseng, grow pot, and make a little whiskey. It's a whole lot rougher than around here. Real back woodsy."

"What brings you to Cedergren? The bright lights? The music? The dancing?"

Louellen smiled. "I was kinda a foster child in a way. My mama died when I was twelve." Her voice became more serious. "I never knew my daddy. Mama said he drove a log truck and just up and left the country one night. After mama died, Granny took me in. Then while I was a freshman in high school, Granny took pneumonia. She was down for six weeks before she died. I didn't have any more folks."

"What did you do?"

"Nothing. The state took me over. They found that Granny had a cousin that lived in Cedergren. Her name was Mrs. Amanda Litchfield, and she owns this restaurant. So that's how I wound up down here, and I've been here ever since."

"Mighty nice of Mrs. Litchfield."

"It was. I just love her to death. But she just had one bedroom, so I had to sleep on a couch in the living room. I didn't mind it, but Mrs. Litchfield said it wasn't fitting for a young woman to grow up like that. Anyway, toward the end of my sophomore year, we had to write a short story in our English class. I wrote about what had happened to me, Mama and Granny dying and all. Anyway, after the papers had been graded, my English teacher, Mrs. Carrington, asked me to stay after school. She asked me if the story was true."

"You were a sophomore?"

"Yeah. But I thought I was grown. About a week later, she asked me to meet with her and another teacher who talked with me for a long time. Asked me about what I wanted to do with my life and a lot of stuff like that. Turned out the other teacher traveled a lot, especially during the summer, and needed somebody to look after her aquarium. She had a spare bedroom that had been used by her son, but he was growed up and gone from home now. I've been there going on two years. I hope I'll be going to college next year. I'm going to study to be a kindergarten teacher."

"What a great story. Sounds like you're going to be a winner."

Louellen laughed. "Thank you for saying that. Maggie always says the same thing."

A jolt went through my system like I'd been struck by a rattler. "You talking about Maggie Lockhart? The biology teacher."

"Kinda set you back some, didn't it Creighton? Soon as I heard some of the men talking at breakfast the other morning, I connected all the dots real quick. It put me in a weird place. I knowed your story from both ends. The men were pretty excited for your daddy about you being back but I was excited for Maggie, and I don't exactly know why."

"I haven't seen her in thirty years."

"She left the day you got back to Cedergren. I'm pretty sure she still don't know because the island where they're staying don't have a telephone. So, while you turning up here has made a splash, she don't know anything about it. Probably won't until she gets back in a couple of weeks."

"How much do you know about us?"

"Enough. I know that Maggie has got a son named Lock, who has some kinda problems. And I know your daddy looks after him. I know you're the daddy and that you and Maggie never got married. Ya'll wasn't even sweethearts. For the longest time I thought she was married to your daddy and they had broke up. I never asked nobody no questions, and nobody ever volunteered anything to me. The one thing I did know was she loves your daddy an awful lot."

"How did you find out about me?"

Louellen thought for a minute. "I guess it was one night about a year ago. She was cleaning out her closet and I was helping her. She brought an old box into the living room. It had all kinds of stuff in it: some of her early report cards, a couple of letters from her sisters, and lots of pictures. Pictures of your daddy, pictures of Lock, pictures of places they'd lived, and an old faded newspaper. After we had looked at the pictures, she started putting them back in the box. I asked her about the newspaper, and she kinda got quiet.

"Finally, she spread the paper open and I could read the headlines. They said something like – *Rescue on the River*. I read the article and thought it was kinda exciting since it told about her and her sisters turning over in some rapids and almost drowning. There was a picture of two folks in a canoe pulling up to the bank. The picture was all faded and wrinkled. But I could still tell it was her in the front of the canoe. The man in the back had a baseball cap pulled down over his eyes and I couldn't see his face, so I asked her who he was.

"She said it was Zeale Roane's boy and his name was Creighton. She turned away from me and dabbed her eyes. 'He's Lock's daddy. I knew him for two days.' Then she folded the paper up and put it back in the box."

A tightness developed inside my stomach and there was no room for any more food – or anything else.

"Another time after Lock had one of his bad spells. She was awful sad and had been crying. She said, 'If Lock had a daddy in his life and I hadn't tried to raise him by myself, I don't believe he would have been like this.' All the time I've known her, that was the only time I ever heard her sound like she was sorry for herself."

I couldn't think of anything to say, and even if I could, I wouldn't have trusted my voice.

Louellen stood up from the table and shrugged. "Bad stuff happens in everybody's life. They say what don't kill us makes us strong. She's real strong. I wish someday I could be as strong as she is. Can I get you anything else?"

"No, thanks, I believe I've had about all I can stand tonight."

*****

Back in Daddy's office, I took the Wild Turkey out of the bottom desk drawer. The first swallow was smooth, the second smoother.

I stood before the paintings and looked at the man with the hidden face, a daddy the artist had never seen. Then the reality slammed into me: I had been the big loser. I had missed the opportunity to raise a son, to be married to a wonderful woman, and to be a part of the growth of a successful company. I had missed life, and I knew damned well I would never travel that path again.

Somewhere after four pulls at the bottle, I lost count.

*****

It was daylight. I had spent the night sleeping in Daddy's office chair with my feet propped up on his desk. My chin was shoved against my chest, and I must have slept in that position all night. I might never be able to walk completely upright again.

I waited seconds before opening my eyes and sure enough the headache was just as bad as I thought it would be. The pain of leaning forward to lace my boots was almost unbearable. I walked carefully out onto the office porch and saw the sun a couple of hours above the horizon.

A long, warm shower helped some. A slice of dry toast and a glass of cold milk almost soothed my churning stomach.

With my cap pulled down over my eyes, trying to keep out any light, I walked carefully across the yard to the jeep. A man wearing faded overalls and a chambray shirt was sitting cross-legged in the bed of a log truck, leaning back on the cab, smoking a pipe.

Without standing, the man extended his hand. "Howdy. I'm Buster Dwyre. We met down at the café the other day. When we was all younger, your daddy and I dropped a many a tree together. I wanted to talk with you before you got away this morning."

"Sure Mr. Dwyre, I remember you." Gingerly, I climbed up on the truck bed and sat.

He shoved his felt hat back on his head and I saw the tan line stopped just above his eyebrows, like Daddy's had when I was a boy.

"Yesterday, I got a call from Cousin Ian. He said you and Vaughn Blackman had come up to see him. Said you was asking about your daddy and some things that had happened a long time ago. Hit got me to thinking. Since you was rattling old bones, I thought I'd give you another story."

"I'm listening."

"I helped your daddy when he was still working in the woods. I was about ten years younger than he was, but he damned near kilt me cross that saw. We lived in a little house tween Christian Springs and Cedergren. He'd stop by in the morning way fore daylight and pick me up. We'd pull that saw all day long, and he'd let me out at the house after dark."

"I remember putting in some long days with Daddy myself."

Dwyer spent some time emptying the bowl of his pipe and scraping the residue with his knife. "I remember hit was in July, when hit was daylight for a long time. We'd be in the woods from about half past five until half past eight and wouldn't even hardly stop for dinner or nothing. We got back to the house, your daddy stopped and let me out. I was so tarred I couldn't hardly drag my ass out of the truck. He pulled his watch out of his pocket looked at it and said, 'Well Buster, another day and not a damn thing done.' I went in the house and told Papa 'That old sumbitch didn't kill me today, but he's going to try again tomorrow.'"

Even with my headache, I couldn't help but laugh. "Tough, wasn't he?"

Dwyre grinned "Damned straight! Anyways, Ian told me about the talk ya'll had and I thought, by gosh, I've got a story he might like to hear. You may have heard it but nobody around today except me and your daddy seed hit."

"Sure, fire away."

"Your folks was a living at Christian Springs when your mama had her second baby. I believe hit was a boy baby. She was having trouble, and your daddy had sent for the doctor – old man named O.C. Evans. I heard that Dr. Evans told your daddy he had company for the night, and he'd try to get out sometime the next day. I was out in the front yard a splitting stove wood when I heard your daddy's old truck coming down the road, running wide open. I mean he had the ears on that old truck laid back. He came a sliding into my yard sideways and told me to get in. Said he was on his way to see the doctor about coming to see your mama. Said your mama was dying. Said if the doctor wouldn't come and see her right now, he was gonna to kill him."

"Going to kill him!"

"What he said. I started to ask your daddy why he wanted me to go with him, but then I changed my mind and just got in the truck. I ain't never had such a ride in my life; I'll bet hit didn't take us fifteen minutes to get down to Cedergren. Zeale didn't wait to turn in the doctor's driveway. Just run across the yard in his truck. He jumped out and run in the house, didn't knock or nothing."

"Were you scared?"

"Damn straight, I was," Dwyre said. "They was five or six men setting around the eating table, all of them wearing dress shirts and neckties. I remember the was candles and a white tablecloth. Zeale just run right up to the table where doc was eating. He hollered, 'Get in the truck.' Old Doc Evans just looked at him like he had no idea who your daddy was. Then your daddy hollered again, 'Get in the truck, damn ye. My wife is a dying and you're going to see her right now. Now, goddammit.' Doc looked at your daddy and said, 'Ah yes. You're that Roane feller. I told you I'd get out there tomorrow.'"

I could picture the scene. "Wrong thing to say, wasn't it?"

Dwyer loaded his pipe, tamping the tobacco with his stubby thumb. "Hell yeah. Your daddy had big old, rough hands, and he just backhanded the doc in the face. The doc fell backwards right in the middle of the eating table. The candles was turned over and the tablecloth caught on far. The other men was trying to get out of the way. None of them ever raised a hand to help the doc or nothing. Your daddy just reached down and got the doc by the collar and pretty much drug him out to the truck. Threw his ass in there like he was a sack of hog feed. I'm standing at the door watching, case the other men decided to come outside. But they just huddled up like chickens that had a fox after them, rat in a corner of that fancy dining room."

"What were you going to do if the men decided to help the doctor?"

"I don't know. Guess I'd busted them in the face. Anyways, your daddy cranked the truck and started out cross the yard. I seed a leather bag on the floor and thought hit to be the doc's. I grabbed hit and was just barely able to jump in the back of the truck before he hit the main road. Tell you one thing. Case I thought the ride down to the doc house was fast, hit didn't hold a candle to the ride back to Christian Springs. I hung on the best I could, but I rolled around in the bed of the truck like a empty beer can."

"Pretty bad, huh?"

"I'd seed fights in the logwoods, but this was the quickest ending I'd ever seed. We got back to Christian Springs and the doc kinda eased out of the truck, like a mouse looking for a cat. I climbed out of back of the truck and handed him his bag. Zeale shoved the doc toward the house, and the first thing I knew that old doc was a going at a full run with your daddy right in behind him. I don't know why, but when they went in the house, I followed them. There was several womenfolk in the house – mostly old women that had helped with a bunch of birthings. The only man was your mama's oldest brother, Frank. The women had done washed the baby and wrapped the pore little thing in a towel. They was pulling the sheet up over your mama's face."

"Mother was already … dead?"

Dwyer nodded. "Your Uncle Frank put his arms around your daddy and said, 'Hits done Zeale. She's gone.' Zeale dropped to his knees beside the bed and put his face against your mama. I'd heard a wildcat squall out before and hit would make the hair stand up on the back of your neck, but I'd never heard nobody make a noise like your daddy made. I guess it was a howl. I don't know how to describe it. Hit was the most sorrowful and scariest thing I ever heard. Hit tore me up pretty bad: I just went out in the front yard and started crying."

Tears were rolling down my cheeks. "I never knew what happened."

"I guess I'm the only person still alive 'sides your daddy that was there that night. The doctor was kinda backed up in a corner. One of the women went to him and took him out on the front porch. Frank come out and told me, 'Get the doctor out of here before Zeale comes around, cause ain't nothing in the world that could stop him from killing him.' I could still hear Zeale howling when I loaded that doc's ass in the truck. I brought him back to Cedergren. Sorry sumbitch was still a jerkin' when I let him out.

"Some of the big shots that was at the doc's house that night let on like a bunch of men from up on the mountain had busted in the house and kidnapped old Doc Evans. Said they fit them, but there was too many of them. Said they set the house a far and left. I told Ma and Papa what I'd seed and they kinda spread the truth.

"Nothing never come of it. I always thought your daddy would have killed the doc that night if hit had come into his head. I was afraid he might hunt him down later and kill him, but I guess he kinda come to his senses. This happened a long time ago, but the strangest thing – I can still hear your daddy howling and hit will still bring the hair up on the back of my neck to this very day."

"How long was it until you saw Daddy again?" I asked.

Dwyer took a kitchen match from under his hatband, struck it with his thumbnail, and held it over the bowl of his pipe. He took a pull from his pipe and blew the match out with a smoky puff. "It was probably three or four days atter they buried your mama. I'd just come in from milking about dark one evening when your daddy pulled up in the yard. He looked awful. Looked like he hadn't shaved in a week, and the ass of his britches was just about to drag the ground.

"He came up on the porch where Ma and Papa was setting and shelling whippoorwill peas. He said he wanted to apologize for getting me in the middle of that scrape, and hit wouldn't never happen again. Wanted to know if I was ready for the woods the next day, and I said yeah. In all the years we worked together, he never talked hit again. Your daddy is a fine man, but when he was younger he had the goddammest temper I ever seed. He changed some after your mama died and a whole lot more atter Miss Maggie's baby was born."

*****

The drive out to the Arn was not too bad as long as I didn't hit any bumps or make any sharp turns.

Daddy and Lock were sitting facing each other in two old lawn chairs. I could tell by Daddy's hand movements he was talking. Lock was listening, his head cocked to the side like a dog watching his master. I parked beside Old Pony and walked down to where they were sitting.

"Gosh," Daddy said. "Looks like you lost bad last night. You must a tried eating your own cooking." He laughed and looked at Lock. Lock stared at me.

"No, I ate at the café last night. Had a good steak. But it was the dessert in your office that did me in. Turkey too close to bedtime isn't good."

"Yep," Daddy said. "I learned that a long time ago. Usually doesn't take more than a couple of rounds until even the most stubborn man gets the general idea. Did you see Louellen last night?"

"Yeah, I did. How did you know?"

"Didn't. But knew it was about time for her to have the late shift. Not had an easy life, has she?"

"No," I said.

Daddy shoved his hat back on his head and looked at me. "Learn anything you didn't already know?"

"Yes. We talked about the woman she lives with."

"Kinda special, isn't she?"

I nodded. "Yeah, both of them are special. Talked with another of your old buddies this morning, Buster Dwyre. He told me some stuff I didn't know."

Daddy looked at me sharply. "Sometimes Buster has a hard time separating the truth from what he thinks he remembers. What kind of stuff did he tell you?"

I fought the tightening in my chest. "He told me about the night Mother died, and the problem you had with the doctor."

"Yeah, well, that was a long time ago. I'm a better man now, more civilized. I try not to think about that night anymore. It hurts too bad. What else?"

"I was thinking maybe you could come home tonight and sleep in your own bed for a change."

Daddy looked at Lock before answering. "What do you think, son? Think you can hold things down out here tonight by yourself?"

Lock nodded and his lips mouthed yes.

Daddy ruffled Lock's hair playfully, like you would a small boy's. "That's about what I figured. You're getting tired of me out here eating all your food, aren't you?"

Daddy started rolling up the tarpaulin he had used as a ground cover. "Tell you what. I'll go home and bring some minnows back with me tomorrow. We'll see if we can catch some crappie around the spillway. How does that sound? You want Rip to stay with you tonight?"

Lock rolled his cap bill. He studied the form of the bill, put the cap on his head, and adjusted it carefully until his eyes were hidden. He nodded again.

Daddy looked at me, shrugged, made an okay gesture, and started walking back up the hill toward Old Pony.

I asked Daddy if he thought Lock would be all right.

"If he says he'll be okay, he'll be okay."

I looked over my shoulder and checked a second time. "Did you notice he's not carrying the rock?"

Daddy nodded and held up his first two fingers in a "V" sign. "I'll take that as a good sign."

*****

I followed Daddy back home, him driving Old Pony and me in the jeep. He weaved from one side of his lane to the other and I wondered just how safe his driving was.

Shadows were creeping across the yard when we got home. Daddy swung his feet out of Old Pony, shoved his hat up on his forehead, and rested an arm on the open door. "It's good to get home. I'm going to fix me some cheese and crackers, drink me a cold beer, take a shower and a nap. If I wake up, we'll go and eat some catfish. I don't, I'll see you in the morning."

Daddy walked into the house, his steps were slow and short. He has finally gotten old, I thought. It was strange seeing his once-powerful frame deteriorating. He had always carried himself so upright, chest out, and chin back, "Like a soldier marching in a hurry," Camran had once said. Now his steps were slow and his head tilted forward as if he was searching the ground for obstructions. I didn't want to see him that way. I wondered how he saw himself. Did he recognize what had happened over the years, or did his stubborn mind still see himself as a man of forty?

I suppose I'll know when I reach his age.

I decided to spend more time in his office, perhaps looking for more photographs, or just looking at the books he had read over the years. The phone rang. I was happy to hear Luther's voice. "Creight, I thought I might catch you there. How have the past few days been for you – you about caught up on the Cedergren gossip?"

"Pretty much."

"You by yourself?"

"Yeah. Daddy's had a hard few days and nights. He's bushed. He's had a beer, and is going to take a nap. If he wakes up, we are going to eat some catfish. Why don't you go with us?

Luther laughed. "If he takes a nap after having a beer, you're not going to see him until daylight. I've got a couple of friends with me here at the house. Why don't we come over and spend some time with you?"

"I'll be here."

*****

Luther, along with two men I had never seen, walked into Daddy's office. I offered Wild Turkey and all three refused. "I hate to drink alone," I said as I poured two fingers into a glass. "But when forced, I will."

Luther made the introductions. "Creight, this is Wade Walker. He's on our legal staff in Charlotte." Walker and I shook hands. "This is Nelson McKelvy. He's with the DA's office in Knoxville, but he is here unofficially. Nelson and I roomed together at UT for a couple of years. Wade is not here representing Roman. He's here as a friend. So, let's just say he isn't here either. Understand?"

"Understood."

A car door slammed. Adam Huntsman, wearing running shoes and shorts came into the office. Luther introduced him to the others while dragging a bench in from the front porch. I took what was becoming my accustomed seat in Daddy's office chair. The two men seated themselves across from me, while Luther and Adam sat on the bench.

Luther opened the conversation. "We've got a problem that looks as if it may be coming to a head. Mr. Roane has put Sheriff Fox in a bad position. He has promised the sheriff for a number of months he would take care of the Lock problem, and as you know, that hasn't happened. Creight, after ya'll had the last run-in with the McCamys, they talked with someone on the district attorney's staff. Not Nelson, but some other assistant."

"What'd they say?"

"Well, they said a lot of stuff, some lies and some half-truths. They said Zeale had tried to kill them and a bunch of other garbage. But they also said they knew who had killed the two men and thrown their bodies off the bluff. They said they knew where he was and that they had almost caught him."

"Oh shit. They're really asking for it," I said.

"They also talked with someone at the TV station and the newspaper." Luther looked down, and then said, "So, you see we've got to do something before this thing blows sky high."

"What happens if we just deny any of this happened? Everyone knows the McCamys are nuts."

McKelvy spoke for the first time. "I'm sorry, but that's not an option. Our office has obligations. I believe within a week an investigation will get underway."

I turned to Roman's attorney. "Mr. Walker, any suggestions?"

"Legally, I don't. The young man hasn't been charged with anything at this point. From a practical standpoint, my suggestion would be get him out of there, maybe out of state, before any charges are filed."

I gave Walker a thumbs up. "Well, I can handle that; I've had experience in disappearing."

For the first time Adam spoke. "Won't work."

"Why not?" Luther and I asked together.

"A number of reasons," Adam said. "While Lock's mental condition is not my strong suit, occasionally I've treated him physically. Creight, he may have appeared relatively stable to you, but he's not. He is in a comfortable place now: he is familiar with his surroundings, and he interacts with Zeale. But he is, and I believe always will be, on the edge of the bubble. Prolonged trauma could cause him to fall into a depressed state from which he would never recover. Worst case scenario: he could kill himself and anyone around him."

"Could Daddy help us get him out."

Adam shook his head. "He won't."

"How do you know that?"

"I've talked with him, more than once," Adam said. "Zeale made it plain, very plain, that as long as he's alive Lock will not be disturbed. And then he said something very scary; he said 'Lock would be taken out of there over his dead body.'"

I studied the seriousness in Adam's face. "Maybe I can talk some sense into him, reason with him."

Luther said, "I've known your father longer than you have. I know when his mind can be changed about something. This isn't one of those times."

Adam nodded in agreement, "I've known your daddy a pretty good while, and I consider us good friends. I've discussed this situation with him. It's like talking to a stump. There's nothing would convince Zeale that Lock would be better off somewhere else."

"What about Maggie? Could she convince him that we've got to do something?"

Luther shook his head. "No. I'm sure …."

The screen door leading out onto the porch slammed closed. Daddy was standing in the doorway wearing his pajama bottoms. He looked at the men gathered in the room. He chewed on his bottom lip, then said, "Boys, this meeting was called without me being invited. But since I'm here, I've appointed myself chairman of the board, and as chairman, I am entitled to make a statement. As long as I am able to draw a breath, under no circumstances will I allow Lock to leave the Arn. Now, this meeting is adjourned. Good night, gentlemen."

The next morning I had breakfast on the table when Daddy came out of his room. It was kind of a peace offering. He poured his coffee and sat at the table across from me. "I laid in bed last night thinking about the meeting you fellers were having out in my office. At first, I thought I ought to apologize for my actions. Then I thought, Hell no! If an apology is due, it's due to me. Ya'll were dealing in my business and I wasn't even invited to the meeting."

I protested, "I didn't have anything to do with the meeting, it just …"

Dismissively, Daddy raised his hand and turned his face away from me. "I know, I know. I also know everybody last night had my best interest at heart. But my best interest is to see after Lock and, to see after Lock, you've got to know him. I'm the only person in this world who knows him. He's in the only environment where he can survive. Take him off the Arn, and you kill him. I don't care what your intentions are."

"But Daddy, it's possible doctors would be able to help him, get him straightened out and…"

"Ain't no straightening out. He is the way he is. The thing that you don't understand is, this has been a long, long downhill slide. You weren't around. You haven't seen the changes that have come over him the past few years."

"But…"

"Ain't no buts. He was the sweetest little boy you ever saw. Minded his mama, studied hard – just a great kid. He's got Maggie's smarts. College was no harder for him than first grade. You've seen his paintings and sculpture. God gives some folks talent, and Lock got more than his share. He was always a little bit standoffish."

Daddy went off into his own world.

"The first unusual thing I saw was when he was about ten. He was spending the summers with me and started asking questions about his daddy. Maggie and I had decided early on we would kinda dance around that question until he was old enough to understand. So I told him his daddy loved him and his mother very much, but something bad had happened and his father had died."

"Died! You told him his father died."

"Yeah. Died. What in the hell should I have told him? That you ran off, had a fit, and just ran off?"

"No. You could have told him that you ran me off, that you didn't see fit to treat me like a man."

"You weren't a man."

"I was. I might not have been but eighteen but I was a man."

Daddy looked down into his coffee cup. "Well, that's all behind us. Nothing either one of us can do anything about it now."

"Did you ever tell him any different? Does he still think his daddy is dead?"

"No. I don't know what he thinks about his daddy. We never talked about it again."

I slammed my mug down and coffee splashed on the oilcloth covering the table. "You know none of this is right, don't you?"

Daddy looked away. "It was a long time ago. What do you want me to say?"

"How about starting with, I'm sorry."

"I can say it. But it wouldn't change anything. You weren't here and I wasn't going to make up some long tale."

I recognized a lost battle when I saw one. "Go on telling me about Lock."

Daddy took a deep breath and continued. "Lock had always had an interest in your canoe, so I took it down to the shop and one of our sheet-metal men patched it up. I'd take Lock out to Hematite Lake and he'd paddle the canoe around, 'Practicing to run the Henderson Brothers,' he would say. He found an old baseball cap of yours and he wore it all the time, pulled down like you always wore yours. He loved to spend time playing around the stone fort, and he'd bug me to tell about the moon-eyes and the Indians.

"We'd taken a picnic out to the fort in the late summer. We were standing looking off over the edge of the bluff when Lock looked at me and said, 'Papa Zeale, I've got something to tell you, if you promise to not be mad.' I promised. Then Lock said, 'I can see yesterday.' You know how much imagination kids have, so I kinda went along with it and said something like, 'that's unusual, but it's okay.'

"Nothing else was said about it, and things just kinda rocked along. That fall we'd come back out to the Arn bird hunting. I figured Lock was big enough to handle your little 20-gauge. Maggie had fixed us some sandwiches, and we're sitting on the fort wall, eating. Lock said, 'Papa Zeale, don't you want to know what I saw?' It took me a minute to remember what he was talking about. It was just like we were continuing our earlier conversation."

"You mean about seeing yesterday?"

Daddy nodded his head. "Yeah. So I asked him, 'What did you see?' Lock said, 'I saw my daddy. He was running Last Chance.' I tried to not show surprise. I said 'You did?' I thought I'd just go along with it, like we were playing. I said 'What did your Daddy look like?' Lock said, 'I can't really tell you because his cap bill was pulled down over his eyes. He was wearing a red St. Louis Cardinal T shirt and it was wet.' I swear to God, Creight, chill bumps the size of marbles rose up the back of my neck because you were wearing a shirt like that when you and Maggie came into Dove Landing."

"He must have seen a picture. There were some newspaper folks around that day."

Daddy's eyes were wet, "No, I checked. I couldn't find any pictures that had been taken that day. Turned out later Maggie had a paper with a picture in it like that, but it wasn't in color and she said Lock had never seen it."

"So, how do you explain it?"

Daddy was wiping water from the corners of his eyes. "I can't. I talked to Maggie about it. She said Lock had never said things like that to her."

"This ever happen again?"

"It would kinda come and go. Maybe he was twelve or thirteen when he stopped telling me things he saw that had happened in the past. Sometimes I would bring it up just to see if he'd talk about it again, but he would always change the subject.

"He finished up down at Baylor and in the summer enrolled at UT. He just whizzed through. Maggie had suggested a couple of schools in New York and Philadelphia for him to get his masters. I forget which one he went to first. I think it was Columbia. But when he got his masters, he just swung into getting his doctorate at the University of Chicago."

"Pretty swanky schools."

Daddy just nodded. "Anyway, he always lived with me in the summer, and we spent a lot of time camping out at the Arn. He loved the outdoors, and I loved being with him. He was always painting. When he would get tired of that, he would do sculpturing. He painted a lot of pictures of the river, did some wildlife stuff, painted a lot of fish and bugs, stuff Maggie encouraged him to paint."

"I wouldn't have thought there a market for paintings of bugs and fishes?"

"Yeah, some folks really got hung up on those pictures. You hardly ever see a painting of a water bug that is six feet high, but he started getting commissions for that kind of thing. Some of the paintings brought fifteen grand or more. The money really didn't mean nothing to him. He would just give it away to some foundation that took his fancy. Folks who bought his paintings wanted him to come and make talks, but that turned him off. He was starting to withdraw from talking with people."

"And this was something new?"

"A little. Seemed like any time folks started showing an interest in what he was doing, he'd want to quit."

"Did Maggie encourage him in his work?"

"Yeah. Looked like the more she encouraged, the more determined he was to not paint. Same thing with his sculpturing. He'd have something almost finished, then he'd take a hammer and break it into little pieces.

"After a while, he got hung up doing Indian stuff. He worked a lot with different kinds of metal and then started working with gold only."

"Where'd the gold come from?"

"I wouldn't ask him," Daddy said. "But I knew he was getting coins out at the fort and melting them down for his work. He never sold any of the gold work. He would just show it to Maggie or me, then he'd melt it down and start something new.

"You said he was starting to withdraw from people. Do you mean everybody?"

Daddy nodded. "Pretty much. He and Maggie had started getting crossways. Especially when she pushed him to finish a painting or sculpture. He finally just quit talking to Maggie altogether. Wouldn't even act like he could see her. He'd still talk with Andy every once and a while but not always."

"But he'd still talk with you?"

Daddy nodded again. "Yeah, things never really changed between us. Some days when he was in one of his low spells, he'd hide from me. If I couldn't find him, I'd go down and ring that big bell at the furnace. Sometimes he'd come and sometimes he wouldn't. Sometimes I'd know he was hiding in the bushes watching me, and I'd take that little penny whistle and blow *Amazing Grace*. Most of the times when I did he'd play *Amazing Grace* back to me. If he didn't show himself pretty soon after I heard that song, I'd know he was all right but just didn't want anybody around."

"What kind of things would ya'll talk about?"

"In the beginning, pretty standard kinda stuff. Politics, sports, what was happening in the world, maybe a little bit of religion. Then he started talking again about being able to see what had happened in the past. Then it was just more and more. Like he was living a long time ago. He said he could see the battle that had taken place at the fort. He would draw pictures showing how the Indians had overrun the fort."

"So, he figured it was the moon-eyes got attacked?"

"Yeah, that was his version. He'd tell me about how the moon-eyes had hidden their gold and their babies in the little cave, how the moon-eyed women screamed while the Indians were scalping them, and how they threw their older children off the cliff before the Indians got to them."

I was trying to get into Lock's head and follow his line of thinking. "Why did he decide on this version?"

"I don't know. Somehow, it fit in with the little bones he and Andy found. Sometimes that kind of talk would go on for a week, then Lock would come back to the present. Part of the time, I could convince him to stay away from the fort, and it would look like he was going to be all right. Then I wouldn't be able to find him for a couple of days, and when I did, he'd be sitting on one of those big stone circles at the fort, crying, his hands over his ears, rocking back and forth. It was scary as the devil."

"You never tried to get help for him again?"

Daddy sighed. "No. We decided that one more round with the doctors and the outside world would make him worse or kill him. The only trouble has been when those two goofs got in here and started poking around. I'm sorry it happened, but it wasn't all Lock's fault. I'd like to think it happened only because they were around the fort, but I'm not sure. Maybe it would have happened if Lock had found them anywhere on the Arn.

"I think he may've reached the point where he believes everybody threatens him. As long as I'm alive, Lock's not going to come out of the Arn. I'd take his life myself before I'd allow him to be caged up somewhere like a mad dog. You understand what I'm saying?"

"You wouldn't take his life. You're not serious?"

Daddy walked to the sink and emptied his coffee. He had not even touched his breakfast. He took his canvas coat from the hook where it always hung, and folded it over his arm, "As serious as a heart attack," he said and walked out.

*****

I called Adam's office and was told he was with a patient, but she'd tell him I called. Ten minutes later, the phone rang. "Sorry about last night," Adam said. "We should've included Zeale from the beginning, but that's water under the bridge."

I told him about the conversation at the kitchen table that morning. He listened without comment until I asked if he thought Daddy was serious with his threat to kill Lock.

Adam said, "I've known Zeale for a long time. Maggie's effort with other doctors was a last resort. You know how that turned out. I believe your daddy's assessment of Lock and how he would respond to being in the outside world is correct. I'm not sure how dangerous he might be to others but Zeale knows him better than anyone else does, and I guess I'd have to agree with him. As to whether he would take Lock's life, I hope that's a bridge we never have to cross. But if I had to make a bet, I'd say he would."

*****

Sheriff Roy Ruby Fox was on his knees in front of a metal filing cabinet with manila folders scattered on the floor around him. He looked up and said, "Hell, I can't ever find anything. I've got to the point to where I can't even remember my ABCs half the time. I'm telling you, Creight, everything they tell you about getting old is the truth, except it's worse." He grabbed the desk and pulled himself up. "Shit! Listen to them knees," he said. "Sounds like somebody grinding rocks."

"You mean I've got bad stuff waiting for me when I get your age?"

Sheriff Fox relit his cold cigar and said, "You don't even want to know."

I sat on an old wooden chair across from the sheriff's desk. "We had a little meeting out at the house last night."

The sheriff nodded and blew a stream of blue smoke toward the ceiling. "What I heard. Heard it ended kinda quick."

"You heard right. Daddy adjourned a meeting where he wasn't even invited."

The sheriff took another draw on his cigar and held the smoke in his lungs. I watched it lazily escape his nostrils, "Yep, Zeale don't take kindly to folks making his decisions for him. Never did."

I smiled. "No, I reckon he's not developed that habit yet. Since you know about the meeting, I assume you know what the discussion was about?"

"Oh yeah. I may be old, but that don't mean I'm stupid. You boys think because you've got high-powered Roman lawyers and assistant DAs at your meeting you're on top of everything. Hell, Zeale and I know fellers way up the ladder, way higher than them. And we ain't no stranger to what's coming down the road. We know, in this day and time, we can't deal with outsiders the way we used to. Damn folks just need to stay out of here and let us look after things in our own way."

"Sheriff, I'm not being disrespectful, but what is your and Daddy's own way?"

The sheriff ground out his cigar in the overflowing ashtray on the corner of the desk, got out of his chair and opened the door. He made a sweeping motion with his hand. "When we decide, you'll be the first to know, I promise."

*****

Roman electricians had installed a keypad that triggered the gate opening mechanism for the Arn's gate. I punched the numbers and the gate opened. On the way toward Hematite Lake, I ran the last sequence of events through my mind. No matter how I tried to analyze things, I was no closer to a solution than in the beginning. The attorney's suggestions, along with those of Luther and Adam, all ran into the stonewall of Daddy and Sheriff Fox. Apparently, Maggie's influence with Lock was nonexistent, and I had no relationship with him. Even if I could establish a rapport with him, time was running out.

I passed grazing buffalo and wild turkeys dusting themselves beside the road. What a wonderful, peaceful place. No wonder the Roanes settled here and never sold any of this plateau. I wished I could see yesterday like Lock could. I wondered about those early William Roanes, if they'd traveled the very same road, and if they'd have allowed their son taken out of here against their will.

I turned left off the road and drove down to the lake. Old Pony was not parked in the accustomed place and neither Daddy nor Lock was around. I ran my fingers through the campfire ashes. They were cool. However, Daddy's canvas coat was hanging over his lawn chair so I knew he had probably been here earlier today. I felt in the jacket pockets, suddenly worried I might find his pistol. Then I was even more worried when I didn't find it. I did find a timber-tally notebook, a pencil stub, and the battered penny whistle.

I looked out over the lake and didn't see anyone. I walked to the edge of the clearing and called Daddy, then Lock. Neither answered. Back at the camp, I pulled the lever on the big bell several times and listened as the deep tones mournfully rolled out over the plateau.

From the edge of the woods came a few halting notes of *Amazing Grace*. I took the penny whistle from Daddy's coat pocket and answered. A long silence, then from the woods a few more notes. This time more recognizable and definitely *Amazing Grace*. I sat in Daddy's chair and after a couple of minutes, I knew Lock was standing behind me. Without turning, I patted the seat of Lock's chair, "Would you like to sit down here beside me?"

Timidly, he moved to my left and sat on the edge of his chair. He stared at me, his head cocked to one side. He was wearing only blue jeans and a baseball cap. His body had almost no fat and he was sinewy, the build of an acrobat. He could have scaled the escarpment with no problem, I thought.

I nodded slightly. He nodded shyly.

For minutes, we sat in silence. A flock of wild geese, early scouts of the coming fall, came in low, cupped their wings and splashed down in the lake not fifty yards from us. I looked at Lock for some reaction. He made a gliding, curving motion with his hand – fingers pressed together with his little finger and thumb extended to the side. I made a similar motion with my hand, except I deliberately kept my fingers and thumb against my hand. Lock shook his head, showed me the back of his hand, and spread his little finger and thumb outward. He looked at me and raised his eyebrows slightly as if to say, "Do you understand?"

I made a hand motion again but this time similar to the one Lock made. He nodded in approval. I touched my chest with my hand and said, "My name is Creight." Lock nodded. I pointed at him and said, "Your name is Lock." He nodded.

I took Daddy's penny whistle and played a few notes of *Dixie*. Lock turned his chair toward me and stared intently at my fingers as they moved up and down the whistle. He took his whistle, put it to his lips and blew the first notes. Abruptly, he lay his whistle down on the ground, but he continued to stare at my hands.

He looked down at his hands, spread his fingers, and studied them intently. He motioned for me to spread my fingers. He extended one hand, palm facing me, fingers spread. I did the same. Our hands were inches apart but he made no effort to touch mine.

Behind me, I heard Old Pony as it came rattling down the hill toward our camp. Daddy got out and trudged down the hill on arthritic knees. Rip came running toward us. I stood so Daddy could have his chair. Rip and Lock were soon on the ground wrestling.

Daddy sat back in his chair and extended his legs. "I couldn't find him earlier this morning. I hollered a few times and Rip did a lot of sniffing around, but neither one of us could come up with anything. Figured he might've gone out to the fort, but when we couldn't find him I thought I'd just come back here and wait for him to show up. You been here long?"

"About an hour."

"Looked like you two were getting ready to play patty-cake."

"No, I don't think so. I was trying to teach him *Dixie,* but he kinda ran out of interest. Can't say as I blame him; I'm probably not much of a teacher."

Rip wandered down to the edge of the lake to get a drink, and Lock sat crossed-legged on the ground. With his fingers spread, he raised his hand in front of Daddy. Daddy raised his hand and their palms met. Lock studied them and then shook his head. He moved over in front of me and again raised his hand with the fingers extended. Lock studied them closely and then inched slowly forward until our palms touched. He nodded and then quickly jerked his hand away.

"He sees the difference," Daddy said. "I think he knows his fingers are more like yours than mine. That's pretty good. More reasoning than I seen from him in a long time. And he touched you. I'll bet other than Andy touching him the other night when he was sewing him up, you're the first person he has touched in three years, except me. I'd say some headway is definitely being made. You should feel pretty honored."

Lock had taken Daddy's canvas coat and spread it on the ground in the shade. He wrapped the coat around his head and curled up in a fetal position.

I leaned forward and put my face in my hands, wanting to hide the tears forming in my eyes. "Pretty honored," I said. "Pretty honored that for the first time I've touched my thirty year-old son. How did things get this screwed up?"

Daddy cleared his throat. "Look at it this way. It could've been worse. You could've never come home, never known him."

"But I missed his good years. I screwed up something awful, Daddy. Something awful. How come? How come?"

"I think it's in our genes. Our side of the family was always flying off the handle and doing dumb things. Daddy did it, I've done it, and I guess it was passed down to you. Maggie's daddy wasn't a saint. He had a bad streak in him.

"Maybe it was all passed down to Lock. Stuff always runs down hill. Maybe it happened because of the way Lock was born. Who knows? I believe it was just a law of nature. All of those genes got mixed up when they came together and something just got twisted - that's just the way it turned out

I waited for Daddy to continue and when he didn't, I asked, "That's your best explanation?"

"Yeah. At this stage in my life, I'm past solving mysteries. I'm just happy with small things: little victories like fishing with Lock, two or three fingers of Turkey at the end of the day, a good night's sleep, a steak with a twice baked, spending time getting reacquainted with you. Heck, I even enjoy a good pee."

I nodded in agreement. "I'm a lot younger than you are and I enjoy some of those same things."

"Money doesn't mean anything anymore. Roman has got so big I don't even recognize it. When more road is behind you than in front of you, it changes your whole outlook on life. You'll know what I'm saying someday. Age doesn't always bring wisdom. Some of the dumbest folks I've ever known were old. But age does bring understanding and acceptance. And that's where I am. I'm playing the hand I've been dealt." Daddy laughed and then added, "Maybe I've got three aces, and I'm just waiting for the fourth. If it's to be, I'll get it."

"And if you don't?" I asked.

Daddy smiled but I knew it was a forced smile. "I'll try to bluff my way though with what I've got. And if that don't work, it just wasn't in the cards. You understand what I'm telling you?"

"I think I do. The hand you are playing might not be as strong as you make out, and you're just waiting for the last card, hoping it makes your hand stronger?"

Daddy took his fly rod from Old Pony. "See you at the house sometime after supper."

"But you're gambling with folks' lives, not cards. What if the last card doesn't help your hand? What'll you do then?"

Daddy was tying a fly on the end of the leader and didn't look up, "Then I might pass to you and see how you play your hand."

Partner's Café was busy. I sat on a stool at the counter and Louellen, cheerful as always, slid a glass of water over to me. "I guess you want a big old steak and a twice baked tater like you and your daddy always get?"

I laughed. "You're a mind reader."

She gave me one of her smiles. "No," she said, "I just know the both of you."

"Not much going on in my head tonight. It's pretty blank."

She smiled again. "Then you get a piece of apple pie tonight, and it'll be on the house. That'll be something for you to think about."

Today's *Knoxville News Sentinel* was stuck between the cash register and the counter. Nothing very exciting on the front page. TVA said something about the lack of rain was making the cost of electricity higher. Folks in Vermont were developing some kind of program where they could adopt a cow and for a hundred and forty dollars send it to South Carolina farmers. Daddy will get a kick out of that, I thought. I could hear him snort. Adopt a cow? Good Lord. What is this world coming to?

The local news section was more interesting. At the bottom of the front page was an aerial photo of the Arn and a caption that read, "Does a Killer Roam these Mountains?" The reporter summarized the two recent deaths at the Arn. He followed with an interview with Iliad McCamy who gave glowing details about how he and his brother had cornered the "alleged killer" – a raving lunatic with hair and beard down to his waist who lived in the trees like some kind of ape. They'd almost captured him when several men intervened. According to McCamy, there'd been a fierce gun battle and they had barely escaped with their lives. McCamy went on to say "the killer" was kin to Breazeale Roane. They described him as the most prominent man in all of the mountains, and said he had protected "the killer" for years. The story ended with the brothers vowing to capture the lunatic before he could escape and kill other innocent people.

Louellen returned with my meal. "You okay? You look like you might be going to throw up."

"Thanks for the compliment. I'm just not hungry."

When she went back to the kitchen to pick up an order, I left a ten on the counter beside my untouched steak.

I was climbing into the jeep when Sheriff Fox's cruiser pulled into the adjacent space. The sheriff stepped out of his cruiser and said, "Evening, Creight."

"Evening, sheriff."

He had a chew of tobacco lodged in the back of his jaw and was firing up the cigar stub clenched between his teeth. He inhaled, and then spit a smoking stream of tobacco onto the pavement. "I've left word a couple of times for Zeale to stop by the office and see me, but he ain't seen fitting to do it. Tell him two fellers with the Tennessee Bureau of Investigation paid me a visit today. Tell him this thing ain't going to go away this time. Tell him I'm running out of excuses and he's running out of time. Tell him these old boys got muscle, and they are going to take over the investigation. I've done everything I could do for him and Lock, but I'm running out of 'could do' pretty quick."

Sheriff Fox reached back in his cruiser and pulled out the same edition of the *News Sentinel* I had read in the café. He flipped it into the jeep. "Here, take this to Zeale. He might want to catch up on what's going on out in the real world."

*****

I sat behind Daddy's desk for an hour, listening to my stomach rumble and trying to find a way out of this mess. I called Adam's home and got only the answering machine. In Atlanta, Vaughn's maid told me he was fishing somewhere down in the Gulf.

I searched my billfold and found the paper where I had written important numbers. I dialed Mr. Bishop's number and got a recording saying the number had been disconnected. It had been years since we had talked, and now I wondered if he might have died.

I dialed information in Atlanta and asked for the number of Dr. Joshua Bishop. The operator asked if I needed the business number or the residential number. I thought any son of Ken Bishop, even if he were a doctor, would have his residence listed. After the second ring, a man's voice answered, "This is Josh Bishop".

"Josh," I said, "this is Bill Creighton. How are you getting along?"

It took fifteen minutes for him to update me. He had two children. His wife had gone back to school. They were involved in church work and mission trips to Guyana, all of the things I'd have expected from him. Yes, his father was in fair health, and so was his mother. They had moved to a condo recently but still lived in Key West. The family got together every couple of months. His father was teaching the children to fish. His mother spoiled them rotten. He gave me his father's phone number and said how glad he was to talk with me again.

I tried to gather my thoughts. I couldn't decide if I was looking for an answer, looking for sympathy, or just looking for a way out.

"Hello," the old man's voice was rough and ragged.

"Mr. Bishop, this is Bill Creighton," I said.

"Who?"

I smiled, picturing my old friend sitting on a balcony watching the sun set over the Keys. "Creight. The feller that followed you around like a puppy."

"Well, I'll be damned, Creight. How are you doing, boy?"

Reminiscing takes a long time when two good friends are conducting it over the phone. Mr. Bishop told me again everything that had happened since I had watched him and Margaret leave my life in Alaska. Then he went back to the first time we met and covered those years between Memphis and Alaska. My part of the conversation consisted mainly of grunts and an occasional, "Yes." Finally, Mr. Bishop said, "You're back in the mountains of east Tennessee, aren't you?"

"How did you know?"

"Because I know you, and I knew you'd do what was right. All the years we worked together, I knew home was calling. Even when you didn't know, I did. It's a call that's strong, isn't it Creight?"

"Yes sir, Mr. Bishop, you're right. Just like you always were."

He chuckled. "Most of the times but not always. Tell me how you're getting along."

And I did. It probably took me longer to cover my few days at home than it did Mr. Bishop to cover the past years of his life. He listened without comment as I poured out all of my misery, sorrow, and frustration.

Finally, he said, "Are you looking for some advice from an old man?"

"Yes sir."

He didn't hesitate a heartbeat. "Get him out. If you can't do it tonight, do it tomorrow, and if you can't do it tomorrow, then do it the next day. You were damn good at hiding. You hid for thirty years so you know how. Just do it! Take that boy and get the hell out. Don't ever look back and don't ever second-guess yourself."

We had reached the point of saying goodbye when Mr. Bishop asked, "Did I tell you about my grandchildren?"

"No sir, but please do."

"Cutest little fellers you ever saw." Mr. Bishop's voice fairly glowed. "I'm teaching them how to fish. They think I'm a pretty good granddaddy. Josh's wife, Kate, even named the first one after me, made me awfully proud. When the second one came along, the little feller came Cesarean. They knew it would be their last baby, and Kate told Josh it was his turn to do the naming."

I said, "Turn about is fair play. Knowing Josh, I bet the second boy was named after Kate's daddy.

"No, they call him Billy," Mr. Bishop said. "Ever since they started dating, Josh had told Kate about this feller that had saved his and Margaret's life. She knew Josh loved this man like a brother, so she was not surprised when he chose to name this last child, William Creighton Bishop."

*****

It was just after eight o'clock, time for one other phone call. There was a long silence after I dialed and the phone rang twice before the answer came. "Aleutian Air, this is Carol."

I stifled a laugh. Mice playing when the cat was away. "Carol, let me speak with Jamiesie."

She responded, "Just a moment while I see if Mr. Cotterill is in his office."

Jamiesie answered immediately. His voice deep and very authoritative. "This is Jim Cotterill."

"No shit! When did you change your name to Jim? And just how far away from where Carol is sitting is your office? As I recall the layout of that hovel, it's less than two feet."

"Hillbilly," Jamiesie shouted. "Don't tell anybody but we're just trying to upgrade our image. Becoming more competitive with the big boys, you know."

"Made any upgrades other than Carol?"

"No, that's about it. But we've washed the windows and fixed the front door. Creight, I hate to bring this up, but I could damn well use some help around here. I'm good but I can't fly two planes at one time. Some of your charters are calling, wanting to confirm trips. What am I supposed to do? You want me to tell them, you are vacationing in the mountains and ain't sure when you're going to be back?"

"I'll be back soon as I can get back. I can't tell you the exact day, but it will be soon. Okay?"

Jamiesie waited before mumbling, "Okay."

"I need some help on something."

"I'll do whatever I can. You know that."

I described the physical characteristics of the Arn, the escarpment, and how the Findhorn River wrapped around it. I told him about Lock and his mental problems. I explained the impending investigation and my urgency to do something. Then I asked, "If this were your problem, how would you try to get Lock off the escarpment and out of the country?"

Jamiesie's answer came back quickly. "Why not just take him by road?"

"I'm afraid that's too risky. The McCamy clan is pretty large, and usually some of them are on the roads around the Arn. I'm afraid if there was any kind of confrontation, Lock might … I don't know what he might do."

"It would take me a little while, but I can bring the float plane down and land somewhere on the river or even in that little lake. We could take him out that way."

"Won't work, Jamiesie. It would take way too long for you to get here and even if we had the time, there would be the problem of landing once we got Lock out. Transferring to another plane from a water landing could be a real problem. It would involve too many people and could get confusing to Lock."

"Tell you what. An old boy I was in the Army with has a helicopter service somewhere in West Virginia, think it is around Charleston. I believe he hauls coal-mining big shots. I could probably get him in there, but it'll take me a while to find him. How does that sound?"

"Pretty big commotion for us mountain folks. Big chopper coming in here.

"Not that big. He'd come down the river under the top of the hills, pop up over the edge of the rim, load, drop back off the edge, and skim the river getting out. He's done the same stuff, except facing automatic weapons fire. It'd be a snap for him, I guarantee it."

"You think you can find him?"

"Yep," Jamiesie said. "Give me a little time. It'll be pretty expensive though. Somewhere in the neighborhood of nine hundred per hour with the clock running from the time he leaves West Virginia until he gets back to his base."

"Jamiesie, we're talking about my son. Money don't mean squat."

"I'll be back with you as soon as I can. Where can I reach you?"

I gave him the number. "I'll be waiting for your call. I appreciate your help. I'll make it up to you, I promise."

"I know you will. Soon as you get back, me and Carol just might take a long trip up north. Build snowmen and stuff like that." He was still laughing as we hung up.

*****

The last of the Wild Turkey went down in two swallows.

So this is how it would be played out. I've got to convince Daddy to let me take Lock off the Arn. Maybe after I tell him about my conversation with Roy Ruby, the convincing will be easier. But the hardest part may be getting Lock in the helicopter because I have no idea how he might react. What happens if he freaks out and just takes off out through the woods?

I closed the office door and started for the house. A beat-up truck rounded the curve in the gravel road and roared through the front yard between the mailbox and the house, its tires spinning wildly, and then disappeared down the road in a cloud of blue exhaust. I couldn't see the driver's face but even in the twilight, I could make out the lettering on the door of the truck: McCamy Plumbing.

"Bastards." I mumbled to myself.

Without turning down the covers or undressing, I stretched out on the bed. My mind tried to formulate our escape. We'd take the chopper down to Knoxville and Luther would arrange for the jet to Alaska. Jamiesie could take some provisions up to our cabin on Hermit's Creek, where we'd have some time for Lock to become acclimated before hard winter set in. It would be a real change in my life but maybe Lock would get better. Maybe a time would come when he'd be able to stay by himself, but, if he couldn't, we'd cross that bridge when we came to it. We'd make it somehow. Our last card would be that fourth ace. I was betting on the luck of the draw.

Lock sat at the edge of the stone fort, dressed in a suit and open-collared shirt, his packed bag at his feet. The wind was whipping the snow around us and it was drifting around the huskies as they lay asleep beside the sled. The helicopter was dropping down out of the clouds but was still hidden by the driving snow. Lock was now standing, a large smile on his face, waving his arms back and forth to draw the attention of the helicopter pilot. Daddy, Louellen and Roy Ruby Fox were sitting on café stools behind Lock. Each had a plate containing a twice-baked potato. The chopper was now plainly visible, and I was horrified to see that it was a pickup truck and Iliad McCamy was leaning out of the open door, fist shaking and cursing.

"Dang, Creight. Wake up. What in the heck are you doing in bed with your clothes on? No wonder you're thrashing around and hollering." Daddy was standing in the darkness at the foot of my bed. "I got heartburn something awful and I can't find my Tums. You got any?"

It took me a couple of seconds to come around, and I was relieved not to hear the helicopter engine and feel blowing snow. "They're in the medicine cabinet over the sink. They may be old but they will beat nothing."

Daddy flipped on the bathroom light and rummaged around in the cabinet before finding the Tums. "Take them with you," I said. "I'll get more tomorrow. What time is it?"

"A little after two. Lock and I got to looking at the stars, and I think we saw Haley's Comet. Time kinda got away from me. Then Roy Ruby pulled me over. Had those damned blue lights flashing like I was some kinda outlaw."

I didn't want to ask but I had to know, "Did he tell you about those fellers from the TBI?"

Daddy turned out the light and from the stairs grumbled, "Yeah."

*****

Daylight. I smelled coffee. Daddy was sitting at the kitchen table drinking coffee and reading yesterday's paper. He looked up as I came into the kitchen, folded his paper, and shoved his reading glasses up on his forehead. "What a bunch of crap." he said. "Makes me wish I had shot both of them and buried them out in the buffalo pasture. Damn fools. That tribe has always been damn fools. If there was ever a good argument for abortion, it's the McCamys."

I was trying to think of the best way to approach Daddy about my plan to take Lock back to Alaska. I had poured a cup of coffee and stood at the window, watching Rip sniffing at a butterfly in the grass near the mailbox. "Daddy, what would you think if ..." I didn't get to finish my sentence, but instead watched a pickup truck veer off the road, and almost exactly follow the tracks from last night across the front yard.

Rip never saw the truck that hit him.

Daddy stood up from the table. "What in the heck was that?"

Rip was laying in the grass, his neck at a strange angle. He was bleeding from his mouth and ears. Daddy dropped to his knees beside him. Rip tried to stand. His back legs collapsed and, if Daddy hadn't caught him, the dog would have fallen.

He pulled Rip close to his chest. Blood continued to run from Rip's mouth. He tried to lick Daddy's hand but lacked the coordination. Tears were running out of Daddy's eyes as he looked up at me, "Get my pistol. It's under the front seat of Old Pony."

I came back with the pistol and watched Daddy, his face distorted in agony, lovingly stroke the top of Rip's head. Then he stood up and turned away from the dog, "Shoot him."

I was stunned. "No, let's take him down to the vet."

Daddy shook his head, "He's all busted up inside, and his neck is broke. A vet can't help him. Put him out of his misery, Creighton."

I held the pistol. It was still in its leather holster. My hand was shaking violently, "I can't. I can't shoot him."

Daddy snatched the pistol from my hand. "Creighton, I've never asked a whole lot from you and, goddammit, when I do, this is what I get." The magnum roared. Rip twitched once and then lay still. Without a word, Daddy jammed the pistol back into its holster, went into the house, and came back with his canvas coat. He wrapped it around Rip, stood with a great effort, and staggered across the yard carrying Rip's body. I hurried ahead of him and started to open the tailgate. Daddy said, "No, open the passenger door; this time Rip is riding in the front seat with me – where he belongs."

*****

I stood in the shower for a long time, letting the warm water run over my body, praying it would wash away the shame that covered me like some kind of green slime. Why didn't I help Daddy and put Rip out of his misery? Such a simple thing. Why did I force an old man to kill his own dog? What was wrong with me? Why couldn't I step up just one time?

After brushing my teeth, I stared at the face in the mirror searching the eyes staring back at me for some weakness. Maybe I needed to see behind the eyes, back into the mind, or maybe into the heart. Maybe that's where the weakness lived - in the heart.

Blood had dried on the grass where Rip died. I took the hose and washed the blood out into the side ditch. I wished I could clean my soul as easily.

I knew Daddy would be at the Arn burying Rip on the edge of the family cemetery. In his hurry to leave or maybe in his anger, he had left his pistol on the porch. I picked it up and shoved it under the front seat of the jeep.

*****

The preacher, David Moody, was on his knees in front of his house pulling grass out of a patch of ivy. He stood, pressed both hands into the small of his back, and then waved.

"Good to see you, Brother Moody," I said.

"Glad you stopped," he said. "Your daddy came by about half an hour ago. I waved but he didn't slow down. In fact, didn't even look up. Kinda strange for him because he usually stops to chew the fat."

I told the preacher about Rip and how it upset Daddy. In the back of my mind, I was thinking about how confession is supposed to be good for the soul.

The preacher removed his gloves. "Oh, I'm so sorry to hear that. I know how much Rip meant to your daddy. They were always together. You know Rip was almost fifteen years old. I gave him to Zeale. Somebody had dumped a sack of puppies down by the creek. I brought them home. All but one died within a couple of days. Your daddy had been fishing. He stopped by to leave me a mess of bass. He saw the pup and said 'Preacher, you don't have any need for a pup like that. Why don't you give it to me?' So that's how Rip and your daddy hooked up."

"I didn't know that. I figured Daddy bought him somewhere."

"This swing suit you?" the preacher asked, motioning to an old wooden swing suspended from a mountain oak limb.

"Brother Moody, I've decided I must be short on something."

The preacher looked at me, his face troubled. "How did you reach that decision?"

"I'm not sure I can put my finger on it. I make bad choices but that's not all. I always make them when Daddy is involved."

Moody smiled. "Looks like to me you've made Zeale pretty happy."

"I can't put my finger exactly on when it started. I guess I was a teenager. I could never do enough to suit him. I'd bust my butt in the logwoods, do as much work as any grown man on the crew. He never seemed to notice. It was like it was expected of me, and I was just doing what I was supposed to do."

Brother Moody looked down at his hands. "You think you're the first son who thought that?"

"Maybe not, but it is hard for me to understand. I made good grades in high school, on the honor roll some of the time, but never got a 'Good job.' Nothing like that. Ever. Most of the boys my age drove too fast, got in car wrecks, fistfights, drank beer, always tried to lay around with some girl out of a moonshine family. I never did any of that."

"Did what you were supposed do, sounds like."

"I tried. Maybe I could've tried harder."

Maybe it was from the stress of the day or maybe it was because I was sitting there with this kind man, but for the first time in my life, I let it out.

"I'd always tried to hold my resentment, tried to not let my disappointment show. I'm sure you've probably heard about the mess on the river, when everybody thought there'd been a big accident. Lot of confusion. Right in front of a lot of people, he really let me have it with both barrels. He said some things I didn't think I deserved. I didn't even try to defend myself. I didn't know how. I just pulled my tail between my legs. I left and … well, you know the rest of the story."

The preacher nodded.

"We've had some edgy times since I've come back, and I've tried to let it slide. Sometimes it's like he still thinks I'm a kid. When Rip was dying today, Daddy asked me to put the poor thing out of his misery. I couldn't do it. He had to shoot him, shoot his own dog. He got awful mad and said something about me always letting him down. You saw him when he came past here, and I'll bet if you could have seen him up close, you would have seen smoke coming out of his ears."

"You may be right but if I was a betting man, I'd bet I would seen tears running down his cheeks. I can't defend his actions. I'm just a listener, and a lot of the time it's best if I forget what I've heard, but sometimes I can't forget. I've been here longer than I like to think. I probably know more about most folks than I should. Some of it good and some of it bad."

"I'm not sure I'm following you."

He looked at me intently. "You will. Just listen. You hadn't been gone too long when we moved to Cedergren. It was my first church and I was as busy as a man could be running around trying to help everybody. I was full of good intentions, but I didn't know doodle. Two months after we moved here, my wife died of an infection she picked up during a simple surgery. I was left with a three-year old child. A little girl we'd named Bobbie.

The preacher laced his fingers together, index fingers and thumbs extended and touching. I thought back to a childhood rhyme that started, "Here's the church and here's the steeple, open the door and count the people."

"I was a new daddy, and without a wife to help me raise Bobbie, I didn't know it but my ship was sinking. Started feeling sorry for myself. Just sat around reading my Bible, looking for answers, and taking care of Bobbie. Kept showing up at church the required three times a week. Made a big show of how well I was looking after Bobbie, and the good sisters kept feeding us their best casseroles and banana pudding. I smiled a lot and thanked them. One evening I was sitting right here in this very swing, watching Bobbie play. Zeale pulled up in the front yard in this ratty old truck. I didn't know much about him but I knew he owned a couple of mills and a bunch of timber."

"You'd never met him before?"

"Oh, he didn't come to church but I'd seen him around town. He walked up and sat down right where you're sitting now. We made some small talk about the weather and politics. Then he said, 'I understand you're feeling pretty sorry for yourself. Folks around town have been talking. You're not feeding your sheep. They're going hungry.'

"The Good Book says 'Be slow to wrath.' I'm not a man that loses his temper but I was getting there. "Well, I'm doing the best I can. I've lost my wife. I've got all these people depending on me for spiritual guidance. I've got this little girl to raise, and I'm the most miserable man since Job. And then I said the dumbest thing I said, You've got no idea what I'm dealing with."

"We sat swinging for a minute and then Zeale said, 'You don't know how lucky you are. You've got your whole life in front of you. You're a young man. You've got this beautiful little girl and you're going to have the chance to raise her. You've got a whole church full of people that love you, and you've got the opportunity to influence generations of folks right here in these mountains. Who knows? You just might help develop somebody that could change the world.'"

"Preacher being preached to," I said.

"Folks tell me you are smart and you used to preach the best sermons they ever heard. You don't know how short this life is. You don't have time to sit around and feel sorry for yourself. You came here to look after the souls of these folks. Now tell me the reason you're not visiting the sick and looking after the folks that are hurting."

"He can be hurtfully blunt, can't he?"

The preacher smiled. "Sort of a slap upside the head. I whined a little more, but I couldn't even convince myself anymore that I was right. Finally I said I've got this little girl to look after and that's the most important thing in the world."

With my newfound knowledge about Daddy, I said, "I know what's coming."

The preacher laughed out loud "I suspect you do and if I had known more about Zeale, I would have known what was coming, too. 'Tell you what,' Zeale said, 'give me a month and I'll have somebody here to take care of the house and your little girl. You'll be free to do the things you were hired to do. You've got to stop wasting your time sitting around here feeling sorry for yourself.'"

I tried to visualize the preacher and Daddy sitting in the swing talking. "Bet you wondered what kind of man this was, coming into your yard and beating up on you."

"I told him, my salary wouldn't allow me to hire a full time housekeeper. Zeale said, 'Don't you worry about her salary, it'll be taken care of, but there are a couple of conditions.' When I asked what the conditions were, Zeale said, 'You've got to stop feeling sorry for yourself, and you've got to get on with your life'"

"So what happened next?"

"Ten days later, Leigh Murphy arrived. She was a middle-aged woman, and I liked her the minute I saw her because she reminded me of my mother. She lived here for fifteen years, until Bobbie went off to college. I never knew what she was paid or how she was paid, and I never asked. But when she got ready to leave, I asked her what she was going to do next. She said move back to west Tennessee. I asked her if she needed a letter of reference, and she gave me a little smile. Like she was sharing a special secret. 'Mr. Breazeale has taken care of me,' she said.

"When Bobbie graduated from college, she got a graduation gift from Mrs. Murphy and a note saying she was living in Spain."

"Daddy still never came to church?"

"No, never did. But let me tell you one more thing. There were some periods when the church fell on lean times. It would need a new roof, or the missions program would need help. Zeale would catch me somewhere when nobody was around and he'd say, 'How much do you need?' Guess I was pretty shameless. I'd just tell him. He'd say, 'Okay, you've got it.' Then he'd always say the same thing, 'Don't tell anybody about this.' Bet he told me that a dozen times over the years."

"Why do you think he did things like that?"

The preacher shook his head. "I've thought a lot about that. I believe he's got a strong concept of what's right, and he thinks everybody should just do it, without any questions. He sets a mighty high standard for himself. The bad part of it is he expects everybody else to meet his standards and sometimes folks won't. Or can't.

"No kidding."

"I'm not sure he can help it," the preacher said. "Folks tell me he's a lot better than when he was a younger man – easier to get along with, that is. I wasn't around when you were growing up, when you were a teenager. I don't know why he was so hard on you. But I'll make a guess. He believed you had the potential to do better, that your bloodline was better than his. But he really didn't know how to help you. He tried, but he just didn't know how. I'll make an observation and you can take it for what it's worth. He learned on you. He got started late with Luther, but Luther benefitted. I benefitted. My church benefitted. I know for a fact Cedergren benefitted. But the biggest beneficiary was Lock. I know there's a problem today, but no boy ever had a finer father figure than Zeale."

We stood and Moody draped his arm around my shoulder. "I believe I know what's in his heart now, and it's mostly good. I'll tell you one other thing, and then I've got to get back to those weeds. I pray for him every night. I asked God to judge him on what's in his heart and to forgive him for how he acts sometimes."

*****

Daddy had parked Old Pony by the edge of the Christian Springs cemetery. He was leaning on his shovel. His shirt wet with sweat, and his hat was shoved back on his head, Rip's grave was open in front of him.

Without much success, I tried to keep my voice steady. "Daddy, I'm really sorry about Rip, and sorry …"

Daddy waved me off and said, "It s okay… it was my job. I shouldn't have tried to put it off on you."

Rip's body, still on Daddy's canvas coat, was beside the grave. Lock came out of the woods carrying a bucket of water. He removed his shirt and dropped to his knees beside the dog. He dipped his shirt in the water bucket, and started washing the blood from Rip's head. I couldn't see his face, but I could tell from the way his sides were heaving that he was crying.

I worried how the death of Rip might depress Lock. "Daddy, you think he should be …?"

"Yeah, I do. It's closure for him … for both of us."

I thought about wrapping Clawed in his favorite blanket and his burial in the back yard.

I put my arm around Daddy's shoulders and we stood there together watching as Lock continued to wash Rip's lifeless body and making the cooing sounds I had grown accustomed to hearing. Finally, I asked, "Think we should go ahead and bury Rip?"

"No," Daddy said. "Let's give him plenty of time to finish with his washing. He's going to miss him something awful. Let him grieve."

Lock finished and carefully rinsed the blood from his shirt before wrapping it around Rip. We gently lowered the dog into the grave and shoveled dirt over him.

"I don't want a fox or coon digging in the grave," Daddy said. "Let's pile some rocks over him." While we did this, Lock stood and watched. He had taken his tin whistle from his pocket and was making an effort to play *Amazing Grace*. Daddy shook his head and smiled. "That's the way we've always said our final goodbyes. I must have told him about it when he was a little boy."

After he had arranged the rocks in a way that suited him, Lock walked out to the edge of the escarpment and sat looking down toward the river. He sat with his arms wrapped around his knees, Daddy's bloody coat around his shoulders.

*****

Daddy put the shovel in the back of Old Pony. "I've got to go back to Cedergren and see Roy Ruby. As much as I'd like to, I can't keep ignoring him. About to get him in trouble and I don't want to do that."

"Let me go with you," I said. "I've been working on something. I believe there's a way of getting Lock away from here."

"You going to get divine intervention or something like it?" Daddy asked, unsuccessful at keeping the sarcasm out of his voice.

I outlined my plan to Daddy, trying to make it sound easy. I painted a rosy picture of the cabin at Hermit's Lake and tried to convince Daddy that Lock would be happy there. I stressed the seclusion of the area. Emphasizing that Lock would seldom be in contact with people.

"You going to take him up there and dump him out like a stray cat? He'd be better off if we fought this thing out right here. Right now. If worse comes to worse, I'll just keep him hid out here on the Arn."

"Not an option, Daddy. He can't stay here and it's reaching a point where you won't be able to protect him. I'm not dumping him. I'll stay with him until he gets comfortable."

"What if he never does?"

"I've thought about that," I said. "Lots of worse places for me to live. I'd move there with him. Permanently. As he becomes more accustomed to his surroundings, I could set up a little operation. I'm pretty well established and I've got enough regular clients that I could bring folks in occasionally, guide a few hunting and fishing trips, things like that."

Daddy shook his head. "Won't work. Even if it does, I'd never see him again. He needs me." Daddy looked at the ground. "And I need him."

"You could come up and visit whenever you wanted to. You could live with us. In fact, why don't you just go in the beginning? It'll work. I know it will."

"Bullshit," Daddy said. "You're dreaming. I'm an old man. I couldn't survive up there, and even if I could, Lock can't. Can't you see, he's got to stay here?"

I was running out of arguments. "What happens to him when you die?"

Daddy was getting into Old Pony, and I knew our conversation was ending, "I'm not figuring on dying any time soon, and even if I do," his voice broke, "maybe Lock and I'll be lucky. Maybe we'll cross over that *dark river* together."

After Daddy left, I went back and sat with Lock. His expression had not changed. He had torn a thin strip of cloth from the lining of Daddy's coat and was plaiting it together with some grass stems. His fingers were slow and a little shaky.

Not expecting an answer, I asked, "What are you making?"

Lock continued with his work as if he didn't hear me. I watched him closely as he made a small knot and held up the finished product for my inspection. It was a necklace, round, very tight, four-plait with a small pouch in the front. The pouch was large enough to hold a small stone. Or a small coin I thought remembering the amulets the men found dead near the stone fort were wearing.

"That's pretty work," I said. Lock nodded and put the necklace in the pocket of the jacket.

Desperate to communicate, I said, "I'm sorry Rip died. I know you loved each other. Nice thing you did, washing him like that. It made Papa Zeale feel better."

With a jerky movement, Lock brought his hands up and covered his eyes. His voice was so soft and so unexpected, I only heard the last of his sentence, "…when I die."

Everyone has jolting experiences in their lives: the unexpected death of a loved one, the loss of a job, contact with an electrical wire, an automobile wreck, or being the victim of a crime. But nothing could have prepared me for the sound of Lock's voice. A surge of something unknown ripped through my body. I could not breath. I fought the impulse to stand, pull him to his feet, and dance for joy.

I put my hand on his shoulder. "I'm sorry, I didn't hear the first part of what you said."

Lock cleared his throat. "Who will wash me when I die?"

"It will be a long time before you die."

Lock removed his hands from his face. Tears had formed in his eyes. "Will you cry for me?"

I struggled to keep my voice from breaking. "I'm older than you are. I will die a long time before you do."

Lock shook his head. "No, I will die first."

I had to know the answer. "Do you know who I am?"

"Yes," he said, looking out over the river. "You are my father."

"How long have you known?"

Lock had taken the amulet from the jacket pocket. "I saw your fingers. They were like mine. I heard you and Papa Zeale talking."

"I wish you had told me sooner."

"I couldn't."

Lock's answers were getting shorter, and his voice was getting softer. I was desperately afraid he was going to stop talking. "But you talk to Papa Zeale."

"Yes." Lock rolled the amulet between his fingers. "I can't talk much. Sometimes, I have lights in my head. My mouth tastes like copper. The words are in my mind, but … they won't come out. They hide in colors … I can't find them. I feel scared and I have to go to a quiet place…I have to hide."

"Papa Zeale says that you have good days sometimes."

"Sometimes I feel like a kite… and the string … holding me is broken. I'm afraid that I will drift off … into something … black and evil. I'm afraid I can't come back … can't come back. Then Papa Zeale comes and … he catches the string and I'm all right."

Frantically, I searched for comforting words. And there were none.

"I'm sick all the time. Sometimes I'm sicker. I can't get my mind to work right. If I could just get something to hold on to. If I could make my mind … be steady."

Lock rubbed the amulet against his temple. "I hear babies crying. Sometimes they talk to me. At night, I talk to them. I don't do it around Papa Zeale … it makes him sad … and them I get sad."

"Papa Zeale tells me you two spend a lot of time out here. He says you fish together and you help him look after the buffalo."

Without much enthusiasm, Lock nodded.

"He tells me you camp out around the old fort sometimes in the summer when it's warm. I used to camp there when I was a boy. Luther and I spent a lot of nights out there. Sometimes we would get scared. Have you ever been scared out at the fort?"

Lock stared at me and nodded.

"You've lived out here almost three years. Pretty long time to live here by yourself. Do you ever get lonesome?"

Lock continued to rub the amulet against his temple. "Sometimes. That is when I cry…when nobody but the babies can hear me."

I wanted to clamp my hands over my ears. I fought nausea and then a sadness settled on my shoulders like Atlas supporting the earth. I could accept Daddy's account of Lock's behavior, but I was not sure that even he knew the depths of Lock's problems.

"I used to live in Alaska. I've got a home there. Nice lakes and the mountains are pretty. Good places to fish and hunt. I would like it if you could come and visit."

Lock's brow wrinkled and he seemed in deep thought. Finally, he extended his arm and laid his index finger across his bicep. Then he made a swimming motion with his hands.

"No, no," I said. "Much bigger."

Lock stretched both arms full length and raised his eyebrows.

"Yes, that big and sometimes bigger," I said. "Maybe you and I could fly up to my house."

Lock studied this thought before shrugging his shoulders in a noncommittal gesture.

"I think you'd really like it, lot of good fishing and not many people around." I wasn't sure how convincing I was, even if Lock was showing some interest. "Think about it, and we'll talk some more later."

Lock shifted the amulet from hand to hand. "Would Papa Zeale go?"

"I'm not sure. Would you like for him to go with us?"

Lock put the amulet into his pocket. He rubbed the lapel of Daddy's canvas jacket against his face. "Yes. He is old. I will need to look after him."

With more cheer than I felt, I said, "I can ask him. Do you think he will?"

Lock didn't answer, but he stood and continued to look off the edge of the escarpment toward the river.

I waited for almost a minute before I decided that Lock ended conservations just like his grandfather did. He just stopped responding. "Probably need to get back to camp," I said and started walking down the hill to the jeep. I was relieved to hear Lock following.

At the jeep, I asked Lock if he wanted to drive. He shook his head and climbed into the passenger seat. We bounced along the dirt road until we reached the campsite at Hematite Lake.

In the early days of our company, we bought blue T-shirts as advertisement for Aleutian Air. They were simple, just the company name over a picture of our floatplane. I had one on under my shirt. I took it off and gave it to Lock. Without a word, he disappeared into the cabin and closed the door. I walked down to the edge of the lake. The late afternoon sun was causing shadows to grow from the western edge, and I watched as they slowly extended toward where I was sitting on the earthen dam.

I thought about what had happened on this day: Rip's death, how tender Lock had been with the body of the dog, how unwilling Daddy had been to even consider my plan to take Lock off the Arn, and my surprise that when I discussed my plan with Lock, while he wasn't very responsive, he didn't seem outwardly opposed. Although my plan would need refining, at least, it was a starting place. It had a lot more possibilities than anything Daddy had offered. Now, my major problem was getting Daddy to go along with it.

Just before dark, Old Pony came down off the ridge toward the campsite. Daddy had two sacks of groceries and a carton of Cokes. "Hey fellers, I've got some chow. Barbecue, baked beans, slaw and tater salad. Got some fried pies to top it off. Kings may eat better than we do, but not tonight." He set the sacks down on the rocks at the fire pit.

"How'd you know I was starving?" I asked.

With a touch of concern in his voice, Daddy asked, "Where's the boy?"

I motioned to the cabin, "In there. You want me to roust him?"

"No," Daddy said quickly. "I'm betting this morning was pretty tough on him. The best thing for him is sleep.

"How did your meeting with the sheriff go?"

Daddy shook his head. "Not too good. Roy Ruby hasn't heard from the TBI today. But he didn't offer any hope in making the thing disappear. He thinks maybe they're putting together a grand jury. It's a case of no news being good news, I reckon."

"I talked some with Lock about taking him to Alaska," I said and then waited for the explosion.

More subdued than I expected, Daddy said, "Creight, you shouldn't have done that. Even if you were going to talk with him about it, you should've waited until I was around. You deliberately went behind my back."

"No, I didn't. If you'd been here, the conversation would've never taken place. You'd have just said no and that would have been the end of it."

Daddy sat in his chair and crossed his legs. He ran his fingers across his face. "How did Lock take to your suggestion?"

"He seemed interested in the size of fish in Alaska."

"And that's it?" Daddy asked, nodding his head as if answering his own question.

"No, not quite. He asked if you would go."

"He asked? Are you saying he talked to you?"

I felt a sense of victory over Daddy's stubbornness. "Yes. We had a long conversation, considering we had never talked at all."

Daddy closed his eyes and shook his head. "Damn. He talked to you."

"Yes. Fathers and sons talk."

"But he doesn't know that you're…"

"Sure he does. He heard us talking. He knew by the shape of our fingers."

Daddy stared at me as if he might detect that I was lying. "And he told you that? With words?"

"Yes. With words. He said you were old and that he would need to look after you." I waited for Lock's words to sink into Daddy's mind. "Puts things in a different light, doesn't it?"

As if he didn't hear me, Daddy stood, unwrapped the barbecue and made sandwiches. I ladled out the beans, slaw and potato salad on paper plates. The Cokes were warm, but they still did a good job washing the barbecue down. We sat in the old, beat-up lawn chairs and ate like it was the first food we'd eaten in a week.

Daddy said, "You want to eat our pies now or wait and see if Lock wakes up?"

"Let's wait," I said. "Let's get this other thing out of the way."

Daddy stared at me, not quite as belligerent as before. "All right, let's go."

"I've given a lot of thought to Lock and what's best for him. I'm not sure my plan is the best thing for me, and it may not be the best for you, but it's the best for Lock."

"You don't know what's best for Lock."

"I think I do. Roy Ruby is at the end of his rope. The next thing that's going to happen is that a search warrant is going to be issued. Going to be men coming out here, state troopers, marshals, Roy Ruby's deputies. It doesn't make any difference. They're going to turn this place upside down. Lock won't be able to hide, and you won't be able to protect him. They'll find him and carry him out like some kind of wild animal. The worst case is they'll kill him."

"What makes you think you've got all the answers?"

"I don't think I have all of them. I just know he can't stay here."

Daddy shook his head. "It'll ruin him. He'll never fit in anywhere else. You know that."

"No, I don't know that and neither do you. Unless you come up with a better plan, I'm taking him out of here. He wants you to go with us. It'll make it a lot easier on me. And him. Be glad for you to go with us but that's your decision, and I can't make it for you. Does it mean anything to you that he wants you to go? That he feels a need to look after you."

Daddy stood and unwrapped one of the fried pies. He took a bite and then violently threw the pie out into the darkness. "Damn you Creighton."

*****

I left Daddy staring out toward the blackness of the lake, his hands jammed in his pockets. I drove out to the stone fort and by the light of the jeep gathered firewood. The small fire did little to erase the pain of my squabble with Daddy.

I thought my relationship with Daddy had grown to be one of man to man - maybe. People had told me that Daddy had changed, mellowed, and that he was easier and more understanding. Perhaps. But not with me. He had little more regard for me now than he did when I was eighteen.

I pulled an oak limb over the fire and watched as it started to burn, long thin streams of smoke snaking up toward the dark sky. I lay back against a rock with my body drained of energy from our argument. Sleep was not immediate but it eventually came.

The moon-eyes came that night.

The men built the fort while the women cooked venison stew over open flames. The older children played and looked after their younger siblings. Two men stood guard while their companions moved the last of the boulders into place. Darkness settled across the encampment. There was no moon. It was the dark nights in August.

The Indians arrived, casting no shadows and making no sounds. Most of the moon-eyes had their heads caved in by the Indians' war clubs before they were even aware of the attackers. While some of the braver women stood shoulder to shoulder and fought alongside their husbands, others huddled along the edge of the escarpment with their children's faces buried in their bosoms.

The Indians made short work of the moon-eyes' first line of defense and attacked the women and children at the edge of the escarpment. The women screamed and pushed their children over the edge into the gorge below. Clutching each other, they followed their children off the edge of the cliff. One young woman lowered her three young children into a crevasse and dropped two deerskin pouches after them. The children quickly and silently disappeared into the gray limestone darkness. She stood and stepped away from the hiding place of her children. A warrior wearing a cap and mantel made from the pelt of a red fox tomahawked her and she fell to the ground. Peace had crowded the fear from her mind; her children were safe.

The warrior dropped to his knees and reached down into the crevasse. His searching hands felt nothing except the cool darkness.

*****

Just after daylight, I dried the dampness from the jeep's seat and drove back to the camp.

Daddy was sitting in his lawn chair with his feet propped up in the second chair. The jeep rattled to a stop and Daddy stirred. I stopped at the wooden box that held the cooking supplies and said, "You got any coffee in here?"

Daddy nodded. I took the coffee pot to the lake, washed it out, and filled it with fresh water. Daddy added twigs to the smoldering fire and when it started to blaze, added larger twigs. I put the pot on the open fire and we both sat.

Exactly as if we were resuming a conversation after a brief pause Daddy said, "You put the monkey on my back, didn't you?"

"If that's what you want to call it."

"A man can't just disappear."

"Yes he can, and he will. There won't be any trace of where he went and really not much evidence he was ever here. Andy won't ever tell anybody. Camran won't. Sherriff Fox sure won't. Lock will be four thousand miles away and might as well be in the craters of the moon."

Daddy thought for a minute before he said, "What about the McCamy brothers? They've seen him. How are you going to shut them up?"

"I'm not. And I'm not going to worry about them. You've said they're big liars and everybody knows it. If they keep on, as a last resort, maybe Logomicino could visit them. Or Camran. He'd enjoy it. Either one of them could give them something else to think about."

Daddy took a peach seed from his pocket and started to work on a half-finished bird. "Got it all figured out, haven't you?"

I nodded. "Pretty much."

"I can't let you do it."

I hoped it would not come to this. "You don't have a choice this time, Daddy. I'm not asking for your permission. You've raised him, but he's my son. This is my decision."

"No goddammit, it's my decision. He's my boy and I've always looked after him. Just because I'm old doesn't mean I'm not capable."

"I didn't say that. Being old doesn't have anything to do with it. You've run things up here for a long time. But there's been changes. Newspapers and TV have changed things. You can't just pen Lock up like he was a bear. Can't tell folks what to do like you used to."

Daddy threw the half carved seed into the fire. He took another dried peach seed from his pocket and started whittling. "Things haven't changed. Roy Ruby will help me. We can do it, I know we can."

"No. You can't. But this is how you can help Lock and me. Go with us. You're not too old to start another life. If you don't like it up there, you can just come back here."

Daddy sat whittling, not looking at me. I could almost hear the wheels turning in his head. "I guess that for the first time in my life, I feel defeated. Cheated, somehow. I'm at a loss. My back's to the wall. I'd hoped I'd never have to come to a decision on this."

"I understand and I'm sorry."

"You think this is the right thing? You think you can pull it off?"

I nodded. "I'll give it my best shot."

"When?"

"Depends on how things fall into place. Three, four, five days at the most."

Daddy leaned forward and rested his elbows on his knees, staring at the ground between his feet. His body rocked slightly as if his mind was digesting information. Accepting and rejecting data.

*****

I got two tin mugs from the wooden box and poured coffee. We sat in the muted light of early dawn drinking, not talking. Finally, Daddy said, "What kind of help you going to need in this?"

"I need Luther to arrange for the plane to meet us in Knoxville. That's it."

"You sure you got everything else covered?"

"Yes," I replied. "What kind of arrangements will you need to make? We'll need to pack you some gear, but we can just buy anything you need when we get to Anchorage."

"Dammit, Creight, you know I'm not going."

"Why? Why not?"

Daddy refilled his coffee cup and took a long drink. "I've lived here in these mountains all my life. Me moving to Alaska would be like taking a magnolia tree and setting it out at the north pole. I fit here but I never would fit there. I'm old, beat up, set in my ways, too old to learn new tricks. I've got other Roane men waiting for me at Christian Springs. In a way, I'm looking forward to spending some time with them."

"Don't talk that way. You've got another hundred thousand miles in you."

"You know that's not true, Creight. I'm an old rotten apple, just waiting to fall off the tree. A little frost, a light breeze and – poof – I'm gone."

"Come on, Daddy. You will be around to show me how to apply for a bed in the old folks' home."

The cabin door opened and Lock came out, digging his fists in his eyes and yawning. I got another cup and filled it with coffee. Lock squatted on the ground between Daddy and me, rubbing the warm cup against his cheek.

Daddy said," Creight tells me you may be going to take a trip with him. May be going to Alaska. Is that right?"

Lock leaned forward and looked up at Daddy. "Papa Zeale, you have to go with us. I have to look after you."

Daddy didn't meet Lock's eyes. "I'll be fine here. I have friends to look after me. Camran. Andy. I'll be fine."

Lock turned to face me, his eyes were wet. "I can't go unless Papa Zeale goes with us."

Daddy said, "I can't go Lock. I have to stay here. But you are going to a good place, and Creight will look after you really good."

Lock was still wearing Daddy's bloody coat over the T-shirt I had given him earlier. He buttoned it against the coolness of the early morning, stood and walked back to the cabin, hands over his eyes, crying.

Daddy rubbed his eyes with his shirtsleeve. "Creighton, I can't do this. I'm too old. I'm tired. I'm wore out. Don't make me be a part of this. "

"You can do this. You've always been a daddy to Lock. From the time you hauled him in the front seat of your truck when he was a baby to now. You've guided him through good and bad years. Don't quit now. Do this last thing for him. Help him. Help me."

Daddy took a peach seed and knife from his pocket, but his hands shook so much he couldn't open the knife.

Without turning to face me, Daddy said, "Do it."

We made another pot of coffee and roasted potatoes in the ashes. "Weirdest breakfast I ever had," Daddy observed. "Let's catch a mess of bream, and we'll have them this afternoon."

We rowed the johnboat along the levy and worked the cattails with our fly rods. We discussed the newspaper article and the interview with the McCamy brothers. Daddy again expressed his opinion that all McCamys should be aborted long before their birth. "Sumbitches had no business killing Rip. What kinda man does things like that?

"I stopped and talked with your buddy the preacher yesterday. He had some nice things to say about you."

"He's a good man," Daddy said. "Talks a lot and wears his collar backwards, but I don't think he can help either one of them."

"Moody said he gave Rip to you?"

"Yep, he did." Daddy looked down. "Rip was a buddy."

"Lock showed a tender side I'd never seen while we were burying Rip. He has a kind side to him."

"Yeah, you're right." Then, as if he needed to change the subject, Daddy asked, "What else did that gossipy old preacher say?"

"He said he prays for you every night."

"Did he really say that? Well, I'll be damned."

*****

Daddy reminisced about his younger days, about when he and Mother married, about Mother's death, about the buying of the timberland from Trevethan and Gunn, about Maggie, and about Lock growing up. He talked some about his father and about his mother dying from a snakebite.

Late afternoon we cleaned the fish and ate. Lock picked the breading from the fried bream but ate little else. "Son, you won't grow up to be bigger than a minute," Daddy joked with Lock.

Wiping the grease from his fingers on the leg of his jeans, Lock asked, "Are you going with me, Papa Zeale?" His voice was tender as that of a child. He reached out and took one of Daddy's rough hands.

I held my breath as Daddy put his arm around Lock's shoulder. "Would that make you happy?"

Lock looked at the ground, "I think it would be a good thing to do."

Daddy didn't respond for a few seconds. Lock had taken Daddy's hand again and was looking deeply into his eyes. "I … I think I can. But I … I might have to come back after a while. Do you think you would be all right?"

Lock nodded and then hugged Daddy's neck. A flock of geese came over and landed in the lake. They swam to the shore and started grazing on the tender grass growing on the levy. Lock wandered off to watch the geese.

I didn't question Daddy any more. I knew he had given the best answer that he was capable of giving.

About midnight, Daddy told me he was going to stay on the Arn that night with Lock, and I should get back to Cedergren to finalize my plans. He asked me to pick up some groceries on my way back, something for breakfast.

I stood to leave. Daddy said, "Did you pick up my pistol yesterday? I think I left it on the porch."

"It's under the seat of the jeep."

"If you don't mind, would you bring it down to me? Can't ever tell, I might need to shoot at a boogeyman tonight."

Briefly, I thought about challenging his need for the handgun, and then thought better. I got the pistol and gave it to Daddy with the warning, "Shoot straight."

Daddy opened the cylinder, ejected the spent cartridge, and slid another shell into its place. Without looking away from the pistol, Daddy said, "Creighton, I'm sorry. When you were growing up … I was a whole lot more like my daddy than I meant to be. I just wanted you to know that. I didn't always do right by you … and I'm sorry."

"Daddy, I…"

He shook his head and motioned me toward the jeep.

I walked back up the hill to the jeep and started to drive off. The headlights swept through the darkness illuminating Daddy sitting in his old chair, the pistol resting on his knee. I stopped and considered going back and hugging him and telling him I loved him and always had. But I thought he might feel awkward so I didn't.

If I had that chance again, I would. A thousand times, I would.

The house and office were dark. With just a twinge of guilty conscience, I rummaged through Daddy's bedroom closet. Under a raincoat on the floor, I found a half case of Wild Turkey. Crafty father, crafty son I thought. I got two glasses from the kitchen and filled one with water. I decided this was a four-finger night – or maybe more.

I sat on the edge of Daddy's bed and had my first drink of the day. I'd already invaded Daddy's privacy, so why not look a bit deeper? His closet was pretty neat, particularly for an old man with no woman to keep things straight. His winter clothes, plaid flannel shirts and brown corduroy pants were separated from his summer khakis by a couple of white shirts and a blue suit. A red and blue striped tie was thrown carelessly over a vacant hanger. A pair of black dress shoes and several pair of work boots were scattered on the closet floor next to the raincoat. A couple of felt hats and some battered hunting caps occupied one end of the closet shelf, a large white box wrapped in yellowed newspaper sat at the other end.

I removed the box from the shelf and put it on the bed.

The newspaper was fragile and partially disintegrated in my hands. An envelope was taped to the top of the box. I knew I was stepping over the boundary of privacy, but I slid my fingers under the flap and found it wasn't sealed. A sheet of rough, lined paper was folded inside. The writing was done with a pencil and had dimmed to the point where it was almost illegible. I took the paper into the kitchen where the light was stronger and spread it on the table. Daddy's rough scrawl read:

Maggie

I want you to have this dress. It was Susan's. She wore it on the day we got married. That was the only time it was ever wore. I can't give it to you in person but when I'm gone it's yours. I believe Susan would be pleased that you have it and I'd like for you to tell Lock that it was his grandmother's.

William Breazeale Roane, December 25, 1965

I wanted to see the dress, but I couldn't open the box. Although I had never seen it, and it was my mother's, and I was combing through my Daddy's belongings like a common burglar, I just couldn't do it. I wasn't sure how I would feel if the dress had deteriorated into a jumble of threads and scattering of buttons. What if it was stained? I wanted to believe it was in pristine condition. If that was the way I saw it my mind, why take the risk it was anything less? I placed the box carefully back on the shelf, turned out the bedroom light and went up to my room.

I sat at my childhood desk, my second four fingers of Turkey in front of me. I couldn't stop thinking of Mother and how she must have looked in her wedding dress.

The Turkey went down without being followed by water. I studied the pencil markings on the desktop. With my pocketknife, I had cut my initials on the surface and then filled in the carving with red ink. I had scratched the interlocking "NY" logo of the New York Yankees just under my initials. I could remember pouring over the Yankee box scores in the Knoxville paper. Somewhere in my desk drawer was a black and white newspaper photograph of Mickey Mantle, standing in the bright sunlight at Yankee Stadium. He had it all: skill, looks, personality, and fame. I took another long drink, this time from the bottle. Poor Mickey, I thought, somebody said the booze got him, cut his career short; others said he could never meet his father's expectations and it haunted him mercilessly. I wondered what kind of demons chased him, what drove a kid from a nowhere town in Oklahoma to the bottom of the bottle.

I was puzzled when I turned the bottle up and it was empty. I tried to stand and found the effort too much.

The dream came just before daylight, at a time intended for peaceful sleep.

Mother was walking down the path to the camp at Hematite, carrying the box containing her wedding dress. A woman was sitting in Daddy's chair, schoolchildren at her feet, reading aloud from a book about little puppies and flying geese. The woman looked up, a Yankee cap pushed back on her head, and smiled as Mother approached. "My husband asked me to give this to you," Mother said. "He didn't have the courage himself. He said you would think him crazy."

The woman took the box from Mother and asked, "Do I know you?"

"Not really, but I've watched you for a long time. You are a good mother to my grandson."

"You're Mrs. Roane, aren't you?"

"Yes, but please call me Susan." There was a long pause before she continued, "He has left there and I thought it would be nice to visit with you while I was carrying out his wishes."

"When did he leave?"

"He left last night and I expect him here today. I've packed a picnic, and we are going to the stone fort. When we were young, we used to sit out there and look down on the river below. It was one of our favorite places. Creighton loved to chase the squirrels that lived in the rocks that had fallen from the fort." Mother took a handkerchief from her sleeve and dabbed at the corners of her eyes. "Zeale and I've missed each other so much."

"Will he be back here?"

"No," Mother replied. *She smiled and pushed a lock of hair from her forehead. "He doesn't need to. He says his work there is over."*

I woke, head pounding, shouting "No! He's not gone! He's still here. He's got to help me finish this! He can't go yet! We need him."

I was fumbling around with the coffee: a feat complicated by a thundering hangover when the phone rang. I considered not answering because I couldn't think of any voice I wanted to hear.

Through the static, Jamiesie Cotterill's voice came booming, "Hey. Hillbilly. What's going on in the land of barefoot, pregnant women?"

"I've got a bad head, Jamiesie. Probably not terminal, but I'm afraid to open both eyes at the same time."

"Moonshine, old buddy. I'll bet you've been dipping into some of that mountain brew," Jamiesie cackled.

Jamiesie's lightheartedness was trying. I needed to get to the point of his call. "What kind of news you got for me this mornin'?"

Jamiesie was now all business, "I got a call in the middle of the night from my West Virginia buddy. Apparently, you folks don't have any idea of the time difference. Hell, I just stayed up, and soon as I finish this call, I'm going back to bed. Anyway, he's got a Bell Jet Ranger. It's down for a scheduled maintenance right now but it'll be ready in three days. Make it sometime this weekend. How does that fit with your needs?"

I tried to clear my head. "Three days … would make it maybe … Saturday?"

"Or Sunday at the latest," Jamiesie responded.

"That'll work."

"Creight, let me come down there. I'm kinda worried about you. I'm not so sure you're all right."

I was trying to make plans and carry on a conversation at the same time. "Yeah, just can't get my prop spinning this morning. Fuel mixture was definitely too rich last night. Give me your West Virginia buddy's name and number, and I'll give him a call."

"It's Willie West and he lives near Cabin Creek, somewhere south of Charleston," Jamiesie said. Then he gave me the phone number.

I had to go over the numbers three times before I got it right. "Jamiesie, have you got stuff up to Hermit's Lake yet?"

"It's done, old buddy. You'll be real proud of me. Carol and I carried chow up yesterday. We spent the night. She was real impressed. She really liked the cabin."

I smiled for the first time today and the pain was significant. "I'm glad you clarified that. I was starting to wonder what impressed her."

"Creight, I can tell you're going to live. I'll be ready when you get here. You coming up in that company jet?"

"I haven't made all of the arrangements yet, but I'm pretty sure we will. I'll get back with you. Let's plan to meet at International. I'm betting it'll be in the middle of the night," I said. Plans were beginning to form in my clearing brain.

"Just give me a heads up. Aleutian Air will have your sorry ass out and at Hermit's Lake in time to fry breakfast eggs," Jamiesie laughed.

"You're a good man, Jamiesie."

Jamiesie laughed again. "That's what partners do, rescue old drunks and damsels in distress."

*****

No one answered at Luther's home, and the receptionist at Roman said he hadn't arrived yet.

Cedergren had one traffic light and it usually didn't work. This morning it did and I stopped. From the left, a rusted pickup turned right and stopped beside me blocking the opposite lane. The greasy haired driver leaned out his window and grinned. "Cousin tells me Zeale's dog was a laying out in the road a licking his ass and got runned over. Just wanted to express how much all the McCamys folks hate hit happened."

I gave him the middle finger as he drove off.

Luther and Sheriff Fox were having a late breakfast at the restaurant. He and Sheriff Fox were sitting at a corner booth, well away from the Brotherhood, leaning forward in deep conversation. I nudged Luther's shoulder. "Scoot over."

Luther moved toward the wall. "Good gosh, Creight. You look like death eating a cracker. You all right?"

Before I could answer, Sheriff Fox said, "I've busted up stills didn't smell as strong as you do this mornin'."

I was not surprised at their comments. "Thank you both for the compliment … been better … been worse." Then I got off my own volley, "Looks like the Brotherhood has dismissed both of you from the club. And it's about time."

Sheriff Fox was lighting his second cigar of the day. He looked at me through a cloud of blue smoke. "Luther and me are working on something that might give Zeale some breathing room."

"Appreciate your work," I said, "but I'm starting to tie up some loose ends that'll take care of everybody's problems."

Luther peered over the top of his coffee cup. "Anything I can do to help?"

"Yes," I replied.

Sheriff Fox scrambled from his seat and said, "I've got a feeling there's nothing I can do. I don't need to be a part of this conversation and I don't want to."

"You're a sage and wise man. You're right. You don't need to hear this."

Louellen set a coffee mug before me and poured. "I'm betting you're not eating breakfast this morning."

Sheriff Fox dropped two dollars on the table. "This'll pay for these two deadbeats' coffee. And you're right, that old boy ain't going to be eating any breakfast this morning. See you later. I've got to go look for outlaws and cattle rustlers, stuff like that."

Luther and I watched out the window as the sheriff backed his cruiser from the curb. He disappeared down the street, the cruiser's long antenna whipping back and forth.

Luther took a swallow of coffee and then made circles on the tabletop with the mug. "How can I help, and how much do I need to know?"

I debated a second with myself before saying, "I'm going to need the jet sometime within the next three or four days."

"How long are you going to need it?"

"Two days."

Luther erased one of the circles. "How many passengers? The pilots need to know for fuel calculations."

"Maybe three, two for sure,"

"And passengers on the return flight?"

I didn't look at him, "I'm not sure, maybe one, maybe none."

I could see sorrow in Luther's eyes as he said, "I hope three go."

"I do too, but the third person is stubborn."

Luther nodded. "Call me. We'll need at least a days notice if you can so I can clear out any charters."

I slid from the seat and Luther followed me. Without saying anything, he shook my hand and left the restaurant, shoulders a little more stooped than usual.

I drained my coffee. As I was starting to leave, Louellen gave me two paper sacks. "Here," she said. "You might get hungry later. When the stuff wears off. I packed some ham and biscuits. There's enough for you to share with Mr. Roane. This little sack has some scraps for Rip."

Why tell Louellen about Rip? Just because I was feeling so rotten, I didn't see any reason her day should be spoiled too.

The trip from Cedergren to the Arn gate was all on smooth road without much bouncing, but the trip from the gate down to the camp at Hematite Lake was something entirely different. The jeep bounced and swayed, a bucking horse on rubber tires. The coffee was starting to work, and the pain in my temples had reached a manageable point – almost.

I gave the jeep's horn a toot, gathered the sacks Louellen had given me, and started my walk down to the camp. The two chairs by the fire pit were empty and I didn't see anybody along the lakeshore. The cabin door was open. For a second, I didn't see the figure stretched out on the floor, covered by a canvas jacket.

"Hey, Daddy," I shouted. "You've picked a pretty sorry place to take a nap." I saw no movement, and walking toward the cabin, shouted again, "Louellen sent you some chow."

He was on his back, coat buttoned, and arms folded across his chest. Atop the coat were two tin whistles twisted together in an "X". His hair had been dampened and brushed back smoothly. A ragged washcloth was crumpled in a battered, enameled washbasin near his head.

Only to its victim is death immediate.

I sat on the edge of the porch, stunned and somewhere between disbelief and reality. Maybe if I didn't look at Daddy any more, but instead walked back up to the jeep, drove back out to the gate and then came back, things would change. Daddy would be sitting in his chair or he and Lock would be down at the lake fishing for bream. He might even look up, shove his hat back on his head, and ask me what was in the paper bags. Maybe I could untwist the whistles, play a few notes, and Daddy would sit up, reach for the other whistle and join me, and we would play *Amazing Grace* together.

Reality erases disbelief and truth comes: a large and ugly presence that won't be ignored. In the noonday sun, I sat on the edge of the porch and looked at his hands, remembering their strength. Once upon a time, they had been brown, calloused, the nails rough, a healing cut on a finger. I could see the fingers as they gripped an axe or tightened on the handle of a chain saw, but now they were lifeless and pale. I took Daddy's cold and stiff hands in mine, willing them to move but knowing they were stilled forever.

I unbuttoned the coat from under his crossed arms. I looked for bloodstains on the front of his clothing, and finding none, I gently rolled him over onto his side. Nothing unusual. I had just started to replace the coat over his body when I thought to examine his neck for bruises. I pulled up on his shirt collar and ran my fingers across his throat. I felt something rough and when I pulled the collar wider, I saw a thin cord, a four-plait made of animal hair and grass. A small pocket woven into the cord contained the likeness of a bird fashioned from gold, wings spread in eternal flight.

The hair on the back of my neck stiffened. No, I thought, not again. I took my knife, cut the cord, and pocketed the amulet.

The water from the basin had been thrown out across the dusty yard, leaving a semicircular slash of dampness. A cigarette, a Picayune, burnt end down, was stuck in the dirt and within the path of the water. I dropped to my knees and examined it. The cigarette had been wet but no way to tell if it had been shoved into the dirt before or after the basin had been emptied.

I stood in the noonday sun, retching again and again until nothing was left in my stomach, and no more tears left to flow from my eyes.

*****

I sat in Old Pony and watched the sun set over Hematite Lake, a fiery ball being extinguished for this day. Finally, I keyed the mike on Daddy's radio and said, "Camran, this is Creight. You hear me?"

Almost immediately, Camran's voice came back. "Gotcha. What can I do for you?"

"I need for you to get in touch with Sheriff Fox. Tell him to meet me at the gate. You come too."

"Okay, it will take me a little bit to round him up. Maybe an hour before we kin get there. Anything wrong?"

"No," I replied, not trusting the open radio channel and not trusting my voice.

*****

The sheriff parked his cruiser inside the gate alongside Camran's truck. While Camran climbed in the back of my jeep, Roy Ruby heaved himself into the passenger's seat. We drove along the rim road, disturbing the buffalo already bedded down for the night, and then turned down the woods road to the camp. After our brief conversation at the gate, nobody said anything until we reached the cabin.

The beam of Roy Ruby's big flashlight searched back and forth across the camp before settling on Daddy's body. The three of us stopped just short of the porch and Roy Ruby said, "And that's the way you found him, just laying on his back like that?"

"Yeah," I said.

Roy Ruby's light played around the edge of the cabin, jumpy like a scared rabbit. Behind me, Camran broke the seal on a bottle of whiskey. I could hear the liquid gurgling down his throat before he said under his breath, "Damn, just goddamn."

Roy Ruby's light searched the woods around the cabin. "Where's the boy?"

I was afraid the sheriff could hear the hammering in my chest. "I don't know. He wasn't here when I got here and I haven't seen him."

The beam of the flashlight settled on Daddy's body again. The sheriff said, "Have you moved anything? Creight, really need you straight with me."

"Sheriff, my daddy's laying dead. What in the world are you talking about?"

Roy Ruby squatted before Daddy, playing the light up and down his body. He took a ballpoint pen from his pocket and pulled the canvas coat away from Daddy's chest. He slid the coat to the edge of the porch where, using another pen, he lifted the flap and looked into the pockets. Using the same method, he looked into Daddy's shirt pockets. The light played down Daddy's body again, stopping at his belt buckle before continuing down to his shoes, and then reversed its path back up to Daddy's head.

"Looks like his hair has been wet and combed," the sheriff said.

"Probably wet from the dew," I responded.

The sheriff's light probed the packed dirt around the cabin and came to rest on a damp place. "Reckon why the ground's dampish? Looks like somebody has slung water on the ground."

"That was me," I lied. "A wash pan was setting on that shelf. I poured some water in it and washed my face."

"You told me you hadn't moved nothing," the sheriff said with irritation.

"Look, sheriff," I replied, trying to keep anger and fear from my voice. "I've just found my daddy dead and I'll tell you everything just as I remember it, but if I miss something ..."

The sheriff held up his hand, "Don't get hot with me. I never had a better friend than Zeale, and there is nothing I'd rather do than just get the hell out of here. But I got to conduct some kind of investigation. You got to admit, with the kind of things that have happened out here, somebody's going to raise some questions as to how Zeale died. I don't want to sound like some kind of dumb ass idiot. You follow me?"

I nodded. "I'm sorry."

"Ain't no need for sorry. I understand your feelings," the sheriff said as he peered at Daddy's body. He took the ballpoint pen again, and this time pulled Daddy's collar away from his neck. He stood and said, "You don't know how relieved I am to not find one of them damn amulet things around his neck."

Camran guzzled the last of the whiskey, and I heard the woo-woo-woo sound of the thrown bottle and then the noise of it crashing down through the woods.

For a fat man the sheriff was quick and he wheeled with his gun drawn, his flashlight following the crashing sound of the bottle. Almost in a whisper he said, "What in hell was that?"

Sheepishly, Camran said, "Take it easy Roy Ruby, I just threw a bottle off down in the woods."

The sheriff took a deep breath. "I sure appreciate it you didn't do shit like that."

Camran said, "Sorry, Roy Ruby."

The sheriff handed the light to me. "Camran, let's roll Zeale over on his side and see if any blood is on his back." I played the light up and down Daddy's back and legs until the sheriff was satisfied he had not overlooked anything.

The sheriff took the light back. "Okay, that's enough for tonight. Camran, I want you to stay here with Zeale. I get back to my car, I'll call Boyd. Somebody will have to come out here tonight and take Zeale to the funeral home."

"No, sheriff. I'll take him back to Cedergren. He's not going out of here in a damned ambulance like some drunk that fell off the back of a flatbed truck." I said.

"I don't think we can do that," the sheriff mumbled, almost to himself.

"Yeah, we can and I'm going to do it. Camran, you drive Old Pony and I'll ride in the back with Daddy," I said, as if Daddy was still alive.

"Well …," the sheriff said, and when he turned to say something to Camran, he must have been surprised to see him loping up through the woods in the darkness toward Daddy's Suburban. He finished his sentence, "Ain't right, but ain't been nothing right this whole night. When we get out of here, I'll radio the office and have them tell Boyd we're coming. Guess I'll ask them to call Adam to get him come down and sign a death certificate. At least we'll have done something right."

"Appreciate this, sheriff. You take my jeep and just punch these numbers into the opener when you get to the gate. We'll be along soon as we can. Just leave the jeep and take the keys." I said, giving him the gate numbers scrawled on a piece of paper sack.

Roy Ruby nodded and squinted at the numbers.

*****

Camran backed Old Pony as far down the trail as he could. We clasped each other's wrists under Daddy's shoulders and behind his knees, and started up the hill. I was surprised he was so light.

I lowered the tailgate and crawled in, pulling Daddy behind me. I sat with my back against the seat and cradled Daddy's head in my lap. In the faint dome light, I could see Camran's cheeks were wet. With a shaky voice, he said, "Creight, he were big. Biggest damned man that ever lived in these mountains, I'll tell you. I heard a feller say once that a man's size is measured by his heart. If there's anything to that, Zeale was a giant."

I only half-heard Camran as I tried to erase the questions whirling through my mind: Where is Lock and is he all right?

Camran was watching me in the rearview mirror and intercepting my thoughts. His eyes narrowed, "I read signs a damn sight better than Roy Ruby. I seed him a looking at them boot tracks. You never wore boots like that and Zeale never. They damned sure ain't the boys. We get Zeale took care of, I'll come back and find the boy." He drove for a minute before saying, "I'll bring my .30 - 30 and take care of anything else needs taking care of too."

"Thank you, Camran. This is pretty close family business. I'll handle it."

He glared at me, his cold grey eyes murderous and lips pulled tight against his teeth, "Dammit, Creighton, this ain't got nothing to do with you handling a damned thing. Zeale was blood to me and … and I loved him. I aim to do this for him."

"No, you won't. I want you to keep off the Arn. This is my hand to play."

The buffalo had bedded back down near the road, and we disturbed their sleep again. They stood, blinking slowly in the headlights, their massive heads turning to follow Old Pony. Wild turkeys roosting in the trees beside the road stirred and gobbled as we went rattling past. How ironic, I thought, the critters given sanctuary in the Arn are the first to view his funeral procession. I couldn't help but wonder, were they the only ones witnessing Daddy's departure?

*****

Just after eleven o'clock, Camran pulled in behind Conall's Funeral Home and backed up to the double doors. Boyd, with two assistants, came out with a gurney. The assistants covered Daddy's body with a white blanket, then disappeared back inside, pushing the gurney in front of them. Boyd shook my hand, a look of genuine sadness on his face. "I'm sorry Creight. It comes to all of us, but I guess we're never ready."

"That's for sure," I mumbled.

"Your daddy had looked way down the road with this, just like everything else in his life. He was pretty specific about things. He wanted a plain pine box. He wanted to be laid to rest at Christian Springs, alongside the other Williams."

"Never left much to chance, did he?"

"No. No, he didn't. He intended to be in control right up to the end."

"And maybe a bit later," I said.

"He just wanted a graveside service. We argued some about that, and I guess it was the only argument I ever won with Zeale. I told him it wouldn't be fair to a lot of folks who would want to just come by and pay their respects. So, there'll be a viewing here from four o'clock tomorrow evening until eight o'clock tomorrow night.

"Brother Moody will say a few words at the graveside." Boyd paused, "Guess that's about it, unless you've got something."

Luther, Roy Ruby and Adam Huntsman were standing together just inside the door, talking softly. Adam shook my hand and wet his lips as if to say something, but no words came out. Trailed by Roy Ruby, Luther came toward me with his arms extended. We embraced and Roy Ruby looked away, embarrassed to be an intruder to the moment or maybe at seeing two grown men being so intimate.

Luther blew his nose. "I know he was your daddy and how much you must be hurting. He was the nearest thing to a daddy I ever had. I knew this day would come, but not like this.

"I know you loved him. He always thought of you and Aunt Winnie as family."

Roy Ruby cleared his throat, "I'm going back out to get the jeep. I'll carry a deputy with me to bring it back. We'll take it up to your daddy's … uh … your house. I'm going to leave a deputy here, and if you need anything else, he can get in contact with me."

As the sheriff drove away, Luther said with a weak smile, "Friends in high places."

I nodded and looked at my watch, surprised it was nearing midnight. "I've bout had it. We've got things to do and I don't know where to start."

"Not that much. Zeale knew this day would come; he's covered everything with Boyd, even down to the pallbearers. So far as I know, there's not a single detail that needs your attention. I've called Brother Moody. He'll be here first thing in the morning to work out the final details with Boyd. I talked with Grant Ellar. The lights were on at *The Mountain News* when I drove past. I'll bet Zeale's obituary is being finalized right now.

"Daddy took care of business, didn't he?"

"Always," Luther said.

"I don't know how to handle this, Luther. What are we going to do about Maggie?"

"I covered that," Luther said. "Logomicino flew out of Charlotte about thirty minutes ago."

Feeling I needed the two-mile walk to clear my head, I refused Luther's offer to drive me home. The night air was refreshing. But it did little to settle my mind.

I learned something when I stepped up on the front porch of Daddy's house. The people that live in the house are what make it home. If I lived here a hundred years, this would never be home again.

I went into Daddy's room, switched on the lights, and just stood and looked. The closet door was open. I knew the wedding dress was still there, along with Daddy's clothes. I took the dress box and laid it on the bed, carefully removed the wrapping, and gently took the fragile dress in my hands. Mother was just a girl when she and Daddy married. Hoping for a sweet fragrance, I smelled the dress but found only mustiness. I searched the box looking for a note, a piece of jewelry, maybe a faded flower but I found nothing. It was probably best. If I had found something, some personal item, I couldn't have coped with it.

I took a wooden hanger from the closet, and carefully hung the dress on it. I moved Daddy's clothes until his blue suit was the only thing hanging in the center of the rod, and then I hung the wedding dress against his suit. I'm sorry, Daddy, I know you wanted Maggie to be the one to open the box, but I wanted you near Mother tonight.

I lay down on Daddy's bed and found comfort in his scent, a scent leaving this earth forever.

We sat on the rocks at the fort, Mother, Daddy and me. The picnic basket contained fried chicken, baked beans, homemade light bread, slaw, and a jug of lemonade.

"We are going to get you a little brother," Daddy said.

"I know," I said. "I know his name."

Mother pulled me up against her and said, "Creighton, we haven't named him yet."

"Yes, Mother, his name is Lock," I said.

"No, son," Daddy said solemnly. "Lock won't be here for a long, long time."

The sun was streaming through the window, birds were singing, and Luther's voice was searching the house for me. "Creight, where are you?"

"Here. Daddy's room." The fuzziness wasn't leaving my head without a fight. While my watch insisted it was a quarter past nine, nothing in my system agreed.

Luther's voice was almost a whisper, "Are you about ready to get up?"

I sat on the edge of the bed with my face in my hands, "Thanks for waking me. Two nights with about an hour's sleep. Guess I must have crashed. Give me ten minutes to shower and I'll be able to think straight."

The shower and clean clothes helped, though not much. Luther was in the kitchen, talking on Daddy's old black, cradle phone. "No, I'm sorry. You should contact Wade Walker. He's in our corporate office in Charlotte. No, I've told you. No interviews today. No, no interviews tomorrow either. That policy will remain in effect." Luther listened a few seconds, and then hung up.

"News folks?" I asked.

Luther nodded, "Persistent as hiccups. I've been fielding calls since six this morning. All the wire services. TV stations down in Knoxville. That was somebody on Charles Kramer's staff. They want to set up interviews. 'Potentially, a great human interest story,' they said. I told them the same thing I told the other networks."

Luther dialed the phone. "Kate, this is Luther. All of my calls from the media are to be routed through Wade."

He turned back to me and smiled. "He's gone to see his mother-in-law in Wyoming. I know for a fact she doesn't have a phone, so that's that,"

"So where are we?" I asked.

Luther turned the pages of a yellow legal pad. "With the exception of opening and closing of the grave, your Daddy pretty much had everything covered."

"What about the casseroles the church ladies will bring by? Did he leave instructions about them?" We both had a good laugh. If Daddy had been with us, he would've laughed too.

*****

Luther suggested breakfast, but I asked to drive by Conall's first to see if Boyd needed anything or had any questions. The funeral home parking lot was full, so we used the back entrance. Boyd was on the phone. He shook his head wearily as he hung up, "It's been like this all morning: one phone call after another, everybody wanting information about Zeale's service."

"Join the crowd," Luther said.

"Did you see the parking lot?" Boyd said. "I've posted that visiting hours are from four to eight, but folks keep coming to the door, asking when they can come in. They'll sit out in their cars and trucks all afternoon. Just waiting until we open. Creight, this visitation is bigger than anything Zeale ever dreamed."

*****

The café was empty. A large wreath hung from the front door and someone was moving around inside. The door was unlocked, so we went in. The cook was walking around in the kitchen. Over in one corner, Louellen was sitting alone, her chin in the palms of her hands reading the paper. She came over and put her arms around me. "I'm so sorry. I'm just so sorry."

I patted her back. "Thank you, Louellen. You were awfully nice to him. He thought a lot of you."

"Mrs. Litchfield said no need to open this morning, but I just didn't know what else to do. I got here and Peanut was already in the kitchen, but we never even turned the grill on. The flower shop came by while ago and put a black wreath on the door," Louellen said before bursting into sobs.

Trying to control my emotions, I said, "Peanut make any coffee?"

Louellen motioned for Luther and me to sit. She returned with three mugs and set them on the table. She tried a smile, "These are on the house, or I guess you could say they are on the table." She sat down and shoved the paper over to me. "Look at that. Ain't that pitiful? I'd have thought Mr. Ellar would have done a better job than that." she said.

In the lower corner of the front page was a three-line blurb: *Mr. William Breazeale Roane, a former resident of Christian Springs, passed away last night. A private graveside service will be conducted tomorrow in the Roane family cemetery.*

I slid the paper over to Luther. "Read that!"

Luther slid the paper back, "Don't have to read it, I was with Mr. Roane when he wrote it. Mr. Ellar was making a joke one morning with the Brotherhood. He told them he would let them write their own obits. Your daddy took him up on it. When he took it down to the paper and gave it to Mr. Ellar, he said 'I don't want you to change a damn word, and I sure as heck don't want you adding anything to it.'"

I shook my head in disbelief. "That's all he wanted?"

"Yep, and exactly what Mr. Ellar gave him."

Louellen folded the paper and took it behind the counter, "Well, I still think it's tacky. I don't care what Mr. Roane said. If I'd been running the paper, I'd have wrote a whole lot more than that."

She went back into the kitchen. I heard the back door slam shut. She came back around the counter, pulled her apron over her head, and dropped it on a table beside us. "I've sent Peanut home, and now I'm going. Stay long as you like, just close the front door when you leave. It'll lock itself. Plenty of coffee in the urn, such as it is."

Luther and I sat alone in the silence of the café, each making mental notes for the day ahead. In the reflection of the café's front window, I could see the round table where the old men usually gathered. Today it was vacant. I turned away, and then looked back, giving images time to materialize. I wanted to see men joking and laughing. I would even have settled for ghostly images, but there was nothing, just emptiness.

Finally, Luther said, "Where is he?"

Slowly I came back to the present, "Where is …?"

"Where's Lock?"

"He's out at the Arn I reckon. Why'd you ask?"

"I talked with Camran about an hour ago. He says something, maybe part of a blue T shirt, was hanging from the barb wire on top of the security gate at the Arn."

"What else did Camran see? Any sign on the ground? Did he see anybody?"

"No. That's all. It may not be anything, maybe the wind blew the cloth up there, or maybe somebody is just pulling a prank."

"Maybe," I said. I didn't want to think about Lock leaving the Arn. I tried not to think about the blue T shirt I had given him. It was something like someone telling you to not think about an elephant.

Luther took me back home. I didn't want to go in the house. It was too soon. No, that's not right. It was too late. Too late to tell Daddy how much I'd missed him in the years I'd been gone; too late to ask him all those questions we always want to ask when a parent dies. Too late. It's all over.

I looked for comfort in Daddy's office. The fireplace, the cluttered desk, his wooden swivel chair, the paintings, the sculpture. The faceless man prominent in the paintings and the sculpture. My face. Gone for thirty years, missing for the entire life of the artist. I could almost hear a judge saying, "Dereliction of parenthood, punishable by no law other than the law of the guilty conscience." No comfort for me in that building.

I crossed the yard. Steering well clear of Daddy's bedroom, I climbed the stairs to my room. I had a white dress shirt. I looked through my old dresser and in the back of the bottom drawer, I found a black tie. It was ragged and outdated, just like I felt.

Looking in the mirror while knotting my tie, I was shocked by the dark circles under my eyes and the shagginess of my beard and hair. I removed my shirt, grabbed some scissors and in a moment, a slightly improved face peered back from the mirror. I was the sole representative of the family.

"Flying the family colors," Daddy always said. I assessed myself in the mirror again and decided they were flying from a tattered flag today.

I drove slowly through town to the funeral home. Now, not only was the parking lot full, but dusty cars and battered pickups were parked along both sides of the road for a half mile. I wondered what Daddy would have thought.

*****

After the doors opened at four, we had a steady stream of visitors.

The first people through the door were the Brotherhood of the Round Table. A kind of honor guard I thought. The old men lined up, hats in hand, and passed Daddy's open coffin.

As I had expected, a lot of old folks showed up because they always do when another old person dies, as a preview of what's waiting for them.

It was half past seven when two men dressed in dark suits came in and looked over the room. The smaller of the two disappeared and came back, trailed by a large gray-haired man. Luther had been talking with the Brotherhood. He hurried over to me and said, "Creight, the man walking toward us is Senator Edison Waggner"

"Luther," the senator fairly boomed. "I was just devastated when I learned of Zeale's death. You are aware of how much his support has meant to me over these past years. Were it not for him, I would probably still be trying cases in a lower court in Knoxville. I know you will miss your mentor terribly."

Luther shook the senator's hand. "Thank you for coming by." Then turning to me he said, "Senator, I'd like to introduce you to Mr. Roane's son, Creighton."

The senator seemed to change gears in almost mid-sentence. "Why, I didn't recall Mr. Roane having a son. I'm sorry we have to meet on such a sad occasion."

We shook hands and I thought, I've known a hundred men just like you. Phony right down to the soles of your shoes.

The senator surveyed the room, nodding, winking, and smiling at other potential voters. "Yes sir," he said. "Your daddy was a fine man and a real friend to me. A real friend."

Luther tugged at the senator's elbow. "Come over here, Senator, some men I'd like for you to meet."

He steered the senator over to the Brotherhood and made introductions. When Luther came back, he said, "I'm starting to read you like a book – it's a lot like reading your daddy. He thought Waggner was a pompous windbag. But he said Waggner was the best of the incompetents, so he supported him. A photograph on the front page of any local paper of your daddy and the senator shaking hands was all it took to sway the upper East Tennessee vote. The senator was truthful when he said he would still be trying cases in some lower court in Knoxville if it hadn't been for the support of your daddy."

I watched the senator working his way around the room, shaking hands and slapping backs. "So he owes Daddy?"

"Big." Luther responded.

Just after eight o'clock, Boyd Conall came to where Luther and I were sitting, "Creight, if it's okay with you, I'm going to start turning out some lights, kinda give folks the notion we need to close. If we don't, some of these folks will be here all night."

"Good idea. This has been a long day. We all need to get some rest."

Soon, Boyd and I were the only people left. "If it's okay with you, Creight, I need to close him for the night."

I agreed. Boyd closed the coffin, and then said, "Let me run you home."

I stood and looked at Daddy's coffin, "Thanks, Boyd, but I'm going to spend this last night with Daddy."

Boyd put his arm around me. "Creight, I'm not sure it's the right…"

I interrupted, "No, Boyd, I'm sure it's exactly the right thing."

Boyd brought a pillow and blanket from an office closet, tossed them on a couch in the lobby, and left for the night.

*****

I roamed the hallway of the empty funeral home, looking at the paintings of all the Conall family members who had attended to the final services of the citizens of Cedergren. I turned on the lights in the display room and looked at the polished coffins with their gleaming handles. I was glad that Daddy was making his last journey in a plain pine box.

I turned out the light and lay on the couch, pulling the blanket under my chin and rolling the pillow into a ball under my head. The grandfather clock in the hall struck ten o'clock. I wondered if sleep would ever come.

I never heard the clock chime the quarter hour.

The wind shivered the river birch leaves and caused small ripples on the lake turning gold in the light of the setting sun. Small butterflies investigated something in the stream that fed the lake and were disturbed when a gray heron silently glided in to perch on an overhanging limb. Somewhere across the lake, Whip-poor-wills were trying to outdo each other – their rolling calls echoing through the night. The sky faded from gold to purple, then to black. Millions of miles away, stars emerged. I could dimly see the outline of the cabin and in the darkness, a shadow materialized from the porch, turned into pale silver, and dissolved.

*****

The rattling of the front door woke me. The luminous hands on my watch showed it was ten after twelve. I switched on the hall light and after looking through the window and seeing no one, unlocked and opened the front door to only the sounds of crickets, katydids, and the far-off barking of a dog. I felt foolish. It was obvious the sound at the door was simply an extension of my dream.

I woke again at half past one to the sound of the door opening and voices. One of Roy Ruby's deputies was standing in the doorway. As I stood up from the couch, his hand momentarily fell toward his pistol. "Sweet Jesus!" he said. "You liked to have scared me to death. I sure didn't expect to see anybody up walking around."

"Well, the feeling is mutual. I didn't expect to see anything walking around either, particularly at this time of night."

The deputy introduced himself as Heck Forbes. "We keep a set of funeral home keys at the office. Sometimes when there has been a death, we come down and open up before the ambulance gets here. I didn't mean to scare you."

I sat back down on the couch and started to put on my shoes. "Has there been a death tonight?"

"Oh no, nothing like that. Roy Ruby called and told me to meet some folks down here and let them in"

"At this time of night?"

The deputy looked over his shoulder and then moved to the side as the bulk of Tony Logomicino filled the doorway behind him. He stepped into the hallway and said, "I'm sorry about Mr. Roane's death."

I nodded, "Thank you for what you've done for Daddy all these years."

He turned and motioned to the woman standing behind him. "This is Maggie Lockhart."

THE BEGINNING OF THE END

I had known this moment was coming. A smarter man would have developed a greeting, some plan, something. I stood slack-jawed, nothing, absolutely nothing. Now I understood what Daddy meant. She is a beautiful woman. Her eyes are a deep blue – blue as the Findhorn – and her smile is sweet and sad at the same time. Maggie took my hand and said, "I am sorry about Papa Zeale's death. As great as the shock was to me, I know it was even greater to you."

"Thank you for coming back."

She nervously ran her hand over her hair. "I must apologize for my appearance. We were preparing for a noon dive when a boat came in and anchored in the cove. They lowered a runabout, and as soon as I saw Logomicino, I knew something was wrong."

"Luther told me Logomicino was going down to get you, but I had no idea when you'd get here."

"We called Luther when we got into Knoxville. He said he would arrange for someone to meet us here. I hope you won't think I'm intruding."

"How could you be intruding? Other than Mother, Daddy loved you more than any woman in the world."

Maggie gave me a sad smile, and I saw the deep dimples in each cheek. "After all these years, I guess I've finally one-upped Papa Zeale, because I can truthfully say, I loved him more than I ever loved any man."

"Not easy to one-up Daddy."

"He gave me shelter and protection in the most vulnerable times of my life. And he never quit, he was always my champion."

Listening to Maggie talk about Daddy, it was difficult not to feel humiliated. "I'm sorry how things turned out. I'm sorry about the problems with your family."

With a cool, calm voice, Maggie said, "You shouldn't be. The problems in my family started long before we moved to Cedergren. I loved my father, but he … he never changed."

A drop of moisture slid down my spine, and I wondered if the air conditioner was working. "Not exactly what I'm talking about. I think if you hadn't been …"

"Pregnant? But I was, and it was a fact of life. Mother could have dealt with it but not Daddy. He was always looking for an excuse to go into a tantrum. Sounds like you have talked with Dr. Blackman or Vaughn," Maggie said her voice little more than a whisper.

"I'm haunted by the thought that … if I had been here, we could have …".

"It is not significant after all these years," Maggie interrupted.

"No, I mean it. I'm just getting to know Lock, and I've seen his work. Daddy has told me some of the problems and, if I had been here, maybe…". My mouth was getting ahead of my brain and I wasn't making any sense.

"A noble thought but probably not very realistic. In some ways, we were both children. Obviously, old enough to have children, but still both of us were very immature. Even if we had married, well, neither of us was prepared for marriage. This way, I grew up in a hurry. I had to. Papa Zeale provided stability. He gave me room to mature, to grow, and he also gave me love, something I'd never had."

"But maybe I could have grown into a husband. Maybe I could've grown up in a hurry like you did."

"I'm assuming you didn't know you were leaving a pregnant girl here in this little town. It's not as if you ran off rather than accepting responsibility. Somehow, I get the sense that you beat yourself up over things that are beyond your control. Is that a fair observation?"

"Maybe. I guess I never thought of it that way."

"This is my philosophy. Many things in this life are beyond our control. We should cope with them. Cope, not solve. Just cope. The circumstances we are able to change - those are the things we concentrate on."

Maggie smoothed her hair once more. I noticed the scattering of silver and I thought Daddy was right. Probably she had no idea how beautiful she was.

The ice was broken. We spent the next hour talking about Daddy, our lives after the Dove Landing incident, and Lock.

Finally, Maggie asked, "How is he? He was so dependent on Papa Zeale, and now with ...," her voice trailed off, and tears welled up in her eyes.

"He's okay," I said, trying to project more confidence than I had.

Maggie looked into my eyes and read me, "But you aren't really sure."

I felt foolish. "Not really, but Camran and I are going out as soon as we can. We'll find him. He'll be all right."

I explained to her my plans to take Lock to Alaska. She just listened, shaking her head occasionally. I could tell it was going to take a lot of convincing. After all, he is just as much her son as mine. No, he is more.

"I've got to get some sleep. Tomorrow will be a long day. This has been a long day. Before I go, I'd like to see Papa Zeale."

"Sure."

We went into the viewing room and were met by a warm breeze flowing in through a partially opened window. I raised the lid and Maggie leaned over the coffin, staring at Daddy. She wiped tears from her eyes.

"I know this is such a cliché, but he looks so natural. And what a nice gesture, Boyd has put one of those peach seed carvings of a dove on his tie. How many of those did I watch Papa Zeale whittle?"

The hair on my neck stiffened as the night breeze sluggishly crept through the open window. There had been no peach-seed carving when we closed the coffin earlier tonight – and the window had certainly been closed.

The gate was open leading into the Arn and the Roane cemetery. Tony Logomicino with two other men directed traffic, diverting all but a few cars.

The Brotherhood carried Daddy to the open grave. We gathered in the shade of the Pitch Pines. I looked at the small gathering: Luther, his sons, Julie, Maggie, the Brotherhood, and Brother Moody. Moody cleared his throat. Timidly, I searched for and found Maggie's hand.

"Mr. Roane was very specific in how his service was to be conducted," Moody said. "He wanted a prayer and one song – that's all. Ordinarily, as most of you know, his word was second only to the Lord here in these mountains. But only his body is here today. His spirit has gone to some other place, to a place of mystery, a place all of us will see someday. Before we have our prayer, I want to read something to you I have read and reread for many years. It is from Longfellow's, *A Psalm of Life*:

> *In the world's broad field of battle,*
> *In the bivouac of Life,*
> *Be not like dumb, driven cattle!*
> *Be a hero in the strife!*
> *Trust no Future, howe'er pleasant!*
> *Let the dead Past bury its dead!*
> *Act, - act in the living Present!*
> *Heart within, and God o'erhead!*

Lives of great men all remind us
We can make our lives sublime,
And, departing, leave behind us
Footprints on the sand of time;
Footprints, that perhaps another,
Sailing o er life's solemn main,
A forlorn and shipwrecked brother,
Seeing, shall take heart again.

Moody said a short prayer. As he said amen, the words of the poem rang in my ears, was this some kind of message Daddy had left behind for me? Be a hero in the strife… act in the living present … footprints on the sand of time … life's solemn main … forlorn and shipwrecked brother … seeing, shall take heart again. With my eyes closed and temples pounding, the cadence and the words of the poem seeped into the crevices of my soul.

Behind us, the moan and wail of bagpipes interrupted the silence. Adam Huntsman came striding along the narrow trail dressed in full Highland garb, the notes of *Amazing Grace* surrounding him. I could hear Daddy say, "We've always done it this way. This is the way we always say goodbye to the Roane men; with *Amazing Grace*."

As Adam came up the hill, the Brotherhood lowered Daddy's body into the grave. When the song ended, Adam was standing at the edge of the open grave. He leaned forward, picked up a handful of dirt, and sprinkled it on the coffin. One by one, the Brotherhood did the same.

David said, "Thank all of you for coming today, and thank you for your part in this service. I'd like to suggest we leave Maggie, Creighton, and Luther and his family here for a time. I have found a great degree of healing in privacy at the end of the service."

A round of handshaking, and slowly the men left the cemetery. Luther whispered that he and his family would leave, allowing Maggie and me to have some time together before the grave was filled.

"Boyd, I know this has been an unusual day and I've got another request. I'd like to fill Daddy's grave myself."

"Sure thing, Creight. It's unusual, but I've seen it done before. I've always thought it a sweet final gesture. Maybe Camran or somebody could come out tomorrow and open the gate so we could get the rest of our equipment."

"I'll ask Camran to give you a call tomorrow morning and ya'll can work out the details." I took a shovel from Boyd's work truck and the funeral director and his crew left.

I took off my tie and started filling the grave. Maggie said, "I'll go out and tell Logomicino to close the gate while we finish up and that we won't need him the rest of the day."

Maggie disappeared down the trail toward the gate, and I turned to the grave again. Just you and me, Daddy. One William Roane looking after another William Roane. You said we've always done it, but we are about to reach the end of the Roanes.

Filling the grave was hard work. I was half through when I straightened up to stretch my aching back. Lock was standing ten feet from me, tears streaming down his cheeks.

He was wearing dirty, torn jeans and old tennis shoes. He was shockingly gaunt. He was wearing the Aleutian Air T-shirt I had given him. It was torn to ribbons and a large part of the back was missing. The ribs on one side of his body were crisscrossed by deep cuts. They had scabbed over and dried blood stained his torn pants. He was expressionless and, except for his tears, absolutely no emotion in his being.

"You've come to help us bury Papa Zeale," I said. Lock nodded. I extended the shovel. Lock grasped the handle tentatively but made no other movement.

"It's okay," I said. "It's like when you helped us bury Rip. We need to do this to show Papa how much we love him. It's okay to cry; I've cried a lot, and I'll probably cry a lot more."

Listlessly, Lock started shoveling dirt into the partially filled grave. His movements were slow. There was no sign of any energy. *You're in one of those low places Daddy talked about* I thought.

"Did you hear Adam playing *Amazing Grace?*"

Lock nodded, then sat cross-legged beside the grave, hands over his face, body shaking softly.

"Your mother is here. Did you see her?"

Lock stopped crying, looked at me, and wiped his face with his dirty hands.

"She'll be back in a minute. Do you want to talk with her?"

Ignoring my question, Lock started filling the grave again.

"You're doing a good job. I'll be back in just a minute."

I walked down the trail to warn Maggie and to prepare her for Lock's appearance. Just out of sight of the cemetery, I met her. "Lock is at Daddy's grave. But he's kinda cut up and bloody. He's not very good."

"I've seen him like that, so I know what to expect," Maggie whispered as we continued back up the trail. "I haven't seen him in three years. I … I … just want to touch him."

Together we walked into the empty clearing.

Lock had disappeared.

*****

It was dark when we left. We had repeatedly called Lock but there was no response. Without success, I tried to convince Maggie that his disappearance had nothing to do with her. "Thanks for trying to make me feel better," she said, "but he and I lost all connection years ago. His condition had been deteriorating for … years. Your daddy insisted we go to the best facility and we chose Mayo. Lock underwent a battery of physical examinations. The doctors were looking for specific symptoms, medical and family history, cultural settings, and environmental factors that would help determine the best treatment."

Hoping Maggie had some insight that Daddy had hidden from me, I asked, "What did they decide?"

"They were baffled. They treated the depression with all manner of drugs and cognitive therapy. Three months went by and no improvement. They reevaluated the medicine and dosage. Nothing positive happened."

"What was he like while all this was going on?"

Maggie took a deep breath and continued with a sigh. "Toward the end, he had totally withdrawn to where he would not respond to me or any of the Mayo staff. Then, one day he attacked the psychiatrist who had worked with him for weeks. Fortunately, two attendants were nearby, but the psychiatrist was seriously injured. The clinic suspended treatment and suggested we try another facility. Really, they asked us to leave. Papa Zeale, Dr. Huntsman and I decided to bring Lock back to Cedergren."

"Was this his first violent episode?"

Maggie shook her head, "No, there had been others but not to this extent. I checked Lock out of the clinic and we started home. He was sullen and withdrawn. An hour south of Rochester, Lock opened the car door and just stepped out. We must have been going fifty. I don't know why he wasn't killed."

"Had he said anything before he jumped?"

Maggie was crying. I put my arm around her. She regained her composure and said, "Just before he jumped, he looked at me and said, 'Why did you do this to me?' He's not spoken to or looked at me since."

"What an awful experience."

Maggie continued, "He was unconscious after hitting the highway. Had massive bruises and a torn ligament in his leg. Two truckers helped get him back in the car, and I took him to a hospital. The scene in the emergency room was somewhere between a nightmare and a war. He turned over tables, broke most of the lights, just destruction. The doctor finally let me in to try to calm him down. He was crouched in the corner like some kind of wild animal, naked, blood and saliva dripping from his chin. It took three orderlies and a policeman to subdue him. They got him sedated. I called Papa Zeale. He and Luther arrived early the next morning.

"Did he get any better after Daddy got there?"

"A little, I guess. At least, he got in the car with Papa Zeale. Luther and I followed them back to Cedergren. Papa Zeale took Lock directly home and Luther convinced me I shouldn't even try to see him for a while. Papa Zeale got some camping stuff, an old flat bottom boat, some clothes and they drove out to the Arn. Papa Zeale was out on the Arn with him for a month without ever coming home. Camran or Luther took groceries out once a week, but I don't think either ever saw Lock."

"And you haven't seen him since?"

"No." Maggie said, and broke into deep, racking sobs.

*****

We turned into Maggie's drive. The porch light came on immediately, and Louellen came down the steps to meet us. The women hugged. Louellen patted Maggie on the back like she would a hurt child.

"I've been so worried about you," Louellen said. "I know this has been one of the worst days of your life. I'll bet you're totally beat. I've got some fresh sweet tea in the refrigerator; ya'll come on in and I'll fix us some. I've got some coconut cake left over from last night."

Maggie looked at me inquiringly. I shook my head, "Thank you, but you're right about this being a long day. I know Maggie is about dead because I am, and I've had more sleep than she has. Let's just call it a day and we'll see how things look in tomorrow's light."

"He's right," Maggie said. "I'm afraid my thinking process is functioning at about ten percent."

Like two best friends, we shook hands and Maggie walked wearily into her house. Louellen asked, "How do you think she's getting along?"

"She's pretty tough," I answered. "She'll be okay after a good night's sleep."

"I'm not trying to be nosey, but did she see Lock? She'd so hoped she would."

"He was there after the service but she didn't get to see him."

"He hid, didn't he?"

"Yes."

"If that just don't beat all. He ain't got no cause to act like that."

*****

I stopped at Person Brothers service station and bought two six-packs of Bud. Lit only by a single street light, Cedergren was deserted.

I parked in front of the courthouse. The clock struck eleven as I opened my third beer. The cruiser eased in beside me. "You got a cold one left for me?" the sheriff asked.

"Damn, sheriff. You're everywhere, aren't you? Looks like you would have something better to do than hassle law-abiding citizens."

The sheriff heaved himself into the seat beside me. "Gus Heckle, my old stove-up deputy that looks after things at night, called and said you was setting out here in the dark drinking beer. I told him I'd take care of things. Now gimme one of them damn beers before I have to haul you in for disobeying an officer of the law."

I shoved the carton over to the sheriff, "Help yourself. But don't make me have to do a citizen's arrest because you were drunk and disorderly."

The sheriff's Adam's apple moved up and down three times before he lowered the can. "Pretty much hit the spot. Worth getting out of bed for, I'd say."

"I appreciate everything you've done for us the last few days. I know things could've been done a lot different the other night. We probably went against everything in the sheriff's handbook, but thank you for helping me get Daddy out."

"Hey, that's our motto: We serve and protect. Gimme another beer." The sheriff pulled the top on his second beer and said, "Since we're being straight up with each other, gimme me an answer to a question. Other night when I drove your jeep out of the Arn, the holster for that big pistol of your daddy's was in the floor board."

"It was?"

"Yeah, it was. Nothing but the empty holster. Where you reckon that pistol is at?"

"I don't know sheriff. You think it might be somewhere around the camp?"

"No, I don't think that. I'm old, Creighton, but I want you to know I can still read people. You told me you found Zeale around noon, but you didn't call Camran until after dark. Six hours in there I don't know where you were at or what in the hell you was a doing."

I opened the fourth beer and took my time before saying, "Sheriff, I don't think you want to know the answer to either of those questions."

"Yeah." The sheriff looked at me for a long time. "I don't reckon I'll ever ask you about any of that again."

I didn't respond.

"Another thing you might be interested in, Creighton. Old lady McCamy was down at the office this evening. Said her boys ain't been home since Zeale died. Wasn't like them, last night was Iliad's birthday. About the whole tribe was at her house waiting to share his birthday supper."

"Bet they just laid out drunk somewhere. They'll be home."

"Sure," the sheriff said. "I know how fond you are of them. If they don't show in a couple more days, may have to get some bloodhounds and look for them. Don't guess you'd mind if we took a look out at the Arn, would you?"

I didn't answer what I knew was not a question.

"Another thing, Creighton: The TBI boys will be up here the middle part of next week." The sheriff's face was lit momentarily as he fired up his cigar. "Not that it would interest you. I just thought I'd tell you."

"Thanks for telling me. Next week, feel free to take as many dogs you want to out to the Arn. Try to stay away from the buffalo. I understand they don't take kindly to dogs. It'll be okay if you take the TBI along for the ride. I'd say next week would be real good."

The sheriff took another long pull on his cigar and the pleasant odor of a Swisher Sweet drifted past my nose. "Figured it would be all right with you and, if you don't mind, I believe I'll take another Bud. Kinda one for the road. I'm assuming you're going home, driving real slow and careful like."

"Yes sir," I said, pulling another beer out of the carton, putting it in the sheriff's outstretched hand.

The sheriff stepped out of the jeep. "Thanks."

I cranked the jeep. The sheriff leaned over and tapped the windshield with his beer can. "Have somebody send me a Christmas card so I'll know everything is okay."

I set Daddy's wind-up alarm clock for half past six, climbed into his bed and lay in the dark, listing to the mechanical tick-tick-tick. Daddy said he'd laid here in this bed many nights feeling sorry for himself. I thought, finally I'm following in your footsteps. It took a while, but I'm doing it.

Daddy sat on the edge of the porch and sharpened his worn Barlow knife on the sole of his work boot. I watched as he fished around in his shirt pocket and pulled out a peach seed. He turned it over in his thick fingers, examined it from all directions, and then started carving.

Without looking up from his whittling, he said, "I had hoped that Lock and I might leave this world together but we didn't. It turned out I was like that ripe apple, I just fell off the tree. I told you I might pass the cards to you and see how you played the hand. Well, Creight, you've got them.

Daddy rolled the partially finished carving over in his fingers, looked at it again, and went back to whittling. You need to get on with this. Don't wait. I wish Lock could get out of there tomorrow. I'll rest better when he's in Alaska."

He stood up. The blade clicked as he shut the knife and dropped it in his pocket. He examined the partially finished carving, the same type dove I'd seen him carve dozens of times, and handed it to me. Here you are – it's all in your hands now. You finish it.

He turned to leave, stopped, and gave me a wry smile. "You know, you cheated Camran out of something he really wanted to do. It was a good day's work you did, taking care of the McCamy brothers. They had it coming. I wished I'd done it a long time ago."

*****

The clock did its job. It started hammering at six thirty, and I put my feet on the floor. I showered and then called Maggie, "Why don't you come over and let me fix you some breakfast."

"I didn't know you could cook."

"There's probably a lot of things you don't know about me. 'Sides, anybody can stir up biscuits and break some eggs. How does half past eight sound?"

"Two scrambled and no grits."

*****

I hustled. I made up the bed, picked up dirty clothes, gave the bathroom a quick scrubbing, and even ran a damp cloth over the kitchen cabinets. Two men batching together needed a housekeeper, or just needed to change houses after a couple months.

The biscuits were ugly, but passable. I found sausage, crumbled it up, and cooked it with the eggs. The old tin percolator was gurgling as Maggie tapped on the screen door. I answered her knock with the standard mountain welcome, "Come on in, if you can get in."

Maggie, wearing a red blouse and black slacks, came straight to the kitchen. "Good morning," she said, taking a mug from the cabinet. "I hope the coffee is strong because I need something to get my heart started this morning."

"I may not be much of a cook, but I make an excellent cup of coffee. And I'm modest too."

Maggie took a sip of the coffee, unfolded a *USA Today* on the kitchen table, and turned to the *Life* section. "Take a look at that," she said.

Above the fold of the page was a color photograph of Daddy, superimposed over an aerial photograph of the Arn. The caption read *Mountain Monarch Mourned*. I spent the next five minutes reading the article, which accurately chronicled Daddy's life from a struggling woodsman to an almost reclusive philanthropic businessman. His love of wildlife conservation and timber management was applauded by heads of various Federal and State agencies. There were favorable interviews with state educators commenting on his commitment to higher education of the people of the Appalachians.

"Daddy would've had a fit," I said after finishing the article.

"Maybe, maybe not. Did you notice not one local person was quoted? Everybody up here in these parts respected Papa Zeale's privacy, even after his death."

"That's a thought, and it says a lot about how folks around here respected him," I said, refolding the paper.

"Okay," Maggie said. "Now let's see your biscuits."

I took two plates from the cabinet and set them on the table. I filled a third plate with the egg-sausage mixture and hot biscuits. Maggie took another drink of coffee and said, "Do you like these dishes?"

"Yeah. I don't remember them being here when I was growing up."

"I brought them to Papa Zeale from Hawaii. He had never seen the ocean, and he wanted to know if this was the color of the Pacific. Lock told him the ocean had a more fishy color. Your daddy laughed and always called them his fishy dishes." She moved the eggs around in her plate, and then said with an unsteady voice, "I'm going to miss him, and Lock will be lost without him."

"We … we need to talk about Lock."

"I don't know how to say this without it sounding strange." Her chin trembled and her voice had a choked quality. "If your daddy had asked me, I would have married him. I can't explain how I felt about him. He was so kind to me before Lock was born, and then all during his growing up years. There was almost a forty year age difference and well .., I can't explain it but I probably loved him more than you did."

"He loved you as much as you loved him."

Maggie took a paper napkin and dabbed at the corners of her eyes, "I hope he knew how much I cared."

"Let's eat breakfast before it's stone cold. Let me tell you about my plans."

After we finished, Maggie insisted we wash the dishes. "You wash and I'll dry," she said. I'm not a romantic but I thought this is nice. Twice, when our elbows touched, I was alive with electricity and wondered if my hair and beard was standing straight out. *It could have been like this*, I thought. Then my chest filled with emotion, and I was afraid to look at Maggie.

I took the damp dishrag, cleaned the table, and still without looking at her said, "Let's go out to Daddy's office. That's where business was always conducted around here."

The little office was cold without Daddy. I sat in one of the straight chairs in front of his desk and gestured for Maggie to sit in the other.

"Let me tell you my plans for Lock," I said.

"I'm not sure I want to hear them," Maggie said, meeting my eyes with a cold stare.

"I don't think there is a choice for any of us."

For the next half hour, I went over what had happened in the past weeks: our encounter with the McCamys at the Arn and them taking their case to the newspaper, the certain indictments, and the sheriff's concern with the TBI preparing to search the Arn. "Finally," I said, "the sheriff told me last night, both Homer and Iliad McCamy are missing. I've got a hunch they've been back out on the Arn again, and …?"

"You've got a hunch …?" Maggie's voice trailed off, leaving a question hanging.

"Yes."

She leaned forward and stared at me. "It's more than a hunch, isn't it?"

"We may leave in the morning. No later than the day after."

Her eyes boring into me again, "You didn't answer my question."

"I answered the best I could. We need to put this behind us, not talk about it anymore."

She leaned back and crossed her arms. "What happens if I disagree with your plans?"

"Then I would ask you what you think we should do. What is your plan?"

"I don't have a plan but I don't want my son to just leave. I might never see him again."

"Do you see him now?"

Tears welled up in Maggie's eyes, "That was cruel."

"I'm not trying to be cruel. I promised Daddy I would look after Lock. Give me a better solution. Tell me how to keep him from being jailed. Tell me how to keep some glory-seeking, half-wit from hunting him down and killing him. Do you think I would take him to some strange place, take him out of his comfort zone, if I had a better solution? For God's sake, Maggie, I'd like to do something right for just one time in my life. Just one time."

Maggie walked around the room, then stopped and opened a drawer in the lower part of the built-in bookcase. She searched the drawer. Not finding what she was looking for, she opened and searched a second drawer. Then, in obvious frustration, searched a third and fourth drawer before saying, "Where is it?"

"What are you looking for?"

"A small, deer-skin sack, smaller than a shoe box. It's always been in one of these lower drawers. For fifteen years it's been here."

"What's in it?"

"Oh … a hammer, some chisels, small things used for a fine finish on a sculpture," she said, frustration growing.

"Why would Daddy have something like that here in his office?"

"They weren't Papa Zeale's, they were Lock's. He left them here and when I asked him why, he said, 'When Papa Zeale's gone, I want them here. It will help me have good memories.'"

"I never saw them," I said, almost defensively.

"Have you noticed anything else missing?"

I looked around the room making a quick inventory. "I don't notice anything."

"Where is the small sculpture that sat by the door?"

"I don't know. I've not been here much since Daddy's death. I just haven't missed it."

Maggie walked over and looked out the window behind Daddy's desk. "Why didn't you look at me when our elbows touched while we washed dishes?"

"I don't know, I just felt like …"

"Why didn't you sit in Papa Zeale's chair when we came to the office a while ago? You are the head of the family now." Maggie said, her back still to me.

"I don't know, I just thought – I didn't feel like I, I … uh …, measure up and …," my words trailed off and I had no answer. I sat with my face in my hands and did not look up until I heard Maggie's footsteps crossing the office floor.

"Where are you going?" I asked.

She didn't answer. But as the screen door slammed, she said, "Call me tonight."

*****

I spent the rest of the morning making phone calls, starting with Willie West. The Jet Ranger was ready, and we agreed an early morning pickup would be best for everybody. He'd flown the Findhorn River with clients and was familiar with the tip of the Arn. "Couldn't miss them damned buffalos and the old rock fort," he said. "Sunday morning at six o'clock, be about daylight. I'll not miss it more than five minutes either way. I'll get you out slicker than a widow's kiss and twice as fast."

The second call was to Aleutian Air. I explained my tentative timetable to Jamiesie and he said, "I'm waiting. When you are thirty minutes out, somebody at the tower can give me a holler. I guarantee you fifteen minutes from the time you hit the ground here, we'll be in the air. We're going to make this thing work. I don't know what kind of trail you're leaving but ain't going to be any sign here. Vanishing into thin air don't even start to describe it."

The raspy voice of Roy Ruby Fox answered, "Sheriff Fox."

"Sheriff, this is Creighton. I'm solving our problem in the morning. I'd appreciate it if you could keep folks off the Arn but if you can't, you can't. I don't believe they're going to find anything out there. Leastways, they're not going to find any of my kin. Let them investigate until the cows come home."

I heard the click of the sheriff's Zippo lighter and then a long exhale, "Anything I can do to help?"

"No, I'm good," I said.

The sheriff's office chair squeaked as he shifted his weight, "Good luck to you."

*****

Luther's secretary said he was just ending a meeting and would be free within fifteen minutes. I parked the old jeep at the front of Roman's small, unpretentious office in a space "Reserved for Mr. Roane." I smiled when I saw grass growing up in the cracks of the pavement.

"Hey. Creight, come on in to my office." After we sat, he said, "I know it sounds crass, but I've had Roman's accountants in, and we're starting to implement some things Mr. Roane wanted done after his death. Personal things. The legal people will come over from Charlotte in a couple of days and we'll open his will. He left a copy with me. Of course, we'll want you here when the original is read."

"I won't be here, so go ahead without me."

"I prefer you to be here. The latest will was written five years ago at a time when Mr. Roane thought you were dead. He'd scheduled a meeting with Roman's lawyers for the end of next week to make major revisions – most of them relating to you and the position he was assigning you with the company."

"Who is the executor of the will?"

"I am, but I am acting in your stead. The will is clear in that. The will states that if you're competent at the time of Mr. Roane's death, you have full power to make all decisions relating to his interest in Roman and all subsidiaries."

Luther opened a folder and pushed a file across his desk to me. "This is the copy of the will."

Without opening the file, I slid it back to Luther. "When the will is opened, you'll not know if I am living or dead and my competency is certainly questionable."

"I'm not sure I'm following you."

"I want the corporate jet at the Roman hanger in Knoxville Sunday. Early morning."

Luther raised his eyebrows, "You're leaving?"

"Yes."

Luther seemed to ponder my answer, "It will be necessary for the plane's logs to show the final destination. You are aware of that, aren't you?"

"It will be a round trip, starting and ending in Knoxville. Lock and I will be on the plane when it leaves, but not on it when it returns. It's as simple as that. Maybe the log will show the trip … I don't know … was just to pick up some fresh salmon."

"You don't think I need to know anything else?"

"No. What you don't know can't hurt you."

Luther rubbed his eyes for a moment, "How do we handle Mr. Roane's affairs?"

"Just as he requested. I assume financial provisions for Maggie are in place?"

Luther nodded, "More than adequate."

"Good. I knew Daddy would've taken care of her. If a trust can be established so I can discreetly access it at some time in the future, I'd appreciate it. I have total faith in you," I said as I stood up from the table.

"What else can I do to help?" Luther asked, his voice shaky.

"Wish me a good trip. Charter Aleutian Air every couple of years. Ask the pilot where the best fishing is. Maybe bring Maggie with you." I tried to smile. "Keep the grass killed out of Daddy's parking space."

*****

Back at the house, I packed my clothes in the beat-up duffle bag that had seen me through so many trips. I took the cigar box with Maggie's daddy's derringer in it and put it on the bed. I carefully repacked Mother's wedding dress, sealing the box the best I could. I loaded everything in the jeep and went back into the house. I didn't go upstairs but I looked in the downstairs rooms: the kitchen, Daddy's bedroom and the living room, and burned their images into my mind.

Back in the office, I looked at Daddy's battered desk, his bookcases, and the paintings. I took the two calendars from the wall, one current, and one for the year 1956. I rolled them up and tied them with a string. I took some half-finished peach seed carvings from Daddy's desk and his old pocketknife. I pulled Daddy's black felt hat on my head and said goodbye to all the memories.

There was no car in Maggie's drive, but I rang the bell and was surprised when Louellen opened the door. With her cheerful smile, Louellen said, "Maggie had to run down to the school to get some kind of records. She'll be back in five minutes."

I gave the box containing Mother's wedding dress to Louellen, and told her there was a note from Daddy inside. I asked her to give it to Maggie. I told her the cigar box contained a pistol that had belonged to Maggie's father. I didn't think the rest of the story was worth telling, so I just let it go.

"Maggie will be awful disappointed she missed you," Louellen said. "You need to give her a call. She was pure tore up when she got back here this mornin'. Stayed in her room for a long time and I could hear her crying. Said she owed you an apology, said she'd said some mean things. Said things had not turned out like they was supposed to. You going to call her tonight, ain't you?"

I nodded and hugged Louellen.

Just before I made the curve at the end of the street, I looked in the rearview mirror and saw Maggie's car turning into her driveway. I saw no reason to go back. A man told me once, "When you've seen Denali, the giant redwoods, or the Grand Canyon, somehow it becomes not worth the effort to see inferior versions."

Maggie had spent too many years around Daddy. My version of manhood would never measure up.

THE ESCAPE

I pressed the numbers on the keypad, the gate opened, and I followed the road out to the camp. It was my first trip to the lake since Daddy's death.

The flat-bottom johnboat was tied to an old bitternut tree at the edge of the lake, but I found no sign of a campfire. I checked the wooden food box. Nothing had been disturbed. No sign that Lock had been back. Even the two beat-up old lawn chairs were just as I'd last seen them.

I drove out toward the old fort, looking for any human footprints in the dusty road. There were only a couple of prints from a buffalo calf and a wallowed-out place where a turkey had dusted. The ruins at the fort were deserted and no sign of a campfire. I stood at the rim of the escarpment and shouted Lock's name. The only response was an echo bouncing mockingly up from the gorge.

Checking alongside the road again, I drove back to the south end of the plateau to the cemetery. Boyd Conall's men had been here earlier in the day and removed their tent and pads. The pall of roses was missing. I thought it inconsiderate of Conall's men to take it.

For the first time, I felt anxiousness. While it was just a little after three and more than three hours before sundown, I didn't want to be searching the woods for him in the dark. I decided to go back to the camp and try ringing the bell Daddy used to call Lock.

I left the jeep parked on the crest of the ridge where the camp road intersected with the road leading to the fort. Maybe Lock would see it and start looking for me. Walking down to the camp, I continued to shout his name. I pulled the bell's rope and the deep peal rolled out through the timber – haunting like the sound something hurt would make. I stopped and shouted Lock's name again.

I saw a splash of color near the old campfire site. There had been nothing when I'd checked earlier. I left the bell and walked through the brush toward the camp. Lock was sitting on the ground between the two lawn chairs; Daddy's canvas coat draped over one knee. The pall of roses was spread across the top of Daddy's chair. As I came out of the brush, Lock stood and looked at me. His eyes were vacant, and he was naked.

"Son, where are your clothes?" I asked, trying to hide my astonishment.

Lock shrugged his shoulders.

I took his hand, "I've got clothes in my bag up at the jeep. Let's get something on you." I slipped the canvas coat over his shoulder.

Without any resistance, and after gathering the pall, Lock followed me up the hill to the jeep. I found a pair of jeans and a shirt. Someone had left a pair of leather, lace-up boots in the back of the jeep. Without any assistance from Lock, I dressed him. But I couldn't get the boots on him. He just sat and looked at the boots as if he had no idea of their function.

My clothes hung on him, and I wondered when he had last eaten. I helped him into the passenger's seat and told him to wait until I came back. He just stared at me as if heavily sedated.

I double-timed back to the camp, opened the wooden box, got crackers, coffee, canned peaches and a couple cans of tuna, and the old coffee pot. I filled a gallon jug from the spring, put everything in a burlap bag, grabbed a Coleman lantern and ran back up the hill. I almost held my breath until I could see Lock still sitting in the jeep where I had left him. I dumped the food in the back seat. Lock, still without any emotion, looked straight ahead.

It was almost five o'clock. I thought how lucky I was to have found him. With only thirteen hours until the helicopter was to take us out, I shuddered at the thought of trying to find him in these heavy woods. He knew the Arn better than I, and he could have hidden from me for weeks.

"Lock, this is what we're going to do," I explained. "We're going to camp out tonight at the fort and then about daylight, a friend is going to come in a helicopter. You and I are going to fly down to Knoxville. We are going to get on Luther's plane. We'll be the only passengers. We will go to sleep and we will wake up in a new place. A place where you'll be safe."

Lock was still non-responsive. Then his head slowly tilted forward and he closed his eyes. His lips were moving but there were no words. A thin stream of saliva escaped the corner of his mouth and ran down his chin. I panicked at the thought he might be having some kind of seizure. I called his name. He slowly raised his head and opened his eyes. He wiped the saliva from his chin and, for a moment, his lips were still. Then they started moving again, but still without sound.

During our trip to the fort, Lock looked straight ahead seemingly unaware of my presence. He sat in the jeep as I unloaded the groceries and started a fire for the coffee. I helped him from the jeep. In slow motion, he walked over to the fort wall and sat. He had carried the boots with him, but instead of putting them on, wrapped them in the canvas jacket and placed them on the ground.

It was almost dark when the coffee was ready. I lit the Coleman lantern and offered Lock a cup of coffee, hoping the caffeine might help pull him out of his lethargy. He took a couple of swallows, then wrapped both hands around the mug and stared at the campfire. I opened a can of tuna and a packet of crackers and sat on the ground facing him.

He looked at the food much the same way as he had the boots, head cocked to the side and eyes half closed. I spread some of the tuna on a cracker and touched it to Lock's lips. He opened his mouth and I pushed the food inside. He chewed and then swallowed. I repeated the process, but this time he turned his head away with his lips pressed tightly together.

After showing him the picture of a peach on the side of a can, using my knife I sawed through the lid, moistened my finger with the sweet juice, and wet his lips. For the first time he showed some interest in eating, but when I gave him the can, he set it down on the ground beside the boots and coat.

I tried to talk with him about the past few days but he remained unresponsive. I felt a need to reassure him about our trip, but again he showed no interest in anything I said.

He took the can of peaches, emptied the tuna can, and with his thumbnail, removed the paper labels from both of them. The fire was dying out. He took two small, burnt sticks from the ashes, smoothed the paper labels across his knee and, with the burnt twigs, started making marks on the paper. I was encouraged by any movement on his part. Afraid to disturb him, I watched him from across the campfire.

Five minutes passed before Lock handed the paper to me.

On the back of a label, he'd sketched a likeness of a man and a little boy fishing. A second sketch was also one of a young man scratching a dog's head, and the third one of a woman reading a book to a little curly-haired boy. On the back of the second label, he had sketched a man, obviously me, holding the hand of a little boy that I assumed was Lock. He took the drawings from my hand and through heavily-lidded eyes stared at me before crushing the drawing of the older man and the boy. He threw it into the fire. He did the same with the drawing of the boy and the dog. He took the drawing of the woman and the boy, and smudged the likeness of the woman until she was unrecognizable.

"Why are you doing this?"

Without answering, Lock erased the boy from the drawing of the man and boy. He folded the paper and stuffed it into my shirt pocket.

"I'm not going anywhere without you," I said. "You can just put the boy back in the drawing. I'm your father and you're my son. We look after each other." I handed the drawing to Lock, but without even unfolding the paper, he stuffed it in my shirt pocket again.

I was puzzled. "What are you trying to tell me? We will be together, I promise."

Lock didn't answer but went back to his seat on the pile of rocks. He folded the canvas coat across his lap and took two items from the coat pockets – the small stone stature and a miniature hammer The dying fire gave little light, and the Coleman lantern was hanging from a limb behind me. Lock was in almost total darkness.

"What are you working on?" I asked. Lock ignored my question but appeared to be tapping on the statue with the small hammer and a delicate chisel. I stood and took a step toward him, but he quickly folded the coat over whatever he had in his lap.

"Okay. If you don't want me to see it, that's all right," I said, sitting back down by the fire. For maybe an hour, Lock continued tapping on the object in his lap. I didn't want to interrupt him, because this was the most interest he had shown in anything since he had come out of the woods earlier in the day. I grew sleepy and stretched out on the ground with my feet toward the fire. I told Lock, "I'm going to take a nap. We've got an early start in the morning. When you get finished with whatever you are workin' on, if you want me to see it, wake me up."

Sometime after midnight, the wind shifted. For a few minutes, it flowed up a crevice out at the end of the point, making the same sound that had scared Luther and me when we were children. I sat up and looked around. Lock was bent over scraping his arm with something. I asked him if he was okay, but he ignored my question.

It was just getting light. It was that time of the morning when the light softens everything and nothing casts a shadow. I woke to a low noise, something between a chant and a moan. Only a wisp of smoke curled up from the dying fire. Lock was squatting five feet away, peering intently at me. He swayed gently from side to side, keeping time with the chanting moan.

"Morning," I said. Lock didn't answer but stopped chanting. "Damn, it's almost six o'clock. We're not even going to have time for coffee. We should be hearing the helicopter pretty soon."

Lock stood. He was naked again. He had shaved his head, his beard, and most of his body hair. The knife must have been dull, because he was bleeding from several cuts on his head and the side of his face. He had covered his body with ashes from the fire, and using red clay had drawn a circle around each eye. He had drawn red lines from the edges of his eyes down to the corners of his mouth and red geometric patterns on his chest. He was wearing the same kind of amulet I had found on Daddy's body.

Stunned at his appearance, I stood. "Heck, Lock. You're going to scare the crap out of the helicopter pilot."

Lock stood in front of me, his pupils small dark dots in a sea of green, staring intently into my face as if I was a long way off and he wasn't sure who I was. Frightened, I stared back, wondering what this was leading to.

He placed his fingers on my lips. He had cried and there were tear stains running through the ashes on his cheeks. "I didn't want to be this way," he said, his voice low. "I can't help it. I wanted to … be better … happy. It's just that my mind won't … Mother … I can't be what … Last night the string broke. Papa Zeale … couldn't catch it. I'm drifting to … I don't know. Help me … find my string and hold me before…"

"Don't be afraid, we're going to be all right," I said soothingly. "This will be a good day. Tomorrow we'll be in another place. A safe place. Just you and me. A daddy and a son."

Lock leaned forward and hugged me. "Daddy," he whispered, "did you hear … the babies crying last night?"

His body was hot and smelled of ashes. There was also an odor and my memory had catalogued that smell. It was the same as my shirt had smelled after I had a horrifying experience with a grizzly: fear and stress.

"Son, it was just the wind."

"No," he whispered, "it was the babies crying. They are … calling me. They want me to save them … come and take …take care of them."

I searched for words of reason and comfort as Lock walked to the edge of the escarpment.

In the distance, I heard the whap-whap-whap of the approaching helicopter. A light wind came up off the river and sucked through the crevice at the edge of the bluff: the same low moaning sound I'd found so frightening when I was a boy. The pulsating sound of the wind grew greater than the hammering of the helicopter rotators.

The fog rising up the canyon walls from the Findhorn was painted red by the rising sun. Lock's low chanting was just audible. Slowly he raised his arms level with his shoulders, his palms up. He tilted his head back and looked up into the paleness of the morning sky.

I believe that long ago, before I was born or the first William Roane came into these mountains, God destined this moment to punish me for my sins, to punish me for all the sins the Roanes had ever committed. Or ever would.

Without bending his legs, his arms still at shoulder height, palms up, Lock leaned forward and disappeared over the edge of the escarpment into the mist.

CHRISTIAN SPRINGS 1996

"Good morning, Jamiesie, and good morning to you, Carol. It is so good to see you two again. Won't you come in and let me get you some coffee and a sweet roll. Please sit over here by the window so you can look out into the gorge. That's the Henderson Brothers rapids just to the left of the sassafras tree.

It has been an eternity since I last saw you. What a wonderful time we had on our visit with you.

Yes, it was too short.

I wish we had too.

It is pretty out here, isn't it? We built this house almost ten years ago. We had an agreement, Creighton could design it providing I chose the colors. I don't know if you remember, but he was almost color blind.

No, all of the lumber came off the Arn, even the logs were hewn from timber standing near Hematite Lake. The fireplace and chimney were taken from parts of the old iron furnace. Have you noticed the dog-irons in the fireplace? Creighton was cleaning up and found them where the tavern had burned more than a century ago. He was as excited as a child.

So you thought Cedergren would be a bigger town? I guess Creighton was selfish about the town, just like Papa Zeale was when the Roman Company was starting. Neither of them wanted the town to grow. Papa Zeale didn't want "lawyer folks" to have offices here, and Creighton had the same belief. So Roman's operational facilities stayed in Charlotte.

No, Luther Sears is still here. He's not visibly active in the company any more. But if you know where to look, you can still see his guidance. Both of his sons are climbing the corporate ladder. Creighton used to tell Luther that the boys would've been smarter if Aunt Winnie had been around while they were growing up to whip their britches, like she did theirs.

Get your bags and let's take them out to the guest house. I'll give you a little time to freshen up. We'll have some lunch, and then I want to take you for a drive around Cedergren and the college. We must share stories about our families.

*****

Yes, that's the same Partner's Café Creighton talked to you about. And yes, that's where the Brotherhood of the Round Table met. They're all gone now. Papa Zeale once described himself as an old leaf on a tree, and that's the way those men were. Papa Zeale was the first leaf to fall. Within five years of his death, they all had fallen from the tree. Sheriff Fox was killed while helping Federal agents raid a still the McCamys were operating up on Daves Creek. Most of the others died in their own beds. Except Camran Grainger. We don't know exactly what happened to him. He went up into the mountains around Dashoga Gap deer hunting a few days before season opened and just never came back. Creighton flew the mountains for days searching for him. No trace of him was ever found. Creighton said he hoped Camran's spirit was happy and would roam the mountains throughout eternity.

I'm sorry Louellen wasn't in. She is a beautiful woman. She married Andy Cailean, a friend of Lock's. They have three of the prettiest little boys you ever saw. Papa Zeale just loved her to death, and she spoiled him.

A codicil in his will left the café to her. She cried when Luther told her what Papa Zeale had done.

Let me drive you around the court square. Don't blink or you'll miss it. There's the Blackman law office. They were early partners with Papa Zeale in the fledgling Roman Company. Over there is Dr. Huntsman's clinic. That clothing store and that hardware store have been in the same family for almost a hundred years. Things don't change here. That's why I love this town.

Even the college didn't change things much. There it is. Waggner State. It has the strongest forestry and wildlife conservation department in the state. Probably in the top five in the southeast. Creighton was so proud of it.

Here is a little history behind it. Senator Waggner long had the support of Papa Zeale and admitted he owed his long tenure in office to him. Creighton didn't like politicians because he believed they ignored the mountain people and saw them as nothing more than votes to be harvested at election time.

Yes, he was strongly opinionated about some things.

Anyway, shortly after Papa Zeale's death, Senator Waggner's term was ending and he had to start campaigning. He came to Creighton and told him how much he had appreciated his father's financial support in the past. Then he asked Creighton to endorse him in the campaign, maybe make some appearances and have some photographs taken together for the local papers.

Really rubbed Creighton the wrong way. He came home for lunch and he was just furious. 'The senator wants to marry us mountain folks, but for just for one night,' Creighton said. 'Well, I'll show him he's through taking from the mountain people and not giving anything in return.' So Creighton refused to support the senator with money or an endorsement.

Yes, he had a pretty short fuse, but in his defense, he worked on making it longer. He was mellowing just like Papa Zeale did.

You bet the senator was sweating. Three months before the election, Senator Waggner came back to Cedergren. He was down by more than twenty points in the polls, and his campaign was practically broke. This time Creighton told the senator he would support him on one condition. Luther told me later the senator acted as if the burdens of the world had been taken off his shoulders. Then Creighton told the senator he wanted a college built here in Cedergren and wanted the senator's promise it would be built during his next term. The senator started talking about the difficulties of getting support in Washington. Creighton cut him off saying, 'My proposal. Take it or leave it.'

Senator Waggner was reelected for two more terms and died in office just before the end of the second term. But before he died, Waggner State was born and completed.

Oh, no. Creight felt it would be pretentious to have the Roane name associated too heavily with the naming of the school. He suggested the name Waggner State. You know how politicians are flattered with things like that. On the day the school was dedicated, they had this big ceremony. Senator Waggner strutted around like a king.

The building on the left and the second building on the right were built through contributions of The Roman Company and North Georgia Global. The first building houses the Center for Wildlife Studies and is named The Lockhart Center. You will recall that Lockhart was my maiden name and the middle name of our son. The other building is The Breazeale Building and it houses the School of Forestry Management. Papa Zeale's mother was a Breazeale. Yes, it can be confusing. The firstborn son was always given a first name of William and then his mother's maiden name. So the genealogy is not too difficult to trace.

Luther leaned on Creighton for two years before he would agree to use the Breazeale name.

The student population is comprised of 75 percent Appalachians and their costs are negligible. The remaining student population consists of gifted kids that ordinarily wouldn't have been able to attend college. I am chairperson of the committee that chooses these students. We require these gifted children to perform one year of community service after graduation. Then the college forgives all of their educational costs.

While we are out this way, let me take you by the airport. Creighton improved the runway but kept it grass and wouldn't allow it to be lengthened enough to serve corporate aircraft. The hanger in the center is where Creighton kept his plane. It is the one we will be using in the morning. Creighton was so proud of that plane. He said it flew like a homesick angel.

Before we go back out to the Arn, I'd like to take you by the Roane home place, the place where Papa Zeale had his office.

Sounds as if Creighton had described it to you accurately. Characteristically, and in keeping with everything about Papa Zeale's personal life, the house was pretty basic. We moved it and Papa Zeale's office out to the Arn. We didn't update the house in any way. Creighton would allow quail hunting buddies to use it. Once Dr. Bishop brought his daddy up from Florida, and they spent a month in the house. I know Creighton must have told you about the effect Mr. Bishop had on his life. He and Creighton were almost like father and son. They spent long days reminiscing.

Oh, yes. A few other people used it, too. Vaughn Blackman was a frequent visitor. When he and Creighton would get together, it would remind you of two fifth-graders. Vaughn died about a year before Creighton. He had a stroke while playing golf and died before they could get him to the hospital. One of his associates called with the news of

Vaughn's death. Creighton's eyes misted up and he went out to the shed where he kept his canoe. I gave him a few minutes before I followed. He had started whittling peach seeds just like Papa Zeale had done. He wouldn't whittle birds, just rabbits and things like that. He had a peach seed in his hand and was just looking at it. I told him I was sorry and the muscles in his jaw tightened. Finally, he said, "We never ran the Findhorn like he wanted to do. We never got to be young again.'

The office sat over there where the muscadine vines are growing. Creighton moved it out behind the house we built. A path leads from our back porch down to it. There is no road. Creighton wanted it that way. After he got sick, Tony would take him down on warm days, 'Living on the sunny side of the river,' Creighton would cheerfully say. You should take a walk down to see it when we get home.

Yes, the same Tony you met that first day when Luther flew up to Alaska. Right after Papa Zeale's death, he and Creighton reached an understanding. They ended up being pretty close friends. Tony was invaluable at the end of Creighton's life.

No, he's still around. If you don't see him this afternoon, he'll be at the airport in the morning.

I know you must be exhausted after flying all night. Let's go home. You two get a nap, maybe take a walk, and then we will have dinner.

*****

I'm glad you took the walk down to the office. It is pretty neat, isn't it?

Sure. And no, it's not too painful. I'll be glad to tell you about our boys.

Lock did all the paintings. Yes, he was talented. He had a great future, but maybe the factors that made him brilliant were the same factors that destroyed him. He did other paintings, but they are scattered about the country. We chased some of them down and bought a couple, but somehow they never had the value to us as those you saw.

I'm glad you noticed the small sculpture. Creighton found it wrapped in Papa Zeale's canvas coat the morning of Lock's death. He believed Lock finished it on his last night on earth. It is the only likeness of Creighton that Lock ever did, and that is what made it so precious to us.

I grieved over him for years before he died, and then years afterward. Lock was the sixth William, you know, going all the way back to William McCree Roane. In medieval times he would have had a fleur-de-lis on his coat of arms denoting that. He would have been a dashing and fierce warrior.

Maybe things would have gotten better if Creighton could have gotten him out and up in your part of the country, but I doubt it.

That's right, if things had gone as planned, this is about the spot they would have lifted off. I talked with Mr. West, the helicopter pilot, the day after Lock died. Mr. West said it was about a quarter past six when he got here. It was still foggy along the river, but the plateau was almost clear. He made a pass and saw a man standing out by the end of the ruins. He set down and did not kill the engine because he knew the urgency to get out quickly.

No, no, it's all right. I don't mind talking about it. Mr. West said the man made no response to the presence of the helicopter. He shut the engine down and once the rotors stopped, he could hear the man crying. He described it as the sound a hurt dog would make.

Oh, he was very apprehensive. He knew from earlier conversations with you and with Creighton that one of his passengers was mentally unstable. He thought Creighton was the unstable passenger, and he was afraid to approach too closely.

It was several minutes before Creighton regained enough composure to identify himself and tell Mr. West what had just happened. Mr. West wanted to fly to Cedergren and contact the sheriff's office. Creighton wouldn't hear of it. They flew the river and within ten minutes found Lock. His body had washed up on a sand bar just below the Henderson Brothers rapids. Mr. West said that considering everything Lock's body had gone through, there was amazingly little damage and there seemed to be a smile on his lips. He said Creighton carried Lock to the helicopter by himself and cradled him in his arms all the way back to Cedergren.

No, I'll be all right. Just give me a minute.

They landed in the front yard at Papa Zeale's house. Creighton carried Lock inside and put him on Papa Zeale's bed. Of course, in a little town like Cedergren, a helicopter setting down causes all kinds of commotion. One of the deputies investigated, and the pilot told him what happened. Sheriff Fox came out to the house but Creighton wouldn't let him in. I got to the house and Sheriff Fox was pacing up and down the front porch, his shirt soaked with perspiration.

After an hour of pleading, Creighton let me in the house. He had washed the sand and debris from Lock's body. He sat beside the bed holding Lock's hand in his. I don't think he recognized me because the only thing he said to me that I could understand was, 'Mother, my son is dead.' If I had known him better, maybe I could have anticipated what was coming.

We buried Lock two days later with all the other men named William Roane at the family cemetery. Creighton didn't leave the cemetery with the rest of us but promised to see me the next day.

It was three months before I saw him again.

He just hid in and lived like a hermit. I don't think anyone but Camran saw him during all that time. The morning of Lock's services, Creighton had Camran bring a bulldozer out to the stone fort. Camran told me he watched Creighton doze the fort to the ground. He totally destroyed it. Covered it with five feet of dirt.

The conservation people and the archeologists had a fit when they found out what had been done, but there was nothing they could do about it. Later, Creighton even mentioned it in his will. He said the site could be uncovered on the hundredth anniversary of his death, and not before.

Camran took canned meat and bread out there. Sometimes he would see Creighton and sometimes he wouldn't. Through Tony, I found out Camran was also taking whisky. I had developed some knowledge of Creighton's thought process, and I knew he shouldn't be out there by himself. Tony threatened Camran, told him he couldn't go out there anymore, and then made him tell where we could find Creighton.

Yes, I know you've been on the threatening end of Tony. Anyway, just like Camran said, we found Creighton in Whetstone Cave. He must have lost forty pounds. He was as filthy as he could be. He was drunk past the point of recognizing anybody, and was so weak he could barely walk. Tony slung him over his shoulder like a sack of feed and carried him up the hill. We brought him back to Dr Huntsman's clinic, and they went to work on him.

It was almost three weeks before they released him. I took him to my house and either Louellen or I was with him all the time for about two more months. Some days it would seem there was no progress. It was pretty discouraging.

I'm not sure, but I think it was just an accumulation of things: Papa Zeale's death, Lock's suicide, and I don't know what else – maybe depression over the turn his life had taken. He would never really talk about it. We got married six months later, but there were always doors in his mind he would not open for me.

Yes, he still had nightmares. They never fully went away. Sometimes weeks would pass and he would be free of them. Then he might have them for two or three nights in a row. I would wake and he would be thrashing around fighting the cover, moaning and cursing. I would hold him for hours. Sometimes he would sob like a baby. He never told me what he was dreaming. He said I didn't need to know.

Creighton said the dreams were like scars. The wounds healed but the scars never went away. They got better, but they never went away. You were with him when he was living in Alaska and … this is not an easy question to ask, and you don't have to answer, but did he ever …? This is silly, I know. Was he ever involved in a killing?

That seemed a recurring theme in his nightmares. He was always hunting two men, and on his really bad nights, he would think he had killed them. Sometime, I would wake up and Creighton wouldn't be in bed. I would find him stumbling around in the dark, sleep walking, looking for Papa Zeale's pistol. After he died, I've thought many times it's probably best Creighton never opened that door. I wouldn't have wanted to go into those dreams.

Oh, we had a wonderful life. You'll see our son tomorrow, but today he and some Boy Scouts are building a wooden tower across the river. He'll be back before you leave.

He is the image of his daddy. Louellen has said it's like Creighton spit in the dirt, and Deuce got up and walked out of it. He has the same build and the same way of walking. You remember the way Creighton walked, always bent over a little and hurrying? Exactly the way Deuce moves.

Yes, we were surprised. Here I was fifty years old and pregnant. We didn't think we would ever have children. I had gone back to teaching, and I didn't tell Creighton I was pregnant until the doctor confirmed it. We had developed a little ritual about washing the supper dishes together. Each night when we finished, we would sit at the kitchen table and tell each other about our day. When I gave him the news, he stared at me slack-jawed for about fifteen seconds before he let out a whoop. He snatched me up from the table, and we danced around the kitchen like schoolchildren.

You probably didn't know how emotional Creighton was. His heart was as tender as a baby's at times. After we finished our dance, he sat back down at the kitchen table, put his head in his arms and cried. He insisted I stop teaching and just stay at home and take care of myself. I laughed him off and told him I needed to finish the semester. And I did, but he monitored me daily about any strange pains, nutrition, and any stress. He reminded me frequently about my difficulties with Lock's birth. He would get a far-away-look in his eyes and tell me for the thousandth time about the death of his mother when she had her second child.

As time went along and things went well, he became less worried. Our lives slowly became normal again. We were finishing the dishes one night about a month before the baby was born and Creighton cleared his throat – always a signal he was about to say something he considered important. He looked at me and said 'I've been giving this some thought. It's not proper for our baby to be around a daddy that cusses, chews tobacco, and drinks.' He hugged me and said, 'Today, I've quit all three.' So far as I know, he never had a drink of whiskey or a chew of tobacco again. Sometimes he would slip and say something bad in front of me, but he would spend the next five minutes apologizing.

When the baby came and it was a boy, Creighton acted like it was the first man-child ever born in these mountains. He strutted around town like a fighting rooster. He handed out cigars and sent announcements to everybody he knew. He wouldn't have it any other way but we name the baby William Lockhart Roane II. We never had the chance to enjoy our first son together, but we would honor his life by giving his brother the same name.

We did consider the confusion that could come about with naming our second son the same as our first. The dilemma solved itself. When we took the baby for his first checkup, Dr. Danny McGinley looked at his chart and said, 'What a long name for such a little boy – I think I'll just call you Deuce.' And that was it, he has been Deuce ever since.

Yes, exactly. We had the rare chance to do something a second time and this time we got it right. He'll carry the Roane name and bloodline forward, and long after we are gone, it will still be here in these mountains. I believe that's the way it should be – it belongs here.

Ironically, Deuce was born on Papa Zeale's birthday. Papa Zeale once told Creighton that he tried to believe in reincarnation, that he wanted to come back and give life another shot. Occasionally, Deuce would do something or say something you would not expect from a child of his age. Creighton would say to Deuce, 'Now who did you say you are?' We laughed about it. But somehow, we always wondered just a little.

I've kept you up long enough and have just talked your ears off. Thank you so much for telling me about the years you and Creighton spent together. In his last days, he would sit before the fireplace at night and recount his 'Alaska days,' as he called them. The Boy Scouts would come over and I'd make hot chocolate. Deuce would say, 'Tell them, Daddy, about the time you ran the bear out of the camp with the skillet,' and he would be off and running. Those are sweet, sweet memories.

Oh, I'm sorry. I thought I'd already told you. I guess you could say the Findhorn River brought us together in the beginning and then separated us at the end. Even in his later years, Creighton still loved to run the river. However, he decided a white-water canoe was too tame, so he started taking a kayak instead.

Oh, I guess he was good. Not as good as he thought, but he managed. It reached a point I didn't want him on the river by himself. It's too dangerous, I would tell him and he would just laugh. But he did start going with some young men and that … led to his undoing.

Last winter, just after the first snow, he and a young photographer took an early morning run down the Findhorn. The young man had significantly overrated his kayak expertise. He flipped going into a two-boulder rapid named Double Bubble. It was probably no more than a high Class III, but he got caught upside down in a hydraulic at the base of the first large boulder. He couldn't roll the kayak, and he panicked. Creighton went in after him and somehow got him free. Both of them were pulled by the swift water to the second boulder. It was undercut and the current was strong.

I don't know if the photographer could have gotten out by himself or not, but Creighton was never afraid of the water, and he just went after him. The current was sucking both of them under the rock. Creighton was able to get his knees against the rock, grab the photographer by the back of his life jacket, and jerk him back away from the rock. The photographer was free but now Creighton was hung up. Half his body was under the rock, with just his head and arms above the water.

He was there maybe forty-five minutes. To the photographer's credit, he caught up with his kayak, took a line out, and ran back upstream to where Creighton was trapped. It was a very dangerous situation for everybody. Finally, the photographer got the line to Creighton, and somehow he managed to get it under his arms.

I was terrified when I found out what had happened. Creighton had been taken to the hospital when Tony came to get me. We thought the worst was over, but the cold water had done vascular damage to his legs and lower part of his torso. A couple of months later, they removed both of Creighton's legs at the hospital over in Charlotte. But gangrene had invaded his system. The doctors found other major circulatory damage and no surgical solution. Seven months after he got trapped, he died.

It was fortunate we had as much time as we did. He put all his affairs in order. He set up trusts, and for a few weeks, lawyers were here every day. The legal mumbo-jumbo was enormous.

After that was over, we spent a lot of time sitting in the sun, out on the deck. Creighton wanted to sit where he could see the river. I had decided to home-school Deuce for those last few months, so the three of us were together almost all of the time. Toward the end, Deuce would crawl up in the bed with Creighton and read to him. Sometimes Deuce would bring photos of the buffalo or just a wild turkey feather. No father and son ever had a stronger bond.

We were in bed one night, the three of us. I was reading and Deuce was rubbing oil on the stumps of Creighton's legs. He was not feeling well that night and was mostly just listening to Deuce talk. Deuce was talking about the river and kayaking. He told Creighton 'When I get grown, I think I can run everything except the Henderson Brothers.'

I knew this was "man talk" and I pretended to be absorbed in my book.

Their conversation continued and Creighton asked Deuce 'Why not run the Henderson Brothers?' Deuce told him 'I'll be afraid because they are too big and scary.' Creighton told him, 'When the right time comes, you'll do it.' Deuce asked 'How will I know when that time comes?' Creighton laughed and said, 'It will be about six months before you're grown.' Deuce leaned forward and whispered, 'Did you run them?'

I got out of bed to let our cat in for the night. When I came back, Deuce was standing up in the bed, his eyes dancing, and his hands over his mouth.

No, I don't know what Creighton told him. I asked once, Deuce didn't answer, just looked at me and smiled.

I wish I could say Creight's last days were easy, but they weren't. He was in a lot of pain but he wouldn't take anything. 'I don't have a lot of time left,' he said, 'I don't want anything to rob us of time together.'

We kept him here at home until the end. One morning, just after daylight, I'd gotten out of bed to make coffee. Creighton had been restless all night, and neither of us had slept very much. When I came back to the bedroom, he was sitting up and leaning against the headboard. I got back in bed and put his head against my shoulder. He was sweating, taking deep breaths and I wasn't sure he was awake until he said, 'I dreamed last night.' I told him I thought he had. He said, 'They weren't bad, I dreamed Lock, Deuce, Daddy and I were fishing out at Hematite. You and Mother brought us some lemonade and cookies.'

He was quiet for a long time and I thought he had gone back to sleep. Then he whispered, 'We shared it didn't we, honey?'

I thought he might be out of his head, and I asked him what we shared.

'Common ground, we shared common ground – at the start and now here at the end. We shared common ground, didn't we?'

I brushed the hair from his forehead, 'We did and we will share more – we are not through.'

He pulled my hand to his lips. 'The day Lock died … I lost my soul … I thought it had collapsed … and fallen … into a dark place … where I would never find it … but you and Deuce …' He took one other deep breath and then he left us."

INFINITY

I hadn't given much thought as to what it would be like when I was dead. I have none of the senses I had when I was alive - yet in death, I sense everything.

I know Jamiesie is the pilot because I recognize his style of flying. He was always a safe pilot. Today, he used every foot of airstrip to gain maximum ground speed before we lifted off.

Deuce is riding in the opposite seat, his little hand clutching the cord that will open the box and set me free. He is a brave boy. I wish he and Daddy could have known each other. He is built out of the Roane mold in so many ways. He is wearing the Cardinal baseball cap we bought in St. Louis last year and the aviator sunglasses he got for his ninth birthday. He is expressionless but I sense his elevated heart rate.

My darling Maggie is in the back seat, leaning forward, her hands cupped around her face as she presses her forehead against the cool window. Maybe she fools the two in the front, but I know her eyes are closed and tears are starting to roll down her cheeks. I want her to know how much I'm missing her and, if I could, I would kiss the tears from her face. I am aware of the ache in her heart, and I want to tell her that she helped heal my soul. I don't want her to be sorry but instead to rejoice in my freedom.

I sense we have been flying north along the Findhorn, and now as we bank to the east, I know the Henderson Brothers rapids are under us. I know the leap of their shining water as it works down through the boulders and then swings in against the edge of the bluff. We turn south and gain elevation to climb over the edge of the escarpment. Now Christian Springs is below us, and north up ahead the waters of Hematite Lake are without a ripple in the stillness of the morning.

The trail leading down to Whetstone Cave is just east of us. I wanted to die in that cave, but I couldn't will myself to do so and I didn't have the courage to throw myself off the bluff into the river. I remember thinking that maybe I would have been better off if I hadn't gotten home but instead died like Clawed – died trying.

But these are shadow thoughts, and the brightness of the last ten years washes them clean. Today, my soul yearns for final release.

We fly the river again and as we approach the Henderson Brothers, Maggie tells Deuce to start pulling the cord. A thin stream of silver ashes trails the plane up the river, then up over the escarpment and northward toward the stone fort. Below, a buffalo bull snorts his displeasure at the low flying plane.

Now, I become aware of Maggie's singing, and my spirit sings along with her.

'Amazing grace, how sweet the sound that saved a wretch like me.
I once was lost but now am found; was blind but now I see.
Yea, when this flesh and heart shall fail, and mortal life shall cease,
I shall possess within the veil, a life of joy and peace.'

Maggie takes Deuce's hand and together they give the cord a final pull – the box empties - I'm now totally free. Jamiesie banks the plane back to the southwest toward Cedergren, and I know Maggie and Deuce are waving goodbye.

Below me, faintly, I hear an old scratchy violin playing and I know it is Amazing Grace. I know they are waiting, all those men named William Roane. We've always gone home to that and now I'm no different – I will have within the veil, a life of joy and peace - and I know - after the end, when it is over – we are all equal.

CPSIA information can be obtained at www.ICGtesting.com
Printed in the USA
LVOW040534080512

280747LV00003B/1/P